Bone Tear: A Love Story

Harry Hauca

PublishAmerica
Baltimore

First printing

This is a work of fiction. Names, characters, places, and incidents either are the product of the author's imagination or are used fictitiously. Any resemblance to actual persons, living or dead, events, or locales is entirely coincidental.

PublishAmerica has allowed this work to remain exactly as the author intended, verbatim, without editorial input.

ISBN: 1-60813-944-1
PUBLISHED BY PUBLISHAMERICA, LLLP
www.publishamerica.com
Baltimore

Printed in the United States of America

PROLOGUE

The stink of blood and split bowels did not faze him but the sounds of the dying men and horses could not be shut out. The lucky died quickly, a fortunate slash across some major artery or a skull-cracking blow with the sword—most would bleed to death slowly, sometimes painfully, their whimpering suggesting surprise and fear more than pain.

He sat on the hillside, head resting on arms as he hugged his bent knees, the dead smell increasing with the rising sun.

Gut wounds, liver wounds are the worst!

His arms and legs, which had earlier been a blur of speed and strength, were now weak, helpless appendages as the juice of combat seeped from them; his brain was just now beginning to actually think.

"Lord?"

"Yes, Glendon?" Without stirring.

"You're covered with blood. Any of it yours?"

Vortimer wearily looked up at his lieutenant. "So are you. Any of it yours?"

Glendon clapped his hands, roared out a laugh and pulled Vortimer to his feet—both men looked over the field of carelessly strewn bodies. His own soldiers walked gingerly on the blood-soaked grass, careful not to slip on the gore. Going from man to man they took whatever valuables their foes might have had, a ring or some fancy bauble and pocketed it.

And if they find one of their comrades heading towards death, a gut or lung wound, they will say a silent prayer and speed him on his journey—a difficult thing to do.

Glendon barely came to Vortimer's shoulder as the two of them began walking, each silently being careful not to slip.

"Many prisoners?"

"Some, most died or fled."

"Don't let the men damage them any more. Get the slaver and see what we can get," Vortimer spat.

Slave traders, like carrion feeders, were one of the necessities of war that few soldiers liked to acknowledge, but they did serve a purpose. Their armies hadn't the manpower or resources to care for prisoners so it was either slay them outright or sell them and get some profit for their labors. Having allegiance only to the victor, traders were adept in several languages, had contacts throughout the civilized world and were friends to all. As much as they were despised, they were treated well—no telling when you might be the one being sold…and some gesture of civility now might make for preferential treatment in the future should Fortune frown. Too, they were a bubbling font of knowledge regarding troop strengths, positions and weaknesses—a characteristic that could be used for information and misdirection.

"Maybe we should kill less, Lord; a dead man has no value."

"One less to encounter in the future, Glendon. Besides, the crows and foxes have to eat."

Vortimer glared at the north horizon that was beginning to darken with rain-thickened clouds. "Have you seen him?"

"No, Lord. I know he is here, though—he must be!"

Vortimer's twisted right leg began to throb gently as the balm of battle began to wear off. Cursing, he knew that by nightfall his leg would be an exquisite agony. Looking about he felt a sudden elation at the recognition of the pain—he was alive to bear it! Drawing his short sword with his right hand, he allowed his shield drop from his left arm and raised both fist and sword, letting out a guttural cry as he looked about. Again he boomed out a ferocious bellow. Glendon looked him in the eye and did the same—cry after cry blanketed the red field as his men all did the same and began walking towards him. The crows were frightened off by the throaty shouts of the men as they began heading towards their lord, fists and swords pointed towards the dimming sun.

Standing on the fallen, twenty, then forty, then a hundred and then hundreds more, crying, blood-covered men shouted in jubilation, not because they were victorious but because they had escaped death…again. Some wept openly, others still had the blaze of killing in their bellies and eyes—it made no difference—their joy was primitive, mindless.

Finally sheathing his sword, the tall lord looked over his exulting troops, silently grateful for their allegiance.

Could be worse, a lot worse! Any more dedication and I could make them into Roman legionnaires!

A thin smile creased his usually impassive face as the shouting and yelling died, the only sound was the freshening breeze from the north.

"If we kill any more, we won't be able to do this again!" He shouted.

A thick laugh rose and a score yelled out "Vortimer!"

"Go now, dress your wounds, weep for and bury your friends—tonight we feast and drink to their memory and our victory!"

As one, they shouted out his name again and again but Vortimer was already heading towards the small cove he had found earlier, Glendon at his side.

"I want to be alone for a moment, I want to bathe this stench from me. Go and do what must be done. Tally up the dead and walking wounded, set up sentries just in case this is some ruse but I don't foresee a counter attack, do you?"

"No, Lord. I will have your tent prepared and a complete census made."

Without replying, Vortimer limped several hundred yards to the hidden salt pond, he had scouted earlier. Past experience had taught him that the seawater cleansed wounds better than anything he knew. He stood on the rocky beach, determined to bathe in spite of the cold. He pulled the heavy leather jacket over his head, unmindful of the new scars embossed on it and dropped it to the ground. Next came the shirt of heavy mail, followed by the thick felt tunic that covered his upper torso. He wanted to stretch but the exertion of just removing his gear made him dizzy. He kicked off his heavy boots and dropped his tights quickly—the rounded stones already numbing his feet.

He stepped into the frigid water, feeling his ankle muscles tighten. Trying to walk rapidly, he stopped when the water reached his crotch, sending his testicles up into his belly.

I will do this.

Taking one deep breath, he knifed his body into the raw water and allowed a scream of shock to bubble up. Surfacing, he stood chest deep and quickly began running his numbed hands through his short hair, and briskly over his face and neck, removing the blood and sweat. He bobbed beneath the surface one more time and massaged his calves, knees and thighs. He stood again and rinsed his torso and buttocks—his body demanding an end to the abuse. Satisfied, he turned and saw an elfin-like creature waiting for him on the shore, holding his clothes. He willed his face to remain impassive and commanded his numb feet to walk slowly towards the shore. Unfeeling from face to soles, he moved awkwardly from the icy bath to the small man holding his garments.

Wordlessly, he sat on the cold stones and began to pull on his tights, his wet legs and blue-numbed fingers making it difficult. He brushed off his feet, pulled on his boots and stood, then put on the felt tunic.

"A delicious victory, young master," the odd man chirped. "Well planned and executed brilliantly! A few miscues which we may discuss at a later date but nothing too serious. I have news."

"What is the news, Varduc?"

"Something is coming, young, frigid, obstinate master. Something from the north."

"Rain?" Asked Vortimer, glancing at the sky.

"Your attempt at humor at my expense is pathetic, young master. Quite frankly, I am often embarrassed by your persistent ignorance, feigned though it may be."

"So, my counselor, my thorn, what is it that comes from the north?"

Here the little man turned away and let the winds buffet his thin face. "Something, young master, something. I am no seer but I feel a stirring, an agitation approaching from that direction."

"An agitation?"

"Something entirely new and different for you, life-changing."

"What is it, damn it?"

The counselor allowed himself a sly grin at Vortimer's impatience.

"A promise, young master…an opportunity. But enough of the future, it is too dark and you are weary, hungry and cold. Let us get drunk together."

The tall, broad-shouldered young man and the wizened fellow in the black robes headed from the shore, the north wind biting their ears and bending the rushes.

CHAPTER ONE

The bloodied hands of the disquieting dream that had awakened her were now a wispy, fleeting memory for the young woman at the window.

It is a sin to sleep on a night like this, she mused as she gazed from her room. The full of the February moon behind the castle had illuminated the fields and bare trees below with a silvery sheen, casting sharp shadows, blotting out the stars. She leaned on her elbows and breathed the cold, damp air deeply—smelling the promise of growth and greenery beneath the thin frost that covered the fields. The ewes were already coming into milk and once more fresh cheese would be plentiful.

Bridget's eyes, no longer sleep-laden, grew accustomed to the slaty landscape below. An errant puff of air blew some strands of dark, thick hair over her eyes and she tossed her head back with a long sigh. The night was quiet and still, yet Bridget felt uneasy. Something foreboding was in the air, something just beyond conscious thought and whatever it was, was not welcome.

What is wrong with me? I can't stand this feeling! Maybe it is the thought of a new season or perhaps it was the celebration of my patron saint that felt…empty, hollow. I have never felt like this before, certainly!

As she turned this thought over and about another breath of night air enveloped her, hardening her nipples, as they lay pressed against the cold wooden sill. *I am becoming quite like Mathilde,* she chided herself. Nevertheless, she haphazardly allowed her fingertips to brush across the point of her left breast, drawing a quick shudder. Enough!

She ignored the tightening sensation and returned to looking at the vista below when she spotted a movement on a slight rise less than several hundred yards from the castle. A stooped figure was walking slowly from the few huts to the edge of the woods on the left. Perhaps it was the size of the figure or the gait, but without doubt, knew it was a woman walking across that rough field, clutching something to her body with both arms. Her steps were small but determined as she trudged in the night, faltering but never stopping. The woman looked over her shoulder and then continued into the darkness of the copse—always shielding whatever it was she held next to her body.

Gazing more deeply at the blackened trees, Bridget's vision blurred as the different darknesses melded into one. A horse whinnying in the courtyard broke the reverie. Turning, she padded across the carpet-strewn floor to the bed, pulled the heavy blanket up and closed her eyes. The only sounds were the blood pulsating and her shallow breathing. Sleep would be an elusive friend as unsettling thoughts raced about, much like the hounds chasing a stag through her father's forest.

She did not want change. Content, happy with her hopes and dreams for the future, any deviation would be unthinkable, unbearable. The younger of two princesses, she was gratefully unmarried; she desired no man and certainly no children! Hadn't she seen too many women die in childbirth or shortly thereafter? No, she was destined for a much longer and happier life. Perhaps as the Abbess had suggested, she would become a member of the order and spend her life in contemplative quiet and prayer and worship of Jesus. And the opportunities that were denied her outside the convent would be there for her in the service of God.

Or there was the slight possibility that her father might send her to a foreign court where she could serve a great queen in a splendid castle where silk was as plentiful as the coarse linen she often wore here. There would be dances and finery and courtiers, men of distinction with polished manners and smooth hands. Yes, that possibility quickened her pulse and made sleep all the more impossible as she fretted and turned. But would she be happy, she wondered? Would any of these alternatives allow her to ride her horse with the abandon she did now, away from her father's eyes? Or to vent her sinful temper that could lead to blinding rage? God knew.

"Sweet Jesus, help me, protect me from the snares of the devil. Please don't let anything happen to me." She whispered. Lying there in the dark she waited for some sign that her prayer had been heard. She drifted off into an uneasy sleep as the earlier dream returned with increased clarity. There was a cloaked person standing before her, the face hidden. Wanting to see this shadow, she walked towards it until the phantom held up its hands, dripping blood.

* * *

A score of miles away, Celestine looked at her darkened fingertips in the wavering candlelight. Blood. Again! She threw back the covers unmindful of the besotted figure lying next to her and rose quickly to the toilet after grasping the candle from the table. Her upper thighs shone wet and red and her cheeks crimsoned with anger and humiliation…again. Oh, they would all blame her for not having a child, for being barren! They wouldn't dare blame the duke, her husband, for this ignominy. She wiped herself as best she could and fastened the woolen pad between her legs.

"Damn him! Damn him!" She hissed.

Lowering the gown, she looked into the imported mirror; her flaxen hair shone like silken strands of gold in the warmth of the candlelight and her unblemished skin was the white of pearl. Her arms and legs were long and supple; her breasts were just large enough to cause men to look at them furtively as they imagined their texture, their feel.

"I am as beautiful a woman as any man could desire," she whispered to the figure in the glass. "Then perhaps my husband is not a man."

What must I do to get this man, my husband, to give me a child? What else is left? I have offered myself, spread myself before him in as many ways possible! Oh, he's all fine and hard at the start, with his huffing and moaning—a pity he cannot finish what so strongly he starts. Why plow the field if you can't plant the seed? She flushed with the humiliating memory of that particular night when she had used her mouth to arouse him, all to bear an heir. But her husband's passion for drink and commerce left little fire for their bed and so she would continue to be called barren and become an object of scorn and pity.

She wanted, no, needed a son, an heir. The kingdom cried out for a male of noble lineage to save it…and she would be the one to bear him. With a strong son she could bargain, and make alliances that would strengthen her power. Oh, she had thought of cuckolding the duke once or twice, but in her heart she knew it would only be a matter of time before some drunken lord boasted of his "conquest." Though she spoke and could act like a whore, she would not become one, she thought.

Gazing into the mirror she thought herself much like a birch—white, slender and delicate. Nothing like Bridget, her sister, *Now there is an oak if ever I saw one! Poor Bridget, my dear sister, with your wide hips, slight breasts and nearly as tall as most men, what do you have with which to entice a man, a husband? And your fierce temper…well, maybe the abbey would be best for you, after all.*

She walked back to the bed and listened to the duke's drunken breathing before climbing in and laid on the far side so as to prevent an accidental, repulsive chambermaid. How would she adapt to life in the convent? Could she change? And if not change, then could she at least hold her tongue?

The prayer completed, she rose and sat in her chair in front of the unshuttered window, taking advantage of the scant gray light that entered. Noticing the pensive mood of her mistress, Mathilde wordlessly began the morning ritual of brushing and combing her chestnut-colored hair, thick and shiny.

As in many closed communities such as the castle, it was those who least needed to know who knew the most and Bridget recognized this.

"Tell me, has anything untoward or out of the ordinary been happening lately, Mathilde?"

Grateful for her lady's confidence she gushed, "La, milady! Your father the king supped with the abbot last night, barely leaving anything behind for the poor serving girl (her source) to eat, just crumbs and a bit of mutton bone, I understand."

Her father was wary of the cleric and anything having to do with the Church of Rome, so having Father Junius there for a meal was odd, she mused. With this bit of information she began to sort through all the possible reasons for the visit—taxes, working on the Sabbath, the prospects for a bountiful harvest this year.

"Did your friend happen to tell you what it was they spoke about?"

"Nay, milady. You know your father when he wants to keep things for only one pair of ears, besides, she had to tend the chickens because one of the hounds had gotten in there and created quite a stir!"

Not just a dinner, a private meeting! That her father would become more active with the Church was unthinkable, no matter how hard she prayed. Was he speaking to him of her going to the convent? Could that have been the subject? Or was she merely trying to bolster her own chances?

"Has milady heard that new song? The one about the smith and the fat maiden?"

Yes, Bridget thought, she probably had, closing her eyes, letting the girl continue to comb her hair and sing the song. Like all of Mathilde's songs, this one would involve a man and a maiden, or possibly two men and a woman or maybe two women and a robust man. Not listening to the words but hearing Mathilde's stunningly crystal voice reverberate throughout the room made the princess think, not for the first time, "How could God have given such an angelic voice, a voice that should sing His praises, to one with the morals of a cat in heat?"

"Round and round about they did play."

But how could she question the Almighty? Who was she to question His wisdom when she scarcely knew how to handle each day?

"Kissing and becoming hard as a rock, she reached around and grabbed his…"

"I think the mistress needn't hear the rest of your filthy tongue, Mathilde. Give it rest, lest it be torn from your mouth." The stentorian voice of her other chambermaid, Gwenthe, rumbled as the song dribbled weakly from Mathilde's lips.

"La, milady has told me she would do that already once this morning."

"Then hush, hussy, and tend to your mistress's hair. Severing your tongue from your mouth would make mistress and me happier, but would break the hearts of many a squire."

Gwenthe, heavy set and outweighing both the princess and Mathilde put together, had been the queen's favorite chambermaid. After the queen's death, she had adopted the princess as her special charge and gave her as much loving care as was in her plodding bulk. Gruff of voice and manner and short-tempered to boot, she had no time for foolishness when the princess was concerned, except for Mathilde who, for reasons known only to the stars, was also a recipient of her crushing love.

Bridget sat, eyes closed, as Mathilde continued to brush; Gwenthe would be going through her things, arranging her wardrobe on the bed.

"Milady is quiet today? Are you all right, my child? Or has Mathilde so dismayed you that you are saddened for the fate of her soiled soul?" Though attempting to interject some bit of levity at Mathilde's expense, Gwenthe's voice betrayed concern over Bridget's lack of spirit.

"No, my dear Gwenthe, though I have prayed long and hard for our sister in Christ, I have merely slept poorly, that's all. All last night, it seemed, I dreamed of something, someone, that made sleep impossible. Did you ever have that? A dream that left the moment you opened your eyes, yet stayed with you when you were awake like, like a shadow?"

"Dreams? Now be very careful of dreams, mistress!" Huffed Gwenthe as she stood in front of the chair, her gray head wagging. "They can be the stuff of children, silly and without sense. Or they can be signs, portents!"

"Portents," Mathilde giggled as she stopped brushing, "dreams are nothing, dear lady. Just stuff that's in your head, like a word. Dreams? They're like snow."

"Snow?" said Bridget turning towards Mathilde.

"Yes, milady. Have you ever seen a fresh bit of snow on the ground? Of course, you have. Well, it was real, no? But where is the snow now? Where goes the snow when the sun shines on it? Gone. Nothing. Like a dream."

"Mathilde, stop your foolishness. Go now and empty the pot and fetch up milady's food."

As she left to obey her senior, Gwenthe leaned close to Bridget, "She's wrong, sweet child. Dreams are the stuff of spirits, both good and bad. I mean not to upset you, princess, but be aware of what is around you. If need be I know a woman who can tell what the dream means."

"That's just it, Gwenthe! I do not remember. If I could recall who or what was in the dream I should be able to forget it or laugh at my foolishness, but I can't! Ah, maybe it is just snow, after all."

Rising from the chair, Bridget removed her evening gown and pulled on the cotton chemise. Gwenthe handed her the garter belt to which she clipped her hose. The tunic she had chosen was one of the princess's favorites—lightly woven, made of wool and with long sleeves, it was dyed a rich, dark green and was embroidered with red and gold thread.

"Oh, I have loved this ever since it was given to me by Lord Glamorgan." She said as her fingers ran along the fine stitching done in the shape of oak leaves. Gwenthe wordlessly handed her the belt with the silver buckle that Bridget cinched around her waist.

"Does milady want to put on the paste"?

"No, no face color today Gwenthe. Today is a day of work and horse." Gwenthe disliked the use of cosmetics by the princess, thinking that the white color made her look like death and the pink like the nether parts of a cat.

"That's a good girl, mistress. If God had wanted you to have the color of a corpse, He'd a made you that way."

As Gwenthe went about straightening the bed, Bridget took the mirror from her dresser and looked at herself. She did not put her hair up because she would be outside for a good part of the day; full, and a glistening chestnut, she allowed it to fall to her shoulders. Her eyes, green with flecks of gold, were clear and bright. Her skin, while it lacked the luster and smoothness of her sister's, was clear and browned from hours spent in the saddle. The tunic, her favorite in so many other ways, could not conceal her hips, however.

For the hundredth time, "I have the hips of a cow."

And for the hundredth time Gwenthe said, "My lady is a princess."

"A princess with thick hips and oaken thighs! Come, I have changed my mind. I shall eat in the hall instead."

Leaving the room and taking the spiral stairs into the hall was much like walking from the inside of a cave with cold, clean air into the midday sun of high summer. The hall, oblong in shape and about four times as long as it was wide, was the center for all the castle's activities. Eating, food preparation from husbandry to the final product, meetings, and judicial matters all had this as their center. The smells of cooking and baking intermingled with the odor of goats and hogs, waste, rotting food, damp earth and smoke.

The stairs ended on a stage upon which sat a long table, well back from the king's ornately carved throne. Mathilde, noticing her mistress now seated at the table, scurried into the kitchen to fetch her food. Though the sun was now above the horizon, the hall was poorly lit and great tapers supplied most of the smoky, quavering light.

Mathilde returned with a heavy tray that she placed on the table away from the princess. In front of her she placed a silver goblet and a shallow bowl. Bridget bowed her head and clasped her hands in front of her. "Holy Father, I give thanks for your blessings, your bounty and your Son. Praise be to God."

Lifting her eyes, she motioned for Mathilde to pour the wine from a crystal flagon. The wine, sweetened with honey and a little water brought an approving smile from Bridget as the rest of the meal was served. Bread, fresh baked and steaming was used to sop up the eggs that were placed in the bowl. A wedge of hard cheese completed the meal that was eaten in silence except for an occasional belch from the princess that brought a disapproving scowl from Gwenthe who stood behind and to the side of the chair. Completing the meal, she stretched appreciatively, the sleepless night forgotten for the moment.

"Fetch me the steward, Gwenthe."

For all her oversight in running the affairs of her father's castle, the princess absolutely depended on the steward, for it was he who kept the affairs in order and who would deal with those with whom the castle would do business. With a slight build, the grace of a dancer and a face that never seemed to have need of a razor, Peter's rise to steward was something of legend, a story to be told over endless goblets of wine.

When her mother the queen had died, she left Bridget few warm memories and the responsibility for managing the castle, a job for which she was poorly equipped and ill prepared. Her father, who had ignored her for years, had little sympathy. "For God's sake, child! Your mother did it and so must you." And oh, how she tried!

She would spend the better part of her day tracking down receipts, vendors and merchants. Checking invoices, counting casks, barrels and flocks, she knew that the servants and household were becoming fat with fraud but could never prove anything. The former steward had an excuse for everything, always. A barrel of wine had fallen and broken, a cart had crushed two sheep, and the laundress had torn the clothes. Always an excuse. Bridget was humiliated by his treatment, his disdain and blatant lies. She felt as helpless and as powerless as a fawn, but as a fawn might run or hide, she could not; and as princess and as a woman, she began to loathe the steward and her own cowardice. Her eyes became downcast in his presence; she stooped as she walked and no longer laughed at all, anytime or anywhere.

There comes a time in the lives of people when destiny presents them with a choice: stay on this same path if you like or choose this one if you dare. It happens many times, sometimes we are aware of it but most often not. And when presented, the choice is there but for a flicker of a moment. The time for the princess came on a day not unlike the many that had preceded it.

Sitting at the table, her breakfast completed, she told Gwenthe to beckon the steward.

Her face was reddened when she returned, caused by something Bridget could not ascertain. "Milady, the steward says that he is very busy, very busy and could you come see him later."

She could have ignored this insult and gone on with her day, mindful of the gross effrontery that had been given. Instead she stood.

"Gwenthe," in a voice barely audible, "tell the steward to come here."

She huffed towards the clanging kitchen and a few moments later there was a great uproar with yelling and cursing as the steward, with ledger in hand, strode importantly towards the princess.

His usually florid face was now scarlet with anger, he slammed the ledger open on the table. "Lookee here, milady. I cannot do me job properly with all these in'truptions."

"Is something the matter then, steward?" she asked, with an equanimity he did not notice.

Looking her dead in the eye and at arm's length, he said with a grin beginning,

"Why, yes indeed! Two barrels of wine broke last night, a sack of flour has gone weevily and wolves killed two sheep."

Whether it was from her years of neglect by her parents, or lack of respect shown woman in general, she did not know. Neither did she know if it was caused by his insolence and willingness to take advantage of her youthful inexperience. It didn't matter. Not now, not ever again.

Fisting her hands she swung at the steward like a man and landed a blow against the side of his head. The steward, taken unawares, was stunned but unhurt. Letting out a yell from somewhere deep within, her other hand rammed straight against his nose from which blood suddenly spurt. As he began to fall away the princess pressed her attack, fighting not with maiden-like slaps, but with wide, rounding punches that more often than not, found their mark. For his part, all the steward could do was to try to protect his face from the battering blows that now had him on the floor.

Yelling and cursing, Bridget stood over the man and began kicking him in the ribs and side of the head, but this was not as satisfying as using her hands. She dropped to her knees and once again began flailing at the head that had now become something more like bloody flesh in the shape of a face. Her anger and rage, no longer held in check, continued to erupt as the pummeling continued. The man, for his part, did nothing except try to evade the blows that came from everywhere! While it might be thought that he was being bested because she was a woman of birth, such was not the case—he was being overpowered.

Still swearing mightily, her arms tiring, she switched to her more feminine weapons and began to use her nails, going for his eyes.

"You son of a whore! You bastard! You cowardly bastard!" as she raked the side of his neck with her nails leaving fresh red rivulets in their wake. Punching and clawing, she changed position, hoping to get a better angle from which to attack and finish him off.

Seeing that the battle had been won long ago, yet startled by her ferocity, Mathilde and Gwenthe stood helplessly by, waiting for the right time to intervene. Some other servants came from the kitchen and stood slack jawed as the assault continued. Gwenthe looked at Mathilde who was as pale as a bowl of milk. "Now."

As of one mind they simultaneously grabbed Bridget's arms and shoulders and peeled her from the motionless form beneath.

"No!" Kicking and screaming at the man as she was lifted, she suddenly went limp and with no more than a final look at the steward, allowed herself to be walked up the stairs. The rage that almost killed the man had also saved him; blinded by her anger, she had not noticed the knife on the table, barely five feet away. Had she but taken it, he would most certainly have been singing with the *castrati*, or worse.

Clucking with concern, the chambermaids washed her damaged hands. Skin had been peeled from most of the knuckles, nails were bent and there were areas of tooth impressions on the fingers. Feeling an inward serenity that was long due, Bridget allowed them to apply a soothing balm and dressings. "I think I shall nap now, Gwenthe, thank you."

She was not even to her room when news of the assault began to spread, first within the kitchen, then to the stables, from there to the knights and squires and then to the trades people and merchants, to the peasants, to the clergy. Each retelling added more carnage until some had heard that in a fit of madness over his thievery, the princess had ripped out the knave's heart, eaten it and thrown the body to the pigs. No one saw, no one knew, whatever became of the battered man.

Ah, but that delicious bit of abandon had been more than two years ago and from that time forward she feared no man nor woman. She stood erect, even if it made her taller than the men around her. She did not care; she was the princess and mistress of the castle. A wan smile crossed her lips as she thought of that day, her day of reckoning and growth.

Peter, the new steward, was something altogether different. With his characteristic fluidity, he walked to her, bowed and presented the day's ledger.

"My princess." He said in a respectful tone as he bowed.

"My steward." She replied, "Sit here and let us go over the foodstuffs."

The remainder of the great hall began to fill with soldiers; those coming from guard duty and those going on. There was the barking of dogs, general clatter and noise as more than a hundred men milled, laughed and ate.

Peter turned the ledger towards her and began to detail precisely what the stores were, what was needed, the projected cost and possible substitutions. While the princess ran over the pages with her eyes, Peter knew it by heart. Not unexpectedly, there had been a dramatic decrease in the number of broken casks and killed sheep. Too, the steward kept meticulous records on repairs being made on the castle. Bridget did not know how he did it, didn't care. She was interested in results and Peter was scrupulously efficient.

"That will be all, Peter. Tomorrow we shall inspect the gates you mentioned and I should like to see the granaries."

With a bow at the waist and a serious expression, he removed the ledger and returned to the kitchen.

She motioned for her two handmaidens, "Gwenthe, Mathilde, today I shall ride."

She pushed back from her chair, and surveyed the noisy hall as she spun on her heel towards the courtyard.

Muddy and filled with milling men and horses, the courtyard held the stables, barracks and training arena for the king's army. The barracks that housed the common soldier and the occasional knight were on the left with the stables for more than fifty horses on the right. Directly in front of the princess was the training area for the warriors. Heavy posts, chewed by countless attacks, stuck out of the ground like rotted teeth as knights and those who would aspire to knighthood, slashed and struck them with broad swords, mace or spear.

The men, clad in tunics and tights, were already sweating in the early morning light. Their swords chopped with dry whacks. Young they were—sinewy, serious and scarred. Battle and war was more than their livelihood, it was their life. Rare was the man who had endured and survived numerous battles to become a seasoned veteran. Young boys with wooden swords did the same thing to the posts as their mentors studied and criticized their moves. Warring, a serious business, guaranteed only death however they risked all for the promise of wealth, fame and honor.

Surveying the sword-swiping group was Lord Glamorgan. With his hands balled into flexing fists, he walked up and down, cursing and uttering oaths at the straining men before him. His black hair, streaked with silver, was matted against his forehead, as he continued bellowing

"Uncle."

Lord Glamorgan twisted around sharply and at once bowed slowly and deliberately and with a broad smile crossing his face. "My lady. I am so pleased to see you but regret that your eyes must witness these poor excuses for fighting men."

Lady Bridget smiled warmly. "Uncle, you have said the same thing to me all these years and yet we continue to win battles, do we not?"

"Fate has given us those victories, certainly not the skills of these men."

"I think you judge them harshly. Uncle, I shall be riding to the Abbey today and would need an escort. Not that I require one, but my father—"

Glamorgan knew only too well what was left unsaid. An attack on the Princess was an attack on the king and his kingdom. Should the Princess suffer a scraped knee, Lord Glamorgan would be held accountable. Not that attacks on nobility were common, but it had happened last year during a festival when some drunken peasants had dehorsed a particularly odious knight and killed him. They were executed, of course—hanged. But this sort of thing had to be guarded against.

"Of course, my Lady. As you wish."

He turned around, "You and you," as he pointed at two young knights, "shall escort the princess at peril of your miserable lives. Get your worthless nags and meet milady by the stables." Sheathing their swords, the two knights grinned at the good fortune that had saved them from the muscle-numbing exercises. They came towards Glamorgan as he beckoned them forward. Sirs Maldwyn and Astorious were vassals of Glamorgan, their lord. As yet unpropertied, they were eager and hungry for battle and glory yet were just as happy to quit the morning toils.

They bowed. "The two of you, take care. The princess is my special charge and I have cherished her since she was a little girl. Mind that she comes to no harm. Kill anyone who even looks crossly at her. And be aware, she rides better than you. Go."

Princess Bridget walked deliberately towards the stable, inhaling the smell deeply. Looking into their faces, she ran her hands over their thick muscular necks and jaws, grinning at their big eyes and pricked ears. A stable boy, his cap removed, bowed awkwardly, speechless.

"Please saddle Alexander"

"Yes 'um." The boy flew to the appropriate stall with the tack dragging from his narrow shoulders. She grinned at the retreating figure and turned to look across the courtyard. With a high fence and two gates, it was separated from the rest of the castle's main structure. She saw the two that would accompany her. Nice looking young men and no doubt courteous, but she had no use for them other than their protection and their ability to fight. Not that she was disinclined towards men, it was just that it was pointless to carry on so. Her destiny lay with the convent and the good Abbess.

His eyes downcast, the stumbling stable boy returned with Alexander, her white stallion. "Oh, sweet Alexander!! And how are you, my big lovely?" She ran her hands along his cheek and over his ears, which he pointed quizzically at the young woman before him. She did not hesitate and in a totally unfashionable manner mounted her steed just as smoothly as any man, her knees gripping the horse's flanks. As soon as she had mounted, Maldwyn and Astorious joined her. Bowing from horseback, they saluted her. "We are honored to have been chosen to accompany milady." Said the raffish-looking Maldwyn.

"Excellent. We shall ride the countryside and thence to the Abbey. Now, let us go."

With Maldwyn leading and Astorious taking up their rear, they headed out the gate leading towards the castle's common area.

The peasants didn't need to be told to make way, anyone on horseback, dressed in finery and escorted by knights, was immediately given a wide berth. The Princess was well known, however, and her masculine riding manner made her easily distinguishable. Women curtsied and men removed their caps and bowed awkwardly as she passed and headed towards the castle gate. The throngs passing to and fro were easily jostled aside by the horses. The knights, though glad to have been set free from their calisthenics, took their job seriously and made sure no one came too near; to have her abused or insulted by some vagabond meant facing the famous brutality of a wrathful Glamorgan.

Bridget, erect and comfortable, looked straight ahead as they headed out the gate and on to the cart-worn path. Once clear of the milling mob, she allowed Alexander to break into an easy canter. Passing through the closely cropped fields on either side, her nostrils were assaulted with the rich, lush scent of the wet dirt. There was no other smell quite like it. The rising sun was now earnestly beginning to dissipate the morning's chill and she allowed the warmth to caress her back. The only sounds she heard were those that involved her excursion. The steady beat of the hooves and the strong breathing of the horses worked their rhythm into her.

Ever since she was a little girl, riding had been a passion that gave a physical and emotional release. Left to her own devices and her tutor by her parents and ignored by her older sister, Bridget obtained an education unlike many of her station. Yes, she could spin and brocade, though it ached her hands and bored her beyond endurance. Taught to read and speak Latin and Greek, she would sit captivated as her Irish tutor spoke of the world outside the twenty or so miles with which she was familiar; of sea serpents and Atlantis and of women warriors and jealous gods and beasts too terrible to describe. Her imagination, once kindled, never died.

And when at last her tutor had tired or became distracted, the young princess stole towards the courtyard and from a respectable distance observed the comings and goings of the knights and their horses. Her matronly guardian did not approve of such actions from a princess and one so young at that, but the overriding rule was to keep her out of the way of her parents. And so it was one day that she met Glamorgan.

Standing beside some casks and holding on to the hand of her governess, she watched as one of the knights, large, loud, with angry eyes and ragged beard, came towards her leading a white pony. He stood before her, looking down as she looked up.

"And who might you be who comes here each day to watch as my men and I work and sweat?"

"Bridget." She said huskily.

"D'ye mean Princess Bridget?" He demanded.

"Yes…I am Princess Bridget." In a voice growing somewhat smaller.

"Ah," he said as he bowed with respect and caring, "your humble servant, Glamorgan, my lady."

And from that day to the present he had become her "uncle" in truth if not in blood as the gruff warrior befriended and became her other, more interesting, mentor. She learned about swords and daggers and armor. Though she was not permitted to do anything resembling warlike behavior in view of others, she was not above grabbing a wooden sword and whacking and thrusting the posts and sacks in private. He allowed her to watch, hidden, as the young men fought and wrestled. She learned about horses and she learned how to ride, not like a woman, but like a man.

It was not unusual for women of station to ride. Indeed, many ladies were as passionate about hunting and falconry as their husbands, it was just that Bridget found it much more comfortable to ride full in the saddle, the ladies be damned! And it made jumping so much easier. Horseback riding was not just a finely honed amusement, it was a rough form of freedom, a living outside the castle where she was in control of her destiny. How was it that she could control so huge and powerful a beast as a horse and yet be told how she must sit, properly, like a lady? Ah, to ride was to live! Away from the castle she would let the sun warm her and the wind twist her hair in wild, cascading knots. Sometimes she would laugh from the sheer joy of galloping through an open field, alive and breathless—the mistress of herself.

She grinned as the little girl memories seeped into her consciousness. Good thoughts and good feelings overpowered the parental neglect and sibling taunts. It would have been easy for one in her position to become spoiled. With servants, tutors, and a family that neither loved nor hated her, she was able to blend her experiences into her own personality without undue influence. Thus she could tell her tutor, Clement, that though she had never seen a unicorn she mightily believed in them and the magic they held. The same argument was also used to bulwark her belief in the Christ God. Though He could not be seen, it was evident that many had and that a God who would become a man and die for the sins of the World, well, that was a God of love.

She also recalled the time she had fallen off her pony and broken her forearm while attempting to jump a small log. Glamorgan had warned her against it, had warned her all the time about learning to ride before she attempted to guide such a large animal over a jump. She remembered two things most vividly of that day. The throbbing pain that would not allow her to make a fist and the sudden pallor of her uncle as sweat beaded over his upper lip. He was so solicitous, it was the first time she had ever seen him flustered as he alternately threatened to kill himself, her or her horse!

"This has never happened, Uncle," she stated flatly as they entered the courtyard.

"What do you mean, my Lady?"

She turned towards him as he held the reins of both their horses, "Uncle, should my father ever learn that I have been injured in this manner he will forbid me from ever riding again, and that will not do. No, not at all. And, you see, he may blame you for my own stupidity and that would not be fair, would it?"

He bent towards her ever so slightly so that an observer would only think that he was straining to hear more clearly. "What do you have in mind, my Princess?" He said in a conspiratorial voice.

For that one moment, Bridget wished her uncle didn't drink so much wine as his fragrant breath washed over her.

"We were out beyond sight of the castle and off the main road, so we were not seen. No one knows of my injury and my tunic is untorn. You will return the horses to the stable and I shall leave and have an unfortunate accident. Unfortunate in that I shall not be able to ride for a while."

He stood up straight, never taking his eyes from her, "My Lady." She dismounted unsteadily and strode into the castle. Glamorgan remarked to himself that she was a damned good liar in spite of the nuns and priests and her only twelve years old! It was later that night as he was making his rounds of the guards that he learned that Princess Bridget had slipped while getting out of her bath and had broken her arm.

A larger grin came upon her face as the Princess recalled that day when she and her uncle became conspirators. Well, logs were meant to be jumped and as she spied one about one hundred yards to her left, she dug her heels into Alexander's flanks and said, "Go, Alexander!"

The horse, unaccustomed to being ridden sedately, sprang forward as the two knights were caught unawares. Alexander went into full stride quickly as he allowed himself to be guided towards the fallen tree. Galloping now, the princess crowed as she glanced at her two hapless guards and then turned again towards her goal. In no time at all, it seemed, she leaned forward and whispered loudly into the horse's ear, "Fly, Alexander!" And he did, with grace, power and dignity. Bridget felt that giddy, weightless feeling as horse and rider became one being, an unthinking animal of action that would not be denied. They landed smoothly and in one fluid motion she brought her horse into a canter and headed back towards the path. Her two companions had not even made it to the jump and they veered towards her in a flurry of excitement and exclamations.

"My Lady! My Lady!" Was all they could say breathlessly as they came up to either flank.

"Alexander and I wanted to jump." She said to no one in particular. "Now let us go about our business and pay more attention." She laughed to herself. Though she did not look at either of them, she knew that they would have flushed faces, embarrassed that the princess, a woman, had ridden better than they. Would they have felt such shame if a prince had done it? Probably not, she thought. As soon they regained the road they came upon several thatched cottages.

Not a village in any sense, most of those of her father's kingdom lived like this. A loose collection of peasants who grazed the sheep, goats and pigs in common and yet tilled the land individually either with mule or oxen, which ever was cheaper. Children, too young to work, mostly naked, were scurrying about and laughing as children do. Two women walked side by side, each holding a suckling infant with an arm and a hip, carrying a bucket of water with the other. As the entourage approached, they bowed their heads clumsily.

"Good day, ladies," said the Princess as she stopped Alexander, "has young mistress Annine given birth yet? She looked quite ready to go light a fortnight ago."

The two women looked at one another quickly and then squinted up at the Princess.

"La, sorry milady, but the babe was born without a heartbeat last evening. A terrible thing it was, but it is God's will. Annine and her man were quite beside themselves at first, but the priest has been fetched and will talk to them, surely."

Born dead. How many had the Princess heard of like this? Countless, it seemed. She shuddered inwardly at the thought of giving birth to a dead, wet thing.

"God's will." She replied and began heading forward once again.

As they rode at a comfortable and easy pace she let her mind wander as Alexander took over. Children. Childbirth. Death. The concepts swirled about her head in a loose lather. No, she would not have children, she would not marry. She was too young to risk death, too scared of that particular void. True, if she had not committed a mortal sin she would go to heaven and be with Jesus and Mary, but the pain frightened her, and the blood and the crying. All of it. Let others of her sex bear children, let Celestine have her heir. Oh, how she admired Celestine's bravery! "Well, good for her," she thought, "not for me."

The disquieting thoughts fled as rapidly as a barn swallow when she heard the bells of the abbey announcing prayer again. Out of sight from the castle yet within sound of its clarion call, the abbey had become the princess's obsession ever since she had decided that she would not, could not, marry.

The choices for women whether of gentility or poverty were not many. Spinsterhood and what? Watching the petty intrigues of the court? She had no power to speak of and certainly no property. Without a husband or child she would be as worthless to the court as she would be to herself. In spite of her education, organizational skills and her facility with languages, she would become a female drone. A frown creased the corner of her otherwise straight mouth. *Become what? Dry of flesh and spirit, the one that is always around but never invited. What would I have to confess? The priest would become so maddeningly bored that I'd have to invent some indiscretions to wake him up. If Celestine ever has that baby I could become the spinster aunt!*

Travel was yet another possibility but one with limited probability as her father would most certainly declare that such extravagances had to have at least some promise of a return to the kingdom, whether via gold, soldiers or alliances and as she was unwilling to marry, why bother?

Why was I created a woman, my God? I have neither the talents nor the desire to be as such around me! Sweet Lord, I know when you were in the Garden you asked that the cup may be passed, yet you drank from it freely, but I am not you, my sweet Lord. Closing her eyes, she tilted her head heavenward so that God might more easily hear her. *My God, you know that I will always love and obey you and your commandments, so forgive me for doubting your eternal wisdom. Yet I know that I can do and be so much more, yet am hindered by my sex, Lord. Did not Eve and all women after have children with pain?*

At this point she came to the crux of her misgivings for at least the thousandth time. Her mother had been taken with a fever after giving birth to her that she never fully recovered and had become an emaciated, breathing thing that looked more like some bent, dead branch. Her decline had been so painfully slow that the princess was old enough to recall her and the smell that had permeated her mother's room. Frightened, she would clutch Gwenthe's large leg and bury her face in her dress with the childhood hope that force and strength and wanting it to go away would make it so. It did when her mother obligingly died and what surprised her the most was Gwenthe's tears and overwhelming sadness so evident on her good, honest face.

And then there was always the excellent possibility that if she did not die immediately after birthing, the baby would die before its second year. Why did God allow that? Why, if He was so loving and merciful, would He do that? How could He break those parents' hearts so? Why did a poor babe, not yet weaned, turn horribly cold at the breast? Why, my dear Lord?

Her eyes still closed, she waited for God to answer, to send her some striking, soul-shattering response, but He did not. Once again she remembered that God had not given Job any answers either, only more questions. Contemplating more, she had the sadly chilling realization of just whom she was questioning so brashly. His Son, He allowed, His only son to be stripped, whipped, mocked and nailed to a cross. What kind of a God would do that? Can any sacrifice I make dare to compare with His? No, never.

"Forgive me Father, for doubting You." She whispered, unheard by her escorts who kept a wary eye on their surprising charge who now appeared to be in some sort of reverie, perhaps praying to herself as they wended their way to the abbey.

Her eyes opened once more, satisfied that she had not blasphemed for asking Him so many questions. She thought of more mortal babies and the pregnant women who bore them. Grotesquely fat, sick and awkward women, their ponderous bellies making even getting up from a chair look painful, never! Their complaints, the vomiting, their swollen breasts as they suckled their children. Well, she was a princess and would have a wet nurse to take care of that part, of course, but for the rest of it, well, it would never happen. *And I probably would not be allowed to ride Alexander!*

She had witnessed many animals giving birth while growing up and was awe struck by the simplicity of the whole thing. Nothing much to it really, messy, but the mare, cow and bitch never seemed to be in any great distress. Then Gwenthe had allowed her to see one of the wayward maids give birth with the hopes that such a spectacle would keep the Princess from any untowards lusting after men before wedlock. Ten years old, she stood in the corner of a crowded room while Gwenthe's plate-sized hand held hers. The cries of the young women only brought scolding laughter from the two women (both married) attending her.

"Well, I sees 'ow your legs are spread again!"

"Don't feel so good this time around, does it now, slut."

A third woman, the midwife, sat on a small stool and kept peering and probing between the open legs, muttering encouragement. Every so often she would place her hand on the taut skin of the belly and give a firm push, but mostly she just let it lie there, feeling the life beneath the undulating abdomen.

The maid, her name forgotten, prayed, cursed and cried out. Watching her give birth was like watching a snake swallow a frog, repulsive yet fascinating. A trembling and shaking Bridget, her eyes widened with fear, seemed to breathe in unison with the straining woman before her. Sweat, lots of sweat and varying shades of blood and crying, that was what she remembered most. That and, "Ah, here's the little bastard, at last."

The wizened woman on the stool deftly grabbed the slippery infant by the heels and smartly struck him on the back and buttocks till he at last began to squall. Taking a finger she drew it through the mouth and placed a coarse blanket around the infant and gave it to the mother. The other two women began trying to determine out who the father was. "Well, with a thing that small, it could be anyone's."

Bridget had never forgotten that spectacle.

The three rode abreast now on the hard packed path; the princess deep within her own thoughts, her mind exercising its freedom as Maldwyn and Artorious became less anxious as they neared their destination. Through a stand of firs on the top of a small ridge they were able to gaze down at the Abbey of The Passionate Cross. Like starlings, figures in black bent to their work in the fields that flanked the road and surrounded the building proper.

The structure itself had been built less than fifty years ago, back when the lands were less populated than at present. The Sisters of Mercy had hoped to have been granted a post in Ireland where it had been rumored that libraries and books were plentiful. But the pope had sent them here instead, to the land of pagans; a land and a people not much removed from human sacrifice. Obedient, they had come and brought with them their plans for a dwelling that was better designed for the hospitable climate of Italy than ragged weather of Britain.

A large two-story square building housed the occupants comfortably and permitted ample room for all their daily activities—which were endless toil and ceaseless prayer with some few moments set aside for food and sleep. By far the most striking thing about the Abbey was its inner courtyard that had been designed much like its Italian counterpart. Small trees, shrubs and flowers blanketed it, as a gravel-covered path snaked its way through the flora. Icons of The Virgin in various hardwoods stood sentinel as there was no marble, nor artisans skilled in that medium in this part of the world. A covered walkway, with carved benches to allow one to sit and pray, surrounded the blessed garden.

As they drew closer to the opened gate, a broad and gentle smile spread across the princess's face.

Yes, this is where I belong; where I may serve my Lord to the best of my poor ability.

As they dismounted a young and haggard novitiate, so designated by her white garb, came up and wordlessly took the reins of the steeds and led the horses to the stable where they would be watered and fed.

"The Reverend Mother is expecting you, my Lady." Said another flushed novitiate, fast on the heels of the one who had taken the horses. Turning to her guards Bridget said bluntly, "I shall be safe here. These are women of God, mind that you are Christian men and behave like it."

Rebuked, the two knights bowed uncomfortably. As she turned to follow the nervous girl, she thought she heard "itch" uttered, but could not be sure and did not let it effect her pace.

For so long the abbey had been her fixation, her redeemer. It was here, she that she belonged. Surrounded by other women, many superbly educated, she would be able worship God in freedom and so much more. She had seen the blessed ladies, sitting at benches in front of the opened windows painstakingly copying manuscripts with an artistry she admired as the new pages were illuminated with skill. Moreover, some of the sisters took it upon themselves to begin translating the works they were copying. It was here that she felt she could best be used; engaging in dialogue with another about the correct tense of a verb or possible meanings for a Greek phrase!

She would work in the field and in the kitchen, of course, but she also knew that ladies of her standing were used in ways more suitable to their talents. Coming to an oaken door with heavy iron bands, the novitiate knocked timidly.

"Reverend Mother, Princess Bridget."

To Bridget it looked as though the young girl fled after her knock, but no matter. She waited patiently, trying to hear something behind the door. But as always, she heard nothing until it opened slowly and noisily to reveal the abbess.

Reverend Mother, Sister Maria, Abbess, stood in the doorway, her hands clasped together. Draped in black robes, the only visible flesh were her hands and face.

The princess dropped to both knees. "Reverend Mother." She said respectfully with head bowed and eyes closed. The presence before her placed both hands on top of her head, then cupped the princess's face, soft as a memory.

"Arise, my child. You honor the abbey and this humble servant of God."

With that, the princess grasped the finely-boned hands of the old nun and kissed them both gently before standing.

Sister Maria's head barely came to the lower part of the Princess's shoulder but her voice, deep and rich, sounded as though it came from within a cave. Mellow and sonorous, it was a voice that caressed the listener and delighted the ear. That words spoken with such beauty might instruct or vilify was secondary; when the shepherds heard the angels, it was with a voice such as this.

"It is so good to see my beloved princess on such a fine morning as God has given us. Come, let us walk about the garden so that we may enjoy His blessings!"

It was the time of year when the cold of the rocks and soil battled with the warming air, heavy with the promise of rain. Allowing the nun to place her hand around arm, they walked silently over the limestone walk; the only sounds were that of some birds trilling invisibly in the garden. The sun, much higher now, warmed their shoulders.

As they walked silently, the princess found herself recalling the time the Abbess had come to the castle to celebrate the Birth of Christ. Some of the men, if not most, had become drunk and loud, celebrating not as Christian men should, but as reminders of the Old Ways.

"May the peace of this day be with us, always." Was all she had said, but somehow it carried over and through the carousing assembly and was heard distinctly throughout the great hall. As of one mind, all speech halted and the eyes of the celebrants followed the track of this black sparrow as she slowly walked to the dais where the king sat. Bowing, she said, "May the Lord hold you in the palm of His hand, King Gwaldner."

"You honor us this day, good sister." And the king rose and actually bowed to the little nun!

Yes, she remembered that day, and yes, Reverend Mother was much like a bird, thin with nervous, dark, clear eyes. Her olive-colored skin was beginning to furrow across the brow and cheeks, but the eyes, dark and deep, had a fire in them. They walked without speaking and as had become their custom, entered the chapel.

Fully two stories high, the room was dominated by a full-size crucifix secured against the wall at one end of the room. The oaken figure of a gaunt and broken Jesus was painted in muted tones; He looked upward, beseechingly, painfully. At either side of the same wall were two small, stained glass windows. One depicted a strident Moses with flowing beard, holding the commandments of God, while the other showed the Virgin crushing a snake's head beneath her foot. A small, unadorned wooden altar sat but a few feet in front of the wall and faced the roomful of chairs before it. The two women knelt on the stone floor as they made the Sign of The Cross.

The Abbess closed her eyes as Bridget began to pray. That she loved the young woman next to her was not a surprise. Bridget, so full of life, so spirited, delighted the older woman. *What does this young one think of me? She sees an old woman, no doubt, but she does not see me as ever being young. Who could believe that an old nun had once been a girl?*

She had grown up in a small farming village just outside Rome. Her family, like all the others, was large and lusty. Three older brothers and two younger sisters helped their parents tend to the grapes, olives and goats and pigs. It was a hard life that showed no distinction between the work of a woman or a man. She had plowed behind the mule with her brothers, hadn't she? And after plucking the ripened olives from the trees she would hurl the heavy baskets to her sister who stood in the waiting cart to stack them. She was always small, this one. The smallest member of a family known for their size, she was gristle and gut. The muscles of her shoulders and thighs rippled beneath the sweaty, sun browned skin as she toiled along side her grunting family. And they had laughter, all of them, a gift of the climate that was both warm and lush.

She sighed. Remembering the warmth of the sun and soil back then did nothing to take away the cold hardness of this barbaric place! But it had been created by God and so it must serve His greater purpose in some way; her knees, spent in a generation of prayer, held firm against the floor as Bridget continued to worship.

Could she ever believe, could anyone believe, that I once had a lover?

His name was Antonius and what a fine, good-looking man he had been! With his dark hair short and lightly oiled, he smelled as sweet and fresh as the morning air. His eyes were the color of shiny leather and full of laughter. They had met for the first time during a day at market when she was unloading the cart. She felt him looking at her long before she spied him standing across the road, leaning against a cart. She looked up swiftly. "Anyone can stand with their arms folded." She muttered sullenly.

"Ah, but no woman can look as beautiful as you working, Bella!"

She recalled the flushing she felt as she turned her head away from the mocking figure and continued her work. When she looked up a few minutes later, he was gone. The next time they had met had been several weeks later during a harvest celebration in a neighboring town. The festival had been preceded by a days worth of labor as they helped neighbors begin the harvest. That night a large fire had been started and the wine and song would begin to dull the aches of their bodies. Joining hands, the crowd circled the fire and began running this way and that around it. That people would stumble and fall was part of the gaiety as the participants became golden shadows before the roaring light. Again, she felt his presence before she saw him looking at her just outside the circle of light. Again, he had his arms folded.

She walked boldly up to him, "Anyone can stand with their arms folded."

"But none can look as lovely as you, Bella."

And they kissed. She didn't know what to expect at first and didn't care. Her arms wrapped around his waist as her mouth reached up to his. With eyes closed her body seemed to explode as their tongues met. Was it the climate, the passion of the celebration? It didn't matter. There was nothing timid or awkward about the jousting of their mouths. Her lips became a gate that opened and closed on his probing tongue; sometimes she would let it enter her mouth and search for hers; other times she would suck on it. Her breathing came deeper and quicker, she felt her thudding heart beat as their bodies pressed together. She knew it was wrong, that she should stop, but also knew that she couldn't. Inhaling his breath was intoxicating; her body became alive to the slightest touch. Their tongues danced willfully, neither asking or receiving quarter.

With one mind they began withdrawing from the crowded fire and backed into the shadows. There was no mystery to either of them when it came to sex; living on a farm and in crowded conditions had removed any sense of modesty, real or feigned, long ago. But the passion! Ah, this field had never been plowed by either.

Holding hands they stumbled in the dark till they came to a fig tree where they lay on the ground. Wordlessly, with gasps, they continued to kiss. Their hands running hurriedly over each other, she felt his hand caress her breast as she pushed it against him. Such exquisite fire! She untied her blouse and his hand touched her tingling nipples, erect and with a sensitivity she had never known. The newness, the excitement was beyond her imagination—she had never known it could be like this! Just when she thought she could not be any more frenzied, she proved herself wrong and began arching her back in an attempt to push her breast towards his mouth.

What little light there was, was just enough for her to see the eyes of her young Antonius; they were not laughing now but were instead deep and intent. She rolled him over in one sudden rush, her body, as if muscled with steel bands, did it without effort. Sitting on his stomach, she wordlessly and quickly pulled off her blouse and bent over, letting his mouth find her right breast, then the left.

His mouth was a magic thing as he began to lick, suck and gently bite her fleshy globes as he squeezed them warmly

She moaned, softly at first, as she inched her hips back slowly while allowing his mouth to caress her breasts. Finally, when she could stretch no longer, she sat up and felt his stiffness through his breeches. From somewhere deep inside a place of her that she never knew existed, a soft growl started. It startled the two of them at first, but neither was of a mind to explain it. Sitting upon him like this she closed her eyes and rocked gently on him, feeling the jolts of fire from each erect nipple run deep between her legs. Growling still, she ripped his shirt easily and began running her fingers along his finely-haired chest. She felt his hips begin to grind with hers and she laughed as she threw her head back. Yes, yes! She was no longer capable of thinking, only feeling, as her nails now dug ragged scratches into his torso.

Wordlessly, she reached back and began to loosen his breeches as he lifted his buttocks up and pulled them down just enough to allow his rod out. Reaching behind with two hands, she grasped it and felt its silky hardness. She squeezed it a little and this brought a gasp from his core, whether of pain or pleasure, she could not tell, nor did she care. With her skirt still on, she rose on her knees and arched her hips just till she felt it part the wet lips. Never had she felt such a sensation, never. Every fiber of her was awake, her body and mind were distinct yet somehow blended and forged into some new creature. Still holding it, she began to sit back ever so slowly, ever so slowly till at last she felt a thrust of pain which startled her at first, but she waited and sat back a bit more, biting her lip to hold back a small cry. It seemed as though she kept sitting back forever, the smallest bit of entry bringing a new delight that raced through her. At last she could sit no further and with eyes closed stayed completely still, allowing the fullness of the moment to consume her. She felt her toes curl. How strange was that?

Then she began to move. She had never seen two people actually make love before. This was some part of her that had never been awakened until now. Her hips pulsed and gyrated as her breathing became long and regular; enjoying the fullness of each stroke as it went up inside her wet delight. For how long this went on she could not tell but at last something changed yet again and that soft growl surfaced once more. No longer seeing, or hearing, her hips began moving with an urgency and rhythm all their own. Faster now, she began clutching and digging her fingers into his chest, at one time pounding it, as her whole body began to dance, her breasts heaving wildly, and then a long paroxysm as her body seemed to contract all at once. It was the joining of fire and water where both existed at the same time; it was a feeling so impossible, so overwhelming that she whimpered.

She did not move as she felt the sweat run from her armpits down her sides. She began sucking huge bellows of air into her starved lungs, as if she had never breathed before. Slowly, very slowly her breathing became more normal and the cool night air began to soothe the heat of their passion. Opening her eyes she gazed into the face of Antonius whose eyes were opened wide as he looked up at her.

"Mother of God! I swear to you that I never thought it could be like that!"

"Good?"

"Yes, good. Wonderful"

They stayed in the same position for a few moments longer, each feeling uncomfortable in ending such an exquisite pleasure till at last Maria said, "My legs are beginning to cramp staying like this." She stood stiffly while he rolled onto his side and began standing and pulling up his pants. Though dark, they found their clothes and hurriedly put themselves together before heading back towards the fire and the shouting throng.

Maria felt the sticky wetness between her thighs as she began walking back. The lewdness of it all brought a small smile to her face and feeling his seed mingling with her own fluids made her begin to tingle again. Without a word, they kissed once more, gently, their tongues rolling, before they reached the perimeter of the bonfire and separated. Her mother thought she had drunk too much wine as she laid quietly in the cart along with her brothers and sisters who were talking and laughing with the silliness of innocence.

Later that night, as she laid in bed with her sisters the youngest whined. "What's that funny smell?" It was all she could do to stop from bursting out in laughter.

"Hush! Your sister probably passed some air!"

In the darkness Maria heard her sister giggle.

But that was a lifetime ago.

The Abbess reached her arm around Bridget's shoulder and hugged her warmly.

No, the Princess will never know what that summer was like! How we met secretly and hurriedly, each time newer and more exciting than the time before as we explored each other with our fingers and tongues.

But that was so long ago. They had been discovered of course; she heard her father say "honor" for the first time—but rather than marry the young man she had chosen to enter the convent. Bold and brazen, she was also a quick learner with a facility for reading and writing that had amazed her teachers. There was no more devout sister in the order and her rise had been swift, sure and tumultuous.

As she kneeled with the Princess next to her, she thought back once again. She had confessed her sins with all due sorrow and fear and had done her penance a hundred fold, yet she never regretted her actions. Surely, one could not live without making mistakes and you could not live fully if you regretted all your misdeeds forever. That God loved her and forgave her was enough. She did not delight in her sins, but neither did she shy from them—she had lived.

Her knees starting to ache, the Abbess cleared her throat and made the Sign of the Cross as did the princess. Silently they stood up and headed towards the door where they dipped their fingers in Holy Water and again crossed themselves.

The chapel bell sounded once again.

"Will you break bread with us, my dear? I am certain the other sisters would enjoy seeing you again." In truth, the Abbess knew the food, though plain, was spicy and filling and she wanted the princess to feel at home here—she wanted Bridget to become one of the Order. For the Abbess had only two loves in her life now: God and the order. The pope, if he were more a man of God than a polititian might have earned some degree of respect, but he was who he was.

Yes, the princess would bring a nice dowry to the order and with that came power and with that power came the responsibility to use it for the promotion of God. The Abbess sighed once more; it had been much easier plucking olives and lifting barrels.

CHAPTER THREE

As her sister was preparing to leave the abbey more than a score of miles away, Celestine sat before the burnished mirror caressing her hair with long strokes of the mother of pearl brush, a gift from some dignitary or other. Gazing at herself, she marveled once more at her ability to mask the emotions of torment and anger that even now coursed through her veins and churned her brain. Indeed, being able to hide her feelings behind a wan smile and placid demeanor even as she plotted feverishly had been a gift she had honed since childhood. Now, as an adult, this gift had become crucial to her marriage and to her role as Duchess to the richest lord of the kingdom.

This is not good; this is not good at all. The simplest peasant can have a baby almost at will. Scrawny and ribbed, they are able to walk around big-bellied in swill while I must sit here and long for a child. They all think that it is my fault, that I am cold and barren, ha! If I could only lay the blame where it belongs, the sot! I must do something; learn some way to get him proper.

That she was well-favored in appearance had also been a gift she embellished over the years with the addition of exquisite and delicate mannerisms. As her body had bloomed into womanhood, so had she learned how best to display and accentuate her charms, a practice that evoked the ire of other women in her circle but which utterly aroused their husbands.

"Wyngeth, fetch my breakfast and prepare my clothes."

Without missing a stroke of the brush, nor turning her head, she knew the old woman she had specifically chosen as her chambermaid would carry out her order.

Young girls do prattle so and their heads are full of mischief. Let my sister keep her little tart. Wyngeth knows to whom she owes her livelihood. One word from me and she'd be a beggar.

She shut her eyes as she began brushing with her left hand now.

What is the worst that can happen if I do not have a male child? My lord may attempt to divorce me or send me to a convent, but he is not that stupid. He knows what a shambles that would make of his estate and holdings. Father would not allow it. But what if I was divorced? What then? Certainly there would be other suitors eager to marry the daughter of the king. But what then? There are none nearly so wealthy or weak-willed as my current husband. There are none that would willingly give up the running of their estate such as Theodorus.

And the convent? Ha! No convent would hold me for long.

She allowed herself the thinnest of grins at the thought of being restricted to a nunnery. How long would it take, she mused, before she controlled the abbey? Though not married more than two years, she had accumulated and hidden enough gold to wield considerable power both with the church and within the kingdom.

Thank the stars for his willingness to allow me to hold court within the property.

One of the duties of the manor's lord was to settle disputes and punish vassals who broke the common law. Theodorus, whose mind chose greater ventures, allowed this duty to be relegated to Celestine with his utmost gratitude as he little liked riding from village to squalid village where he heard the most absurd complaints. Better to give his wife this arduous task.

Ah, husband! If only you knew how quickly those shillings and coppers add up. Would any other lord allow me this freedom? Doubtful.

So, for the moment divorce and being sent to the convent are not likely to occur. He could die. Hunting and falls from horses happen with regularity. Or maybe he could catch the fever? That would make me a widow with the three things men most desire: beauty, wealth and a way to the throne.

She allowed herself a sigh as she heard Wyngeth set the plates behind her. Wordlessly she arose from the mirror and sat down at the table, smelling the still warm bread with large inhalations, its yeasty vapors causing a growling within her stomach.

No. The chances of him dying suddenly and soon is too much to leave to chance.

Celestine tore a corner off the loaf and dredged it over the tub of butter before dipping it into the honey. Chewing slowly, savoring the flavors, she allowed herself the freedom to eat without calculating. The wine, gently warmed, was spiced as she liked it and she allowed its glow to warm her belly. She fingered through the baked perch, taking only the whitest meat. Her hunger satisfied, she dipped her fingers in a bowl containing water with vinegar and wiped them on a cloth. She closed her eyes and leaned back on the chair, her hands clasped.

I must have a child.

"Are my clothes prepared, Wyngeth?"

"Yes, milady."

"Go then. Have them prepare a coach with a pair and inform the sergeant-at-arms."

As the old woman removed the foodstuffs from the table, Celestine walked over to the bench where her garments had been laid out. As it was yet cold, a heavier silk gown was needed along with a light woolen cape. Dropping her linen robe to the floor, Celestine replaced the pad between her legs and tossed the bloodied one into the fire where it began to hiss angrily.

Dressing with deliberation before the mirror, the young woman checked the fall of the dress and examined it for any loose stitching or stains. A light purple, it highlighted her flaxen hair that she allowed to hang loosely on her shoulders. A pair of softest leather boots completed her dressing as she glanced one last time in the mirror to apprise her form and figure. Satisfied, she quit her chambers for the long second story hall.

Though considerably smaller than her father's castle, the manor house of her husband was more extravagant and infinitely more comfortable. The floor of the hall was made from closely hewn boards upon which a single, thick carpet padded footfalls and prevented drafts. Finely crafted candelabra from the smiths of Italy were regularly spaced and provided illumination. Upon the walls were hung oil paintings of old family members or biblical scenes. Not that she cared for those. Her favorite was the tapestry of the birth of Venus, which hung downstairs and dominated the large hall.

Her husband had balked when she first proposed hanging it above the large fireplace. "It is too immodest, too pagan." He protested.

"But husband," she replied, "it is of the finest craftsmanship. And how is it immodest? Her breasts are demurely hidden; her demeanor is virtuous and is in no wise enticing. Too, it lightens up the room. And what care you of 'pagan'? Truly. You are not a Jew yet you would have that old rag of David slinging a stone at Goliath there. Since when does my husband care what these Roman priests think? Or are you in someway intimidated by them that you must relinquish your good taste for fine art?" David and Goliath, forever fixed in battle were relegated to the darker north end.

The Hall, unlike the one of the castle, had wooden floors in place of earth. Here, because so many tramped through, there were no carpets but a fine layer of straw was used to keep down the dust and filth. With her cloak affixed, she strode purposefully through the kitchen, ignored the curtsies and bows and headed out the rear entrance. Behind the manor was a small pen for the animals that would be used to feed those within. Chickens, goats and pigs were in fragrant abundance as she waited with no little impatience for her carriage to come from the stables.

The teamster soon appeared with two chestnut stallions pulling the black-lacquered carriage that stopped before her. As they did not have the extravagance of a footman, the driver, who was also a groom, jumped unceremoniously to the ground, bowed with respect and opened the carriage door. Celestine, standing on a hewn stone, lightly raised her dress and stepped into the carriage confines. As he closed the door behind her, she said, "Do you know where the Stones are?"

"Yes, milady."

"Then we shall go there immediately and for your own sake you will drive rapidly and softly. Do you understand?"

The youth, who was used to the contradictory demands of his mistress, nodded. He could blame the slow ride on the horses, but he would be responsible for the comfort of the duchess.

"Yes, milady."

Though the sun was well up by the time they left, the chill surrounded Celestine as she pulled the cowl onto her head and hid her hands well within the folds of the cape. Closing her eyes, she allowed the creaking and coarse rocking of the carriage to lull her into an uneasy sleep; one where she was aware of her surroundings yet oblivious to them. A perfect time to allow her thoughts to return to the pressing matters at hand.

The time has certainly come to do something. It is a new season, soon the barley and wheat will be planted and soon harvested. Before the next harvest I shall be pregnant. There is no other way.

Allowing her thoughts to drift thus, she worked out the ramifications of having a child. That it would be a male she had no doubt, none.

He will be a healthy, strong baby. I shall get the best wet nurses available, import them if I must. I shall let Theodorus arrange for his classical training and education, yet we must keep him close by, he shall not be fostered, too dangerous. Father shall have to remain healthy and keep the other nobles at bay for at least a few more years. What can I do to help him? That will have to be looked into. My son, my prince, will be more fiercely protected than any bear cub! And if father should die? Theodorus has the largest amount of vassals, he would be regent until my son reached maturity, and I know I could keep Theodorus from too many grave errors in judgment. The vassalage would know where the real power of the throne lay! Who to cajole? Who to crush?

She allowed the various permutations of intrigue and power to play themselves out till at last she sensed the carriage stopping. With her eyes still closed, she felt the driver leap from his seat and only opened them when the carriage door was unbolted.

"I can go no further milady."

She let him hold her hand as she alighted from the coach to the wet grass below. She glanced at the two knights that had accompanied them.

"You shall wait here till I return."

The older of the two said, "Yes, milady."

The Stones were located several hundred yards from where the carriage had stopped. Celestine peered at the thick forest till at last she spied the familiar footpath that entered it. Barely more than a rabbit's run, the path wended over thick roots and coarse rock. The trees, not yet in full leaf, still hid the sun and what was once a chill became cold; she could see her breath as she labored alone along the broken forest floor. Stopping to rest, she noticed that hers was the only presence. No bird sang and no wind stirred the silent branches above. Was it any wonder that the priests told the people that this land was cursed, stained by the devil? But the peasants knew better.

The trail began a gradual climb, not steep, but long. Her lungs begged her to stop but she did not, could not. Her legs, long, strong and nimble, found their way till at last the forest ended as suddenly to reveal an overgrown clearing.

This is where it is, this is where it begins. Already I can sense that feeling.

Fully two hundred yards in diameter, the unwooded area was thin stubble. Unmindful of the hard earth, Celestine walked confidently towards the middle of the clearing till at last she stood in the center.

Head high, there were nineteen stones making a circle that was circumscribed by the silent trees. Dark and gray, the rocks stood unblemished by moss or lichens. Of no particular shape, they were more tall than broad and were more or less equally spaced from each other. Their surfaces were rough, cold and angular. Four of the monoliths had strange engravings on them in a language no one knew. Not Latin, not Greek, but something much older. She did not know how she knew this. These four inscribed stones stood exactly opposite one another and had she cared to connect a string to them, would have divided the circle into four equal parts.

She stood and closed her eyes as she raised her arms with palms up.

She had been here many times, of course. First as a child when, after hearing

44

of the strange place, pleaded with her father to allow her to be taken to see them. The princess, who treated most people with a polite disdain, had a special reverence for the stony circle ever since that first time when she felt a gentle tugging at her belly and felt her heart flutter within her skinny body, all knees and elbows. Oddly enough, she was the only individual so affected. As others walked, talked and even sat on the rocks, she sat quiet at their epicenter, allowing whatever it was that was present at this place to touch her.

Too, there had been times when she did not feel the pull of the stones and she would be disappointed and at a loss to explain why the cold earth did not warm her being. But nothing that happened before could compare with the feelings that now coursed through her veins like warmed oil. She began to notice a gentle thrumming, as if the taut cord of a harp had suddenly connected her belly to the center of the earth. Gentle it was, yet powerful, overwhelming with its gentle, infinite intensity. The cold disappeared as though the sun concentrated its glow upon the woman on the earth below; her skin felt flush and alive, radiant with energy as though cord was plucked by an unseen energy. She kicked off her boots, needing to curl her toes into the soil.

Time was not, only being. Her body, her brain, was no longer her own but now under the control of the Stones. The Stones, placed there before the Christ suckled, eons before the God of the desert was known, watched in silence as the woman stood before them. She saw voices and heard colors unknown as her senses grappled and reeled with the enormity of time and space. She heard the birth of winds in a land of ice and snow, and saw languages born. She knew that the Stones were the Land, the essence of the Earth and creation. The Stones maybe had not been placed at all but had grown from deep under the dirt. They were old, present before air was breathed and the wind felt. They had seen all, were all. Silent sentinels of this patch of earth, they focused the energy of the universe for those sensitive enough to feel it.

Celestine had not come here for revelations, to speak with gods or demons, but to affirm her purpose. Never one to bargain, she would bend to no deity. Now, with her senses caught up in the Essential whirlwind, being one with creation, she swore a silent oath. She would be the vessel that would carry the new king. Her womb would be his first temple; she would become his holy place. How could it be otherwise now that she was one with the Cosmos?

She had seen things or felt she had. Awareness began to leak into her consciousness; her shoulders throbbed as she lowered her arms to her side. She began pulling in deep lungfuls of air, as though she had held her breath too long during some childhood game. Her head drooped. She saw that her menstrual blood had run freely down her leg and now stained the ground.

After a few moments she felt the warmth radiate from her body to be replaced by the chill that bathed her skin with prickly flesh and for the first time she noticed her sweat-saturated clothes. Her eyes opened at last to new surroundings. Never had she been so affected here, never. She had heard the stories and the legends but thought them the stuff of childish fancy or a subject for some storyteller but now she knew.

Feeling weak, she willed her body for conscious control as she pulled on her boots—not caring that her foot was red with the thin blood. She turned around, gazing hard at each and every rock as if expecting them to have altered their shapes or color. The sun had hardly moved a whit, she noticed. As if Time had stood still.

What a silly thought.

With cautious and deliberate steps she walked into the waiting trees to emerge a short time later to find the two knights sitting against the wagon wheels, laughing at a story the groom was telling them. They stood up hurriedly as she approached.

"Is everything all right, milady," asked the senior knight.

"Why yes, of course. Why do you ask?"

"Begging your lady's pardon but you just all of a sudden looks so tired like."

"No, nothing. I am quite fine really, actually. Thank you."

How would it be if I took them right here? One after another, rolling on the ground like animals? And they are young, we would do it again, making the soil muddy with our fluids— covering ourselves!

She smiled bemusedly at the thought as she held up her hand for the groom to assist her into the carriage.

"Go to where this road forks and go to the north. There we shall come to a dwelling hard by where I will speak with the tenant."

"Yes, milady."

The two knights mounted their steeds as the groom turned the carriage around. Each of the three remarked silently to themselves to keep away from the stones or the power that was there. How else could their beautiful mistress appear even more desirable?

As the carriage bumped along the rutted path, Celestine allowed her mind to come more into focus. Had she heard music while in the circle? It seemed as though deep harmonies had at all times been coursing through her, vibrating her spine.

Looking at the fields as they rode by she watched idly as the peasants plowed behind the straining oxen. Others used horses and she had even seen both horse and oxen yoked together. Soon they would begin the plantings, God knew. Wheat for the bread and barley for the beer took up most of the land while smaller patches grew cabbages, turnips, fruits and beans of all descriptions. It was not too much longer when she felt the carriage come to a stop and heard the groom dismount.

"Here we are milady."

Reaching down once more, she allowed the groom to offer his hand as she stepped from the carriage.

On one side of the road the land flattened out to soft, gentle rolling hills broken into patches by the tilling. On the other side was a forest, her husband's forest. Actually it was all his land bestowed upon him by her father, the king. Duke Theodorus, then leased various parcels to his lesser nobles who then let it out again to the peasants or what few freemen there were. The fruits of the land and taxes flowed to the king.

A rough cottage stood alone next to the forest. This in itself was unusual as the serfs generally clumped their dwellings together to share the labor and the harvest. Surrounded by a small garden, the cottage had both chickens and a goat walking through it. A woman, short and with black hair emerged from the door as the princess approached. Wiping her hands on her coarse dress, the woman walked timidly to the princess to whom she offered an awkward curtsy.

"Good day, milady"

How old can she be? Not very, judging by her skin.

"Are you the mistress of this house?"

"Yes, milady, I am. My husband be working in the fields."

"Good. Then you and I shall have a little chat."

Celestine began walking towards the hovel as the young woman shooed some errant chickens out of the way.

The inside was just as the princess had pictured. The dirt floor was covered with all manner of droppings. What furniture there was consisted of a table and a sturdy chair that sat rather drunkenly. The fireplace held a large cauldron that hung on a hook above the coals. There were two competing odors: animal and smoke, neither of which would relinquish the fight.

The lady of the house pulled the chair towards the princess who said, "Thank you, no. I have been riding all day and prefer to stand."

"Yes, milady." Her eyes glancing towards the floor and at an errant chicken who just walked in.

"What is your name?"

This was most unusual. The Princess Celestine did not come out here often and when she did it was to levy fines or sell licenses for one thing or another. She began to become frightened and wary at the same time.

"My name, my name is Calgwyn, milady."

"And have you any children, Calgwyn?"

"No, two were miscarried, milady."

"Oh, such a pity. Let us step outside, shall we?"

The proposition was little more than the princess telling Calgwyn to step outside away from the fetid smells.

Walking along the edge of the forest Celestine remarked on the large number of crows in the oaks.

"La! They always seems to be around here, milady."

Turning to face her, Celestine said, "I have heard that you are quite an accomplished healer. That you have the gift of selecting the correct herbs and barks for ailments. Is that true?"

Standing to her full height, she looked the princess directly in the eye. "It was no gift, I tell you, but was learned from my mother and she from her mother and from her mother before that. The woods, the earth, the land can cure, not me, mistress."

"And how are you repaid for this skill, my dear?"

"Oh, some times with chickens, or game or a few coppers, or at harvest time a few sheaves of wheat or grain."

"You did say the land, did you not? You know who owns the land, Calgwyn? And do you know who can tax you for its use?"

"Yes, milady." She replied nervously, not liking how this conversation was turning out at all.

"But let us talk of nicer things, shall we? You and I are women of the earth, Calgwyn. Oh, I may not drudge in it as do you, but I know its importance, its potency. Calgwyn, let me ask you something? Can you keep a secret? Not a secret between landlord and tenant, but one between two women of the earth."

Instinctively Calgwyn discerned the inferred threat. "Though I am telling you this and have the power to make your pitiful life worse, I would rather we do this as equals."

"Yes, milady. Of course. How may I help you?"

Knowing of no way to put it delicately and not much caring, Celestine said, "It is my husband. He cannot get the job done, cannot satisfy me. Do you understand or need I be more blunt?"

Her head spinning with the disclosure, Calgwyn was beside herself with excitement but struggled to maintain her composure. "I understand, milady. Fully."

"I want to have a child, sweet Calgwyn. What do you have in your store of roots and herbs that can help?"

Calgwyn's initial reaction was one of amazement that so great a lady as the duchess would come to her, come to her for assistance in so delicate a matter as this! Placing their different backgrounds aside, she rounded her arm around Celestine's waist.

The duchess's immediate thought was to shrug this unwanted familiarity off, but she hesitated. *I need this woman. God help me, but I need her. No, more than that, my child needs this woman.*

Allowing her arm to remain, Celestine walked wordlessly as Calgwyn commiserated with her problem.

"You ain' the only lady to have had such problems, milady. There be more like that than you'd know. But us, we women, keep it to ourselves, don't we? I could tell you stories!"

"Have you helped them, then?"

"Of course!"

Hope! Had there ever been a more beautiful word; a word that dangled the tantalizing possibility of fulfillment!

"But first, milady, we have much to speak of. The herbs and roots can only do so much. I can do no miracles."

The accompanying knights remained mounted as they watched with curiosity as their lady and the peasant woman walked along with heads close together, talking, sometimes laughing. Well, no business of theirs. Finally turning around and heading back, the two women parted at the cottage and the duchess, face flushed, stepped lightly into the waiting carriage.

"We may go home now."

Looking at the men plowing the dark fields she muttered, "Soon the planting will begin."

Calgwyn, her chest feeling like it would burst with pride, was already rummaging and cataloging what stores she had, mentally noting what it was she would need to gather.

An odd one, that, but I can do this thing. She is, after all, a woman. Take away the money and the beauty and strip her finery and she is a woman just like me. I can do this thing and the rewards will be wonderful! Maybe move into the manor itself! Now, wouldn't that be something! No more pottage!

Her hands sorting through the jars mindlessly, Calgwyn began to feel the string of her past tugging at her. The knowledge that was given to her as had been given to her mother by her grandmother, all that culminating with her.

Ah, the trick isn't what plant to use, but what part! Garlic, onion, Toywort, all things that come from the earth, living and growing things are wondrous if used properly.

Allowing herself a small smile at "growing things" she wondered what life within four stout walls and wooden floors would be like.

Celestine looked vacantly at the villeins working the fields, watching as they struggled to hold the plow upright behind the straining teams; the heavy earth reluctantly being turned over. Only after that was done and the earth was somewhat drier would they plow again and begin planting. The beans, peas, barley and oats would go in first; the wheat and hay would be sown on the larger fields of the lord. Here and there she spied a woman guiding the team along as the man followed.

How ironic. Even here it is evident that women do the leading as the hapless man is led along. Did he know where he was being led? She knows, that woman knows exactly where she is going and is allowing him to do most of the work. Yes, I can lead as ably, better, than my husband. This is one ox that won't be led along by his nose, no, not at all! What was it Calgwyn had spoken of? There are things I must do, quiet and subtle things that, along with her medicines, will make him if not a raging bull at least a capable man. I have been blind! Trying to push him rather than lead him. What other counsel had she given? That Celestine would have to act as if Theodorous was the most magnificent of lovers!

They both laughed like children when Calgwyn mentioned that.

"It is true, milady! They are little different than the cock that struts proudly about his hens. Believe me, trust in me. If you really want him stiff and strong enough, you must first become the hen—easy, soft…available. You don't see no hen walking around with her bum up in the air, do you?" They laughed again.

Not at the thought of a presenting hen, but of Celestine being easy, soft, available. The thought of being other than who she was rankled her but only in small measure. That she could delude and deceive her husband into believing she loved him would be no easy feat, but it was one that might prove to be fun...and didn't the goal justify the deception? But just as the fields had to be well prepared long before the planting, she realized that this was an enterprise that must be started immediately.

Upon arriving at the manor she went to her rooms and had Wyngeth bring a comfortable change of clothes along with some bread, cheese and honeyed wine which she finished off hurriedly; she had not realized how famished she had become. The day had been long and though the Stones fortified her spirit, they had taxed her body.

What would those other Stones be like? The ones in a ring I have heard of, that stood as high as two men! What powers might they hold?

But for now the secrets of the large stones would have to wait as Celestine had more immediate plans. Sitting once again before the mirror, she began smiling at herself, looking happy. Then looking coy, now petulant. Each expression brought with it her studied appreciation for the arch of her brows or the narrowing of her eyes. Now she tried looking aroused, sexually hungry; now she felt she looked like a fool. When the time came for it she'd have no need to invent. Again she went back to the more mundane expressions and as she did so, began formulating conversations she would have with her husband. There was no doubt in her mind that she could become the most obedient of wives; demure, decorous and docility would weave themselves into the tapestry of her new behavior. The longer she thought of her new façade, the more thrilling it became.

She began the conquest of her husband with as much forethought as a general planning a campaign, only quicker. She knew her strengths well enough but now she'd have to assess the weaknesses, those little flaws that might render all her schemes futile. While she fully knew the weaknesses of Theodorus, she knew little of his strengths and how these might be used for her own end.

But this is no battle, more like a siege. Everything, all I do must now have but one purpose. I shall become the most devoted and dutiful of wives; even though it galls me, I must not let it show, ever. Let us begin now.

"Wyngeth...Wyngeth come here, please."

Facing her chambermaid she said in as soft as voice as possible, "Please remove the utensils. I shall lie down for a while but you must rouse me as soon as my husband returns. Do you understand? As soon as his horse steps onto the grounds I want to be awakened to greet him."

"Of course, milady."

"Oh, and tell cook that I should very much appreciate it if he prepared something special tonight. Will you do that, please?"

"Certainly, milady," as she bowed herself slowly and with wonder out of the room.

There. That wasn't too difficult. Slow, go slowly, prepare with care.

With that she walked over to her bed, removed her slippers and pulled the covers up, their heaviness enveloping her warmly. The day had been keenly strenuous and rewarding but the physical and emotional fatigue now began exacting its toll. As she drifted into a sweet sleep, visions of sweating plowmen in fields of chest high stones, more tall than broad, laced her dreams.

She wakened even as she heard Wyngeth's footfalls approaching her room. As she heard her door open she stated, "That is quite all right, Wyngeth, I am awake. Tell me, where is my lord?"

Lighting two candles, Wyngeth replied. "He has just given his horse to the groom, milady."

"Ah, good. Thank you, Wyngeth. Fetch me my brush, please."

Brushing her hair quickly, removing whatever twists had dared attempt to tangle it, took little time. Wyngeth watched speechlessly as her mistress straightened her tunic after splashing her eyes with water from an awaiting basin.

"Thank you, Wyngeth. I shall join my husband in the hall."

Duke Theodorus stood before the great fireplace that was easily as tall as a horse, rubbing his hands together and briskly holding them up to the roaring flames. Of average height and build with a rapidly expanding waist, he moved and spoke easily among both nobles and his tenants. While not physically imposing, his financial holdings were his true strength. A bold knight in his youth, he began amassing land as the fortunes of his lord, the king, improved. Then, by dint of various friends on the continent, he was able to speculate and trade both luckily and wisely. His marriage to the princess was just one more good investment.

"Good evening, my lord."

Startled, he looked at the approaching figure of his wife who carried a finely crafted goblet of wine. Handing it to him and placing a gentle kiss on his cheek she said, "Here, let me help you out of that heavy coat. Let the fire warm you."

"Why, thank you, my dear. Thank you." Removing the coat, she tossed it over the back of a tall chair.

"Does the wine please you? It is from the cask you purchased from Italy."

"Those Romans, they do know how to make wine."

"Were you ever there, my husband? I have heard such stories of their buildings and cities that are beyond belief."

Sipping and savoring rather than swilling his wine, the duke shook his head.

"A pity, that. I would have thought you would have traveled in your youth."

"Travel is for those who can afford the time, my dear. Things were hot enough here, I can tell you."

"Here," pulling a heavy oaken chair closer, "sit down. Let the wine warm you within as the fire warms you without." Silent, she tugged his boots off after he took the proffered seat. When done, she sat on the floor with her back to the chair, facing the hearth.

That wasn't so bad, and the fire does feel good and I am so hungry again!

"Is my husband hungry? I have asked cook to prepare something special."

"My stomach growls, Lady. It was a long, hard day."

Look commiserative.

"Let me go see if it is prepared then."

Leaving the duke staring into the leaping flames, she hurried to the kitchen where she had the servants bring the meal on a small table to where they were sitting. A chair was pulled over for the princess who shooed the two servants away as she poured Theodorus more wine. "Our favorite, chicken with mushrooms and onion."

As they ate, Celestine asked gentle questions about his doings, the estate, how much food was salted away, did he think they would have a good year? She listened raptly, hanging on each and every syllable; nodding when it was required and smiling when appropriate.

I can do this thing.

Satisfied, they turned from the meal and once more looked into the flames. The duchess turned her torso just so, knowing that the combination of light and shadow highlighted both her figure and her hair. She brushed the top of his hand with her fingertips.

"Is my husband tired after so long a day? I am tired just hearing about all you did. Shall we go to bed, then?"

Nodding, she stood after he did and held his hand as they walked towards the hall and the stairs to the upper chambers. Shedding all their clothes quietly, they went under the covers quickly. She kissed him softly on the lips and placed her cheek against his chest, her left arm flung across his chest. He had not noticed her pad in the dark room, but it would make no difference.

I can do this; I will do this. The land demands it; the kingdom demands it.

The rhythmic heaving of his chest soon lulled the princess to sleep where the nineteen stones would speak to her.

CHAPTER FOUR

The weeks passed quickly and the sun began lingering, bathing the sodden ground with warmth and light. When frost at last became a bad memory, the populace went mad with activity for now plowing and planting would begin in earnest. The return of the migratory fowl coincided with the resurgence of fishing; the land slowly shed its grays and browns for a carpet of green punctuated with splays of lavender and goldencrown. Beekeepers began planning where best to place their hives. Everyone was thankful for having survived another winter…as they prepared for the next with optimism and sweat.

No one was immune to the changed atmosphere, certainly not Bridget who now rode daily. She relished the caress of the sun and air on her face and tolerated the endless drizzling as they brought the hope of a bountiful harvest. It was good to be alive.

She stood looking at the battlements from her window, something she was doing most every night as the dream with the bloody hands rubbed away her sleep with fearful regularity. What was once a scary nuisance had now become so frightening it filled her days with anticipatory despair, her nights with dread. The apparition had changed only slightly—sometimes the angle of her vision was different or the figure was sharper or the blood more red.

Neither Mathilde nor Gwenthe were aware of these nightly torments, only that their mistress appeared haggard at times. Certainly she drank more wine than was her custom, but what of that? That the princess was young and ripe led them to believe the insistent stirrings of womanhood were at last roiling within her, just as the land was budding. Both women had definite solutions for their mistress's distress: Gwenthe believed Bridget's heart needed to love and be loved; Mathilde's was estimably more direct and physical. "She needs a man to hold and to hold her." Said Gwenthe.

"Nay," Mathilde retorted, "she doesn't need his arms!"

They chuckled in sympathy over Bridget. What could they do but be there when the princess sought their help and counsel?

For as far as Bridget could spy from her window, bonfires dotted the landscape.

Why must they begin planting during the full of the moon? Is it better for the seeds? And can't they sing something other than, "One for my master, one for my house. One for the rook and one for the mouse?"

Dear Jesus, am I losing my mind? Please help me. This dream has to be from the devil to torment me, your poor servant. Please, dear Lord, I only wish to sleep in peace. What have I done? What do you need me to do? I will do whatever you ask gladly.

Easter was fast approaching and the celebration of the resurrection of Jesus would be both joyous and riotous. The feasting and worship would last for a week with enormous quantities of food and ale consumed. There would be fairs and markets with trinkets and wares that had been crafted during the long winter nights. Games would be played with several hundred peasants pitted against one another. Tables would groan with the weight of food as both rich and poor gave thanks for the rebirth of their savior and of the land that had been dead.

My Lord, please give me a sign. Tell me what I must do.

Silence.

Never had she felt so alone, so cut off. Surrounded by servants, doted on by chambermaids, she felt exposed and friendless. There was no one with whom she could confide all that swirled around her mind—certain that her nightly torment was no longer a dream but a terrible portent. She couldn't mention this to the abbess as it had the flavor of deviltry and what would she think of the princess then?

Gwenthe and Mathilde would agree that it was an omen, one that should be brought to the attention of someone versed in the Old Ways. But if she did that then wasn't she denying Christ and putting her soul in jeopardy?

Perhaps someone knows how to make a tea that would rid me of this damned curse? I shall have to ask Gwenthe, she knows more of the old folk around the castle.

And what of her father, the king? He had been acting so strangely towards her lately. Usually treated with kindly neglect, she found herself being asked more and more to dine with him. Looking and sounding very uncomfortable he asked her such simple questions: How did she think this year's harvest would be? Did she trust the nobles? What were her feelings towards the church? At first taken by surprise, she would answer briefly, never elaborating, never asking questions in return. Her father would listen intently, sometimes arching a brow, other times smiling, but always giving weight to each word. Eventually she felt more comfortable with this man who was more king than father, more stranger than friend.

"And what do you think of your sister?" He asked as they pulled apart a joint of mutton.

""Celestine? Celestine is beautiful and lovely and I miss having her here, father."

"Do you really? I thought she tormented you rather badly when you two were younger."

"That was so many years ago. We were just children then. I would like to have her to talk with about things."

He arched his left brow. "Things?"

"I should just like her company, father…a friend. Haven't you any friends?"

He looked at her deeply, eyes narrowing, before he sighed and sat back. "A friend? A king has no friends, my dear. He may have allies and he may have counselors, both of whom may be his enemy, but he will never have a friend…unless you count one of the hounds."

With that they broke into laughter and finished the meal with general bantering.

And this morning they would ride together to view his lands, he said, north of the Wythe. She had no idea why he wanted her company. Could it be that he remembered her love of riding? Or how as a youngster she played on the stone beach as the waves crashed along the far rocky shore. It had been so long, too long ago.

Oh, things were so simple then! That was before the dreams, before managing the castle. All I cared about was playing and spinning in circles with my arms spread out till I fell down, too dizzy to stand. I wish I could dance once more.

What infrequent entertainments there were in the castle, there were always musicians and dancing. While she lacked the natural grace of her sister, she possessed an innate sense of timing, which was awakened by lute and drum. She would close her eyes as she and the melody became one, allowing her body to lose all sense of self and boundary. There was a peace that came with the rhythmical movement that was close to that achieved through deep prayer or breathless rides on Alexander.

Sighing, she returned to bed and prayed for a dreamless sleep.

Long before the sun rose she lay in bed and listened as the castle noisily awoke. It was not often that the king went on a journey and there was much to prepare. The kitchen staff had been awake most of the night, cooking and packing foodstuffs as the king's men readied their horses and equipment. There would be two contingents of knights: the first would consist of ten men who would depart several hours before the main party—their purpose was to scout the best routes and choose each night's encampment. The bulk of the party would serve as escort for the king and princess.

She climbed wearily out of bed but was filled with excitement as the novelty of the adventure was at hand.

"Hurry milady! It is time to be up and about and dressed!" Gwenthe grumbled as she burst through the heavy door.

"Are my things readied?"

"That they are, my dear. Even now Mathilde is seeing to their being stowed on the cart along with our things."

Splashing water on her face, she threw on her tights and tunic and followed in Gwenthe's great wake down the stairs to the hall already filled with the knights, laughing and eating as they made ready.

"Good morning, daughter! Let us break our fast together!" Bellowed her father, already sitting at the table and eating. "It will be several days before we eat as well, I promise you."

"Good morning, father. Yes, I am hungry."

Together they ate their fill of bread, thick with honey and hard cheese as servants bustled about.

The courtyard was misty gray as they awaited their mounts. Gwenthe and Mathilde were seated uncomfortably in one of the carts that carried tents and provisions. A stable hand appeared out of the gloom with the king's horse and Alexander. Bridget mounted confidently while the king required some assistance. In all, their party consisted of sixty soldiers in light, leather armor, two carts filled with supplies and two dogs that followed the king wherever he went. Banners indicating the king's presence were carried at the fore of the procession as they headed out the main gate.

The eastern sky was just beginning to blush when they heard the bells from the abbey...the princess said a silent prayer as her father road stoically and silently before her. Somewhere behind she heard Mathilde's shrill protestations rise and fall in a steady stream. All else was silent except for the heavy hooves of the horses and the creaking of their leather and metal harnesses.

This is too boring! Alexander and I do not plod...

Still, the newness of riding with the king and his finest men blunted the monotony. Feeling as though she would fall asleep as she rode, her languor was broken by her father who turned around and said, "Not much by the way of jumping logs, is it? Still, you won't break your arm."

Startled by his voice and flustered that he knew of her riding accident, Bridget kept her eyes forward and remained silent. Relishing his daughter's discomfiture, he added, "It is the king's job to know what goes on within his walls."

She continued to ride in silence, her face flushed.

And so they proceeded, the sun slowly rising on their right as they passed several mud and timber hovels. On either side they witnessed the farmers working the fields...or women tending to scrawny children and noisy chickens. Unused to seeing such a spectacle as their king riding by, they stopped from their labors and removed their caps while bowing clumsily.

Stopping frequently at streams to water the horses and to stretch, they ate wedges of hard cheese followed with wine.

"Father, I have to go."

"Umh, go where, my dear?"

Bridget raised her eyes and sighed, "I have to pee."

"Of course, of course...right. I shall order the men to stay over there. Be sure to ask your ladies as well."

Gwenthe and Mathilde needed no urging as they had been uncomfortable for quite some time but lacked the wherewithal to request a respite. Muttering about the unseemliness of it all, Gwenthe let herself be led by Mathilde and the princess into some nearby trees.

"Now how am I supposed to go about this, milady?"

"Don't be such an old lady," laughed Mathilde as she lifted her own dress and squatted as she leaned against a tree, her back towards them.

"She is devil's spawn, no doubt." Grumbled Gwenthe whose ill humor had graduated to black. She hadn't done something like this since she was a young girl, much leaner and more limber. Leaning her bulk against a tree, she squatted as the princess held her hands to keep her from falling.

"Please don' look at me milady, I feel a fool."

Meanwhile Mathilde who had finished was beside herself with laughter at the sight.

"Oh my! Oh my!" She howled. Finally the princess began giggling until she was no longer able to maintain Gwenthe who went down in a pile of curses, oaths and wet grass.

"This is no laughing matter! This is not fit for no woman, no!"

Bridget and Mathilde helped her up and began to straighten her soiled dress, laughing now forgotten. The princess took herself to a further tree and did her function with quiet resignation.

I wish I were a man.

They returned to the waiting men who were already mounted and looking at the trio as they exited the woods.

As the sun rose she noticed the knights begin to sweat despite their light armor but they seemed in good spirits as now there was some bantering and joking amongst them. Every few miles they would change positions in the ranks, yet maintain a disciplined and orderly train. Mathilde had thankfully fallen asleep and Gwenthe, the incident in the woods forgotten, was pointing at some new meadow or staring at the hawks circling above. Larks skittered swiftly around them and every so often pheasants or quail exploded from the ground as the dogs roused them.

The land on either side consisted of high broad hills, light gray in the distance; nearer, there were heavy forests from which a curious deer would peer and then return to scrounging the short grasses. What dwellings there were had been abandoned and were now just odd mounds of mud and sticks as the land began its slow reclamation. Bridget could see where fields had once been, where low, stone fences had already begun to spill. They rode silently, daughter and father, each wrapped within their own thoughts as the rhythmic swaying of the horses lulled them into a graceful stupor. Climbing a long hill made them more alert as the horses strained till at last they reached the top. Meadows and ponds surrounded by trees filled the landscape to all horizons as the sun bathed it all in golden hue. Below them ran a river, cold looking and broad. "There it is," said the king, "the Wythe."

Sitting back on Alexander as he stepped his way down, Bridget thought she had never beheld such a beautiful vista.

"Father, why do no people live here?"

"Later. First let's cross the river and make camp with the others."

So taken was the princess by the enormity of the land, that she had overlooked the men who had gone on before and who had already begun pitching tents on a rise across the river. Directed by a knight on the other side, they crossed where the water was shallow but angry. Though not quite to his stifle, Bridget felt Alexander straining to keep upright as he fought the river's power while walking on the moss-slicked rocks. Reaching the other side, she watched as the men, in some secret silence, reworked the cart bearing her two ladies with ropes and an extra horse to cross in grand style and dry.

Though accustomed to riding further, Bridget had never spent so much time in the saddle and so she dismounted with gratitude and a small prayer as she stretched and rubbed the backs of her legs. The knights had shed their armor and were busily setting up the camp that would hold their sovereign that night. With silent efficiency, they broke into several groups. Some began cutting trees that were then trimmed and sharpened into stakes three times a man's height. These were driven into trenches that others had dug until the immediate perimeter bristled with the menacing spikes facing outward. Other men were building fires and setting up cooking areas and tents; several went to hunt fresh meat. The majority were at post, not toiling, but looking about ceaselessly for someone, anyone, who had no business being there. Life in the castle was fine and good but this was their life, to serve their lord.

The long ride and the heady excitement produced a sudden weariness that left Bridget leaden limbed and weary. Her tent was next to her father's and already Gwenthe and Mathilde were bustling in and out, setting up the rough pallets and arranging candles.

"I am going to nap," she said as she stretched out on the skin-covered cot.

"But milady…"

"Mathilde, not a word."

Mathilde, who normally ignored such commands with blissful ignorance, was silenced by the no nonsense timbre in the princess's voice. Looking at Gwenthe sharply, they closed the tent and set themselves on stools outside to watch the gathering gloom.

The princess did not move, her breathing was deep and regular and if she dreamed of the dreadful figure, she did not remember nor awaken.

It seemed as though she had just closed her eyes when she felt the gentle hand of Mathilde on her shoulder, "Milady, awake…it is time to eat and your father is waiting for you."

With the thick taste of sleep in her mouth, she found her father sitting on a log by a roaring fire, his two dogs beside him, their heads resting on folded paws.

Wordlessly, she sat beside him as he handed her a goblet. Never had water tasted so remarkably sweet, so tasteful, and she drank it noisily, removing the staleness from her throat. Smiling, he handed her a joint of meat. "They killed a boar."

"Good." She bit into the greasy meat, savoring its richness, not bothered by the juice that dribbled down her chin. She hadn't realized how hungry she was until she finished her first mouthful. Once more she ripped into it, the charred skin crackling as she chewed greedily.

"Good." She repeated between mouthfuls.

"You will at least allow the dogs to have the bone." He remarked wryly.

"Perhaps."

At last sated, she tossed the meatless bone to the furthest dog that ran off with it into the shadows as the other followed.

"I have never been that hungry, ever."

Father and daughter, king and princess, stared into the dancing flames before them, luxuriating in the warmth that kept the chilly night away. Each allowed their private thoughts to be fanned by the chuckling fire that sporadically snapped sparks into the star strewn sky above.

"There are no inns in these parts because there are no people, no travelers. And there are no people because of the Vikings."

"But this is good ground, father. Can't you defend it? Don't you have enough vassals in your service?"

Ah! "defend". Was ever there a more troubling word? The child knows nothing about my squabbling nobles. Each with his own fiefdom, each with his own petty trickeries; they defend only that which is theirs! Even now, as I travel here, they may be plotting some mischief.

For a fleeting moment he thought of that old bear, bleeding yet fighting the snarling wolves. He watched the flames tickle a wave of sparks into the night.

"The problem is not in the amount of men we have, but in having the right amount at the right place." He lied. He had considered dividing the land among any three of his nobles but knew the outcome would be disastrous. Each would protect his own tract without regard for the welfare of his neighbor, not realizing that what was good for one was good for all. Oh, they might send a paltry war party but would keep the bulk of their troops at home on some excuse or other. That they trusted no one was both blessing and curse; they could not rise against him nor could they supply the troops he most desperately needed.

Their pitifully puny intrigues will be the death of us all.

62

Bridget shuddered when her father said "Vikings;" the very thought of them and their barbarous ways made the night suddenly sinister and dangerous; she peered around for the sentries. Unruly children were threatened with being sold to the savages when they did not mind their parents. It was well known that the sea raiders sacrificed virgins as they launched each new longboat, drinking her blood as well. The sporadic raids along coastal villages netted them goods, livestock and slaves. And she had heard that their vicious women fought at the sides of their men.

"What will you do, father?"

"I'm not sure yet." He lied once more.

Together they stared wordlessly into the flames, the warmth suddenly not as comforting as before.

"Why are we here? Why did you bring me here with you?" She blurted.

He kept looking into the fire, the crags of his face accentuated by the wavering shadows.

Dare I tell her now? The time is not yet right.

"I came here to think and to ponder. What will the Vikings do this season, where will they set ashore? How we may best fight them and where."

"And why am I here?"

"Because this is your land, Bridget."

She barked a laugh, "No, father. This is not my land, this is your land, your kingdom. It is not mine, I want none of it."

Dear child, it is mine to give or to withhold, and as surely as I am king, this will be yours…and your husband's…and mine as well.

"Ah, well. You know what I mean," he said as he looked into her eyes, "but it getting late and I have not napped as you and these old bones are getting weary. Tomorrow we ride and let us hope for clear weather."

Placing his hand on her shoulder he pushed himself up from the log and straightened. The dogs ran from the dark as if he had called them, wordlessly the king walked the twenty paces to his tent and went inside with the pushing hounds.

He looks so sad, tired. I never knew these things. Why hadn't he confided in me before? But what could I do? What can I do now? I haven't knights, no soldiers. It is so unfair! If I were a man I'd be a prince, able to command my men to defend the land from the damned Vikings myself!

With that last thought she squinted into the dark, looking for the sentinels; she saw their dark outlines against the black hills. Turning to the cheerless fire, she felt more alone, more helpless than ever. Now she slung the smothering burden of her father's woes upon herself and had no way of shrugging it off. Resting her elbows on her knees, she looked into the flames until at last the circle of light barely reached her feet. Sighing, she stood and entered her tent where Mathilde and Gwenthe slept noisily. Throwing the skins over herself as she lay down, she curled up, attempting to conserve the heat absorbed from the fire. With this new and disturbing information given her she thought she would never fall asleep. She was wrong.

The birds here are no different than the birds at home—noisy!

She opened her eyes and allowed them to grow accustomed to the dim light of the tent's lone candle. She slipped from beneath the covers and pulled on her boots, making sure not to disturb the two sleeping women who were oblivious to the raucous sound of the birds heralding the dawn.

How do they do that? How do they know when the sun will rise when it is still black as a crow's back?

Stepping out beyond the tent she first smelled the damp ash of last night's fire before she saw it's light pink glow. She walked over to it and kicked some scraps of branches into it with the toe of her boot. Satisfied as small flames awakened, she looked around the sleeping camp as she pulled her skin tightly over her shoulders to ward off the morning chill. Fog had drifted in during the night, obscuring all but the nearest tents. She could not see the river below but heard it in spite of the winged chorus above when she strained her ears. The air was still and damp, the ground wet and cold, yet there was a gentle sweetness to this special time when the night had not yet ended and the day not yet begun. It had been a special time for her ever since she was a child. There was the knowledge that the rustling things of the night were about to retire and that the solid things of the day were waiting; it was a time for her and God to be alone. A horse whinnied but the fog confused the direction from which it came. The eastern sky lightened one miserly shade as crows from the tops of some high, hidden trees joined the chorus and made her chuckle at their audacity. Grinning, she began to build the fire in earnest, forgetting that she hadn't been visited by the hooded figure last night.

The sun was well above the horizon before it began burning away the heavy ground fog. Bridget had a credible fire going as Gwenthe and Mathilde emerged from the tent and warmed their hands and faces against the chill.

"Milady, I do love you like a daughter but I cannot do this again! I am too old and the night air hurts these old joints so! And trying to sleep next to Mathilde is like lying next to a snake, all squirmy."

Mathilde laughed loudly and could barely keep a straight face at Gwenthe's complaints. "No milady, it is me who should complain at old Gwenthe! Milady, she passes gas all night, I thought I should choke or at least die! And the noises were so loud that I thought it would startle the horses. And that isn't all…

"You lying hussy! I'll box your ears when I catch you."

And certainly she would have had not the princess started laughing so hard it brought tears to her eyes. "My two most trusted women! One a snake and the other a bag of gas! Oh, this is just not possible!" And then they all started laughing and were still doing so as the king joined the circle from out of the fog.

"So, is this the way the day will begin, Bridget? By you and your women cackling loud enough to waken the dead?"

Gwenthe and Mathilde curtsied hurriedly and left the fire immediately but Bridget could hear the gentle humor in his voice.

"Good morning, father! I am famished! When shall we eat?"

"Just as soon as my men get stirring and the guards changed. Let me warm myself by your fire, there." He stood rubbing his hands together before the flames, shifting his weight from foot to foot and stretching away the stiffness of sleep.

From out of the lightening fog came a soldier carrying a heavy iron pot that held the hot and steaming remains of last night's dinner which the two dug in to with gusto. What was the magic of this place that made ordinary food so succulent? Around them, shouting shadows were moving about and breaking camp. To Bridget it had the excitement of a fair—the motion, the shouts and the seeming pandemonium—it was a new thing, an adventure.

A half dozen soldiers appeared and began stowing the contents of her tent into the cart where Gwenthe and Mathilde feasted on honey heavy bread. Just as their horses were being hitched, a soldier appeared leading the king's mount and Alexander. They mounted without comment as they joined the ranks already filing through the mist into the lowlands somewhere ahead.

The sunshine didn't melt the fog by degrees, it burst it wide open as after only few miles they found themselves in full daylight with a blue sky arching from horizon to horizon. The air was so crisp it had a taste and Bridget found herself inhaling large lungfuls for the sheer joy of breathing, as if it were the most marvelous thing she had ever done. The highlands to the east and west were no long blurred by distance but stood as stark as the nearest elm. For hours they ranged, noting the streams turning into ponds and the ponds joining other ponds and becoming lakes so beautiful they took her breath away. Her brain worked feverishly trying to etch all she saw into memory that could be relished at her leisure. The rivers and their directions, unusual trees, hills and bogs—all were cataloged behind her eyes.

Sweet Jesus! You are so mighty in your power! Did your father create all this beauty? Was this like the Garden?

After their third break and a bit of bread with cheese, Bridget went to her father sitting beneath an oak thick with age, "Father, how much longer before we reach the end?"

"Tired, are we?"

"To the contrary, this is all just so…"

"Beautiful?" he finished for her.

"No, it is more than beautiful, far above that."

He arched his eyebrow.

"It is…pure, father. I can think of no other word."

Expecting a laugh, she was relieved when the king closed his eyes for a moment, bowed his head and upon raising it, looked at her and said, "Yes, 'pure' is the exact word."

The rest of the day was spent in the saddle, traveling through meadows where not even the Romans had built a road. Bridget luxuriated in the assault upon her senses and even Alexander would break into spontaneous gallops.

"I have heard you are quite the rider, Bridget. Is it your skill or Alexander's talent?" Her father teased.

Laughing, she dug her heels into the horse's flanks and burst into full gallop. *Yes! Yes! Yes!*

With Alexander in full stride, she again became one with him; rider and mount were indistinguishable—an entity of strength, grace and purpose as they hurdled a fallen tree and then a stream. Surging to the top of the steep bank, she wheeled him about and rode along its crest, his flying mane now covering her hands as they gripped the reins. The horse turned as though he read her thoughts and splashed across the stream again, pounding back towards the party.

Puffing, she said, "It is our genius, father."

"So it appears," he whimsied as she fell into line behind him, now beginning to sweat, feeling the great beast's heart throbbing against her thighs.

If possible, the supper that night was more delicious and the water sweeter than the one before. As the king was in discussion with his men, she was able to sit in silent reverie before the crackling fire.

When do I tell him that I want to go with the abbess? What will he say? What can he say? Would that Celestine were here! She might be able to help, her with her husband...maybe they could get mercenaries to defend against the Vikings. Would she appreciate this place, this beauty?

She smiled at the thought of Celestine, beautiful and delicate, riding across open fields with her blond hair tangling behind in the wind. She waited in vain for her father to come to the diminishing fire. Feeling her eyes staying closed longer and longer, she went to her tent where Gwenthe and Mathilde were already asleep, this time on separate pallets. She smiled as she recalled the morning's bantering. Pulling off her boots, she slipped beneath the covers and curled on her side.

"Holy Father, thank you for all your blessings and thank you..." she fell asleep.

Her night was riddled with a variety of dreams: the abbess riding Alexander, Vikings praying, her father yelling at someone. The faceless, hooded figure was in all these segments but on the side, as a spectator, watching and observing all she did.

This morning the cluttering of her two women preparing to eat awakened her.

Mathilde, noisy and irreverent, chided the princess for her laziness.

Is there anything so wonderful as a stretch? Or a warm bed?

Pulling on her boots, she ignored Mathilde (thus riling her more) and stepped out into the morning chill. The sun was already above the horizon as she joined her father who was eating greedily.

"Ah, my lay-a-bed daughter!" He cried as she sat beside him. "Here, last night's meat is even better today!"

Hungrier than ever, she ate and drank rapidly as she could see the tents being broken down.

"I am told that tonight we shall sleep before the great sea." He stated calmly.

Bridget felt her heart jump. How long had it been since she had seen an ocean or walked on the wrinkled shore? Not since she was a little girl, of course, so many years, a lifetime ago. She continued eating, only allowing an "Oh", to escape between mouthfuls.

"Is that all? I thought you would have been more affected?" With that he stood suddenly, flinging a piece of meat into the morning's fire as he strode briskly towards his men who were even now preparing the horses.

Why did I do that? Why didn't I let him know that of course I am excited. And why should he become so angry about how I feel?

No longer hungry, she allowed Alexander to be brought to her and mounted listlessly as the troops continued north once more.

The sun was warm but a cold breeze blew into their faces as they continued. Riding behind her father, she began to notice subtle changes in the landscape. The land seemed to rise and became less hilly; there were fewer streams to cross and the highlands, once so prominent, had now disappeared. Her father continued to ignore her so she ate with her women when they stopped to eat.

"This is the last of the bread, milady," Gwenthe noted unhappily as she chewed her slice with satisfaction.

"And how much longer will we be out here, milady?" asked Mathilde. "Certainly not too much longer, I hope. I miss my own bed!"

"I think," quipped Gwenthe, "that she misses not using her bed, milady."

"La! And that too!"

"Men!" said Bridget suddenly. "Who can understand them? For years you know how my father never paid me any mind. Then he becomes the father I always wanted, laughing with me, listening to me. Then we come here and he's fine one moment and the next he is cold as stone." Bridget averted her eyes from the two women as she spoke and continued to eat in silence after her brief outburst.

"But milady," said Mathilde, suddenly somber, "he is not just a man, nor is he only a father. He is the king!" Gwenthe nodded and looked from Mathilde to the princess who stood rigidly as she walked briskly towards Alexander, ignoring them both. They looked at one another and shrugged as they piled themselves into the cart, pulling furs closer around their shoulders as the sun did nothing to warm the air that now had a bite to it.

The closer they neared their destination the more the mood of the travelers changed. The soldiers no longer bantered and had now grown silent. The wind wormed its way through the tiniest of seams and chilled the spots of exposed flesh. Bridget pulled her tunic tighter, wishing she had gloves but acted indifferently as the wind teared her eyes. The longer they traveled, the more the wind buffeted both horse and rider. She kept her face down to protect her eyes from the cold sting and was surprised when Alexander stopped. Looking up she saw the riders in front of her on a crest, looking out upon the heaving sea.

Nothing big grew there, just mean, scabrous brush that clung to the wind-whipped earth with grim determination and a few twisted, unfamiliar trees, no taller than she. Squinting, she saw the unbroken horizon and the dark gray waters below. The wind ripped into the side of the cliff upon which they stood and rushed up to meet them, trying to push them back. The resulting maelstrom rocked the onlookers as they sat stoically on their horses. The waves below crashed and thundered against the craggy shore in mountains of green and white. Even this high up she could taste the salty mist on her lips; Bridget was struck by the savagery of the place. There would be no girlish walks along the beach this day.

What kind of men call this place home? Who can travel on these towering, angry waters? Vikings.

She shuddered more from the thought than from the cold that numbed her hands and was now caressing her bones. As of one mind the company turned towards a small depression that protected them from some, but not all, of the angry wind. Some soldiers scrambled to put up the tents that slapped loudly as others rode off seeking scarce wood. Bridget had never been this cold, not even during snowstorms. The tents protected them from the worst but the mist-laden gale continued its attack, trying to rip the flimsy skins of cloth from the earth.

Dear God! I am scared! I cannot believe that I am being frightened by a lot of noise and wind! Let Gwenthe and Mathilde hide, shivering beneath the skins!

Determined, she left the tent and climbed to the top of the rise, facing directly into the wind. There was something here for her, she knew. She no longer felt the warmth ebb from her bones; the elemental tumult had now become a song of powers that were old, so old they were as oblivious to time as she was to the assault she faced. How powerful were the waves? Where did they come from? Where had they been? And what creatures hid just beneath them? She felt the earth shudder from their force even at this great distance. Her cape slapped behind her as she lifted her arms.

Go ahead, you do not frighten me any longer. I feel your anger and your power, but I no longer tremble, a cowering child!

She was being cleansed somehow, she felt more than thought; then she no longer thought at all as thinking soiled the currents now running through her. Feet planted solidly, oblivious, she had the same sensation as when she and Alexander rode as one, but with a difference: she was no longer the rider but the ridden.

The wind screamed as it whipped stinging sand against her exposed face and hands as she opened her mouth and let the salt-tinged grains tease her tongue. Row upon row, the angry waves punished the unyielding shore as the wind sang a plaintive song that she alone could hear.

"Milady! Milady! Come in, come back!" She heard Mathilde's voice being spun away by the wind even as Mathilde clasped her shoulder.

La! Look at her! Has she gone mad? This is no place for anyone.

Together they walked, slipped down the slippery bank as the wind pushed them from the back. Gwenthe was up and waiting for them with a dry skin and blanket that she threw over Bridget as she pushed her rudely onto her cot. Gasping, the two women stood over the princess who looked at them through calm, empty eyes.

"Gwenthe! Do you see her expression?" She whispered.

"Yes, I know. That same look as when she finished ripping into the old steward. Kind of scary, eh?" Before them the princess sat, the corners of her mouth tilting slightly up, "Oh, you two! I am fine, really. I am just a little hungry, that's all—and a little cold, now."

At that moment a soldier entered the tent, clutching a sack, "Can't find the wood to make a fire tonight, ladies. But you got the best of what we got," he said as he handed the food to Mathilde. Opening it quickly, Mathilde pulled out strips of smoked fish and handfuls of shelled nuts. "If this is their best…" but Bridget had snatched the bag and pulled out a greasy, eyeless fish and began pulling at the meat with hungry teeth. Following her lead, Gwenthe and Mathilde sat and the three of them ate silently around the lantern, unmindful of the shaking tent. They completed their meal with long pulls from a skin filled with water.

Exhausted and at peace, Bridget allowed herself to be snugged into her cot as Gwenthe and Mathilde made themselves ready for the night.

What was it her old Irish tutor had said, something about the Greeks? Ah, the Elements! Yes! That is why this is such an angry place! Wind, Water and Earth coming together, kissing one another angrily—all that's missing is Fire. Now that is strange, why would I think of them kissing?

She woke once during the night, aroused by the sudden silence, absolute and complete. Closing her eyes once more, she descended into a dreamless sleep.

The party awakened to a dull gray dawn, the sun a smudge on the horizon. The wind had blown itself into a comfortable breeze that would have been refreshing had it not been so cold. Climbing to the crest once more, Bridget looked upon the sea with its long, gray waves thudding onto the shore below.

My God! What a difference between this morning and last evening! Not only has the color of the water changed, but the size and shape of the waves…and even their speed!

She was unaware of how long she stood there, watching the endless parade of waves grow from dark creases to slow moving fluid behemoths that embraced the shore with deliberate thunder. Unmindful of what was happening in the camp, she was surprised when she turned around to see the morning fires started with Gwenthe and Mathilde by one, rubbing their hands together, driving the chill from their bones.

"La, good morning, milady," said Mathilde. "You're up and about, come sit with us and get warm." Gwenthe sat in a miserable silence, content to keep her agony to herself.

It was not too much longer before a soldier appeared with some food; cold and greasy, it was still a feast. "Where is my father?" She asked of the retreating man.

"He was up and out earlier, milady. Gone to scout to the east of here with a few of the others."

Shrugging, Bridget finished her meal indifferently, wishing the sun higher and brighter on this forsaken place. The harsh landscape held no redeeming qualities, at least none of which she was aware. The bleakness had a profound affect on Bridget who now found herself fidgeting and restless. Uncomfortable, she went to the tent and climbed back into the bed, not from tiredness but from boredom.

Where did he go? Why didn't he take me with him? I can ride as well, no, better than any of them! I hate this doing nothing…and this cold!

Slowly she drifted off into that uncomfortable realm that is neither sleep nor wakefulness; she could distinguish sounds and distant conversations but could not link them to anything worth being awake about. She was surprised then when she woke to find the sun well up and the sky a brighter gray—her mouth was thick with its own taste.

"Time for lunch, milady?"

"No…yes, thank you, Mathilde—and something to drink. My mouth tastes like I chewed on rabbit fur."

Laughing, Mathilde ran over to a nearby fire and returned quickly. "La, cooked rabbit…without the fur!" As she handed Bridget the skewered animal. Sinking her teeth into the warm, dry meat, she chewed it carefully, trying to rid her mouth of the taste…she did the same with the water.

"Has my father returned?"

"Indeed he has, and left again, that way." She pointed to the west.

Dropping by the fire she ate sullenly.

This damned place! Where did he go this time and why didn't he bring me with him? I would have gotten up! And this rabbit was cooked too long and is tasteless. Damn.

Tossing the remains into the flames she walked over the crest to look at the ocean once more. The rocks below now had some of their weed-covered sides exposed and in between waves she could see the dark tendrils undulate in the clear water.

What is it about this place then? The ocean is so large and…changeable. Look at it now; a child could swim in it…even Celestine! And yesterday this same water could destroy anything.

Looking to the horizon, she pictured ships, Viking ships with their terrible square sails against the sky, firmly billowed. Then that thought disappeared and she thought of Jesus in the boat with the apostles.

They may have been fishermen, my Lord, but they weren't Vikings, were they? How could they have been so frightened after all the miracles you had shown them? Didn't you get tired of their doubts, their whining? I would have. Maybe you would have had better luck if you had more women.

Feeling suddenly blasphemous at the thought, she stared at the heaving waters once more, determined not to think but to wait till her father returned.

What little sun there was, was just touching the horizon when the king and his party returned, noisy and hungry. Bridget got up slowly and deliberately, holding her questions with cool resolve as she headed back to her tent—the king would tell her in his good time, meanwhile she would remain indifferent.

In a short while she was called out to join him in his tent. The king, his face still flushed with the day's exertions, stood over a makeshift table upon which a map lay.

"Ah, Bridget! Good day, no? No, not really good at all was it…this weather can creep into your soul, can't it? Here, sit down," he continued as he pulled over a stool, "and we shall eat together. I believe they were able to snare some few rabbits and I do have some wine to make them more agreeable."

Bridget sat on the proffered seat and accepted the wine gratefully, consciously averting her eyes from the table. The drink, red and strong, tasted wonderful and she finished it in two noisy swallows. Even as she put it down one of his men returned with a platter of broiled meat. "Yes," said the king, "a fine meal with fine wine!"

Father and daughter grabbed for the food eagerly and pulled the dry meat from the bones with their teeth. Bridget poured herself another goblet of wine before reaching for the next rabbit. The only sound was that of their chewing and drinking mouths; Bridget tossed the bones to the dogs, as did her father. The wine coursed through her rapidly and she felt her face warm, a good feeling. Her belly taut, Bridget found her goblet empty once more—again she filled it, feeling the glow reaching from her face to her limbs now.

"So, how did you spend your day, my dear?" He asked after tossing the last carcass to the waiting hounds.

"Well, after I found myself alone, I went to the cliffs once more and waited and looked at the ocean."

"And then?"

"Slept poorly for a while, that's all."

The wine has gone directly to my head! I feel so thick and clumsy. No, no, no! No more! Why is he asking me all these things? What in earth did he do today? Where did he go? Well, maybe just another and drink it slowly. What is this map all about? I'll be damned if I ask him, though. Let him play his games, they don't concern me anyway. Damn, but that wine tastes good.

Looking directly at the king she poured herself another serving from the flagon of wine, now dry.

"Well," he said with a hint of pride, "I went scouting the shoreline, both east and west of here." He felt decidedly uncomfortable when she did not ask why he had done this thing—she only looked into his eyes and nodded as she sipped from her goblet.

"Here," he said, suddenly standing over the map, "this is what we found."

Bridget stood slowly, deliberately, making sure her feet went the way she wanted them. *Am I drunk? Me? Yes, I think I am. Now, be careful, say nothing and look interested, but not very. My lips are numb, now why did that happen? I can't feel them! Let's see what this damned map is all about.*

She knew immediately that it was a map of her father's kingdom, roughly drawn, crude, it showed the Wythe connecting both coasts, their castle and the larger manors of the various lords and the roads that laced them together. There were no roads north of the great river, though.

"We are here," he pointed to a small "x".

"And what are those circles?"

There were three small circles, two to the east and one to the west of where they were.

"Those are beaches, potential harbors, Bridget."

"And what of that? Places to fish? Swim? Besides, I much prefer to swim in a pond or river; I do not like the taste of salt and it burns my eyes and besides…"

"These are where the Northmen will land."

"Oh."

I'm an idiot! Of course, why else would he ride all the way here? Keep quiet and say nothing! Go swimming! I am so much a fool! Oh, why did I drink this much and talk so stupidly!

Avoiding his eyes, she looked intently at the map, determined not to utter another senseless syllable.

"How do you know they will land at these spots?"

The king seemingly unaware of her discomfiture did not appear to notice her thickened voice. "They will land at any of these places because they have landed there before and because they have no other choices. They beach their crafts and so need protected areas to prevent them from being turned into splinters." He said as he nodded in the direction of outside. "And they need to be able to load and unload their men."

Bridget looked at the map intently as she leaned on the table with both hands, knowing she had to say something to reflect the gravity of the conversation.

"Why wouldn't they land further south?"

"Too close to our main strongholds. Our armies could be summoned quickly and their escape cutoff—they may be savages, but they are cunning savages!"

"Why would they land here at all? What would be their gain?"

"Look, Bridget, closely at the map." She looked.

"Now, what do you see between those circles and my castle, here," he pointed.

"Nothing."

"That's right, nothing. No opposition and they have already destroyed what villages were there before, so there would be no warning when they landed or where they were. In short, they could land, make a hard march and be at my castle's door within two, maybe three days." He cherished this cold assessment, held it closely, looking for other possibilities; finding none, he sighed.

Bridget peered at the map with new respect; finding the Wythe, she was able to determine approximately what swamps and lakes they had passed—what were plains, what were forests.

"But what of your vassals? Surely they could be commanded…"

Bridget jumped as he crashed his palm on the table. "The nobles, those loyal vassals of mine? Ha! I'd sooner trust a priest, Bridget. All they care for is their own skin and fear, fear that I may gain a little too much power and rid myself of them."

"But surely uncle…Glamorgan…"

"Glamorgan is the only true man among the vipers but even he would have to watch behind him, and I can't really blame him, can you?"

Sobered by the gravity of her father's revelations and secretly delighted by his decision to share then with her, Bridget nodded silently, eyes fixed on the man before her.

Quietly, feeling her heart beating, she said, "What will you do, my lord?"

Why did I call him "lord"? Have I ever called him that before? He looks so troubled, melancholy—there must be something he can do, he is still king!

Lifting his expressionless face, he looked into her eyes, "I do not know," he lied. "I am not yet sure…what would you suggest, princess?"

He called me princess! "I do not know enough to offer an intelligent solution, lord, this is all new to me yet is well-known to you. Know that I would do anything to help you, father."

"Would you, Bridget?"

Surprised that he would even ask such a question, Bridget came around the table and grasped his hands with hers, "You are my father and my king. I would be less than a daughter if I did not help you any way I could."

He looked into the eyes of the young woman, his daughter, for what seemed to Bridget to be a long time. *He looks as if he has something important to say.*

"Thank you, Bridget. I am sorry to have troubled you with all this," as he waved his hand over the map.

"No, father, this is something you should have shared with me long ago."

"I suppose you are right…but it is getting late and we have discussed much and tomorrow we head back." He kissed her cheek gently, wondering if Judas felt the way he did at this moment.

"Goodnight, father…thank you for your trust." With that Bridget stood stiffly, left the tent and strode unsteadily towards her tent.

Whoa! I am still feeling the effects of that wine! Easy now, easy. Breathe deeply, long and slow…I never knew my father had such troubles, never. Why didn't he come to me before? Is it because I am only a woman? Doesn't he know I would do anything within my power to help him?

She shook her head in disbelief that her father had waited so long to confess all these things…men! For all his power and authority he was still just a man after all. She lay down on her bed, closed her eyes and felt the room spin around her. Breathing deeply, she opened her eyes, hoping to diminish the flooding vertigo. She didn't know how long it took but sleep, when it came, was shallow— unrefreshing…and the Hooded Man was back that night.

She felt her shoulder being roughly shaken as her head did its best to keep still—anything to lessen the pain that was attempting to lift her scalp off.

Oh, nothing can make this worse!

"Does milady want to eat inside? It's raining."

"Do we have any willow tea, Gwenthe?"

"No, milady. Just water."

"Then just water will have to do…and no food today, thank you."

Grudgingly she pulled on a woolen cape before walking out into the flat, cold rain. Once more she walked up the hill, slipping slightly on the wet grass, till she stood looking at the ocean once more…but there was nothing. All before her was gray—no horizon, no sky.

How do they do it, these Vikings? What special magic do they have that can guide them through days like this?

Disappointed that she would not have one long, last view of the mighty sea, she walked sullenly towards where her tent recently had been.

"Ah, Bridget! Not the best weather to ride in but at least we are heading back."

"Yes, father."

Mounting Alexander, she grimaced at the feel of the wet saddle and pulled the hood of her cape over her head. Any elation she felt last night was lost somewhere between her sodden bottom and pounding head, right there in her unsteady stomach.

"Alexander," she whispered, "slowly please." The horse, sensing a weakness in his rider, lumbered along, his head bobbing in an easy rhythm.

Why do horses smell more when they're wet? My God, what happened to me last night? Oh, I hate feeling this way! Sweet Lord, I just want to get home. What must Mathilde and Gwenthe be feeling? I hardly spoke with them this morning.

The hooded band rode at a steady pace as the rain fell in steady sheets. Feeling somewhat more clearheaded than when she first began, Bridget glanced over her shoulder. The men in their sodden capes were slouched over to keep the rain from their faces.

These are the men who are to defend my father? Afraid of getting wet? I'll wager the Vikings run naked in weather like this!

Bridget sat taller and straighter, ignoring as best she could the new cold rivulets that ran down her back and abdomen.

Does it take a woman to do this? Then I shall be that woman. Perhaps I cannot wield a broad sword as strongly as they, but I can at least ride bravely. Pfaw! Look at them curdling! No matter what happens, no matter how terrible I am feeling, no one will know it from me. They won't say it but they will see how a woman, a strong woman, can suffer more bravely than they.

Braced, Bridget sat tall in the saddle, looking directly ahead, knowing that the men behind were watching. She found that if she let her mind wander, the discomfort seemed to lessen somewhat, not entirely, but at least become more bearable. And so she concentrated on the matter at hand—the Vikings. How many would come? How many ships? Where would they land? Do they bring horses with them? Women? She pictured the crude map of the night before— believing a child could have drawn a better one—where would they camp? How much provisions do they carry? From the Vikings she concentrated on what little she knew of her father's vassals, but she knew as little of them as she did of the raiders from the north.

Where have I been these few years not to have noticed what was going on?

But deep within her she knew the answer—she had been ignored, plain and simple. Her place was within the castle and her duties did not extend beyond its management. With that she straightened herself the more, pulling her shoulders back the way a true horseman rides, the way Uncle Glamorgan had shown her.

When at last she had exhausted what little she knew of the nobility, she prayed. Over and over she prayed in whispers till the Pater Nosters became hypnotic, the words becoming soothing sounds that overcame the boredom and the discomfort. She was very much asleep yet very much awake—so that when at last they stopped for some food it came as a surprise. Stealing a fast look behind her she noticed something remarkable—the men had pulled back their hoods and now sat erect and bold, oblivious to the heat-thieving drizzle. Encouraged by what she saw, she leapt off Alexander and joined her father beneath a tree. Pointless, actually, because the scratchy, leafless branches did nothing to discourage the rain that fell heavier now; even the king's dogs looked miserable, trying to hide beneath the cart carrying Mathilde and Gwenthe who were hidden somewhere beneath the folded tents and tarpaulins.

"Bah! Weather not fit for traveling, Bridget."

"Really, father? I know it is a little uncomfortable, but this is a doable thing, a necessity."

"Perhaps you're right, but I look forward to returning to a big fireplace and warm clothes."

"And a warm bath!"

"Yes, and that too. Come, the longer we stay here the longer we are from home and this inactivity chills the bones even more—I have seen men die under warmer conditions than this!"

They ate as they rode, believing that whatever time they saved brought them that much sooner to the confines of the comfortable castle. When at last they stopped, the night fires were the first line of business, even before the tents. The knights who had ridden earlier had three of them burning strongly, ready to warm the backs and fronts of the bedraggled party.

Don't shiver! Don't rush. First tether Alexander, then go see how Gwenthe and Mathilde are faring... **then** *go to the fire. Show them, show them all what stuff I am made of, no matter how much I want to stand before those flames!*

Feeling herself being watched by the men standing in front of the fires, Bridget walked with calm deliberation and tied Alexander next to the other horses. Then she walked over to the cart to find her ladies hidden beneath the skins as the tents were just now being set up. Thumping on the cart she yelled, "Where are my two ladies?"

A muffled voice (Mathilde's?) escaped, "I don't know, milady! But I am sure they never want to do this kind of thing again! What can I tell them?"

Bridget did all she could to stifle the laughter at the forlorn impertinence. "Well, tell them that their mistress feels just fine and wishes they would rouse themselves shortly...or the king's hounds will be given their supper!" Turning back, she headed towards the fire closest to her father's tent and found him there with his heavy cape off and drying on some branches, the steam wisping. She followed suit and soon the two of them alternately warmed their fronts and backs, grateful that the soaking rain had become a heavy mist.

"I will be eating alone in my tent tonight, Bridget, getting my things dry and getting warm. I would suggest you do the same—you don't want a fever."

"Yes, I agree, getting out of these heavy wet things will feel wonderful."

Shortly thereafter his tent was up and the king left for the cold comfort of its dry interior. Bridget stood rubbing her hands briskly, becoming inpatient with the laggards putting up her's but maintaining her equanimity. When at last it was done it was all she could do to walk over nonchalantly, as if she didn't care whether she was wet or dry, cold or comfortable. Once inside she stripped hurriedly and curled beneath the blankets, allowing the long-repressed shivers to wrack her body spasmodically. Gwenthe and Mathilde appeared shortly, carrying a metal pot, "Stew, milady! They scared up some rabbits and found some early onions!"

Uncovering only her head, Bridget reached greedily for the bowl of steaming warmth, sipping the hot fluid rapidly, not allowing the chunks of stringy meat to settle to the bottom. Her two ladies stood close by, clucking as they hung her sodden clothes and filled the bowl. Gwenthe began rubbing Bridget's arms rapidly, almost causing her to spill the stew that at last began to heat her innards and stop the trembling.

"Here, milady," said Gwenthe, "pull this here dry cap over your head and keep it on—it'll keep your toes warm." Too tired and cold to argue, Bridget complied with the foolishness as she continued drinking the pungent stew, relishing the taste, appreciating that her hands no longer trembled uncontrollably.

"I will pray for better weather tomorrow, milady." Said Mathilde earnestly.

"Will you, Mathilde? That would be nice, I think. I too will pray...but from my bed. I do not know when I have ever felt so tired and the stew was so good— and now I am just starting to feel warm."

Closing her eyes, she felt the women place more covers on her; the gentle heaviness pressuring her into a sleep that knew no cold...but he was there, the Hooded Man. The area was lighter and for the first time she could distinguish vague, unmoving shapes...and there was a chill spilling out from the shadowy hood that seemed to make her bones brittle and her joints stiff...and she felt a terror unlike any other as he held up his misshapen, bloody hands. Just like that— no voice or face—a specter, but she was so afraid! She tried to speak to it but words would not come and that made her feel more helpless, vulnerable. She tried to scream but was mute. Frustrated and terrified, she began gasping, attempting to get as much air into her as possible so that she might bellow and vent her fears and anger for being so afraid.

She woke suddenly to see the inside of the tent, dark except for one flickering candle. She looked around rapidly, hoping and praying that she was alone. Feeling foolish for her childish fears, she let out a thin whistle of air as she laid back down, eyes open, heart pounding still. She could not measure how long she had been asleep, she only knew that she was no longer cold and that there was a comforting sting to her fingers and toes which meant they were getting warm.

Dear God! When will these dreams stop haunting me? I promise that I will be especially prayerful this Easter, I promise—only stop this torment I beg of you!

Eyes closed, she tried to think of friendlier things: a warm bath, the Abbess, hot bread. Miserable, a dreamless sleep at last cloaked her with its healing forgetfulness once more.

"Should we waken her now?" Asked Mathilde.

"No, let her sleep till the last moment, poor child! Getting all chilled like that and then tossing and turning all night with those pitiful whimpers—no wonder she looks so haggard!"

"Maybe it was from too much wine?" Mathilde replied.

Looking at one another, the two women shrugged and sighed simultaneously, hoping that their mistress would confide in them so that they could rid her of vexations, protect her. It was not until the morning meal was almost completed that Gwenthe reluctantly shook Bridget's shoulder.

"Ah," she grumbled, "good morning Gwenthe. Is it time to get up already?"

"La, yes, milady and time to eat, too. The rain has stopped, thank goodness and your things are mostly dry—but you must get up now and eat."

I feel as though I haven't slept at all... did I ever really sleep? At least I am no longer cold! Lord help me, your humble servant, please.

Naked, she stood and stretched quickly before putting on her trousers and tunic that smelled strongly of smoke and though not wet, were not fully dry. Shivering, she walked outside to greet her father whose tent was already being packed.

"Ah, Bridget! I was about to go awaken you myself! Here, have a mug of hot soup. We have been blessed with fair weather this morning, eh? Perhaps the sun will even come out!"

Wordlessly, Bridget took the cup and drank its hot contents slowly and without enthusiasm—glancing at the gray skies as her father gestured, "It looks like it might clear later." She offered.

"Well, let's be about it then. Are you well? You do look as though the trip has been too much for you."

Bridget stiffened perceptibly. "No, my lord, the ride has been refreshing— I only slept but little last night—praying for good weather so your men might not falter from the cold and damp."

"Ah!" he laughed, "well put!"

Though her body screamed for rest, Bridget mounted Alexander deftly, pulling hard at the reins, turning him swiftly as she rode round the camp, letting the knights see her.

They rode hard that day, the lure of comfort strong in their memories, hoping to cross the Wythe sooner rather than later. The sky cleared as promised and all enjoyed the splay of the sun on their garments. Fed by the recent rain, the river ran angrily and it took extra time to find a suitable crossing site; one that would allow them just enough time to make camp on the other side. The cart had a rough time of it and Gwenthe and Mathilde transferred to two horses midstream amidst their oaths and supplications. The laughing knights did what was necessary, transporting them to the other side with nary a drop of water on them. Mathilde looked warmly on the young man who had cupped her breast while holding her on his mount. "La, milady! He truly is a gallant one, that," she told Bridget, safe on the other side.

"To be sure." She replied dryly.

Camp, their last, was raised swiftly. All anyone could think of was the promise of tomorrow's return to the castle. The king fairly bubbled over the evening's meal as Bridget, quiet and thoughtful, ate slowly; her enthusiasm tempered with the prospect that tonight she might share her sleep with the Hooded Man. Leaving her father, wishing he had dulling wine, she sat in front of her fire, staring thoughtlessly at the crackling flames. It was not until Gwenthe came for her that she realized how long she had sat there. Sighing, she entered the dimly lit tent and crawled into her bed after removing her boots. She lay there, eyes open, attempting not to think.

What foolishness is this! No dream, no matter how awful, has ever hurt anyone! How can I be so strong during the day, yet so fearful at night? What is a dream? I have never seen a spirit when awake. What is it then about sleep that makes one so different? There is more to fear in the reality of day than in all the torments of dreams.

Slowly, sleep crept behind her faltering eyes, closing the day and opening the night. What dreams there were, whirled about as the Hooded Man waited and watched.

She was awake before any of them, at once glad that sleep had come and gone without her waking. Pulling on her boots, she tossed the tent flap aside and walked out. The eastern sky was just beginning to lighten and she already knew that the day would be gloriously clear and warm. The travails of the other day forgotten, she stretched and yawned, feeling her sinews tighten and joints crack crisply.

Thank you, Jesus, for a good night. Thank you, Jesus, for this beautiful sunrise!

She closed her eyes, inhaling the wet air deeply, hearing the morning birds as the stars began to fade. The camp awoke early and noisily as the men joked merrily; even the horses seemed skittish, pawing at the ground restlessly, eager to start. Breakfast was little more than water, some dried apples and nuts; Bridget helped her women load the cart, tossing skins and pallets haphazardly into the cart; enjoying the labor and the strength of her arms.

"Come on then, Mathilde! Put some muscle into it!" Cried Bridget as they worked under the disapproving eyes of Gwenthe who thought it unseemly for a princess to toil like some common villein. It was a short time later that they began to recognize familiar landmarks; the abbey bell sounded sweetly, heralding the return of the king to his throne. With an excitement she did not think possible, Bridget smiled wildly at the bowing bands of peasants, grateful for all the comforts she would soon enjoy. The knights abandoned their loose formation and tightened into two columns, sitting proudly and defiantly.

The usual throng in front of the castle fell back respectfully as they entered, banners flying. The band continued through the courtyard and into the stables where upon waiting grooms and stable boys set upon them with much fussing.

"My dear," said the king as he dismounted with Bridget, "I am going to my rooms to see what has been going on since we left. What will you do?"

"A bath! A warm, soaking bath and then clean garments and if I do not fall asleep I will see my steward—but in all honesty I do not think I will see him until tomorrow," she laughed.

Walking towards the entrance the king saw Pardorous, his advisor.

"Sire, welcome home! I have some news from…"

"I have ridden hard and long and I am tired and unless it is about Saxons two days from here, you can tell me in my quarters. Now, allow me to warm these old joints with a hot tub." Bowing, Pardorous stepped aside, knowing that his king might be in a more receptive manner when comfortable.

Bridget waited until Alexander was safe in his stable and being fed and watered before going to the castle where Gwenthe and Mathilde were quickly warming water for milady's bath.

Slow and deliberate. Don't look to be in too much of a hurry—let them believe you could ride for another week if needed. Give the water time to heat!

She smiled at her little duplicity as she strolled to the castle, savoring the healing bath in her imagination.

I will strip, soak and sup in that tub—and if I could I might even sleep in it till I got all wrinkly.

The king was already in his tub, his eyes closed contentedly, when his counselor entered.

"What is so important that it cannot wait till tomorrow?" He asked tiredly.

"It will be too late, Sire. Tomorrow the Archbishop of Londinium will be here—with a marriage proposal for your daughter, Princess Bridget."

CHAPTER FIVE

"Damn!" The king slapped his wet hand on the side of the tub, "I had hoped for a little more time!"

"But sire, you yourself said time was crucial! The priest did his job too well, I think."

"And you, have you heard anything yet from your other inquiries? I want to have a choice in this matter, no matter how poor the candidates."

"Yes, sire. Another messenger came the day before yesterday to announce that another courier should be here tomorrow, also."

Grumbling, the king stood up and stepped out of the steaming water and began to towel vigorously, his head awhirl with what was happening too damn quickly!

I have done this to myself. . . but it had to be done! There is no fighting the gods in this. What has been done, is done. Now I shall have to hold on to this bucking stallion I have created and see how the bones fly!

Dressing slowly he turned to his advisor and placed his hand on his shoulder. "I have had no choice in this matter, Pardorus. We, you and I, shall have to choose the right man; a mistake will be disastrous. You have kept silent on this matter, no?"

"Of course! But the nobles will wonder why a prince of the church is coming to visit, particularly as you have shown no inclination to the Christ."

"My nobles!" He spat, "A scummier pack would be hard to find. . .except for Glamorgan. What is your opinion of him? Be honest, now is not the time to be polite." "He is a steady man, my lord. Stalwart. He appears honest and without ambition. He has served you well."

"Yes. I agree. He will be our anchor in the coming storm."

"Sire?"

"The rest of them will mewl like peeved kittens with no teat to suck. Glamorgan will remain steady. Now, please inform my daughter that I request her presence and notify the steward of the coming of the archbishop. How many in his party?"

"A goodly number."

"Very well, have the kitchen prepare for twenty guests. Tell Bridget I shall meet her in the hall."

"Certainly, lord." Bowing, Pardorus left the king to complete his dressing.

Bridget was just stepping out of her tepid bath when Gwenthe entered with a towel and news that the king had summoned to meet her in the hall.

What? So early? I thought all he wanted to do was rest? What can he ever want to talk about? The coming Easter celebration? What does he have to tell me now that could not wait till tomorrow?

She shivered a little at the possible implication of her thoughts—something important was at hand! She dressed hurriedly, barely drying her thick hair. The fatigue of the trip was forgotten as she headed down the stairs to meet with her father.

She found him sitting in his heavy chair by the table, looking solemn. She was somewhat surprised to hear so much commotion from the kitchen but gave it no thought.

"Father?"

He motioned towards the chair closest to him, "Have a seat, Bridget. I should like to discuss something with you." Sitting, Bridget became suddenly uncomfortable. The tone of his voice belied the expression on his face.

Looking hard into her eyes he said, "The archbishop of Londinium will be here tomorrow."

"Really? Why, that is wonderful, father! It will be so good to meet someone who—"

"He is here carrying a proposal of marriage for you."

"What?"

"Yes, a proposal of marriage. You have heard of marriage?"

The king had heard of men's eyes clouding over but he had never known just how frightening it was until now. Her usually green eyes sparked with gold chips as her skin paled; having dealt with men under moments of extreme pressure, he knew this was a bad sign—better for him if her face had become florid. For her part, Bridget felt a cold rage surge; she felt her pulse slamming through her temples as she stood and crashed her fist on the table just in front of her startled father.

"Never! Never! I will not marry; I do not want to marry! Who does the church think they are, making such a proposal?" Her face scant inches from his face.

"It was I who made the proposal for you, Bridget."

Stunned, she slumped back to her seat, looking at the man before her with dark, angry eyes.

"How dare you? How could you do this to me?"

"How could I not? You are a woman and a princess and my flesh. It is your duty."

"This is my duty!" She lunged forward, drawing her right arm back

"Don't dare think of me as some sniveling steward, child! Do not flatter yourself that you can strike your king, your father!"

"I have no father!" She yelled back, her arm still cocked. "What father would want his flesh and blood to suffer so?"

"Then attend to this, mistress! I am your king!"

Unable to vent her anger physically, tears of rage appeared.

"And why would my king want me to marry?" She spat.

"Because it is your duty for me and for the kingdom."

"What are you talking about?"

"Is this the same woman who only a night ago claimed that she would do anything to help me preserve the territories?"

Crashing her fist down, she shouted, "You tricked me! Damn you! You tricked me into saying that!"

"I did no such thing and one more outburst like that and I will forget that I am your father and act more like a king."

"Ha! You've known all along, haven't you? And you didn't have the backbone to tell me earlier! Well, I won't marry! I will enter the convent, something I have always wanted to do."

"Is that so? And what would your dear abbess say to taking in one more penniless woman—for I will certainly strip you of any inheritance and dowry. And you, so prideful of your thick hair! How will you feel when it is shorn from your scalp? I do not picture you on hands and knees, scrubbing floors and emptying pots!" Bridget's dream world crashed all about her; the hopes which she had built into mighty monuments were now shards of despair.

"Then I shall seek sanctuary."

"Think before you act, Bridget. Your irrationality serves you no purpose. The abbey, the priests, are here only because I allow them. They care for our sick and poor and give the peasants a reason for living their miserable lives. No, there will be no sanctuary, not for us."

Sitting now, her cheeks wet with anger, she breathed long and slow while glowering at the king. "You deceived me. You didn't even ask me."

"I had no choice, Bridget. I had to see the kind of woman you had become and I am well pleased."

"Please don't try to appease me! Not now, not ever. From now on I want only the truth. You have heard of truth?"

Stung, the king sat back. "You already know the truth."

"Then tell me, what will be my dowry? What ever could you offer to entice a man to marry me?"

"All the land north of the Wythe will be yours, you and your husband's."

Bridget sat back, wiping away angry tears from her face with the back of her hand, stunned into silence at the enormity of the prospect placed before her.

Satisfied that he had quieted her for the moment, the king continued. "But such a territory has a great price. Your husband, with my help, will have to defend against the Vikings and my churlish vassals. He will take care of the north and I shall control the south; I cannot do both." "I see." She sniffed. "And who will this man be?"

"I have not yet decided."

"Then I have no say in this matter?" Her voice rising.

"You want the truth? No, you do not. This is a matter of state, not the heart."

"Very well, then." Standing, she scraped the chair back noisily and headed towards the stairs.

The king let this insult pass, knowing that to push too hard might set her off on another rampage.

"Bridget, your anger can be a formidable weapon, keep it hidden."

"Yes, my lord," she replied without turning, walking steadfastly towards the door.

Hearing the earlier shouts, Gwenthe and Mathilde were anxiously waiting for their princess.

"Milady?"

"Enough Gwenthe! Get me a flagon of wine."

"But milady?"

"Now, Gwenthe! Not tomorrow, now!"

Both ladies bowed swiftly out of the room as Bridget paced rapidly about her quarters, attempting to dissolve the rage that pumped through her veins.

Never! Never would I have believed that this could happen to me! To me! How could he do this to me? I don't want to marry! Sweet Jesus, now I know how you felt in the Garden. Was Judas much like my father? How could he betray me like this? What happened to all my prayers? All I wanted was to serve you in the convent and you betrayed me too. What is the use of prayer if you never get what you want?

Feeling the rage begin to rekindle, she stopped and began to breathe long, slow breaths, her eyes closed. She heard the door open as Gwenthe and Mathilde returned. Mathilde looked frightened but Gwenthe had a scowl.

"Gwenthe, I am sorry I raged so, but…"

"It is all right, milady. You are a princess, I am but a serving woman."

"Stop that, Gwenthe. It does not become you! Accept the apology of a woman who has been misused and betrayed."

"Betrayed, milady? How so?"

Pouring herself a cup of wine, she said, "By my father, my king! He is finding me a husband!"

Gwenthe and Mathilde looked at one another rapidly, neither quite knowing what to say. Mathilde was about to laugh till she saw Gwenthe's raised brow and stifled it in her throat.

"Oh, milady," said Gwenthe consolingly, "what will you do?"

"I don't know Gwenthe, I really do not know. I will go see the abbess tomorrow, however and ask her advice. You and Mathilde may go now. Let me think this out."

"Of course, child. Know that we will help you anyway we can." They said as they closed the door behind them. Once outside Mathilde could hardly keep her voice in a whisper, "She is going to be married! Oh, milady, what will you do?" She said in rough parody of Gwenthe. "You would think she was going to the gallows the way she carries on."

Gwenthe shook her head, "Foolish child! It does not matter what you and I think, it is what she thinks! That is what is important to her and what we must help her with." Bridget sat on her bed, sipping the wine without pleasure. She stood and flung the cup into the fireplace, knowing that a clear head was needed, not drunken imaginations. She lay back, eyes closed, trying to view the crushing enormity of what had just happened with an objective eye. She looked at it from all sides and angles, turning it up and around—mentally examining the situation while looking for a solution.

I could just run away and abandon it all—disowned, penniless. And he is so right about the Abbess. If I seek sanctuary he will raze the whole thing, but where would I go? I would just be destroying the whole thing! My God, why have you let this happen to me? The man! The Hooded Man!

At once she sat up, startled by the crackling cold reality of what she now just realized.

It is him! It has to be him! That is what the dreams are all about! This man, my intended husband and the Hooded Man are one! And where did he get the blood? Whose blood is it, mine? The Vikings?

Another consideration suddenly pierced her already frothing thoughts and stabbed down to her belly.

A child! He will want to have children, certainly! The blood must be my own and he is holding it up to me in my dream, mocking me! No! No! I shall never have children, never become pregnant!

Trembling now, tears of fear pressed from behind her eyes as she buried her face in the covers. Her sobbing was long, hard and breathless as it wracked through her convulsing body. Bridget was unaware of how long this went on; she only knew that she was beyond exhaustion—fear and anger had drained all her strength, too tired now to even cry.

She did not go under the covers, preferring not to move anymore. She knew she would not sleep, she would pray instead. If the marriage was inescapable, so be it.

But I shall never have his child! Never!

All the conflicting thoughts and images of the past hour ricocheted through her skull; prayer was impossible as she tossed and fretted all night, looking for some way out, some resolution. The anger and rage she felt earlier melted into inky despair. She did not hate her father, not really, but she certainly would not, could not trust him again, ever. She felt as helpless as some mare at auction, being poked, examined and sold to the highest bidder; she flushed at the ignominy of being used as bait for the slathering jowls of some man. Disheartened, the morning bells of the abbey stirred her to her knees where she tried to pray with no success.

Even Jesus knew betrayal.

She was preparing to leave, to see the Abbess, when Gwenthe and Mathilde entered.

"Milady," said Mathilde, "we are here for you."

89

With that simple utterance Bridget felt tears begin to well up when she thought no more could come.

"Oh, Mathilde!" She cried and grasped her by the shoulders and buried her face on Mathilde's shoulder, letting the tears flow freely now.

"There, there, milady." Tutted Gwenthe. "You are a princess, sure enough, and tears come hard when they do."

Together they sat Bridget down and began to prepare her morning things. "First, go wash that face of yours and don't look at your dark eyes! Mathilde will brush your hair and I will fetch your breakfast. Now go, child."Rudderless, Bridget accepted direction with quiet relief and went to wash.

The king had not slept either, reviewing potential suitors for his daughter before the archbishop came to make his appeal. They all had worthy qualities; they all had defects: an only son meant that he could inherit his father's property and thus have divided loyalties; no experience in warfare but with many men was another. Feeling penned in and tired, the king had Pardorus review the final proposal.

"Prince Vortimer, youngest of three male children sired by King Harald of the Mercian kingdom."

"Three sons? Poor man!" Muttered the king, knowing what it was like to have older brothers. There would be intrigues brought on by various nobles, favoring one youth over the other. Or the two younger would plot to overthrow the eldest; or the eldest son would make sure his two siblings met with unfortunate accidents—thus were dynasties created.

"Fine, he survived, he has no hope of succession. What else?"

"His father kept him from harm's way by sending him to King Augustinus of Italy as a youth."

"A common enough practice, keeping the pups from the wolves and one another. Go on, do I have to ask you for every damn thing!"

"He is a leader of men having distinguished himself against the Saxons, Franks and Turks. He is some ten years older than your daughter, or fifteen, it is unclear here. He is well traveled, speaks Greek and Latin, of course. He can bring three hundred and fifty fighting men with their squires, women and such."

"Christian?""From what it says here, not very. Probably when it suits him."

"Vortimer it is. Damn, I am tired and so are you. Now, let us prepare to meet this prince of the church in graciousness and solicitude. One more thing, notify the Sergeant-at-Arms that my daughter is to be closely escorted—under no circumstances is she to be allowed to go further than the abbey. Make it understood that their heads will be gone if she is not here by evening."

"Is she under arrest, Lord?"

"No. I am just tired and am being careful—six men, two in front, two in the rear and one on each side—and I meant what I said about executing them for failure."

"Yes, lord." Bowing, Pardorus left to do as he was bid and to make sure the steward was getting all prepared for the coming of the prelate.

The king laid back on his bed and closed his eyes, weary and spent from the demands of intrigue, kingship and fatherhood.

Vortimer, Vortimer what kind of man are you? A battler certainly, but can you stand alone? Can you think? The king fell into a sudden and dreamless sleep.

Princess Bridget had finished her breakfast and was heading for the stables where she was met by a stern faced Glamorgan. "And where might you be going today, milady?"

"Why, to the abbey, uncle."

"We'll get Alexander ready for you as soon as your escort prepares."

"As usual, uncle."

"As usual, princess." He bowed.

It was not too much longer when Bridget, surrounded by her grim escorts, felt truly trapped. It was no use pretending that this was not happening; she was a prisoner as much as any shackled felon.

Finally, towards the noon hour, Pardorus came to the king's chambers, "He approaches, sire."

"Then," said the king, "let us make him welcome."

The king freshened briskly and headed to the hall where benches and tables were prepared, warm smells from the kitchen mingled with that of the fresh hay strewn on the rough floor.

"Sire, his excellency, the Archbishop of Londinium, Timothy."

King Gwaldner knew, as did all those in power, that church offices were bought and sold to finance the pope's powerful armies, but even with this knowledge he was taken aback by the brash young man that thundered into his hall.

"Damn me if this hasn't been the most hellacious trip I have ever been on! Have you no decent inns? Of course you don't! Or if you do you have kept them hidden from decent, honest travelers!"

Barely bearded and dressed in fine linen with a fur-lined cape, the prelate continued his tirade as he stomped towards the king who sat impassively.

"And wine! They call that cat piss they serve, wine! Well, the ale is good enough but I reckon to have been shorted too many times to count! Might as well have been robbed by highwaymen, at least they are honest about it! Ah, King Gwaldner! I bear greetings from his excellency, the pope, himself!"

Determined to ignore the lack of civility, King Gwaldner stood, a weak smile shadowing his face.

"Your Excellency, welcome."

"Ah, yes! King Gwaldner!" He went directly to the throne and clasped the king with warmth and noise. "Damned if I'm not glad to be have some decent shelter, at last! Thank you, thank you! And I bring gifts! Knowing how your land is unblessed by a favorable climate, I have brought dates and figs, two barrels, from my own fields and his holiness bids you enjoy two casks of his finest wine, along with a goodly supply of olive oil. I was sorely tempted to crack the wine open myself after tasting the piss that passes for wine in these parts, but I changed to the ale instead! No wonder the Romans hated this country, fit for savages, no? Well, enough—we have much to discuss and we are famished." He flourished his hand towards the small group that remained silent and stood raggedly by Pardorus.

There were perhaps ten soldiers, guards, a few tonsured clerics and one woman, young with black hair down to her shoulders.

"Ah, that's Marissa," said the archbishop, "my companion. My wife cannot abide this abominable climate and I cannot abide a cold bed!"

"Indeed. Then let us make you comfortable first. My men shall direct you and yours to your quarters where you may refresh yourselves. Afterwards we shall dine heartily in my quarters."

""Ah, splendid idea!" He said looking at Marissa, "After so arduous a ride it will be good to have clean linens and a bath."

"Good! That settles it then! Consider my house, yours." Bowing, Timothy smiled, silent as he was led by Pardorus to his chambers, not far from the king's.

Even before Timothy began fondling Marissa, Bridget was being hastily escorted to the abbess. Knocking on the heavy door, she was surprised as always that the old nun was able to open it by herself.

"Oh, Reverend Mother! I am so sorry to disturb you but things have happened and I have no one to turn to."

"Dear child, what can possibly be troubling one so young and healthy?" Her sonorous voice was a balm to Bridget who stood fidgeting as the old nun clutched at her elbow and led her to the courtyard.

"My father wants me to marry—he is making me get married! What can I do? What can you do for me? I know in my heart that God wants me to serve Him here with you and the other good sisters. I am at a loss!"

Damn him! Damn the king! This is not what I nor this little one had planned! What to do, what to do.

With a countenance that radiated tranquility, the old woman allowed herself to be escorted to the small chapel where they found a novitiate lying on the floor face down, her arms and legs spread in silent penance. "Go to your cell, sister, while we pray."

The girl, because she was certainly not old enough to be called a woman, arose stiffly and silently and fled, leaving Bridget and Sister Maria alone.

"Come," she crooned, "let us pray for guidance." She held on to Bridget's elbow as she dropped painfully to her knees. Making the sign of the cross and bowing her head, the old nun's head was swirling with Bridget's declaration.

Damn the king! How could he do this! Well, I suppose he is not so foolish as I or anyone else had hoped. Now, what do I do with this little one here? Ah, it would have been so good to have had her here as one of us; a large dowry, inheritance, she would have helped us immeasurably. Too, the folk seem to respect her—damn! So, what would happen if I gave her sanctuary? How would that old bastard respond? Not favorably. The only thing that keeps us going is his meager gifts and they would cease. Too, he would strip his poor daughter of any dowry and she'd become just another novitiate, one more toiler for Christ. And as God as my judge, the king is not above arranging for mishaps, I am sure! A fire here or there, livestock missing—any number of hidden things to get us to leave. He wouldn't do it outright, I believe, too crafty.

And what would happen if I some how arranged for his daughter to run away, to escape from his influence? First, he'd disown her, of course. And where would she go? And how would all this help me? It wouldn't, it would only provoke him.

She shifted her screaming knees on the cold stone floor, looking, as did all the nuns, for a soft spot on the granite.

What to do, what to do? I did not come this far to be thwarted, not by some petty king! How to turn this adversity to my advantage, that is the trick. Let me counsel Bridget in this marriage, encourage it a little. The king would know of it, of course, my acquiescence lending some support to his plans. So, if she marries obediently, I would not only have a grudgingly thankful father, but someone close to the court! Bridget would trust me with secrets and details heretofore unknown…and with her love I might perhaps influence both husband and father! Perhaps losing Bridget is a godsend!

Making the sign of the cross, the old abbess used the kneeling princess as a crutch and stood, her old knees making little snapping noises—Bridget followed obediently.

"All things," she began, "serve God. Did you know that, Bridget? Our Father knows the number of hairs on our heads; he knows when a bird dies. Our God is all knowing; His wisdom was before the earth itself."

Bridget nodded dumbly, not liking where this conversation appeared to be heading.

"God has a plan for us, my dear. A plan that brings Him honor and glory; a plan that is unknown to us and one that may be difficult. Perhaps it is not in His plan that you should join us here."

"Oh, Sister! But I wanted it so much!"

"Hush, now! It is not what we want, but what He wants of us! The clay does not tell the potter what shape it wants to take," she chided. "Perhaps our Father has greater things for you to do, other ways to serve Him?"

"How?"

"Well, perhaps it shall be your mission to bring your husband to Christ. That would be a noble, holy thing, something that only a wife could do."

Sister Maria continued walking around the courtyard, hoping her words would soothe the young woman's anxiety.

"But I am frightened, Sister! This is something so new to me, alien."

"Hush, child. You are a princess as well as a follower of Christ. Give to Caesar the things that belong to him; and give to God the things that are His." They had completed a circuit and were now by the gates of the abbey where the princess's escorts stood. The old nun motioned for one of them to fetch Alexander. Lifting her mouth close to Bridget's ear, she whispered, "Remember child, if, God forbid, your husband was slain, we do accept widows in the order."

She kissed the abbess respectfully, disheartened that no miracle had come to save her. Riding between her escorts she listlessly observed dark clouds draping gray veils of rain behind them.

Those clouds are from the south, no doubt that is where he is from.

The thought of suicide crossed her mind for the briefest moments and was discarded as cowardly and sinful—no man was worth an eternity of hell.

Bridget lay in her on the bed, emotionally fractured and physically exhausted from trying to evade the inevitable. Knowing the archbishop was there made her feel as though bags of sand were being placed on her chest, crushing her breath away.

"Would milady like something to eat," asked a solicitous Gwenthe.

"No thank you. I just want to lie here and think."

Gwenthe sat on the side of the bed and began brushing Bridget's thick, wavy hair. Not speaking, she looked at the fine features of the princess, disregarding the darkened eyes. A look of pity crossed her face then disappeared. She took her index finger and began running it ever so softly across Bridget's forehead and down and around her cheek and chin and then back up and over her eye brows; the touch of her worn finger softened Bridget's expression and she began breathing more slowly, her body becoming limp by degrees until her lips parted slightly.

"Sleep milady, sleep softly." She began humming an old song from her childhood, the words forgotten but the melody remaining as sharp as yesterday as she continued her fingertip caress. Satisfied that the princess was at last asleep, she covered her lightly and left the room, quiet as a shadow.

While Bridget slept her father was just welcoming the archbishop to his room where the table was crammed with joints of mutton, fowl and fish. "Damned if this isn't the feast I had been looking forward to! My compliments, my compliments! From the inns one would think all you ate was rabbit and beans!"

Pardorous pulled out a chair for the archbishop who sat soundly, thumping his elbows on the table as he reached for a goblet of wine.

"Would you first like to give thanks, your excellency?"

"Ah, yes, quite right, sire."

Clasping his hands tightly in front of him, Timothy bowed his head, "*In vino, veritas*. My apologies, sir, but I could think of nothing else to be grateful for. Let us drink to each other's health instead."

After the toast, the assault on the food began. Tasting and picking from this meat and that, the bones were tossed on the floor. Having the edge taken off appetite, Timothy began praising the king for his wisdom in seeking a suitable match for Bridget.

"*Natuo abhorret a vacuor*," he continued; pleased with his play on words. "You need, your kingdom requires, a man of some wealth, influence and power. The church has such a man; a man much thought of by his holiness, I might add."

"What do you mean?"

"Well," Timothy continued, "his holiness, in spite of his own bellicosities, is very interested in assisting you. So interested that he would send some three hundred of his own troops to augment those of the man I am prepared to recommend."

"And why," asked Pardorous, "is the pope so concerned? We are too many miles from Rome to be of any interest or worth."

"Nonsense! The pope will do all in his considerable power to assist those who would defeat the barbarians."

You lie poorly for a priest, thought Gwaldner

"Leo, in spite of his problems with defending Rome from the Saracens, is willing to send troops of his own here to help you! We must do all we can to help each other, sire."

Sipping from his goblet, the king looked hard at the bishop.

How much did you have to pay for your position, you officious bastard? But I do enjoy your wine…very much.

"So, who does the church propose be my son-in-law?"

"Ah! That it what I like about you people…direct and to the point! First and foremost, he is wealthy and will be able to bring a goodly number of his own force along with some mercenaries."

"How many?"

"Of his own troops, two hundred men. That, along with the three hundred of the pope's would make a considerable deterrent. As for the mercenaries, I confess that I do not know their number."

"A goodly amount—tell me of the man, their leader. Who is he? An army, no matter the size, is a mob unless there is a competent person in charge."

"Hs name is Augustus, son of Augustinus, a proud son of a warrior father."

The king moved his eyes quickly to Pardorous who acknowledged it with the scantest of nods—Vortimer had been under the tutelage of Augustinus! Timothy, more concerned with the bone he was picking, never noticed.

"Yes, Augustus has been well-schooled in the art and science of war, my lord.

"And he is a Christian?"

"Of course, sire! Washed in the blood of Christ by the pope himself!"

"Tell me," asked the king as he leaned towards the bishop, "has he been baptized by the blood of his enemies?"

"My lord?"

"Has this Augustus actually fought? Has he had blood run down his sword and cover his hands? Has he led men into battle? How does he handle reversals?"

Timothy sat back, startled by the king's sudden passion. "My lord, his father has been the staunchest of the pope's allies…"

Gwaldner exploded, "I asked for a man, a warrior to lead soldiers into bloody battle! Not some gelding dressed up like a warhorse!"

"Sire, I am certain that with the number of his troops at his disposal he could successfully apply all that he has learned!"

By God! How could he come all the way here to offer me up some fop who has studied "the art and science of war"?

Controlling the ire he felt welling up, the king poured himself some wine and offered some to Pardorous who sat expressionless.

"The pope must have much confidence in Augustus to gamble with the fortunes of my kingdom."

"Sire, it is no gamble! Leo is certain that with the blessings of God and enough men, the Vikings can be routed!"

Gwaldner sat back in his chair, appearing to look thoughtful.

"This is a grave matter; one that requires our studied attention. We must give it some thought."

"Not to press you too closely, lord, but young Augustus is a valuable and much sought out young man for obvious reasons. His holiness wants this match but the decision, your decision, must be forthcoming. I have been instructed to return with your election."

"We are too much with the world, Timothy. Here, have you tried some of the fish yet? This is a matter that must be given some deal of thought, the pope's impatience not withstanding—we shall inform you this evening…but meanwhile let's feast…and did I thank you for your so-generous gifts? The oil and dates will be a welcome addition to our table."

Nodding as his fingers plucked at the fish, Timothy broke off delicate chunks.

"Certainly, lord. The affairs of state can be a burden," he belched.

The meal continued as the conversation turned to more mundane matters—weather, crops, politics. Sated at last, both men stood and hugged; Timothy retreated to his quarters and the waiting Marissa while the king and Pardorous sat mutely for a brief time.

"Vortimer?" Sighed the king at last.

"Vortimer, lord, is the only choice." Echoed Pardorous.

"The pope must think me a fool! Trying to place an army loyal to him at my doorstep under the guise of helping me! Might as well have foxes guard chickens!"

Pardorous smiled weakly as the king continued to enumerate the rest of Augustus's deficiencies.

"But can Vortimer be successful, sire?"

"Successful? He has no choice but to succeed, no choice. How quickly can he be here?"

Pardorous shrugged, "A fortnight...two at the most."

"This must be done quickly. Send the messengers tonight—inform the king that we should be honored to have his son marry Bridget. Say...a week's betrothal before the ceremony? I think that should serve the purpose, don't you?"

"Of course, sire."

The evening came later now, allowing for more work to be done in the fields as the population readied for the dual holiday of Easter, unmindful of the events that were rapidly unfolding in their sovereign's castle. The peasants, bound to the land owned by the king, worked the earth as hard as it worked them; the reward for unending labor was avoiding starvation. Life, though bleak, was not without its enjoyments; the first of these was beer—one of the few things not taxed and could be me made by anyone—usually the women. Whether Old or Christian, holidays were celebrated with copious amounts of the brew.

In her room Bridget was able to listen to the comings and goings of the servants and of the general population in the courtyard. Her brief rest had given her a momentary reprieve from the troubles vexing her; feeling refreshed, she lay in her bed and stared at the ceiling.

What will he be like, this man? Will he be older than me? Not too much older, I hope...or maybe that would be the best thing. Where will he come from? Will he be common and coarse? I hope he can at least read! What sort of lover will he be? Sweet Jesus! I never thought I would be thinking such things—ever! But what will it be like? What would happen if I refuse? What could he do—divorce me and send me to the convent? This is something that requires careful thought.

What will Celestine think? She will probably tease me just as she has always done! Perhaps she may help me now—I know everything and nothing about a marriage bed!

Mathilde entered the room, closed the shutters and began replenishing the fire as the nights were still cold.

"Are you feeling better, milady? Perhaps a cup of broth?"

"No, Mathilde, thank you. May I ask you something?"

"Of course, milady."

"Then sit here next to me. Tell me, what is it like to be with a man?"

"Milady?"

"I mean, I know how to do it, but what does it feel like? Does it hurt? Why is so much made of it, anyway?"

Sitting next to Bridget on the bed, Mathilde began to giggle. "Oh, milady! It is painful at first; I cannot lie to you. Sort of a burning pain that gradually becomes uncomfortable and then everything else happens!"

"Everything else?"

"Well, maybe not the first time, maybe not the second or third! But eventually, if you have a good man or learn what to do, it is wonderful! You feel as though you are no longer in a bed or a barn floor, but someplace else. It is difficult to describe, milady, I am not pretending to be mysterious, but I am just ignorant of the words!"

Grasping Bridget's hands with her own, Mathilde closed her eyes. "It is unlike any sensation you have ever felt! Your body no longer listens to your head and all feelings radiate from inside of you...it is wonderful. I cannot think of how else to describe it, not now...maybe later if I give it some thought."

"Mathilde," Bridget became grave, how is it you have never had a child? How come you have done all these...things, and have never gotten pregnant?"

"There are ways for a woman with the knowledge to do everything and not have a baby milady...the proper timing is important and then there are things that you can do that can, you know..."

"No, I do not! And I am feeling like a child and I don't like it one bit! Never mind—forget that I ever asked, Mathilde...and not a word of this to Gwenthe, do you understand?"

"Yes, milady, but Gwenthe is an old woman and wise; she has a wisdom of many things, many things...and she would not blush as much as you, I swear!"

Damn! Why must I be betrayed by my ignorance of something so mundane and common?

"Where is my father?"

"He is in his quarters, preparing to see the bishop in private."

"Has he asked for me then? Am I not allowed some small part in this or am I supposed to just let them decide my future?"

"Your father has not requested you...but may I get you some dinner?"

Slapping her palms on the bed, Bridget stood and walked angrily to the window. "Yes, something to eat and drink is what I need right now."

Dear Lord, what have I done to deserve this? I have prayed tirelessly to be allowed to serve you in quiet celibacy and yet you permit. . .this, to happen to me! Very well, if this is your choosing, so be it. I have no idea what I am supposed to do—I only know that I don't want it and cannot accept any part of it. If this is your will then the fruits will also be yours.

Looking out the window she could see distant fires dotting the landscape, places where people who had no troubles could sit around and sing and talk; where who you married, if ever, was your own choice.

If I were a man this wouldn't be happening!

She tasted the bile beginning to rise at the unfairness of it all.

The king and Pardorous awaited Timothy in the king's room—large and lit by heavy candles—a sense of excitation laced with dread permeated the air.

"What we do here, Sire, may well determine our fate."

"Yes, I know that only too well—but what else is there to be done? If we had done nothing we would meet disaster from either the Vikings or a coalition of some of the nobles. At least the barbarians would be honest about it, eh? And if we accept Leo's puppet, what then? It would only be a matter of time before our balls would be cut off and Augustus would be the cock to reckon with! No, Pardorous, as flimsy as it may appear, Vortimer is our best and only hope."

"How so, lord?"

"By ceding the land and its defense to my son-in-law, I keep the Vikings at bay for at least another season and with a minimum of manpower. This will allow me to deal with the others. Too, with the exception of Glamorgan, the nobles will instantly dislike an interloper—their pride will prevent them from seeking any alliances with Vortimer. As a matter of fact, they will probably do all in their power to see that he fails. They will do this unobtrusively, of course. They lack the strength and courage to defy me openly. They are a house full of toothless harlots in the presence of some new, young beauty, Pardorous—their jealousy, hatred and ultimately, fear, will be our assets."

The counselor nodded with grim resignation, acknowledging that the future would be "interesting".

"How do we reject Augustus without outwardly provoking the church too much, Pardorous?"

"I have been giving that some thought, sire. Let me handle Timothy in my own way. Just know that I find this groveling as distasteful as anything I have ever done! Particularly before one who is such a boorish ass! It would go much easier for me just to send him on his way with a swift boot…but decorum…"

"Yes, we have enough enemies to contend with right now," sighed the king. "It would have been so much easier to send the pope Timothy's head in a basket."

"At least there'd be no misinterpreting our thoughts." Pardorous laughed as the king joined him. "I will sweeten our rejection, sire, so much so that Timothy will thank God that Augustus is not the one."

"Do that," said the king, "and keep this creeping Christian at bay."

It was not much later when a sharp knock on the door announced the prelate's arrival. A guard pushed open the door and Timothy, beaming and preened, entered noisily.

"Good evening, sire. Good evening, dear counselor." He bowed graciously to both men.

"Ah, Timothy," greeted Pardorous as he pulled up a chair for the young man, "we were just discussing you and the magnificence of your office. Here, have a seat by us. We have so many questions to ask, so many things of importance to discuss." Pardorous looked at the king and nodded towards the door. The king, taken somewhat off guard, looked hard at his counselor when he finally realized what he had to do. Going to the door, he opened it and dismissed the two guards.

"Trust and privacy are rare commodities, are they not?" Said Pardorous as he poured ale for the three of them. "I imagine that you must have much the same problem in Rome as we do here in this mean place?"

"To be sure," grunted Timothy, "even worse. There, not even prayer is sacred! Why, just speaking in jest has led many to lose their favor and fortunes. Petty intriguers, it seems, carry more weight with the court than those who earnestly seek to serve. A pox on the bastards, I say! Men of honor should join together and crush them with our heels! Ah, yes! Some of your fine ale! You do brew wonderful ale! Sometimes it is just as satisfying as our wine."

"We lack the temperate climate of your home, I fear," said the king easily, "but our beer is second to none!" With this all three drank in agreement and Pardorous refilled the goblets from the cask. Sitting between the clergyman and the king, the counselor smiled warmly at Timothy, "Now, let us get to the matter at hand—the marriage of Bridget to this young Augustus—we approve."

With this announcement Timothy drank deeply with a wide smile that, to the king, looked oily. "The pope shall be pleased, gentlemen, greatly pleased at the news."

"He is a young man, of course," Pardorous continued, "untested in battle and with troops of questionable loyalty but even that does little to diminish his worth."

Timothy began to protest when Pardorous continued, "I mean, after all, mercenaries! And the popish troops are sworn to the pope, no?"

"The mercenaries are well paid," Timothy growled, "and the pope's men are at the disposal of Augustus—they are sworn to him!"

"Ah," continued Pardorous, "but they will be so far removed from Rome that they may forget their allegiances, particularly when they see the Vikings for the first time…and as for the mercenaries, well, my king has many wealthy enemies." The king nodded sagely.

"Augustus will do fine," Timothy said. "Why with just a little help from you," he looked at the king, "the Vikings will be beaten."

"That is just it," said the king, "I can not promise him anything except, perhaps, some few villeins and the help of one of my vassals."

"Tell me," Pardorous asked, "what will the pope's mind be when young Augustus is killed? Will he be angry with us? Surely, we do not want the papal wrath upon us!"

"What do you mean?"

"Rome has no friends here, Timothy. As sure as I sit here before you, Augustus will be dead within the year, killed either outright or by some treachery—of this I have no doubt. What will Leo do then? Send us another suitor for the widow Bridget? How long before the well of eligible men runs dry? How long before the pope turns his back on us completely?"

"What are you proposing?"

"Only this," Pardorous drew closer to Timothy, "who will help us next season?"

Staring into his cup, Timothy discerned a crack in the negotiation and began to force a wedge. "Perhaps this solemn news places the matter in another light," he said.

"How so?" asked the king.

"My lord, the pope, to whom I am sworn spiritually and politically might have a jaundiced eye should Augustus meet an untimely death."

"We would not want to anger the pope," said the king quickly.

Ignoring the king, Timothy continued, "Augustus is a true and good man. His mettle only awaits to be seen. It would be a grave loss for all if he should die before his time."

"But what of the Vikings?" Pardorous protested.

"Well," said the prelate, "perhaps you can find an interim solution? Maybe find some other suitor who is more…disposable. The pope has enemies at his own gate, you know. He would be foolish to place Augustus at such risk with questionable chance of victory."

"But what are we to do?" The king pleaded.

"To do? I know not, but be assured that I will pray for you! Truly, God will find the means to deliver you from the Northmen if you will only come to know His will."

The king and Pardorous let a loud sigh escape.

"I, we, are at a loss," said Pardorous, the resignation in his voice touching Timothy who nodded sagely.

"I will go to my chambers now," said the churchman, "and will pray for you with all my heart. We shall leave before dawn, if it pleases you."

"Prayers in place of swords? Would that the savages were Christians," said Pardorous to Timothy's back as he retreated towards the door.

Turning, Timothy bowed deeply. "My lords, my intercessory prayer is all I can give."

He closed the great door behind him.

The king and Pardorous stood as they listened to the heavy steps of Timothy finally grow silent.

"Like seducing a whore," said the king.

"Easier, sire, easier."

"The messengers are sent for Vortimer?"

"The most swift, lord."

"Ha! Well, we are in his prayers! Cold comfort, that."

"Amen," Pardorous grinned, "amen".

"We have done well, I think, I hope. Now are our fortunes placed in the hands of a stranger—we must be careful to give him the help he needs without weakening our own position."

"Success, sire, is never guaranteed. Know that I will do all in my power to see our enemies vanquished."

"And what of Bridget, Pardorous? Will she be of the same mind, do you think?"

The old man sat and looked thoughtfully at his king. "Great travails make for great people, sire. She is headstrong, willful and with great...passion. Much like her father and mother."

The king smiled ruefully. "Ah, but you have not answered my question."

"As a fine sword is forged by white heat, so shall Bridget be tempered. She needs only a purpose and then woe to those who stand in her way. There is something, a resolve or strength, in her character of which even she is unaware, I believe," said Pardorous.

"You echo my own thinking. Let us retire now and clear our heads. We have much to do before Vortimer comes."

"That we do, sire. That we do."

As the king and his counselor made for their beds, Bridget lay awake in hers, watching the dancing shadows thrown from the fireplace and listening to the night sounds from deep within the castle.

Is this the end, then? No friends, no chance, no hope...what will this man be? Will he be like Celestine's husband...all belly and wine. Or perhaps he may be like Uncle Glamorgan?

She rolled over and stared out the unshuttered window, the last twenty-four hours playing over and over in her head. It was somewhere below the reach of her conscious thought that a change began in her. Cornered like some wild boar, all avenues of escape closed, a steely resolve began to form from somewhere deep and cold within. She was unaware of her jaw tightening, nor did she notice her quickening heart; but suddenly there came a tranquility and serenity born from acceptance of the impossible. And with the acceptance came the determination not to seek other ways to escape, but to fight.

Impossibly, sleep blanketed her at last and the Hooded Man did not come.

CHAPTER SIX

For half a year the sun had been struggling for domination, each day lingering some few precious seconds longer that achingly became minutes. Spinning and revolving, the planets danced to their ethereal music; forever changing, forever constant, the seasons marked by the simplest earth-tiller. Long before the jealous god presented Himself to desert shepherds, the people had worshiped and prayed to those who controlled the planets, for they told when to sow and when to gather.

The minutes of increasing sunlight slowly turned into hours as the night of winter grudgingly loosened its grip. And the great stones that were placed by ancient sky watchers measured the timeless births and deaths of the seasons. The sun bathed the land with its warmth, coaxing it into life yet again—Eostre would be celebrated when at last light and dark were once again equal—the beginning of summer, the resurrection of the land.

The fields were bursting with life as the buds pushed through the rough dirt—riots of wild flowers and clover sprung up; trees began to leaf. The rains, once cold and bitter, were now the blood of life and prayed for. No matter their station, from the richest to the most poor, Eostre was a time of celebration and hope. Families gathered eggs, decorated the shells and gave them as gifts to friends, family and to their lord, who would in turn prepare a great feast for his vassals—in this way acknowledging the great work before them. Secret groves and grottoes were visited and the goddess prayed to—for no amount of endless sweat guaranteed the crops would be spared from the ravages of insects, disease or vermin...the prosperous secretly sacrificed bull, their blood sanctifying the earth.

Bridget, it seemed, was the only one not caught up in the riotous season.

What can I do about this, all this...marriage? Nothing, therefore it is pointless to fight in this way. What was it Uncle Glamorgan used to say? "If you can't beat your opponents with strength, beat them with speed! And if you can't beat them with speed, beat them with cunning!" Well, I will just have to be cunning.

Stretching in bed, Bridget began planning her day; thoughts of her approaching husband were momentarily placed in the back of her mind, to be mulled over later.

"Gwenthe! Mathilde! Where are the two of you? Come, the sun is already up!"

The door opened hurriedly, the two serving women scurried in as breathlessly as if they had just run up the stairs.

"La, milady! I haven't seen you this way in some time! What sorts of dreams did you have last night? Was it about?..."

"Enough, Mathilde. I have much to do and much to prepare for the upcoming Easter celebration. I will not tolerate any prattle about 'dreams' and 'portents' and such. My marriage is of no concern to me right now...no concern whatsoever. I do not care a whit about whom he is or what he is like or what he looks like. Why should I?"

"Of course, milady," said Gwenthe. "Mathilde, you brush milady's hair while I fetch her clothes. What will you be doing today, milady, so that I may get the proper garments?"

"Work and riding to the abbey...simple clothes would be best, I think."

At that moment the clang of the abbey bell leaked through the castle walls and Bridget grabbed the hands of her servants and pulled them both to the bed where they knelt and began to pray hurriedly, more concerned with the speaking than their praying. The prayer completed, Bridget hurried back to the chair and waited for the morning's preamble to end.

So much to do, so much to do! First, I must see my father and get my affairs straightened out once and for all. Then I must see Peter and see to it that he is preparing for Easter and then, and then...to the abbess for her blessing.

Mathilde had barely finished the last stroke when Bridget sprung from the chair and began pulling on her clothes. "Where is my father now? Is he still inside?"

"Yes, milady, I believe he is eating in his room this morning."

"Then I shall have my food there as well," she said as she pulled the tunic over her head, negating all Mathilde's efforts.

"Do you think that wise?" Asked Gwenthe.

"Wisdom has nothing to do with! I am his daughter, the Princess Bridget! The sooner he stops treating me like some, some commodity, the better off we and the kingdom shall be!" With that she thundered through the door as her two women listened to her thudding steps pounding along the hall.

The two guards posted by the door were not there for ornamentation and brought Bridget to an abrupt halt. While it was true that the castle was guarded heavily against an invasion, it was also true that more had been slain by the sly knife than the heavy sword.

"State your business, milady."

"I want to see my father, the king."

"Stand back."

Knocking heavily, one of the guards announced Bridget as the other watched closely, his expression flat but his body poised. The door opened slowly, "Of course, let her in."

Bridget walked in slowly, attempting to compose herself as she did so. "Father, we have things to discuss."

"Yes, of course we do. Sit here," as he pulled a chair from the table.

"I am just now eating, will you join me?"

"My women will bring my food here, I did not know whether or not you were eating."

"Fine, but do enjoy some of the fine wine brought by our visitor from Rome," he said as he poured her a goblet. Father and daughter sat quietly as they watched the sky lighten.

"So, what brings you here so early?"

"The truth is all I want…and my freedom."

"Your ladies are slow. Here, try some bread with the honey. Do you think we shall have a good harvest this year, Bridget? What do you think, eh?" He asked as he gazed out the window.

Whatever does this have to do with me? Doesn't he have the decency to at least recognize my wants?

"I don't know, father. Who can predict what the weather will do or how the harvests will fare?"

"Well, you really should concern yourself with what goes on with your lands—you have to. Our, your strength comes from the bent backs there in the fields, in the mud."

"Tell me what I need to know."

"Such as?"

"Such as my intended husband, who is he? Tell me all you know about him."

"Certainly, of course! You have every reason to want to know about him and

I will tell you all. He is from the south and he is the youngest of three sons; therefore he stands little chance of succeeding to his father's throne. Too, just his living this long lends me to believe that he either has his wits about him, is fleet of foot or damned lucky! He will need all three here, I assure you."

"And he is how old?" She asked, holding her breath, praying fervently that he would not be an old man.

"I believe he is ten years your senior."

She let out a silent prayer of thanks.

"Let's see, what else," the king continued, "he is a tried warrior and triumphant soldier. He has lost some campaigns, I believe, but he does not lack for perseverance. I am told that his men would follow him to the end of the earth. His name is Vortimer."

"Of course, they are following him here."

Laughing, the king shook his head, "Bridget, you have a quick mind and a quick tongue—best hone one and dampen the other—never let on as to what you are thinking until you are certain of the other person. Next question."

"Is he a Christian?"

"If he is, I am unaware of its importance to him."

Bridget mulled the reply momentarily and placed it where she could think about it later. "And why Vortimer? Why not Augustus?"

"Augustus would be the mongrel of Rome, eating scraps from the pope's table and willing to do anything for greater fare! I bear no ill will against the Christ but the church, that church is another matter! How long before the cur's master told it to abandon us or worse. No, Bridget, Augustus would become a greater threat than the Vikings."

Bridget stood away from the table and knelt before her father who looked at her impassively.

"I am Bridget, daughter of Gwaldner, princess and mistress of his castle. Soon I shall be wed to the man upon whom the fortunes of my people will depend. I swear allegiance to my father, my king."

The king looked into her eyes, searching for what lay behind them. "I have told you all, Bridget, my daughter, princess and mistress of my castle."

"And I speak the truth also, and would ask that I no longer be treated as a prisoner here or anywhere else."

Standing, the king took her hands and raised her up, the corners of his mouth barely rising. "Princess Bridget, your allegiance is cherished and will never be questioned. Your feast of Easter is approaching, make the appropriate arrangements."

Bowing, Bridget backed toward the door where she straightened to her full height.

"My lord."

"My daughter."

Opening the door, Bridget walked firmly past the guards and down the hall where she met Gwenthe and Mathilde carrying her food.

"Never mind...I shall eat downstairs instead."

Walking with long, purposeful strides, she came to the hall and sat down quickly, oblivious to the changing of the guards.

Speaking between rushed mouthfuls of food, Bridget had the steward brought to her.

"Milady," said Peter as he began to open the ledger.

"No, my dear Peter, not today. Do you know what feast is upon us?"

"Why of course, Eostre is begun and all the..." seeing his mistress's face sour, he stopped.

"Why, of course! Easter is upon us, the celebration of Jesus rising from the dead! This Sunday Father Junius will hold a special service and..."

"Yes," replied Bridget, somewhat mollified, "we need to go over the foodstuffs for the feast and celebration. All my father's vassals, ladies and generals will be here and I intend that nothing goes undone."

"Of course, milady, it shall be as you wish. Now, permit me to show you here..." and Peter opened the ledger so both he and Bridget could read the inventory of the foods, wines and sweets. Their heads bent over, Peter began taking mental notes as they discussed the number of lambs and barrels of ale required for upwards of one hundred people who were accustomed to the finest. Bridget did not know for how long they sat discussing the festivities until she looked up and noticed the hall deserted, light cascading through its dusty interior.

"I think that should be all, Peter. I leave it to you to have enough help to gather, prepare and serve, is that clear?"

"Of course, milady! This will be an Easter that none shall soon forget!"

Peter walks like a dancing maid, I swear. Now what? I want to ride. I have to get out of here and think.

She motioned to Mathilde and told her to see that Alexander was readied and then sat back in the heavy chair as she lifted her booted feet to the table.

Princess…prince…princess…prince. This is impossible! I cannot get comfortable with the thought, let alone the actuality, of a man in my life. My life! She struck her heel against the table. Sighing, she straightened herself and walked aimlessly toward the stables where she found a groom holding Alexander's reins. She clutched the great horse's mane and swung one leg powerfully over his back. Looking around she saw that no one took any particular interest—good, just as she wanted it.

The sun was full up now and she unconsciously raised her face to soak in its warmth, leaving the castle at an easy canter. The hypnotic rhythm of the ride allowed her thoughts to drift about, haphazardly completing connections that were at once discarded to make room for new ones. The pores of her spirit soaked in the bursting smells and sounds of the new summer; bees, birds and blossoms thickened the air. Unmindful of where she was going, she let Alexander choose—it was enough just to be out.

She turned around suddenly and saw that she was not being followed by anyone at any distance and this was more disturbing than pleasing.

I am the Princess Bridget, daughter of Gwaldner…and on my own.

Letting the newness of her independence seep into her, she gave a sudden start!

Celestine! Celestine, my sister! She can help me! She is a married woman with a wealthy husband and no children. How does she do it? What tricks does she use? What is it like to be with a man?

She let the thoughts tumble about for a few moments, angry with herself for not having considered earlier what a boon Celestine could be.

It is a full day's ride to Celestine and she might not even be there once I arrived. Better to see her on Easter where we can sit and talk in private.

She felt herself flush at the possible direction the conversation would inevitably lead.

I am Princess Bridget…I am Princess Bridget…with God as my witness, I will do this.

Allowing Alexander to ramble where he wished, they reached a noisy stream, swollen by the new rains. Bridget dismounted and sat beneath the tendrils of a willow as the horse drank. Closing her eyes, she escaped the maelstrom of events and emotions vying for her attention—she only wanted to sit and sleep, the energy she felt earlier having vanished and in its place a grim resignation began entrenching itself as if preparing for a long siege.

Why bother with the abbess? It is unseemly to go on sniveling and with no hope of deliverance…I am the Princess Bridget and I have given my father allegiance…what will be, will be.

She fell into the thinnest veil of sleep and found the Hooded Man waiting.

* * *

A day's ride away Celestine was in an uncontrolled rage within her room. Anything that could be broken or splintered lay on the floor around her as she searched for something else to destroy. The blood hammered through her ears as she began shredding the blankets of her bed with malevolent strength; guttural sounds from deep within sprung from her clenched teeth. Still frenzied, she began pulling the heavy drawers from the oaken dresser, the heavy thudding as they hit the floor vibrated up her legs and made her smile tightly.

Marriage! Marriage! How could Bridget do this?! Whatever is my father thinking! Is he mad? All he requires is right here, right here! No! No! No! This cannot be! What of my child? What of my plans! Damn him! Damn my father and damn my husband!

She was heading for the shutters when she glimpsed herself in the toilet's mirror and charged towards it. Looking, she saw herself flushed and bedraggled, the blond strands of hair stuck to her sweaty face. She breathed deeply, willing calmness, letting the fury seep from her bowels until she no longer felt the blood pounding her temples. Her arms and legs trembled at the rampage's end and she suddenly felt weak and faint but continued looking at her reflection.

Is this what it has come to, then? All these weeks of humiliating servitude for nothing? The planning, the discreetly placed herbs in his food, keeping him away from the bottle—all for nothing? All this just so Bridget can get the jewel of the kingdom, that cow? There is no justice here, no justice at all!

Sensing her ire building again, she paused and closed her eyes, gulping lungs of air in deep breaths.

Wait and think…think! What has happened yet? Nothing. The other nobles only sense something is afoot, they have not been told officially yet…that we have eyes and ears throughout the kingdom has helped immeasurably and was worth every copper.

Celestine turned and surveyed the havoc that had once been her bedroom.

Did I do that? Well, Wyngeth will have a time of it, won't she? What to do…what to do. Who is this Vortimer? What manner of man? Certainly stronger than Theodorus; no doubt Bridget, with those hips, would become pregnant just kissing him. Damn my father! If he had given us the land, we could have defended it, mercenaries are cheap enough.

"Wyngeth! Wyngeth!"

The old woman entered the room and carefully averted her eyes away from the carnage that had been done.

"Wyngeth, clean this room and do not disturb me!"

"As you wish." She said as she closed the door to Celestine's private room where she sat looking into the mirror, thinking.

Would it be possible to kill Bridget before she had a child? Or if not do it myself, could I arrange to have it done?

She didn't think she could actually slip the blade between her sister's ribs but perhaps there were other, less obvious ways. Poison? Calgwyn knew every root and leaf that grew, perhaps there could be something there...Or maybe Bridget could be attacked by thieves and killed? But that would entail accomplices and no amount of money could promise silence and then would begin an unending series of murders, each becoming more complicated, more dangerous. She gazed at her reflection, marveling at how much her appearance had changed since the rampage ended. Grinning, she heard Wyngeth's laboring behind the door.

The Stones have spoken to me—I will bear a son—of that there is no doubt, but this new development has unraveled what had been my perfectly knit plan. Damn! How could I have neglected Bridget, my one loose thread?

She felt the beginning of what would become a knee-bending headache.

Let's see, nothing has happened...yet. Bridget is still unwed and that dismal possibility only means that she and Vortimer will possess the richest land, they will not necessarily be the wealthiest for the land is valueless until it produces. So that means that they will be, for the most part, penniless...and my husband is still the most wealthy!

She began rubbing her temples, wincing.

I must call Calgwyn for some of her tea...of course! If Calgwyn can produce an elixir to help plant a baby, then she must have knowledge of how to prevent them! There must be a way, there must be a way to keep Bridget fallow!

"Wyngeth!"

The door opened slowly as the bent form of the old woman appeared.

"Fetch me Calgwyn immediately!"

The door closed again as Celestine tilted her head back, trying to ignore the pulsating pain and concentrate on the promise of Calgwyn's elixirs.

Yes, of course! She must know countless concoctions...but how to get Bridget to take them? Can we place someone in her kitchen? Damn, this pain! It is impossible to think with such agony!

Closing her eyes seemed to help somewhat as she continued massaging her head while keeping it perfectly still. She remained motionless even though she heard the door open and Calgwyn's solicitous voice.

"My head, my swelling brain…you must bring me something…use your magic. I cannot bear this excruciating torment!"

Seeing the prostrate form of her mistress alarmed the young woman who was so accustomed to seeing Celestine in control of herself and those about her. Her hands trembling, she touched Celestine's forehead with all the gentleness at her command.

"Does this happen often, milady?"

"Please, Calgwyn, please not now—just make it go away," she pleaded.

"I must know."

Celestine laughed weakly. "Only one time before, when I found out how dismal my marriage would be."

"Then I will get something for you straight—it is unpleasant tasting, however."

Celsestine waved her hand in weak dismissal and Calgwyn bowed hurriedly out, her eyes widening as she noticed the carnage that Wyngeth was attempting to repair. She fairly flew down the hall and stairs into the kitchen where a special section had been set aside for her personal use. Her face no longer showed the anxiety she had felt initially for she was at home here among her various herbs and remedies. Confident, her eyes darted among the baskets and jars with their dried leaves and roots.

Willow, yes, willow and…

She paused…was it worth using helmetflower? She mentally began judging the risks and benefits—too much meant death, too little meant nothing but palpitations. With a firm certainty she began boiling the willow bark as she fumbled among the jars for the helmetflower.

They think this is all so easy—magic! If only they knew! It is not just the plant that is important but which part as well. And each new season the potency changes somehow, maybe it is the weather? Or where or when it is harvested? There is so much too know! What may be harmless this year may kill the next.

Finding the lethal plant at last, she began to grind it gingerly, careful to keep it away from her skin, remembering how her mother had warned her. She daintily tapped the dry powder into the goblet and then poured in the steaming willow tea. Mixing and blowing to cool it, she returned to Celestine's apartment.

Celestine's condition had deteriorated even further, low moans with muted sobs rattled Calgwyn's normal confidence. Wordlessly, she reached around and placed the warm goblet on Celestine's lips.

She must be ill, poor dear! Doesn't even notice how foul tasting this brew is!

Sitting on a stool by her side, Calgwyn reached for Ceslestine's hand and held it daintily, carefully placing her index finger over the inside of milady's wrist, mindful of the pulse beating there...too much of the helmet flower would cause an erratic rhythm that would eventually quicken and then...stop. She gave her more of the astringent brew.

"This will help, milady. I know it will."

Celestine let out a pained sigh. "It must help, I have to much to do and too little time, Calgwyn. Give me more."

Still fearful of the possible consequences, Calgwyn hesitated. "This works best only if taken over a period of time, milady—slowly. Too much can...overwhelm and place you into a stupor, just sip it slowly."

Allowing herself to be guided was unfamiliar for Celestine who did not much relish passivity, of not being in control—but what could she do? Sipping a few drops, she laid her head back while her eyes remained closed.

"There is one thing else you must do, Calgwyn." She whispered weakly, her brow furrowed. Leaning her ear towards milady's lips, Calgwyn waited.

"By whatever means necessary, how may a pregnancy be averted? What potions do you possess, dear Calgwyn? Think on it, it will be important...but now I just want to rest until this agony subsides."

Standing, the young woman looked down at her mistress, perplexed. Hadn't she been brought to the manor for just the exact opposite reason? Maybe the pain had addled her brain in some way? Calgwyn was never able to maintain any detachment when she treated the sick, be they animal or human, she looked down at Celestine with genuine pity. Wanting to do more, she fetched a small cloth, wetted it in a basin and applied it to Celestine's forehead.

Milady can't be serious about this, can she? We have worked so hard (she grinned at her little joke) *to get her husband to where he can now at least plow the field! Next we have to get Theodorus to sow the seed properly—wasn't that the plan? Well, so long as I am in her house and under her good graces, milady's desires are my desires...but for now there is nothing to do but wait until this pain leaves her.*

Sitting beside her once more, Calgwyn deftly felt for Celestine's pulse, found it steady and gave her another sip of the tepid brew.

Odd people, these nobles. Can't do what comes natural and when you finally get them to where they asked to be taken, they want to go back!

* * *

If someone had happened upon Bridget as she laid sleeping against the tree, they would first be struck by her hair—thick and wavy, it cascaded down her shoulders in rich, shiny chestnut. That she was long of limb did not take away from her appearance—rather, it made her more unique, challenging. Her shoulders were large for a woman but not out of proportion to the rest of her. The face, edged by her hair, was somewhat oval in shape with finely defined eye brows. Her nose was decidedly feminine, straight, narrow and gently rounded. One could watch her eyes as they twitched beneath the lids, her forehead wrinkling and her lips tugging sharply. At rest, her mouth was straight, somewhat wide but entirely in character with the whole of her face. Her skin was clear, smooth and tinted by the air and sun. The head was supported by a neck that was short and thin that at first glance would appear too flimsy to support it, until the capable muscles and tendons corded as she turned her head slightly. Her breasts, moving with each breath beneath the tunic were ample and firm.

The sleeping figure of Bridget was not a restful one, for even in sleep there was little rest. The cowled-thing was there, sharper and more menacing than prior appearances.

What is he doing? Why is he here? I feel as though I can't move but I must...odd, I want to move towards him to see...see what? He's holding them up for me. Is he showing them or is he threatening? I see everything and I see nothing! Woods and trees and there is a horse somewhere, somewhere. And I still can't see his face—there is no sun to mask it in shadow and yet, and yet it remains so. Oh, so cold...so very cold—he's reaching his hands towards me to...

Bridget's body flinched itself awake and for a moment the princess did not move or breathe—waiting to make sure that it was safe to do so. Finally moving, she took in a shuddering lungsful of air and shook her body to full alertness.

Why do I have these dreams, these terrible dreams? A gift from God or a torment from the devil? How far the sun has traveled! Where is Alexander?

Spying the horse some twenty yards downstream, Bridget walked towards the great beast, threw her arms around his powerful neck and hugged him firmly. The Hooded Man had always frightened, terrified her, yet today's dream was even more disturbing. Not only were the images clearer but now she seemed enthralled and captivated by the figure. She shook at the recollection, made the Sign of the Cross and dropped to her knees to drink from the stream. Cupping her hands, she doused her face, trying to wash away the lingering memory of the phantom.

Leaning against the great beast, Bridget idly brushed his coarse mane through her fingers. "Life is never what we expect it to be, Alexander. Remember that! You might have been a mount for some great nobleman, or perhaps you might be pulling some plow, who knows, who knows?" The horse, sensitive to the touch and voice of Bridget, lowered his head and stared at her with bulbous, brown eyes. She continued her gentle pampering, sighing wistfully into the shade, trying not to think and failing.

Easter is almost upon us, my intended husband will arrive shortly thereafter. Is there some significance in the timing? Or is it all just happenstance like, like the rains? What will he be like, this Vortimer? My father tells me all and yet he tells me nothing! I know nothing! I am so ill-equipped for this.

She felt her belly rumbling. Should she go to the abbey as planned or go back to the castle where so much remained undone? *As God as my witness, I love her dearly but what does she know about living, about Life?* Deciding that she would do neither in a hurry, Bridget grasped the reins and began walking back to the castle as Alexander followed, puzzled but compliant. *Ha! What would she do with a man in her bed?* Here she sniggered at the thought of the frail abbess with some virile, loud, big-bellied man grappling to mount her. She made the Sign of the Cross hurriedly, ashamed at thinking such a thing.

Look at me! Last week I would never have entertained such an idea but oh how things have changed. She smiled slightly as the thought lingered a bit longer, playing around in her brain. *But what if it's me? What will I be like? No, more importantly, what will **he** be like? Will he smell? Will he be as coarse and vulgar as the rest of them? What will he think of me? What does it actually feel like?*

Living as they did, the actual practice of the act was no mystery to anyone. The proximity of the shameless animals allowed one and all to observe the precise mechanisms of copulation. *So why is it I am afraid? Why? Because I have never done it before! Bridget, the big virgin bride! Is that what they will call me, Bridget the Big?* She shuddered at the thought of such a terrible name and yearned not for the first time that she shared her sister's charms.

Celestine, Celestine my hope, Celestine my dear sister! She is the only one I can speak with— the only one who can help me through all this. She would not be so cruel as she was when we were children, would she? No, certainly not.

Her pace quickened at the prospect of Celestine's aid. Too, she learned a new truth, that things over which she had no control were best placed on the back shelf until time and chance allowed some action. Her despair changed to confidence as she mounted. Her marriage may not have been in her control but the preparation for the Easter feast was.

The logistics in preparing for so important a feast was something that Bridget relished. With Peter beside her, the two of them spent the next few days deciding how many and what kinds of animals would be slaughtered, how prepared and how presented. Bridget thought the great tables and benches should be placed one way and Peter preferred another. Showing the princess how his idea would ease the service and the movement of guests, Peter prevailed. Bridget threw herself into her work, making life difficult for the servants who swept and scrubbed till their fingers bled. Of particular concern were the rats, lazy, brazen and well fed.

Bringing in cats and terriers she began the assault—the dogs by day and the cats by night. In addition, she had men on tall ladders remove the nesting birds from the high rafters and scrape the thick droppings from the beams.

"I don't want any bird shitting on the food or the guests, understood?"

Air no longer existed in the Great Hall, in its place was a nose-clogging dust that made everything, including patience, gritty—but Bridget would not be swayed from what she felt was a mission. *The feast of Easter will be celebrated here...I will be married here! There is no reason it has to smell and look like a barn.*

One morning, while Bridget badgered the steward, Mathilde and Gwenthe were straightening her room. "What do you think?" asked Mathilde.

Sighing from across the room, Gwenthe shrugged and said flatly, "I knows what I think. What do you think?"

"I think milady is doing her best not to think about what's important, mistress."

"And what would that be, girl?"

"Why getting married, of course! Here she is, not caring a whit about anything except this Easter feast. She goes to bed each night, exhausted and sleeping like the dead. It isn't right...I love her dearly but this ain' right."

"I think," huffed Gwenthe, "I think this is the first time you and me are of the same mind. Milady is scared, Mathilde—dreadfully afraid—I feel it, don't you? She got no other way to treat it, though." The two women let their statements stew and blend for a while as they kept up their pretense of cleaning.

"What will happen to us after she marries, Gwenthe?"

"Child, we will love her the more and do our best to help her."

"We'll stay in her service, then?"

"No fear of that, Mathilde. What I do fear is what is to become of her after the marriage."

"How so?"

"Child, she will be the richest and poorest of women with all that land…and a new wife married to who knows what! Ah, she'll need us, and you and me will be there for her, I swear. You?"

"I swear also, Gwenthe, but I am scared!"

"Of what, child?"

"That's just it, I don't know!"

"Ah, that is precisely how our lady feels, like a child easing into a black cave, not knowing what's in there."

Mathilde nodded, her face grim, her eyes determined, "I swear," she repeated.

"As do I child, as do I—but for now we have things to prepare for…the wedding, like a babe, will come on its own."

The black morning of Easter Sunday found Bridget lying fully awake in her bed. The clamoring of the castle staff and her own excitement over the day had made sleep impossible. Over and over she had reviewed the preparations, hoping that nothing had been left undone. Sighing, she swung her legs from the bed and lit some candles, bathing her room with their waxy glow. Fidgeting, she went to her unshuttered window and looked out into the night, hoping to see anything that might distract her—but nothing. Soon Easter would be past and that would leave her with only one all-consuming affair to consider, her marriage.

Who are you Vortimer? Where are you? What kind of man are you? Are you sleeping now and what do you dream of? Have you had many women, Vortimer, my husband? Will you find me too tall? Well, I do not really care. I never wanted this, you know. I do not want to disappoint you, but I did not choose this mantle, it was slung over me!

She managed to banish the unsettling thoughts for a moment, thinking of nothing, wondering when Gwenthe and Mathilde would come for her. She listened to the distant sounds of tables and benches being pulled around the Great Hall below; the muffled shouts and laughter of the servants filtered into her room. From behind, she heard Gwenthe and Mathilde enter noisily.

"Ah!" cried Mathilde. "My lady is up early and a good thing, too! The sun'll be up shortly and Father Junius is determined to have his service done at the proper time! That fat, little priest is down there now, getting things ready and ordering everyone about as if he were the master! Come, milady! Let's get you freshened up and dressed."

Turning, Bridget watched as Mathilde poured a basin of hot water and Gwenthe huffed around, looking for suitable, holiday clothing.

"Gwenthe, is all in readiness downstairs?"

"Well, milady, I don't know if everything is ready," she said, "but that Peter of yours is making a list of enemies from the staff, I can tell you…a long list!" She laughed. "But why so glum, milady? Everything will be all right."

"Oh, I know that Gwenthe, just thinking is all. Are the guests arrived?"

"They be coming in, milady. Some of your father's people slept here, others in tents outside the castle…oh, it'll be a great day!"

Bridget dutifully washed from the warm basin, allowing the water to remove the fatigue from her eyes. Sitting now, she let Mathilde brush the tangles from her thick hair as her head was tugged this way and that. "La, milady! You have the finest head of hair! It graces you, somehow…but what a torment to maintain!"

From the tall dresser Gwenthe layed out a long white gown, unadorned yet elegant, Bridget did not recognize it. "Where did that come from?" She asked.

"Ah, milady," said Gwenthe, "this has been here for some time but you never had no reason to wear it before today. Here, let's get it on."

Bridget stood and allowed herself to be fit into it. Mathilde and Gwenthe looked at their mistress with wide eyes as the princess stood before them. The gown, tight around the torso with snug sleeves draped her gracefully.

"Well," demanded Bridget, "what is it? What is the matter with this thing?"

"Why, nothing, milady," said Gwenthe. "You look…regal."

"Yes!" cried Mathilde. "The exact word! Milady doesn't look like herself at all!"

Grimacing, Bridget spun around, letting the gown fill out. Gwenthe went to her dresser and pulled out a golden crucifix which she placed around Bridget's neck. The cold metal hung between the curves of her breasts.

"La, many men'll come to worship there, milady!" Mathilde quipped.

"Why? It is only a simple cross."

Mathilde looked over at Gwenthe who gave a reproving look.

"Hush, Mathilde! My lady has many more important things on her mind today. Now you just get her ready to go downstairs."

"Tell me, Gwenthe, is my sister here?"

"I believe I saw the duchess and the duke just entering, milady."

"Well, let us not keep her waiting. Come, finish with this damned gown and let me go!"

The two women frittered and fussed with Bridget's gown—a tug here, a pull there. Their hands simultaneously smoothed and primped until Bridget at last had had enough.

"Come! My guests have arrived and I need to see my dear Celestine."

Striding purposefully from her room with Mathilde and Gwenthe in tow, Bridget made her way down to the great hall. The surging celebrants were divided with the most noteworthy and their ladies towards the front with chairs; lesser folk were clustered towards the rear where they stood. The sky outside was just beginning to lighten when Bridget finally spied Celestine.

"Celestine! Dearest sister!" She cried as she ran unceremoniously up to her and hugged her close. "It is so good to see you! Oh, I have so much to tell you."

Celestine smiled warmly and held her Bridget to her breast, kissing her warmly on both cheeks. "My! But you have grown so, little one! I feel the fool for not seeing you more often, dearest Bridget! Ah, but you are no longer 'little one', are you? Look at you! A large, beautiful woman! And that dress does so accentuate you, my dear." She continued planting kisses on Bridget's cheeks, hugging her close and laughing excitedly.

"Celestine," Bridget at last had the opportunity to whisper in her ear, "I must speak with you later…in private."

"Why, of course, dear. Theodorus and I shall be here all day, at least. I am told that our father has a great deal to discuss with the lords."

"Good. Let's sit in the front as is our right."

Lord! She has filled out so! She is all woman, certainly—but still so ungainly. Now comes the most difficult part.

She allowed Bridget to grasp her hand and together with Theodorus went to the front table where they sat. Bridget leaned over to face Celestine's husband. "My lord duke forgive me my insolence, I pray. It is just that I have not seen my sister for so long…"

"It is quite all right, sister-in-law. My wife has been anxious to see you as well."

Sitting back clasping hands with Celestine, Bridget became more aware of the noisy throng behind her. The muted clamor was punctuated with sparks of laughter and robust backslapping as men who had not seen each other over the long winter, met once again. Bridget was certain that some, if not most, were just this side of being drunk. Turning around, her eyes darted over the general crowd. She nodded to those familiar faces and then noticed a peculiar thing—when she glanced at someone directly, they quickly averted their eyes, a look of displeasure in their expression.

Whatever is that about? Here I have spent so much effort for this feast and they look at me as if I were a beggar!

Bridget unconsciously stiffened and sat taller as she faced forward, suddenly aware that everyone was staring at her. Indeed, the noise had dropped markedly and now all she heard was an occasional cough or shuffling. Suddenly, the air in the hall had become thick and Bridget felt the hairs on her neck become rigid with the tension.

"Stand! Stand for King Gwaldner!" Announced Pardorous as he walked briskly onto the raised platform in front of them. At once the crowd hushed and everyone, including Bridget stood reverentially as her father strode forward. His rough shoulders were covered with a heavy cloak of crimson and his golden crown, worn only for ceremony, sat firmly on his head.

"My friends," he boomed, "we are gathered here today to celebrate rebirth and renewal! It is a time for new beginnings as we struggle here together, our foes around us…but not today!" This last was met with a general roar of approval as the crowd allowed itself to be enveloped by the robust man before them.

"Today, my lords, is not about you or me, but about Jesus. Jesus who did his duty and triumphed—just as we shall triumph!" He leapt from the platform, sending up a small cloud of dust and began walking among the crowd, slapping the backs and shoulders of his many nobles and kissing their women respectfully.

Not once did he mention Easter! Isn't that what this day is supposed to be about? He does move strongly, no doubting his vitality!

He returned to the front of the hall after greeting the majority of his vassals and kissed Celestine and Bridget warmly. "It has been a long time since I have seen you Celestine…beautiful as ever! Your husband and I must make sure that you see more of us here."

"Of course, father, my lord."

"Now enough of that 'my lord'! I am your father and this is your sister."

"I understand, father. You needn't say any more. Bridget and I are sisters, now, perhaps we can become friends!" She strengthened her grip on Bridget's hand.

Bridget felt a warmth flow from her sister and kissed her quickly on the cheek, moved by the sweet sentiment. At that moment Father Junius approached the lectern where a small altar had been placed. The crowd grew respectfully quiet for the most part, as the florid man huffed an Easter greeting and made The Sign of The Cross. Bridget bowed her head and followed suit, trying to say the *Pater Noster* in time with the priest whose voice was half that of her father's!

Bridget tried mightily to focus on the priest and on his words but could not. It seemed to her that things were going too fast and that she did not have time to reflect on what was going on around her. There was the seeming coldness from the lords in attendance and Celestine's radiant warmth and promise of friendship when Bridget needed it most. Father Junius was speaking about the angel at the tomb but Bridget was only aware of a sense of impending dread. She turned her head around and saw numerous sets of eyes looking at her disapprovingly. Turning forward, she closed her eyes tight and began her own prayer. "Sweet Jesus, Sweet Jesus…" Over and over, hoping that fervent repetition would erase her feeling of discomfort—it didn't.

A dog began barking from the rear of the assembly, causing some laughter and waking her father whose head was listing towards his right. Father Junius looked up from his book and started speaking quickly, sensing that what little attention he had enjoyed had just been lost. Bridget joined those others who took the consecrated bread and wine but she missed the comfort it had given her in the past…her mouth was dry with mindless anxiety.

Returning to her seat, she closed her eyes and once again began her litany, hoping to find some worthiness there. It was not much longer until the little priest excused the celebrants who were growing noisy with impatience. At once her father stood, turned to the crowd and roared, "Today we feast and celebrate!"

Servants appeared and began lugging the heavy tables and benches into place quickly. Under the direction of Peter, the king's table was set up first and as if by magic goblets of wine along with food appeared. Bridget looked about aimlessly and grabbed the first available goblet and downed it quickly—then grabbed another.

"Celestine I must speak with you, now! In my room!" Cried Bridget.

"Of course," she replied,"but first I must take leave of my lord, my husband." Whispering in Theodorus's ear rapidly, she turned and followed Bridget up the stairs.

Closing the door behind them Bridget burst into tears and hugged Celestine closely.

"Why, little one, what is the matter?" Celestine asked.

"I am to be married, Celestine! Married!" She sobbed.

"And what, my dear, is so wrong with that?"

"I don't want to be married!" She blubbered as Celestine's heart nearly burst from joy.

"Oh, my poor, dear sister!" As she allowed Bridget to complete her crying, rocking her gently, kissing the top of her head.

"Why are you so frightened? What scares the princess who rides like a whirlwind?"

Bridget smiled at this and sat on her bed. "You've heard I can ride?"

"Who has not?"

"Celsestine, you must promise not to breathe a word of this to anyone. Swear?"

"Of course, dear. Now tell your older sister what really troubles you."

"I have never been with a man but more than that, I do not want to have a child."

Celestine looked blankly at Bridget who drank from her goblet, overcome by the amazing good fortune that had been placed in her hand. She felt as though an immense stone had been taken from her shoulders! Bridget's surprising confession now made many of her schemes unnecessary.

Easy, easy now. Tread softly and let Bridget lead the way.

Finished with the wine, Bridget sighed. "I just don't know who to turn to for help, Celestine? Will you help me?"

"Of course!"

Of course!

"First, who is this man? There have been rumors."

Better to play ignorant.

"His name is Vortimer, out of the south. Father said he wants me to marry him so that Vortimer can deal with the Vikings while he strengthens his own position."

No secrets there.

"Celestine, you must help me! I must not have a baby or get pregnant! Can you help me?"

"There, there, little one! Of course I can. What else are sisters for if not to help one another? Now here, wipe away those tears, princess. They are unseemly for one of our position! Trust in me, Bridget. You must put yourself in my hands and be honest with me in all matters, no matter how distasteful they may be. Do you understand, my dear?"

"Oh, Celestine! Thank you! Thank you!"

"That you are to be married is something we can do nothing about, not now. You can, however, accept it gracefully and make father happy. Can you do that?"

"Yes," Bridget sniffed.

As Bridget was being comforted, the king was announcing the impending marriage to his most powerful nobles who sat at his table. "This day, I declare that Bridget, my daughter, shall wed Prince Vortimer, formerly of Mercia! I know that these rumors have been present and I wish to bring them to an end here and now!"

The treacherous thoughts that darted through the minds of the nobles were not given voice, not yet. Being a guest at the table of the king precluded active dissent.

"Congratulations my lord, on a wise union," said Glamorgan who stood and offered his cup in toast. "What shall be her dowry?"

"The land," said the king, "north of the Wythe."

Glamorgan's face turned scarlet. "I see. Well, here's to health, long life and many children!" The other nobles banged the table with their hands in affirmation. All that land, all that power in the hands of a stranger would require more careful consideration at another, cooler time.

Just as Glamorgan sat, Bridget and Celestine joined the table to robust shouts of happiness and good luck. Celestine sat by her husband and Bridget stood to receive the cries of congratulations, her face blushing.

"I am the Princess Bridget." She declared firmly. "Like you all, I do my duty. I pray for your blessings for our success."

Once more hands thumped the table soundly in appreciation of the young woman who stood before them. Before taking her seat, Bridget put her mouth to Celestine's ear, "You will stay to help me?"

"Of course, dear. There is no place else I would rather be than by your side," Celestine cooed. "Now go sit, eat and enjoy. All will be well, I promise you."

CHAPTER SEVEN

The celebration had gone precisely as Bridget had feared with many of the guests sleeping drunkenly in straw-strewn corners. As it was, the princess sat at the table with her father and sister and accepted the cool congratulations of the lords and their ladies with a hug from the former and a kiss from the latter.

"Milady." Said Lord Glamorgan as he came up from behind.

"Uncle!" Cried Bridget as she stood and faced the large-chested man. "It is so good to see you!"

"Nay, milady. No more 'uncle,' I am sorry to say. What with you getting married and being mistress over the north and all. 'Lord Glamorgan' will satisfy my ears...my heart will hear 'uncle'."

"Oh, no! Has it come to this then? Just know that I have loved you when I was a child and cherish you now that I am an adult."

"I shall always be your servant, milady." He said and hugged her warmly before she sat next to Celestine.

"A good man."

"Yes, a very good man." Bridget confirmed.

The rest of the evening overwhelmed Bridget—the noise, food and wine blended poorly with her anxieties and put her in a state of emotional and numbness. She sat dumb as Celestine pointed out this lord and that lady as she described their individual quirks. "I have heard," said Celestine wickedly, "that Lady Ernesta sleeps with a lot more than her husband."

"No!" Bridget protested. "I see her at services all the time!"

Celestine merely grinned.

The trays of food, buckets of ale and flagons of wine were endless, it seemed. Bridget picked at the mutton and chicken but drank her wine greedily as she sat and observed the goings on around her. Every so often she squeezed Celestine's hand, getting some degree of support from her sister whose beauty and serenity seemed to increase even as the revelers became sloppy.

What I wouldn't give to be as splendid as Celestine! Is that jealousy? I don't think so. How does she remain so aloof from the rest of them? Yet they all come to greet her and kiss her hand, don't they? Is it just her looks or something else? What quality does she possess? Or perhaps it is that she and her husband are wealthy?

Feeling low, Bridget drank morosely as her sister continued to charm and delight the rest of the table with her witticisms and observations. It went on for hours till at last the carousers began showing signs of exhaustion. Seeing that the food and drink had at last gained the advantage, King Gwaldner stood unsteadily—the rest of the fellowship followed suit. "My friends, my boon allies! Today we have celebrated together the start of a new beginning for our kingdom! The marriage of my daughter, Bridget, to Vortimer, will ensure our future successes!" The crowd bellowed its approval at the brave words and it looked as though they were about to start taking drunken oaths of fealty until the king continued. "We are at the start of a new season and much work must be done. I know you have great distances to travel and so I must bid you all a farewell for a short time, but we shall feast again at the wedding, I can assure you of that!" Another great roar followed the king as he kissed Bridget with fatherly fondness. At that, he turned and quit the Great Hall and headed to his quarters, his servants close behind.

"Celestine, I am tired…let's go to my room."

With her sister supporting Bridget, the two women threaded their way through the throng till they at last reached Bridget's room where Gwenthe and Mathilde were waiting. Flinging herself onto the bed, Bridget pulled Celestine with her. "I am so tired and there are so many things going on. Dear Celestine— you will help me, no?"

Even before the laughing Celestine could reply, Bridget had closed her eyes and fallen into a stupor. To the two women she said, "Go, I shall take care of my sister."

Gwenthe and Mathilde were not accustomed to taking orders from any but Bridget, but Celestine's assured voice and commanding manner left no doubt as to who was in charge—they left without a murmur as Celestine stood and began to disrobe as she looked at the prostrate form of Bridget. "Yes, my poppet, I shall take good care of you."

Leaving just one candle lit, Celestine pulled the blankets over them. "I will take very good care of you."

Bridget's first thought, many hours later, was that her brain was swelling and would soon split her skull. Her tongue rolled around her mouth, looking for the mouse that had nested there. Trying not to move her head, she opened an eye that was stabbed by the mid-morning sun.

"Ah! Good morning, sister. How are you feeling? Did you know you snore vilely? Come, it is long past time to get up and we have so much to do."

"You stayed here, Celestine?" Bridget groaned.

"Of course! Isn't that what you wanted, poppet? Come, go to your toilet and freshen yourself. Breakfast awaits and I have sent your women away," Celestine answered.

Bridget felt her ire rise as childhood memories of Celestine's overbearing manner surfaced.

Idiot! That was years ago—she is here for me now, when I need her most!

Bridget pushed slowly to her elbows, her head throbbing. She steadied herself and then rose shakily from the bed to her private room, noticing on the way that Celestine seemed unnaturally radiant. Splashing water on her face, Bridget stretched and ran her tongue along her mouth, deciding that no mouse could ever have built a nest there. She returned to find Celestine sitting quietly at the table that held their food. Even though her stomach was in knots, Bridget managed to down a few mouthfuls that she washed down with large amounts of water.

"Feeling better?"

"Much, Celestine. Thank you," she lied.

"Think nothing of it. It is what I am here for—to give you the education and knowledge I never had. Do you understand? Are you quite up to this?"

"Yes."

"Good, because I understand that your intended will be here within the week. My husband's wealth is not just in gold, but also in knowledge and friends who curry his favor."

"A week!" "A week, a month...what difference would it make? The result would remain the same, no? Now, get yourself dressed and a bit more awake and we can begin, dear one."

Bridget dressed stiffly, her head not yet used to sudden movements. She was conscious that she missed Mathilde's brushing of her hair. Celestine watched coolly, averting her eyes when modesty required.

"My dear," Celestine said earnestly, "we can go outside to have our discussions but I really believe that the privacy here would be so much better."

"As you wish, I am your servant and in your debt."

"Fine. Now tell me, have you known any men?"

"Celestine! Please…"

"Bridget! I only ask this because I need to know! Forget all your golden dreams of love, the reality is bleaker and less forgiving than you could ever imagine. We will discuss matters that will make us both blush but need to be said, do you understand? Do you think I enjoy this?"

"No," Bridget said with remorse in her heart, "I appreciate more than you know, your counsel. In answer to your question, I am a virgin."

The goddess is good.

"There, that wasn't so bad, was it? I was, I was also woefully ignorant."

"Celestine, tell me—what is it like, really? Lying with a man, I mean?" Bridget crimsoned.

"There will be little time for blushing, Bridget. What is it like? Tell me this, you've seen the animals in the house and in the fields—do they look as though they enjoy it?"

Bridget thought for a moment. Had she ever seen any horse or dog actually act as though there was any pleasure in the act? "No."

"Well, it is the same for us, then, Bridget. It is simply an obligation that one must endure."

"But what about all the songs? And all those who carry on about it?"

"Songs! Written by men who would as soon stick their pricks in sheep! And the poetry and the passion? Meant for whores, my dear." Celestine said flatly.

"But Mathilde goes on as if it were the most miraculous thing on earth!"

"Mathilde," said Celestine, "is little more than a slut, my dear. Suitable for a stableboy or some lonesome squire now and then. Don't let her idle chatter cloud the fact that you are a lady and she is a toy."

Bridget took this cold observation objectively. True, she knew what Mathilde did was against God's word, but she was such a kind and free-spirited girl. No mistress had a more devoted servant, of that there was no doubt. Too, Mathilde made her laugh. Sadly, though, Bridget agreed that her sister was right.

"But what do we do then, Celestine?"

"My dear, we do out duty."

"And what precisely is that?"

Celestine took a deep breath and cast her eyes upward before looking at Bridget. "We open our legs, let them enter us and plant their seed."

Determined not to be embarrassed any further, Bridget continued brazenly. "What does it feel like?"

"The first time, as you are a virgin, will be painful, quite painful as he enters. You will bleed and cry and he will not care. You notice how the animals' members are inconsequential until they mate? Same thing with men, Bridget. They become aroused and it becomes longer and very stiff."

Would that my husband's could.

Bridget sat quietly for a moment. Absorbing this new information with calm dignity was proving difficult. "How long does it last? How long does it take?"

"Oh, sometimes in no time at all…moments, really. Other times it seems to go on forever, their pushing and grunting. I have heard that some ladies have fallen asleep during the event!"

"You're joking now!" But one look at Celestine's face told Bridget that she was not.

Sensing that Bridget had been given enough for the moment, Celestine walked over to the window and gazed at the vastness of the tranquil fields and rolling hills. "You know," she said with just the proper amount of wistfulness, "I had forgotten just how lovely it is being here. We did have fun, didn't we?"

"You had fun," replied Bridget who now stood next to her, "but you were cruel to me!" Bridget and Celestine now hugged one another as they stood in the morning sun.

"Celestine, I am scared."

"It will be all right, dear."

"But there is something else, something I have never told any one!"

Celestine held her breath, hoping but not really believing.

"I don't want to have a baby! There, I've said it!" she cried as she buried her face into Celestine's neck and began blubbering. "I am so scared, I am so afraid that I might die and I am afraid of the pain and the blood! Marriage itself doesn't frighten me, I just don't want children."

Do I tell her about the Hooded Man with the blood-covered hands? She would think me mad. No, this is enough for her to know. It feels good to have finally shared this burden with someone else.

Her sister stood mute as she stroked Bridget's hair, letting the spasmodic sobs course through her. Stunned by Bridget's revelation, Celestine was content to remain still and silent as the warp and woof of her plans and possibilities shuttled feverishly in her brain.

I went to the Stones to pray and my prayers have been answered! This alters my plan, but so much for the better! Yes, my dear Bridget…thank you, thank you. It would have been easier if you had gone into the convent, of course, but this, this is almost as good.

Slowly, I must go with care and caution here. My sister is not my enemy, but an ally! Vortimer is the one I shall have to be wary of! How true are Bridget's feelings? Do they run strong and deep enough, I wonder? So far I have her abhorrence of the wedding bed and her outright fear of getting pregnant…how wonderful!

"Sshh, poppet…here, dry your eyes and go clean your face." Celestine said with sisterly concern. When Bridget had at last returned, Celestine sat her down on the bed and held her hands in hers. "Bridget, I stayed here to help you as one sister for another—but I see now that there is a great deal more involved here, but I do not want you to worry, ever. From now on we shall speak as woman to woman, no secrets between us, understood?"

Bridget nodded dumbly, gratitude leaping from her eyes.

"How is your Latin, Bridget?"

"Why, fine, I think. Why?"

Celestine smiled a wickedly small grin. "Si non caste, tamen caute," she whispered.

Bridget closed her eyes, furrowing her brow. "If not chaste, then cautious?"

"Exactly!" Celestine cried, clapping her hands. "There are ways to prevent the seed from being fertilized and methods to keep from becoming big-bellied."

Again, Bridget sighed, had any sister been in such debt to another sister? "I cannot find the words to express my gratitude, Celestine, they fail me. Just know that my love for you is unsurpassed!"

Again they hugged as they sat on the bed.

"The things I am going to instruct you in may sound shocking and distasteful, Bridget, but as the consequences are grave so must the remedies be…extreme. However, I am certain that we will be successful."

Bridget nodded nervously, uncertain as to how 'extreme' the remedies were. She only knew that she would do whatever was asked no matter what was asked. Together they sat, their arms around one another—the comforter and the comforted. Needing time to collect her thoughts and choose what new course to take, Celestine suggested that they would go for a ride. Bridget wanted to saddle Alexander but deferred to Celestine's wanting a carriage. "I only want us to get some fresh air," said Celestine, "not go jumping logs."

As they walked through the hall, Bridget was pleased to notice how much of yesterday's damage had been repaired. Passing through the kitchen, Celestine snatched some cheese and bread. Compared to the emotionally thickened air of her room, the early afternoon air was sweet and exhilarating. Their escort had been given instructions to go no place in particular and to keep a respectable distance from the two. In spite of the clattering wheels on the heavily rutted road the guards were able to hear whooping laughs that bracketed the loud, excited chatter of the sisters.

Celestine is right! She is always right! It is such a pleasure just to sit, even though the ride of carriage is brutal! Not particularly fast, but then, we have no place to go. And she is so funny! I never knew her to have a sense of humor—she was always so mean. A pity we wasted our childhood in petty squabbles.

"There! Have the driver pull over by that elm, Bridget," Celestine cried. "We can eat as we sit under the tree." Directing the escort to stay well out of earshot, the sisters sat with their backs pressed against the coarse bark, delighting in the fragrant breeze that twisted their hair.

"Why is life so complicated, Celestine?" All I wanted to do was to go into the convent and work and pray. Is that such a terrible thing to want?"

"No, poppet, it is not…not for a peasant, at least. But we have our duty to perform. Being noble does not guarantee our life is without sacrifice—even more than the peasants! Think about it, we must fight and struggle and do our best to maintain our kingdom and all they do is work. Do you think they care who is their king? No, they have it easier than us, I do believe."

Bridget nodded, not really thinking but relishing the moment. Sharing childhood indiscretions had released the oppressive tensions of earlier. Here it was enough to get kissed by the sun and caressed by the air. Somehow, someway, this particular moment seemed so harmonious. Her marriage felt as remote and unreal as the pyramids she had once heard about.

"Why did you want to join the abbey?" Celestine asked suddenly, shaking Bridget back to the present.

"Oh, I don't know…what else was there? Father would not have me travel abroad," she replied morosely. "When you have, I suppose "had" is more proper, no intentions of marrying, there is not much else left, is there? Besides, I am a Christian! Serving Christ would be better than becoming an old maid, living in the castle and bored to death! No, the abbey was the only way out."

Celestine mulled her sister's reply, turning the ramifications over and over in her mind till at last she too let out a long sigh. "Feeling better, poppet? Here, have some of this cheese."

Bridget was hungrier than she had realized and ate voraciously, washing the meal down with a generous amount of water from a skin. For her part, Celsestine picked the tiniest morsels and chewed thoughtfully, never allowing a crumb to fall. Satisfied at last, they stood stiffly, held hands and walked to their waiting escorts. Silent for the ride back, Celestine and Bridget stared blankly at the countryside as they were tossed inside the rattling carriage. The sun was midway to setting by the time they entered the castle gates and both felt spent after what had been a most unusual day. Returning to Bridget's room, the two kicked off their boots and tumbled onto the bed, laughing at their foolishness.

"Si non caste, tamen caute," said Celestine suddenly.

"If not chaste, careful." Bridget giggled."I am going to show you this one thing, Bridget, and then I do think we shall have had enough for one day. Now, let us imagine that he has had his way and he has spurted his seed. What do you do?"

"Why, I don't really know." Bridget protested. "What do I do?"

"Come," Celestine grabbed Bridget's hand and took her into the toilet. "You squat down like this," Bridget copied Celestine's lead and squatted with her buttocks barely off the floor, "and sneeze!"

"What! Sneeze as I squat?"

"I told you we had to use extreme measures, Bridget. This is one way to help expel his seed from your vault. Do you understand?"

"Yes, sister," Bridget replied and then sneezed.

"Now, I have sent for my woman who is wise in the use of medicines. She will be here the day after tomorrow and will instruct us in their use. Do not worry, poppet! We shall make certain that his seed and yours never meld. If not chaste…"

"…careful," Bridget said emphatically as she stood. "But won't he think this behavior odd?"

"Who cares? Besides, he will either be huffing and puffing or if you are lucky, asleep. No, my dear, he will just think you are wiping your thighs or some such."

Returning to the bedroom, Celestine had Gwenthe and Mathilde bring her fresh clothes. Bridget sat, observing how her sister commanded so easily—regretting that she lacked Celestine's imposing aura.

True, she does get her way but she doesn't seem to have earned their respect. Is that so important, though? She would never think of speaking 'with' my ladies, she speaks 'to' them, if you can call it that—more like decreeing. Would I be comfortable with that? I don't know—is it worth it? I get accomplished what needs to be done and I believe I am respected without being feared—is it worth it? How are you supposed to get things done properly?

Bridget thought back to the day she thrashed the steward and how things had changed instantly. She was neither feared nor treated condescendingly, she thought. She was treated with the respect due her station and given the courtesy she herself gave.

Yes! That's the difference! Celestine treats the servants as if they were only servants, nothing more. I treat them as people who are servants! I like my way better...I could not maintain her aloofness for very long.

Feeling smugly superior in this one instance, Bridget smiled and began humming a childhood song, nameless and missing long stretches of words, it made her feel good. Celestine finished changing into a fresh tunic that was cinched with a thin leather belt that was worked with fine silver embellishments.

"Celestine, I am tired and am sure that you are, also. I know I have much to learn and am grateful for all that we have done today, really—but can we bring our lessons to a pause? My poor head is reeling!"

"Of course! I understand fully, my dear. Now, no more talk of marriage, men and sex—agreed? What shall we speak of then?" The prolonged pause brought a sudden rush of uncontrolled laughter, bringing tears to their eyes and pain to their sides as they fell back onto the bed, weak from laughter. It was Celestine who first brought herself under control as she wiped her eyes and cheeks. "Let me tell you about the court."

Celestine began her tattles with a wicked grin as Bridget, eyes closed, listened in mute amazement. It was as if Celestine was privy to every scandalous act committed in the kingdom and beyond! Bridget nodded when courtesy required and asked the appropriate questions to show that she was not yet asleep, though weariness tugged her bones and eyes. Celestine, however, was warming to her new found role and would not let Bridget retreat so easily. Didn't Bridget owe her this much, at least? Celestine had spent her money wisely and broadly, discovering the soft underbellies of those powerful enough to matter and now she needed Bridget to acknowledge her craftiness in such affairs. Disgruntled by her sister's seeming lack of interest, she let Bridget finally doze and she prepared for bed. Though it was warm during the day, the night still had a chilly bite and blankets were still needed.

Celestine changed into a light gown and insinuated herself beneath the covers, allowing the fully clothed Bridget to sleep above them. A single candle was enough illumination for their needs.

The gods must laugh at the cruel irony here and I hate them for it! Here I am, wanting an heir yet teaching my sister how not to become pregnant! How unfair it is! I would give my all to be Bridget right now, the fool! She hasn't a clue as to just how lucky she is! The ninny, being afraid of giving birth… now that is an irony! She can't know the significance of her namesake, can she?

Fretting, Celestine turned to look at the sleeping figure next to her, noticing the pained expression on Bridget's face and the fluttering movement beneath her eyelids.

What is the little one dreaming of? Squats and sneezes? Penetration and pumping? Oh, that I could watch those dreams and learn what weaknesses they reveal.

The Hooded Man had returned to Bridget's sleeping world. Not that he had actually left, he had just stayed in the background or somewhere just to the side—just out of vision, he had been glance worthy—but tonight he was in full, dreadful view.

This place, the trees are the same as before, only more distinct. What colors are the leaves? I can't tell. And what is that smell, blood? Does blood smell that strong that it leaves a taste in your mouth? I am walking towards, no, I am walking away from a fallen tree. There he is! Why is he here and what is he doing? Why does he do this to me?

Bridget felt her heart racing even though she slept, as though her spirit had not yet decided which world to favor. The phantom appeared from no direction and all directions at once—he just was. Once more he held up his dripping hands and appeared to examine them, then he looked at Bridget from beneath the cowl and then again back at his hands. It was impossible for Bridget to understand why he was doing this—she wanted to scream at the Hooded Man but was too horrified to think what he might do. Suddenly, she realized her error. He wasn't examining his wet, red hands at all; he was looking past them to Bridget's feet. Feeling an unspeakable terror, Bridget tried to avert her eyes but could not. Looking down, she saw her boots were blood-covered and gleaming wetly.

She willed herself awake with a cry and sat up with the energy of an uncoiling spring. Panting, she looked around the poorly lit room, not really seeing, only assuring herself that there was no danger and no Hooded Man. It took a few moments for Bridget to ascertain that she was safe in her bed, fully clothed with the slack-jawed Celestine lying beside her.

My God! It has never been that powerful before, that vivid! Do I tell Celestine? She is doing so much for me already and this is probably just my fears following me as I sleep. Yet it feels different, more like a warning.

Quietly removing her tunic, Bridget pulled the covers over her and listened to the slow and steady breathing of her sister. Closing her eyes, she reviewed the horrifying premonition as cooly as possible. The phantom had made her look at her soaked boots, hadn't he? Whose blood was on them? Bridget shuddered—hers? And if so, from where? She did not recall a painful wound, yet there was enough blood to smell and soak her boots through. There was something else but she could not quite bring it into focus, something unimportant it seemed had been overpowered by the brutishness of the dream. Maybe she would recall it later.

It was too dark. Getting up, she lit another taper and returned without disturbing Celestine. Bridget closed her eyes and tried to banish all thought; breathing deeply and rhythmically, she intuitively knew that The Man, The Hooded Man had gone off chuckling into the night. Bridget's last thought before she slipped into dreamless sleep was wondering what precisely his dark mission was.

Bridget woke with a start, the sky just beginning to lighten, as Gwenthe and Mathilde entered the room with breakfast for the two women. Wordlessly, she held her finger to her lips at both of them, allowing the still sleeping Celestine to remain undisturbed. Getting up, she changed rapidly as the smell of warm bread, honey and butter filled her nostrils. The recollection of last night's dream did nothing to dampen her spirit or her appetite this morning. She was alive and wound-free, wasn't she? Kissing the two servants, she had them leave, knowing that Celestine and she would discussion that which should never be overheard.

Sitting and eating, Bridget watched out the window, marveling at the sun's slow and steady rise.

"You may live in the castle, sister, but you awaken like a tenant," Celestine finally muttered. "You keep the hours of a peasant, not a princess."

Bridget laughed, "If not chaste, careful! Come, my lay-a bed sister, you have much to teach and I have much to learn," as she yanked Celestine up.

Grudgingly, the elder sister went to her toilet, infinitely regretting that she would not be able to care for her hair today or for the remainder of the week. They ate rapidly, Bridget sucking the sticky honey from her fingertips. When at last they were done and the sun was full up, Celestine began the day's lesson.

She began with Bridget's monthly flow, avowing that no man would ever have intercourse with a woman during that time and Bridget agreed, thinking how repulsive that would be! "He might, however, insist on the Italian way." Celestine said.

"The Italian way?"

"How can I put this delicately...I can't. He may put it up your arse." She said bluntly.

"Sister! What are you saying? Why, that is unnatural and depraved! Even animals don't do that!" Bridget protested.

"True enough, but you cannot get pregnant in that manner, can you? Then again, he may want something else."

Bridget looked hard at her sister, "What else?"

"Again, I cannot put this as I should, but he may want you to use your mouth."

Bridget wanted to yell at her sister to stop joking but one look told Bridget that she was not. "This is beyond endurance, Celestine, utterly unbelievable."

"Again, as distasteful as it may be, you cannot become pregnant...if not chaste..."

"Careful!" Bridget spat.

And so their day flew, with Bridget's sensibilities being shredded and trampled by Celestine's impious and graphic tutelage. "My dear," she said, seeing the dismayed look on Bridget's face, "you don't actually have to do all these things. These are just alternatives, possibilities that may come to pass or may not. The best thing is to get him drunk, though."

"Really?"

"Oh, yes. It increases their passion but diminishes their capabilities, trust me."

They spoke of which positions could influence conception and various suppositories.

"Remember this most of all! You are most fertile after your cycle, so for that time in particular be 'careful'."

"I feel as though I should be writing this down, Celestine."

"Nonsense! When the time comes, all this will come back to you in a rush. Besides, I shall be with you until 'he' arrives and will hammer it repeatedly into your brain so that it will become a part of your nature. Calgwyn, my woman, should be here by tomorrow and she will have more things to share with us. Oh, she is quite good. An expert in the use of roots and wild things, I know."

Yes, Calgwyn's remedies and advice have worked their magic, haven't they? Theodorus is becoming quite the buck, it is only a matter of time, now. Keeping this one without a brat while I become big-bellied with the next successor is all that needs to be done. Perhaps Calgwyn has some potion that can make me more fertile, I shall have to ask her.

The remainder of the day was spent sharing childhood memories and remarking how swiftly time now seemed to pass. Once more they left the castle and went for a ride in the carriage, delighting in the pastoral quietude of serfs performing back-bowing labors. They ate and drank as they rode, fruitlessly trying to keep from dribbling as they sucked on the wineskin. They could do nothing but laugh at their ineptitude; two sisters on holiday.

They returned to the castle just as the sun was beginning to set and in stalls and windows the glow of candles appeared. Entering by the rear, they paraded through the ever-bustling kitchen and up to Bridget's quarters where they found Gwenthe and Mathilde waiting patiently. Celestine dismissed them imperiously and sat down breathlessly, tired from their ride and the long day. Bridget sat cross-legged on the bed, holding the good feelings that coursed through her.

Celestine, I never knew you like this when we were younger. I wish you could have been this kind to me then! No matter—what is done, is gone. I shall cherish you now. Soon we will go to bed—you with a clear heart and me with dread. I can't share this with you, not now. You have given me the gift of your time and knowledge, that is enough.

Tossing off her fears with a feigned nonchalance, Bridget stood and prepared for bed as Celestine sat with her eyes closed. "Come, Celestine. You are as tired as me and the bed beckons."

Celestine roused herself and snuffed all but two candles and changed quietly, the promise of sleep tantalizing her. She could not recall the last time she went to bed without some stratagem regarding her husband, and this was so innocent.

Bridget, I do not have visions and I do not hate you—I only wish that you will have a simple life without troubles or children—but I have a duty to perform, a task to complete and an heir to bear.

Kissing Bridget softly on the cheek, she turned on her left side and whatever plots were brewing were quickly erased with sleep. Bridget remained rigidly alert, uncertain. She prayed silently, putting herself and all she held dear into the hand of God for safe keeping—hoping that He would hold the Hooded Man at bay or remove him completely. She realized that fear had become a double-edged blade: by day, the impending marriage and all its uncertainties—by night, the certainty of her demon. Any interlude from these fears was as welcome as an old friend. Celestine, for her part, helped by allaying her daytime misgivings but at night Bridget was on her own. Except for her sister's regular breaths, Bridget heard nothing. In minuscule increments, Bridget's brow relaxed and her shoulders slumped till sweet oblivion smothered her thoughts.

The Hooded Man did not come. Dreamless and fearless, Bridget slept deeply, waking only once at the sound of horses far below. From habit, she was awake as the castle was beginning to stir.

Sweet Jesus, thank you for freeing me from him. I pray that your angels would return this demon to his hell so he could burn forever in the fires of his own torment...amen.

It was not much longer before Bridget heard Gwenthe and Mathilde enter. Getting up softly, she kissed each of them on the cheek, a gleeful look on her face after so refreshing a sleep. "Be quiet for now and let my sister sleep."

Gwenthe harrumphed that a visitor for Celestine, a woman, had arrived hours earlier and had spent the night in the kitchen keeping warm and trying to sleep. "Feed her, then, Gwenthe and bring her up after my sister and I refresh ourselves. What is her name?" she whispered.

"Calgwyn." Hissed Mathilde.

"Go. I will awaken Celestine. Give us some time and bring up Calgwyn with our food."

Bowing, they left as Bridget shook Celestine's shoulders gently. "What is it, poppet?" She groaned. "What is so important that it cannot wait until daybreak?"

"We have your visitor here—Calgwyn."

Snapping her eyes open, Celestine turned to Bridget. "Good. Let me get ready and let me do all the talking, understood? She is a wise woman but you can trust no one these days, can you?"

"No, I suppose not...but Mathilde and Gwenthe..."

"Enjoy the easy life in the castle, nothing more. Trust no one."

With that, Celestine went to wash the grime from her eyes and not for the first time, longed to have her hair brushed. When she returned she found Bridget dressed and ready to receive. "Remember, Bridget, I shall do the talking and you will do the nodding and agreeing."

"As you wish."

It was not but a few moments more when a dull knock announced Gwenthe with Calgwyn and Mathilde with a tray of food. "This is her, miladies."

Every bone in Calgwyn's body ached. Each fiber of sinew screamed for attention, yet the woman stood placidly and bowed respectfully. For all her years, she had never ridden a horse as fast or as far as she had last night. For her, a horse was used to pull a plow or cart. Or to help rip out a stump. She was not accustomed to actually sitting on a horse as her escorts led her relentlessly. Her hands and forearms were tight from the misery of clutching the reins so fiercely for so long.

Dismissing Gwenthe and Mathilde, Celestine said, "My dear, so good of you to come so quickly."

Dismayed by Calgwyn's haggard appearance, Bridget stood and began to offer her a chair. "Quite right, Bridget. She does look as though the ride has taken a toll."

Glancing at the two princesses, Calgwyn saw two conflicting beauties. She knew Celestine well enough—beautiful as the ice-sheathed branches when the sun made them sparkle so bright it hurt your eyes. The sister had a different kind of beauty, though. She could not describe it because she could only sense it. That was the essential difference, she realized: Celestine was artifice, Bridget was genuine.

Sitting gingerly, she smiled at Bridget warmly, "Thank you, milady."

"So good of you to come."

"Calgwyn," interrupted Celestine, "my sister has a friend, a very close friend, who is being forced into an odious marriage with an impious man. Bridget and I have discussed ways to prevent her from becoming heavy. My question is this: what do you have in your closet that can assure a child never happens?"

Was she telling the truth about a "friend"? Calgwyn doubted it. Still, Celestine had formidable power that had benefited her family. That same power could just as easily make life painful and short—of that she had no doubt. So what if her sister didn't want to become pregnant? She wouldn't be the first.

She directed herself to Celestine. "What kind of man is he, old or young?"

"Young." Chirped Bridget, which brought a reproving glance from her sister.

"Young." Muttered Celestine.

Calgwyn mentally dismissed several possibilities. Short of a blow to the head, there was nothing that could stop a youngish man from having his way. "I do know of some things that may be of some help to your friend. They are drunk after the event, though. I am told it is does not taste too badly, milady. But as in all things, there is no absolute certainty in its effectiveness. If it is God's will..."

"Blast God's will! We are talking about life and death here! How effective is it?" Celestine shot back.

"It is very effective, milady…and there are several varieties. The only problem is that I am unfamiliar with this area and don't know where they grow. I will have to seek, harvest and prepare them from my own land."

"Good," clapped Celestine. "Leave now and begin immediately."

"Celestine," Bridget protested. "Look at her! She's exhausted."

"Life and death for your friend, isn't that the key thing, sister?" Celestine snapped. To Calgwyn, "Grab something from the kitchen. You can eat as you ride."

Dismissed, she stood stiffly, bowed to both and left, knowing she should have expected such treatment from Celestine. True, there was work to be done and quickly, too. A pity to waste such hips, though. She recalled a certain yew that had an odd shape, whose nettles would do nicely if not made too strong. Those, brewed with the roots of the Christmas Rose should be just the thing for Bridget, she thought. Spying some mutton in the kitchen, she grabbed it and a wedge of cheese as she sought out her escort.

"There," said Celsestine, "that wasn't too bad, was it, poppet?"

Bridget shook her head, relieved that the final piece to this monstrous charade was completed. "I feel like such a fool, Celestine," she muttered quietly. "All my life I have been ignorant of the things that really mattered, you understand? I ignored all the possibilities except the one that I fashioned for myself—so here I am, forever in your debt."

"Your safety and happiness are now my cause, Bridget. Just know how much I love you and how much I shall try to keep you from harm's way." They hugged clumsily, neither Bridget nor Celestine accustomed to receiving or giving succor.

"You have learned much, Bridget, and I appreciate how you may be overwhelmed. So let us have a holiday! What would you desire right now?"

"A bath! A long, hot bath! And I want Mathilde to do my hair."

Celestine laughed at her sister's passionate reply. "I think that is a splendid idea and one in which I should like to take part. Do you have two tubs? Good! Then fetch your women and let us indulge ourselves."

It was not too much later that the sisters each sat in opposing tubs—Mathilde brushing Bridget's thick hair as Gwenthe attended to Celestine's. Bridget felt the tension of the past few days melt from her shoulders and back as the warm water coddled her. The strong strokes pulling at her hair removed the tightness from her neck as well. When they had completed attending to the sisters, Gwenthe and Mathilde left, leaving them soak. Bridget sipped wine from a goblet, obtaining warmth from within and without. She hadn't felt this good in weeks!

Celestine felt relaxed as well. Keeping up the appearance of sisterly concern had been taxing but worth it. Now, at last, there was nothing left to do but review what had been taught. "Squat and sneeze?"

"Squat and sneeze," Bridget giggled. Discussing the various ways to prevent implantation, they stopped only when the water became uncomfortably cool.

That afternoon and the next few days were spent in idle urgency as Bridget attempted to ignore the pending arrival of Vortimer.

"He comes the day after tomorrow." Gwenthe told Bridget one morning.

"We are prepared for Lord Vortimer," Celestine snapped. "All that needs to be done now is to find a suitable dress for my sister. Our father should be taking care of everything else—this is his idea, after all."

"La!" said Mathilde. "The king is having Peter prepare for over a hundred—that'd be Vortimer, his men and also his father, Lord Finiseld. Then he had better prepare for the rest of the nobles and some of their men, too."

"Bridget, my darling, I must go to my home and husband. I leave you with your two women who will prepare your clothes and such. Do you understand?

"I understand completely." She replied. "I have kept you for too long. I am confident in all matters, Celestine."

"Good! Then I will ride hard and return in time to see this Vortimer." They hugged one last time and Bridget was, at last, alone. Gwenthe and Mathilde tutted about in a calm frenzy, calling for the seamstress, as Bridget allowed herself to be sized and fitted.

This is it then. My destiny approaches and I stand here trying to choose the appropriate fabric with the correct color! This is a mockery of all that I hold important. Well, he wants a bride and a bride he shall have! I will be the most perfect bride.

She ate alone in her room that night. The food was tasteless and her belly felt weak. No matter how hard she tried to ignore it, Vortimer's impending arrival filled her heart. Restless, she paced and prayed, a multitude of thoughts badgering her. Too, there was the Hooded Man. She knew he was still there, waiting to greet her when she slept—she did not give him the opportunity. Lying in bed, she spent the night in wakeful turmoil.

The morning was frenzied, no one noticed that Bridget had not slept and if they did, ascribed it to virginal nervousness. Her room was strewn with bolts of cotton and swatches of silk. Her ladies, instead of attempting to reverse the tide, were swept up by it all.

"There was a messenger in the kitchen, milady. Grave-faced, he was, and strongly built. He says his lord will be here by noon tomorrow!" said Mathilde.

By noon! Protocol dictates that they should wait outside until met by one of father's men— Pardorus? Then we will sit in the Hall and wait…my entire life seems like it has been one of waiting and I am tired of it! We cannot fit them all, so they will set up tents and the entire castle will be in tumult! Well, let Peter handle it. This damn thing does not fit and I refuse to have anything cover my head! Lord, I am so tired.

It was not until well past supper that the flood of people and fabric at last ebbed. Exhausted from doing nothing but being the focus of everyone's attention, Bridget felt suddenly alone and uncomfortable with the silence. Ill at ease, she quit her room and went to the landing that overlooked the hall. Sitting on the floor, hidden by the shadows, Bridget looked down on the goings on below. Peter was busily directing the staff with threats and insults. She could hear the fowl being slaughtered in the kitchen.

A sudden sadness overcame her. While her childhood had lacked love and laughter, there was something to be said for the comfort that familiarity and affluence provided. Still, she wished she had laughed more as a child—who knew when she would laugh again, if ever? She recognized the heavy steps of Gwenthe coming from behind and barely turned her head to greet her. Gwenthe placed her thick hands on Bridget's shoulders and used them as a prop to sit down heavily.

"What's the matter, child?"

"I don't know. Yes, I do know, really, Gwenthe. I just feel so sad all of a sudden. It seems as though my entire life I have been waiting or preparing for something, but this?"

"What?"

"This marriage! Why should I have to marry?" she cried.

Bridget had never seen anyone's face cloud with anger until now. Clamping her neck tightly, Gwenthe pulled the surprised princess towards her so that she could hiss in her ear. "Dear child, I have loved you since before you was born and for all these years I have stood quiet as you whined when you didn't get your way— but no more! Why do you have to get married? Look down there below—see those servants? That's why you have to marry—for them! Why do you think they work so tirelessly, because they love you? They work here because they don't ever want to have to work out in the fields and die hard! You're not marrying for your father, you're marrying to help preserve what pitiful little your people have."

Shocked by the vehemence of the outburst, Bridget looked at Gwenthe squarely. "And I was thinking how the only friend I had, the only one I could turn to back then, was you." At that Bridget buried her face in Gwenthe's great bosom and began weeping softly. All the uncertainty and fears of the past few weeks surfaced in the tears that soaked the big woman's dress. Gwenthe held Bridget and rocked her gently.

"My dreams, my dreams are all gone, Gwenthe," she sobbed.

"Child," Gwenthe cooed, "perhaps they are yet to begin. Here now, dry your face, that's it. And forgive this old woman for speaking her mind, but know that the bleakest of times can come just before the brightest."

Composed, Bridget asked, "And is this the bleakest of times?"

Gwenthe let out a long sigh and pursed her lips. "Well, as we are sharing our thoughts, I have one more thing to tell you. Something that no one else knows as I have kept it locked in my heart for all these years."

"What, Gwenthe?"

"It is your name, princess."

"And what of my name?" She asked.

Gwenthe looked far away before she began haltingly. "I served your mother for many years and it was she who made me promise to look after you before she died."

This was common knowledge and Bridget nodded, encouraging Gwenthe to continue. "Well, your mother always had a difficult time delivering. There was stillborns before you and your sister." This, too, was a known but quietly kept fact. "Well, your mother knew that she was going to die after you, dear, she did. And she didn't want you to have the same troubles she did and so she…"

"What, Gwenthe, what?"

"You wasn't named after no Saint Bridget. You was named after Brigid, goddess of fertility and birth."

Bridget felt the blood run from her face and knew that if she hadn't already been sitting down she would have collapsed. "No," she whispered.

"Yes, dear. I was never going to tell you, thinking as how you were going to the convent and all—but now…"

Bridget nodded dumbly, feeling as though the last shred of her past had been flicked casually away. "How," she asked quietly, "did I come to be called 'Bridget'?"

"Oh, those priests were furious and baptized you Bridget...but we all called you Brigid up until your mother died."

"Thank you, Gwenthe, for your candor and devotion. You realize how this changes things but doesn't effect anything, don't you?" Bridget stood slowly and helped the large woman up as well. "I am going to my room, now. I am fine, thank you. I just want to be alone for a while."

"Did I do right, milady?"

"You did admirably, Gwenthe. Thank you. Now go to your rooms and prepare my things for tomorrow, for tomorrow begins a new day."

Bridget walked to her room and slowly shut the heavy door behind her, locking out the castle's sounds.

I feel so odd! Why is that? I feel as though a great weight has been lifted off my back. For all these years I believed I was named after a saint only to learn I was named after a goddess of fertility. Me! It's as though everything I did up until this moment has been a sham, meaningless—yet I don't feel betrayed...I feel...good!

Bridget paced aimlessly, straightening a candle here, a chair there.

Is it blasphemous to feel resurrected? I feel reborn! Free! It's as if all the questions I have never known have been answered. Was I consecrated to Brigid? Gwenthe may know. Named after a goddess!

With a calmness that had eluded her for months, Bridget snuffed all but one candle, stripped and went beneath the covers. There was something elementally good about feeling the coarse blanket against her skin. She began to feel giddy—not even Celestine was so-named! And Vortimer? Who cared? Maybe Gwenthe was right—perhaps now her dreams were about to begin. Or perhaps they'd be nightmares where the Hooded Man reigned. As Bridget shed her past intellectually and emotionally, the more at ease she became. Who she was, was no longer. What she was becoming no longer held the terror it did. She slept with the innocence and anticipation of an infant, eager for a new day.

The Hooded Man was there again, but changed. It seemed to Bridget that as repulsed as she was, she followed when he beckoned but the dream was muddied and disjointed and she felt as though the colors changed somehow. Then the apparition was gone and she slept noiselessly once more.

To Peter the steward had fallen the thankless task of preparing not only for the king's nobles but for visiting royalty. The princess was of no help and the king never was. Determined to make it look simple, he drove his workers without mercy. With curses and threats, vast amounts of food were readied and prepared; makeshift barracks were slammed together and extra feed for the horses was obtained. Everything was taken from the unfortunate peasants who happened to live close-by—well, they would get by, somehow.

Gwenthe and Mathilde found their princess sound asleep, apparently oblivious to the clamoring castle and the gravity of the day. "Come, milady!" Gwenthe chided. "Today is not the day to remain in bed! Goodness! You must bathe, Mathilde must do your hair, your gown must be checked, everything must be perfect!"

"Nothing is perfect, Gwenthe. Nothing. Now, prepare my bath and bring some food—I'll not starve waiting for this Vortimer. Mathilde, see to it that the seamstress is finished and you will brush my hair as I bathe."

Scurrying about, the two women did as they were told. Bridget stepped into the steaming tub, letting the heat loosen her tightened muscles. Mathilde could not contain her excitement and went on and on about who was all ready in the castle and who was about to arrive.

"Is my sister here, yet?"

"No, milady. Not yet." Mathilde placed some sweet smelling oil in Bridget's hair and brushed it firmly, making it glisten thickly. "You seem very calm, milady."

"I am Mathilde, very. I am prepared."

Squat and sneeze.

"Pardon my asking, but ain' you a little excited?"

Wine.

"A bit, I suppose."

"Well, I wonder what he looks like."

"Who?"

"Your husband, milady, who else?"

Just lie still. . . fall asleep.

"Mathilde, what he looks like and how he acts is out of our hands. He will be what he will be." Exasperated by Bridget's nonchalance, she tugged viciously at a stubborn knot.

"Take care, Mathilde, please."

"Yes, milady. Sorry."

What's the rush? To wait? Better to lie here in the water and think of nothing.

It was not until her ladies insisted that Bridget finally left the comforting tub and allowed herself to be dressed. She was not accustomed to the tight gown—

pinched at the waist with long clinging sleeves, it made each breath a chore; the tops of her breasts swelled with each inhalation. Fawn-colored, it contrasted nicely with the dark hair that hung about her shoulders. Standing erect as Mathilde secured the same golden crucifix she had worn for Easter, Bridget turned to Gwenthe. "Well?"

"My lady! You look grand!"

Mathilde came around to examine her mistress. "You, you are lovely, milady!"

Knowing they only tried to humor her, Bridget discounted their comments and instead began to fidget. "Come, let's go to the castle wall and keep watch—anything but stay in here."

Passing several servants and guards on her way to the parapet, Bridget was somewhat surprised by their bows but accepted them with a tight smile.

It was a fine, warm day and crowds of farmers, merchants and vendors milled within and without the castle walls. Here and there carts were drawn by oxen or horses no longer able to pull a plow. There was a healthy cursing and hawking of wares. Everything, even the air, seemed alive and vibrant. Looking at the horizon, Bridget stood tall between Gwenthe and Mathilde. "He will come from that direction," she said to no one in particular and squinted as she shaded her eyes from the southern sun.

Why am I here like this? Fool that I am! I just need something to do but I am sure anyone who sees me thinks I must be panting with anticipation. Damn it all!

It was not too much longer when Bridget spied a certain haziness sifting over the trees—dust kicked up by horses, many horses, his horses! A lone rider came tearing down the road that led to the castle gate, a messenger, no doubt, to announce the impending arrival. Soon Bridget and Gwenthe noticed the cloud and clapped their hands excitedly which Bridget thought very childlike.

Closer now, like some thick thundercloud, they came, till at last two riders carrying great red and golden banners could be seen. They proceeded with the deliberate grace and gravity the situation warranted. Behind them Bridget saw two columns of mounted men, over a hundred, and numerous carts bringing up the rear. The general clamor of the mob below increased as the small army came closer. Even Bridget was awed by the sight.

Which one is he? Who among you is Vortimer?

As was customary, the travelers stayed well away from the castle, acknowledging that they were on a peaceful mission and meant no harm. Bridget watched them dismount and studied the disciplined manner in which they began to set up camp. She saw Pardorous leave from the castle accompanied by two escorts with her father's banners slapping the air.

He will see the king and Vortimer and make inquiries as to their needs and the needs of their men. He will bring Vortimer, his father and several of their principal lieutenants to refresh themselves here, as is only befitting their rank. The rest will come later.

True enough, Bridget watched as Pardorous led a group of twenty riders through the castle gate, but they rode too rapidly and being so high up, she was unable to distinguish any features.

Gwenthe placed her meaty arm around Bridget's waist. "I think it is time we go to your room, milady."

"I do believe you are right," she whispered.

Getting to her room, Bridget was overcome with a tiredness so profound that she could barely keep her eyes open. Excusing her women, she went to lie down, but sleep would not come.

He is here! Vortimer, who are you to rip my life away like this! And what do your hands look like? Do you wear a long, heavy cape with a billowing hood, Vortimer? Are you laughing at some joke being made about me? Do you know me? Can you know me?

She must have dozed because the next thing she knew, Gwenthe and Bridget were in her room lighting the candles. "It is time we go down, milady."

"Everyone is here? Celestine is here?"

"Everyone, milady." Said Mathilde as she gave Bridget's hair a few quick strokes and fluffed her gown.

The hall was a tumult of noise as Vortimer's men and her father's had gotten over their initial distrust and were now vying as to who was the strongest, the loudest and drunkest. The newcomers differed only in that few sported beards and those were trimmed. Standing behind a rough, heavy beam, Bridget peered around, hoping to spy Vortimer through the smoky haze. As if reading her mind, Mathilde cried, "There he is, milady. Over there to the right!"

Standing just beneath a bright torch was a tall man, not the tallest Bridget had ever seen and certainly not the tallest man there, but tall enough. What set him apart were his shoulders which looked solid and powerful. His face was set and occasionally he spoke to the man beside him. They laughed together and Bridget saw him look furtively about, a goblet of wine in his hand. His hair was dark and short in the Roman manner and he was beardless. He had no extraordinary facial deformities that Bridget could see—his face was oval and his mouth was firm

147

and straight. She saw his lips make an effort to smile, but they failed. There was an air about him that she noticed quickly, a sense of quiet power and confidence.

He is not a handsome man, but his eyes! So deep and what, sad? No, not sad eyes but something more exquisite. There is a gentle melancholy behind them that mutes his smile, so.

Bridget watched Vortimer intently, saw the easy, unruffled manner in his carriage and person. Again, he looked towards the main banquet table and said something to his companion who shook his head and then looked directly at her! Vortimer's eyes followed and locked onto Bridget's who was caught unawares.

"My God, Glendon! Have you ever seen a more beautiful woman?" Vortimer exclaimed.

"That's the sister, lord. Yours is there, hiding behind that beam to the right of the table." Even in the dust-filled hall, Vortimer was struck by Bridget's green eyes that pierced through the gloom and made him momentarily hold his breath. Powerful and strong, fiery. He watched her brief confusion at being discovered spying and watched as she made her way to the table, next to her father.

"Hips like that can do some damage." Remarked his lieutenant.

"Quiet! You are talking about my future wife." Vortimer laughed.

The king stood and the entire room did the same, all talk ceasing immediately.

"My dear friends, old and new! We are gathered here tonight to forge a new bond! One that will strengthen both our kingdoms!" He boomed. The hands of the multitude thundered the table tops with agreement. "And this bond will be confirmed by the marriage of my daughter, Princess Bridget," he placed his hand on her shoulder, "and Prince Vortimer!" Again, thunderous affirmation accompanied by excited shouts crashed between the walls.

"He's easy on the eyes, milady," Mathilde whispered into Bridget's ear.

"Hush!"

Vortimer was led by Peter towards the end of the table where introductions were made.

The king watched as Vortimer walked with a heavy limp. "What is this?" he hissed to Pardorous who stood next to him.

"Lord, no one ever told me he was lame! I swear!"

"Are there any more surprises? Tell me now!"

"My lord, I swear!"

Bridget had seen the painful way Vortimer walked, as if his right knee and hip were misaligned.

A cripple! I am going to marry a cripple!

A silent moan escaped her lips as she stood tall, no longer looking at Vortimer, but straight ahead. She only looked over at him when he was introduced to Celestine and her husband. He had a quiet, calm voice as he bowed respectfully.

He stood before her now, a good head taller than she and yes, his shoulders and chest were just as large as she first thought. She looked into his eyes and again felt herself becoming lost in their depth. Up close, Vortimer saw the gold flecks swimming in Bridget's eyes. Bridget heard Peter say something but could not quite comprehend it. She bowed as did Vortimer, a faint smile on his face, "My lady."

"I have brought you a gift, milady. A small token of what I hope will become a bright future." Turning towards his man, he took the shawl he was carrying and handed it to Bridget with great care.

It was made of coarse silk the color of grass and was stiffened by fine, gold threads that had intricately been woven into it. Pearls and precious stones were sown into it as well.

"It is beautiful, my lord and I thank you from the bottom of my heart. Did some other lady not want it?"

Acting as if he was unaware of the insult, Vortimer said, "Actually, it did belong to another woman, my mother, who is ill and unable to make the journey. She wants it to bring the happiness she has had, to you."

You fool! Why did you ever say that to him!

"I shall wear it always," she said and placed it over her shoulders.

Vortimer was introduced to the remaining nobles and ladies until at last he was given a big hug by the king who then had him sit next to Bridget. Vortimer, usually confident, was decidedly uncomfortable. He had met greater and wealthier nobles, of course, but he wasn't marrying into their families. And why did she keep looking at his hands? True, she had a beauty that was not easily discerned, but her behavior struck him as very odd.

When at last all the introductions had been made, the king stood as he motioned for Vortimer and Bridget to sit. "Lords, ladies, men! A toast to these two who will be wed within the week!"

The clamoring washed over Bridget who sat speechless.

Within the week!

CHAPTER EIGHT

What does she find so fascinating about my hands? A beautiful woman, big though. Glendon is right, hips like that might make for rough riding, she seems robust enough, nothing dainty about this one—not like some of those others. I wonder if those stories about her are true? She looks able enough to box a man's ears! That must have been a sight! Enough of this!

"Is there something wrong with my hands, milady?"

"Why, no! No! They are perfectly fine hands! I just think that hands can tell a lot about people."

"Really? And what do my hands tell you about me?"

God! What made me say something so foolish? He must think me an ass!

"They are the hands of a strong man," she gripped his right hand firmly, "some small scars here—not the hands of a scholar."

"No, not by any means a scholar! My tutors will be dismayed to learn that their patience was for naught. What else?"

Gwenthe and Mathilde, hiding in the shadows, nudged each other excitedly when they saw Bridget and Vortimer clasping hands. "See," said Mathilde, "she is taken with him already!"

"Hush, now!" said Gwenthe.

Even her grip is firm! From riding so long, perhaps? What kind of wife is she going to make? What kind of mate? I hate this! She does have the loveliest hair! And her smile appears genuine enough... no duplicity in this one. And her eyes! I could lose myself in those green pools—has any other?

His eyes! No, they are not sad eyes, they are the eyes of what? An old soul! There is some melancholy there, some secret sadness. Vortimer, you are not the man I expected. Who are you? What are you about?

"They are strong hands. A broken bone here, I think," as she pressed the large knuckle of his small finger.

"Yes."

My God! How does she do that? And I can tell much from your touch. You are shy, aren't you? I can see how your face has flushed and though you are strong, you may be capable of great gentleness.

These are not the hands of the Hooded Man, too large. And though scarred and calloused, they are cared for—no dirt beneath the nails…something else…his fingers are delicate!

Round about them the Great Hall continued noisily. Under other circumstances the opposing men might have taken the field against one another, but now they had to become uneasy allies. Wary at first, the ale turned their mutual animosity into boastful strutting. Who was the largest? The strongest? Shouts and cries erupted from table to table, men stood up and challenged each other violently, only to be hooted down by the derisive shouts of their companions. Half-eaten chicken bones were thrown from table to table.

"Who can piss as far as Edmuch?"

"His sister!"

Arm wrestling and loud guffaws at the losers' expense filled the air along with meaningless insults and empty boasts. Five musicians seated close to the king played on, determined not to be drowned out by the rabble. Bridget dropped his hand, closed her eyes and began swaying slowly to the rhythms that coursed through her.

What is it about the music? No. No time for thought…

Vortimer watched as Bridget's lips curled up in a faint and distant smile; her upper torso, it seemed, was attuned to a rhythm not easily discerned or felt by the pressing bodies around him or the whirling dancers on the floor—subtle in some way, deeper. Bridget's face transformed minutely—what angles there were, rounded and softened, giving her face an ageless appearance.

Cracking her eyes suddenly open she turned to Vortimer, "Do you dance? No, of course you don't." Before the startled young man could reply, she stood and headed down the long table where she pressed Celestine's shoulder. "We must dance, sister."

Celestine had no time to finish her quips to the attentive ears, so insistent was Bridget's grip.

"What the hell are you doing?" She whispered fiercely into Bridget's ear as they headed toward the other twirling figures on the floor. "You know I do not dance!"

"Ah, dearest sister, I do."

Bridget firmly grasped Celestine's pale hands and began leading her in complex twirls and twists. Back and forth, round and round—Celestine following Bridget who spun to a more primal rhythm. While the others moved with their feet, Bridget danced with her soul—eyes closed—her body undulating, unconscious of those around her.

"Bridget! What has gotten into you?" Celestine barked, hiding her discomfort from their fellow dancers and audience.

"Why, sister? What can you mean?"

"Damn it! I saw you hold his hand!" They spun apart.

"Interesting things, hands" They came together.

"You must cease this stupidity at once!" Celestine, smaller and weaker, grasped Bridget's forearm firmly and led her hurriedly away from the spinning and laughing.

"Bridget," she said when they had retreated to a dark corner, "what is the matter with you?"

"Why, nothing! I just like to dance and he is lame! Did you see him limp?"

Is she drunk? Mad? Both? Oh, I have certainly seen his bad leg, but has she noticed the muscles of his legs, even the gimpy one, beneath his tights? And his shoulders? Too, there is something about his eyes—has she seen into those? No, she is too naive. And the set of his jaw?

"Why did you hold his hand?"

"That was a mistake," Bridget seemed to come out of a reverie, "a mistake."

"For God's sake, You must not encourage him! You must not touch him!"

Bridget wrapped her arms around Celestine clumsily. "Oh, I don't know what came over me, Celestine! I really don't!

"There is much confusion here, poppet! Go back to your seat and be reserved! Remember who you are! Is this the shawl he gave you?"

"Yes, his mother's"

Celestine slid her thumb and index finger over the stiff fabric, marveling at its craftsmanship with a detached expression. "Is that all he brought?"

"Yes! Isn't it a marvel?"

"It is nice. Now, get back to your seat and do not encourage him! Whatever have I taught you!"

"Yes, sister."

At that, Bridget and Celestine parted—Bridget with her eyes down, Celestine with a peeved expression.

Vortimer watched the two sisters intently, noting that although Celestine had the studied grace of a willow's tendril swaying with the wind, Bridget's form was coarser and for some odd reason, more appealing.

Celestine listens to the music and dances—Bridget feels and moves to it.

Surprised by his sudden insight, he watched as they traded words as they left the dance floor, he startled by the malicious look on Celestine's face as her eyes locked onto his.

No! Why would my future sister-in-law hate me?

Caught unawares, he smiled quickly at her as she pulled Bridget to a far, dark corner.

"My lord, he is here."

Vortimer sat back in his chair, so the conversation between him and his lieutenant, Glendon, would not easily be overheard. "Where?"

"You know how he is, lord. He flits like a bug! You only see him out of the corner of your eye and then there he is, standing before you!"

"Well, we knew he would be here, didn't we?"

"Yes, lord."

"Thank you, Glendon." Vortimer said emotionlessly as he sat forward once more.

Varduc! My mysterious and wonderful counselor, how is it that you manage to be just when and where you are most needed? Where are you now, my diminutive friend? In the back, hiding in some shadows? Or are you standing beneath some table?

Vortimer let his breath out in a hiss and laughed silently at his little joke as Bridget returned to her seat.

Varduc, my enigmatic friend, what do you make of all this? How many times have I spoken to you about Life, particularly after some deep scar? Did you know this was to be my fate? I did not. In all honesty I thought that I would end dead on some battlefield... or captured. But who would ransom me? Not my father and certainly not my brothers! Marriage! I never would have guessed it! Here I am, about to become my own master, my Fate in my own hands! And all I have to do, all I have to do is defeat the Vikings and hold onto the richest land in these parts! That's all!

Vortimer let out a small whistle from between his lips, searching the boisterous room for Varduc, knowing it was pointless.

How many battles? How many more? Is this my fate, Varduc? Will you stand by me? You know what I can and cannot do...I lack so much! I am no Caesar, more an Alexander. That Roman was a politician, the Greek was a warrior! What was it he did to the Gordian Knot? Cleave it with his sword, no? Isn't that the only true solution?

Vortimer vaguely noted that the musicians had stopped playing and that Bridget was now quietly sitting beside him, gulping her wine in long drafts. A juggler appeared and began entertaining before the main table, his hands deftly balancing three crystal globes as he sang bawdy songs to his audience. No one was immune to his venomous tongue—Glamorgan's bachelorhood, the drinking of Theodorous, the girth of the priest. He sang his ditties before each victim, much to the delight of those closest, man or woman, who thumped the table heartily. He bypassed Celestine and stood before Vortimer—the crowd quieted.

"There came a man, a warrior from the South," he sang, "and Vortimer was his name. Strong in all his parts...except that he is lame!" Vortimer's eyes narrowed, his lips pursed.

"We wonder if his twisted hip and his twisted knee, will bring to the bridal bed woe and apathy!"

"What did you say, my lord?" Bridget asked Vortimer.

Reluctantly, he replied, "Would he sing as sweet with his throat slit?"

"My lord! This is all in jest and sport, nothing more!"

The juggler moved in front of Bridget. "Sweet Bridget took the steward and nearly beat him dead! What will she do to Vort'mer on their wedding bed? Her robust breasts and healthy hips could certainly take a score...we pray for the soul (and more) of poor ol' Vortimer!"

Vortimer watched with amusement as the crimson rose from the bottom of Bridget's throat to her ears. Even from the side he could see her eyes with their flickering green fire as the golden flecks flared malevolently. She sucked in her cheeks and began twisting her lips, a fury building.

"Tis nothing but good sport, my lady, nothing more." He whispered loudly, relishing her discomfort.

With a gut-wrenching effort she turned to Vortimer, smiled and said, "Yes, my lord, all in jest."

I knew it! I knew someone would say something about my size! Damn, Vortimer and damn this fool! Suddenly, she recalled something her father had said about curbing her anger, hiding her emotions. *It is much more difficult than I thought...but it can be done.*

Both Bridget and Vortimer sat stiffly, carefully avoiding looking at one another, making sure their hands did not touch as Vortimer sipped from his goblet and she gulped from hers—slamming it down when empty.

The musicians began again but this time Bridget had not the ears to hear, she only wished this ordeal, this evening was over. Looking straight ahead, she glimpsed a young man, a gangly youth, toward the back. He was short, little more than a boy, and had the oddest bobbing movements—like a bird, she thought—arms, head, legs, all moving in quick, decisive jerks.

"Is it your custom to bring children with you, Lord?" She asked Vortimer.

Turning and looking at her he replied matter-of-factly, "We do not bring children, lady. My men are quite sufficient."

"Then who is that strange child among the crowd? He is not from here."

Following her eyes he replied, "I see no one…perhaps the wine has clouded your eyes, or the light is insufficient."

Just as she was about to argue about the quality of her vision, the boy stood before the two of them, a shy grin on his face—but he was no boy.

What an odd creature! He stands little taller than the table. Staring hard, she saw something else, he was old, so very old. *His hair is so fine, so wispy, no thicker than a strand from a spider's web and the palest yellow I ever saw. His face had the smooth blush of youth lined with the skinny creases of age but his eyes are such a lively blue and clear as air.*

"Well, young master," the creature piped to Vortimer, "aren't you going to introduce me to this fine woman, this lady, your betrothed? Or are you too sullen for your own good?"

Vortimer stared hard at the little man before standing and smiling. "Princess Bridget, my lady, allow me to present my counselor, Varduc."

The odd man bowed his head quickly, "Young mistress, I must apologize for the ill-mannered man, your intended husband, sitting beside you. You would think him not much more than a clod but I can assure you, he is much more than that," he chirped.

Smiling at the incongruous figure before her and the insults tossed at Vortimer, Bridget reached out and offered her hand to Varduc who obliged with his. Just as their fingertips touched, Bridget felt herself overwhelmed, flooded with feelings and perceptions that made her weak: the smell of freshly baked bread, her mother's hair, new mown hay, roses and salty mist combined with the sounds of spring birds and summer thunder. There was children's laughter, an old song, heavy rain and a crackling fire. Her mouth tasted honey and cold water and strawberries. She felt the warmth of the sun flush upon her and a gentle breeze and a soft caress upon her cheek. There were countless sunsets that cried to be captured and star-filled skies and dawns that broke her heart with their beauty…and more. Bridget's eyes were opened, but she did not see, blinded by the magnificence of the beauty that poured through her—she could taste the sunlight and feel the scent of the bread…and then it was gone.

"It is my honor to meet you, young mistress," said Varduc who quickly pressed his lips to her fingers.

Vortimer watched Bridget closely, smiling inwardly at the bedazzled expression on Bridget who replied incoherently back to his counselor who was already flitting away.

"An interesting man, my counselor."

"Is he really a man?"

Vortimer allowed a small chuckle to escape, "Well, we are pretty sure he is."

At that moment Pardorus appeared and whispered hurriedly to Vortimer who nodded, mumbled his apologies to Bridget, stood and left as Pardorus led him away. For her part, Bridget was glad he was gone, one less distraction in a night that screamed for stability.

Vortimer, my intended husband, is not the demon who haunts my dreams—I know that. As a matter of fact, I don't feel his presence at all, thank God! Or do I thank the goddess?

She reached for her wine goblet, hesitated and then stopped.

Too much, and I need a clearer head and a place to think! The musicians do play well…I feel like dancing again. And that what's his name, Varduc? What happened? I can still feel the shadows of the experience. Oh, to be able to return there, to that feeling! Does it happen each time he touches someone? I would embrace him forever, husband or no!

She sat quietly, feeling the silken shawl on her bare shoulders, watching the boisterous assemblage drink, dance, sing and swear before her.

Is this my betrothal? It is no better than any of the other feasts we have had here…no, we do not always have musicians—and that damned jester! I deserve more than this and am entitled to more respect!

She reached for her goblet and drank deeply.

Vortimer, if it were not for my dowry you wouldn't even be here, damn you! Damn my father!

Vortimer chose that moment to return and sat next to Bridget, perplexed by the sullen expression on her face. "I am afraid that my men and I must leave shortly." He said quickly. She said nothing, ignoring the young man, looking blankly ahead.

Her father stood wobbly, a goblet in his hand, the music stopped and the dancers ceased. The general din quickly became a ragged silence. When it was at last quiet, he toasted the gathering. "My friends, new and old, this evening's merriment has been one of both joy and sadness: the loss of a daughter, the gaining of a son! Well, not quite yet." All laughed.

"I have made it known to Lord Vortimer that he should go to examine his dowry, with my fondest blessing. I have sworn my love to him and he has sworn his allegiance to me." Bridget noticed that the resulting shouts of encouragement were more enthusiastic from Vortimer's men than from her father's.

Bending close to her ear, Vortimer said, "I must go with my men, my lady. The night has been lively and interesting but the sun will rise early and we need to get an early start."

Looking directly into his deep, dark eyes, Bridget said, "Yes, of course! We will need to get an early start!"

"What do you mean, 'we'? You didn't think that you were coming did you?"

"Think it?" She spat. "I know it!"

Standing now and looking perplexed, he replied, "Absolutely not! This is not going to be some dainty jaunt, my lady. With all due respect, it is no place for a woman, particularly the one who will be my wife. It is out of the question."

Bridget stood now, her face the picture of serenity but inside she felt that familiar dark cloud of anger beginning to roil. From across the room, Mathilde and Gwenthe observed the two of them stand and exchange words in a less than amiable fashion. "Oh, no!" said Gwenthe, "look at her face!"

"Just like with steward!" Mathilde squealed.

Vortimer looked squarely at Bridget, sure that his concern for her welfare had banished the silly notion of riding with him and his men from her head. Bridget stood more erect, not much shorter than the arrogant man before her.

Slow! Slow! This cannot happen here, not in front of all these people! I cannot let this wet beast win over me! What did father say, control? I am the Princess Bridget, I am the Princess Bridget!

Sucking in two large lungsful of air, she began calmly. "First, sir, I am the Princess Bridget. The land you want to see is my dowry for you, should we become wife and husband." She placed a strong inflection on 'should' that Vortimer noted without expression. "Second, I have traveled these lands and am familiar with its lay and can be a resource. My father's guides may be good men but I sometimes question their intelligence. Third, should we become wife and husband, my place will be by your side, ruling our land as lord and lady." Again, she inflected 'should'.

What is this all about? I don't need her to slow us. Doesn't she know what we will be doing? This is just not the time or place for a woman to be and she carries on like a petulant child! How can I do the right thing?

"My lady, your reasoning is without a flaw, however this will be a difficult expedition with none of the niceties you or your women are accustomed to."

"Women? What women, sir?"

"Aren't you going to have your ladies accompany you? Who will take care of your essential needs and swear to the company that your honor was not molested?"

Bridget could barely stifle the laugh that wanted to explode. "Lord Vortimer, be aware that I am quite capable of taking care of my essential needs. As to my honor and yours, a chaperone might have its place, were there some carnal temptations, but I can assure you that none exist and after this evening I doubt they will ever become a nuisance."

Vortimer waited for an instant. "As you wish, I too agree with your observations. I am reluctant, but you may come. Just know that you will not become a nuisance or delay our work, agreed?"

"Who are you to let me come?" She stamped her right foot. "I am the Princess Bridget and I come and go as I choose!"

"What did you just do? Did you just stamp your foot? I cannot believe I am seeing and hearing this! You want to come, I acquiesce—but that isn't good enough. What do you want, an invitation? Did you just stamp your left foot?" Vortimer laughed.

"At least I have the strength to stamp both my feet...and dance, too." She retorted.

Vortimer's eyes narrowed and his face hardened as he felt a steel bolt of rancor run through him. "We leave before dawn." He spun sharply and limped rapidly away, his broad shoulders barging anyone not sober enough to notice his cold scowl.

"Fine," Bridget sniffed, "didn't even have the courtesy to say good night." She beckoned Gwenthe and Mathilde who were bubbling with questions that she ignored, stating only that she was going to bed and that two sets of riding clothes should be laid out. Passing by the great kitchen that was still abuzz with activity, she snagged Peter and told him to make sure Alexander was ready for an early ride, very early.

Vortimer snatched his mount from the stable boy who was flustered by the anger apparent in the new lord's manner. The courtyard gate could not open quickly enough for Vortimer who rode as quickly as he dared back to his encampment, small fires in front of rows of tents glowed invitingly. The camp had grown even in the short time they had been in the castle. Stragglers of all kinds had started to follow his small band: artisans, smiths, carpenters, and men and women with no ties, looking for adventure and fortune. Giving his horse to a guard, he strode quickly to his tent and pulled back the flap noisily.

"What are you doing here?" He demanded of Varduc who sat cross-legged on Glendon's cot.

"Why," giggled Varduc, "I am here to serve you, young master. Wasn't this the most extraordinary night! Did you feel the lightening in the air? It fairly crackled. And the food and the wine, superb! Ah, it was a night filled with the wonders and mysteries of promise. And your intended bride! A woman of unsurpassed beauty!"

Vortimer flopped on his own cot and closed his eyes. Long experience had taught him that Varduc would not, could not, be dissuaded when the spirit of speech was in him.

""Beauty"? You are speaking about Bridget, aren't you? Bridget who could fit in my clothes. The same Bridget who drinks too much! The same Bridget..."

"Yes, of course that Bridget," Varduc chuckled. "A most intriguing young woman."

"Intriguing, perhaps, but certainly not beautiful."

Varduc made a derisive noise and talked more loudly. "Young master, you only see with your eyes! Haven't you learned anything over these years? The beauty you see is as real as...mist and lasts about as long, but beauty, true beauty lies within."

"Well, my intended keeps it well-hidden."

"Ah," replied Varduc, "therein lies a problem. The young mistress is not yet fully aware of her strengths, like you she is full of doubts."

Vortimer rolled on his side, his back facing Varduc and farted.

"I tell you this young master, she is the most beautiful woman I have ever seen."

"Have you had many women, Varduc?"

The little man smiled, closed his eyes and laughed. "No, young master, I have never had a woman! Upon reflection I do believe it was they who had me!"

Vortimer could not stop himself from laughing and rolled over again and propped his head on his arm, looking at the enigma before him. "Tell me about her, then. Give me the counsel I need."

"She is, like all women, a great mystery! She is a woman of the earth and sea.

Like any woman she is capable of great love and greater hate. Her strength lies in her frailties and sensitivities...she is much like you, only more so. Within her lies the capabilities of being your greatest treasure or curse. Whichever one she becomes will be up to you, young master," he held his palms up and shrugged, "it will make for an interesting time."

"Do you see the future, Varduc? Or do you just enjoy tormenting me?"

"See the future? Torment you? No, I was not blessed with that sight—but I can see the past and into the souls of some very few and heed me well, treat Bridget like the woman she is and you will have an ally the likes of which you cannot imagine. Treat her poorly and, well...I would weep at your funeral for your stupidity, not for your death—all men die."

Vortimer's attention sparked when he heard 'heed me well'. Two times before he had not listened and both times led to pain. The first time had been when he was a gangly youth; Varduc told him not to go to the river where Glendon had been fishing. A fight followed over some childhood trespass and Vortimer's nose was broken. Several years later Varduc warned him about competing in a 'friendly' tournament. The result of which was his twisted leg that healed badly and almost killed him. Vortimer was determined to listen this time.

"What do I do, Varduc?"

"Do you recall when you were a young boy and had caught that wren in your trap? And when you held it in your clumsy fingers, you could feel its little heart beating and chest puffing? Even then you were aware enough to know that you could crush and kill it if you did not treat it gently, kindly. I believe you should treat the princess the same way."

"And how do I do that, counselor?"

Varduc hopped off the bed and walked over to the young man's cot and looked him in the eye. "I really don't know, young master. I was hoping you could instruct me."

The little man turned quickly and left whistling, leaving Vortimer with an unspoken question on his lips. He lay on his back once more. Like all soldiers he was blessed with the knack of being able to go to sleep quickly, regardless of his surroundings. His last thought before he fell asleep and one which he forgot was this: he recalled the bird vividly but it was years later when he first met Varduc.

As Vortimer was just closing his eyes, Bridget paced about her room.

The insolence of this man! Slow him, my arse! What does he want, a woman or a wife?

As soon as that idea struck her, she paused to take in the enormity of the idea.

She sat disconsolately on the side of her bed and rested her head on her hands, just now beginning to feel the effects of the night's wine.

I don't know what to do, I really don't. Celestine taught me all about the other thing but never how to behave during situations like this, everyday conflicts. What do I do now?

Sighing, she threw herself back on her bed and closed her eyes.

I am going to be the wife of the man with the biggest shoulders and limp I have ever seen! How ironic! "Bridget the Big" and "Vort'mer the Lame!" What a pair! He did have those lovely eyes though, so deep and clear... but he angers so easily! His hands were nice, too. Thank God they did not belong to the hands of the Hooded Man, I would have died! As a matter of fact, I felt a sense of reassurance, not fear, when I held them in mine.

Her lips curled imperceptibly as she recalled holding his hands in hers; she began stroking the stiff fabric of the shawl that lay about her and held it up for closer inspection. She ran the soft silk over her lips, delighted by the whispering feel of it. She felt the coarser strands of gold, wondering how it could have been spun so fine. Looking at it closely, she saw how the pearls and varied gems were woven into it, marveling at the intricacy and detail.

This must have taken an age to weave! Regardless of him, I will wear it always!

Snuggling the shawl, she closed her eyes and tried to forget all that had happened, only hoping that sleep, peaceful and restorative, would come.

Too soon, Bridget found herself being shaken by Mathilde who was urging her to get up and get herself ready.

"Come! I've fetched your clothes and things! Have a bit of something to eat, milady."

"Mathilde, you harridan, it is still dark!" Bridget groaned.

"I don't know about being called a 'hairy thing', milady. I only know you's wanted to be up and ready. You can see Vortimer's camp starting to get going from the ramparts. Gwenthe has not slept a wink, poor dear, worrying about you and getting all your things together."

"Nothing to worry about," Bridget muttered as she stumbled to the toilet where she rinsed the sludge from her mouth. "I fell asleep in my gown."

"That you did," said Mathilde who tossed her a tunic, belt and tights. "Now, put those on double-quick and come down to the kitchen."

Struggling out of her gown, Bridget quickly put on the loose-fitting tunic and cinched it with a simple leather belt. Glancing at the bed, she grabbed the silken scarf and placed it behind her neck and beneath her arms. The tights felt good against her legs as she pulled on her boots and hurried down the stairs to the kitchen. Gwenthe and Mathilde were there, as were a few of the cooks. "We packed some extra food and placed it in sacks on a pack horse for you, milady," Said Gwenthe who huffed and puffed with eyes swollen from lack of sleep."You don't know what to expect on this trip and I must say that I don't care one whit for this foolishness you are planning! An unmarried woman, my princess, out and about with a small army! It isn't proper, it ain't!" Gwenthe scolded.

"Hush, my dear, sweet Gwenthe. I am your princess and I love you and Mathilde so very much! I will be fine, I swear! I only go to see what is mine, that's all. And how much more protected can I be than surrounded by an army! As for 'him', you have no cause to worry, I promise you that!" Bridget declared as she ate a cooked egg and sopped it with a fistful of bread. "No cause to worry, at all."

"Very well, then," said Gwenthe with dark resignation in her voice. "Alexander is ready as is your pack horse. Go, and be careful at all times."

Bridget sniggered a bit when Gwenthe said 'careful'.

"I will always be careful, dear Gwenthe. Here, kiss me and let me go."

All three hugged and kissed in the warm kitchen before Bridget left for the dark stable where she found Alexander saddled and with his ears pointed with curiosity at such an early ride.

"Ah, now don't you worry too, Alexander," chided Bridget, "this will be an adventure."

Along side her were Maldwyn and Astorious, the vassals of Glamorgan, the same men she had one time eluded on her trip to the abbey and who had accompanied them on the trip north. Readying their horses in the dark stable, they nodded in respect as their hands continued tightening the cinches.

"Good morning, gentlemen." Bridget said hurriedly as she mounted deftly. She laughed as she took the lead of the packhorse from the puzzled groom and cried, "Today we ride!"

Bridget wanted to do two things very badly: ride to Vortimer's camp quickly and get it over with and ride slowly to relish the last quiet remnants of the night…she rode slowly, allowing the baggage on the trailing horse to settle and the excitement of what was happening to build.

My life was never like this—it used to be fine! Peter and I ran the castle, I took care of father's affairs, I prayed, saw the abbess regularly—the seasons came and went. When did it change?

She thought this over as they headed through the gate towards the wavering campfires.

With Vortimer! Everything was in its place until this absurd 'marriage'. I was happy and content and... she thought for a few paces...*bored.*

This intrusive, totally foreign idea startled her for a moment.

I was bored! Look at me now! Mistress of a great land, riding towards who knows what in the black of night!

Bridget felt her heart race as the thought of all that had happened and all that could happen, enveloped her. Quickly she recalled those days with Celestine, reviewing hurriedly what she had been taught—if not chaste, careful! Squat and sneeze! She shivered at the thought. Too, there was the Hooded Man.

What part does he play in all this? I only know that I did not feel his presence or that sense of dread with Vortimer or his men. And what of that odd creature, Varduc? And what of my namesake, Brigid?

Her early morning optimism fading quickly, Bridget chucked her heels into Alexander's flanks. *Today we ride.*

Even at this early hour, Bridget was surprised at the enormity of the camp. Soldiers were busily breaking down their tents and packing their horses; shouts and curses of encouragement added to the general confusion. Spying the largest tent, Bridget headed towards it.

"I wouldn't go there, milady, he's in a foul mood." Bridget turned and looked at the barrel of a man that had pulled up beside her.

"Ah, yes. We met last night, you are..."

"Glendon, milady, captain to Vortimer."

"Yes, Glendon! Pardon my for not recalling your name but there were so many people, so much confusion..."

"Don't worry, milady, I understand how things can get confusing—like this," as he waved his thick arm towards the sprawling camp. "But it'll all get done, no worry there." Glancing at Alexander, he smiled appreciatively at the horse and the way Bridget handled him. "Nice looking mount, milady."

"Thank you, Glendon. You have no idea how grateful I am to find a familiar face in all this crowd. When do we depart? I saw two men saddle with me and I believe they are to be our guides; they should be here quick enough."

"No doubt about that, milady. Here, let me take your packhorse. There's no need for you to be worrying about that."

Bridget smiled graciously at the solicitous behavior being given her and with the mildest of protests allowed the reins to be taken.

"Not to fret, milady. We'll look after your things, I promise." Glendon turned his head and let out a volley of curses to anyone and everyone, letting them know he doubted their ancestry and gender. He cantered off, Bridget's pack animal in tow, leaving Bridget just as confused as before.

At least one of them seems civil enough! I am the princess Bridget. I am the princess Bridget! When are we going to start? The eastern sky is getting full light!

As if governed by a common mind, Bridget saw the soldiers mounting their horses, ready and prepared in two columns. There were no more campfires and not one tent was spied.

"Lively now! Lively, you lazy bastards!" Glendon bellowed as he rode up and down their ranks. "Milady, come with me to the fore." Bridget followed obediently.

After all, isn't this where I belong?

She saw Astorious and Maldwyn flanking the tall figure of Vortimer and fell behind them.

"Good morning, my lord Vortimer." She said happily.

Vortimer turned, nodded and muttered something under his breath that sounded like 'good morning, milady'.

Undaunted, Bridget sat taller and struck up a conversation with Glendon who rode beside her.

At least he seems likable enough and if Vortimer chooses to ignore me, so be it! I shall just ignore him!

From Glendon she learned that there would be more than a thousand people within two weeks. Then there would be numerous freemen with their families: millers, joiners, smiths, carpenters, farriers—all young, all eager for adventure and the possibility of fortune.

Fine and wonderful to have such a large population so rapidly but who will feed them? How will the land be apportioned? How will we know who to tax and how much? Where will we get supplies?

The troop headed north with the sky to their right becoming brighter, painting the underbelly of the clouds crimson and purple. They passed several of the small hamlets where grandfathers, fathers and sons were already out working the fields that were dotted with large straw figures. Vortimer remarked loudly that it was pleasing to see that the people still worshiped the goddess.

"The goddess!" Snapped Bridget. "I thought those images were there to frighten the rooks!"

"Nay, milady," said Vortimer who turned to look at her, a small smile on his face, "those effigies are there to bring a blessing to the crops and those that work the fields. Can't much blame them, can you?"

Feeling that she was being baited, Bridget ignored the remark and instead looked at Vortimer's back and the horse he rode.

He is a big man! He seems to sit well enough but I can't say much for his nag. Why doesn't he ride a better horse? Can't we go faster than this?

The foggy morning promised a steamy afternoon. Bridget watched as Vortimer studied a map supplied by the guides. Maldwyn or Astorious would point to one landmark, a large tree or rock outcropping, and show where it was on the chart.

I can't believe how the land has changed since I last rode here! The trees are fully greened and the fields and meadows are so lush! The rains have been good to us.

"Healthy looking land, milady," remarked Glendon as though reading her thoughts.

"Yes, yes it is Glendon. It is going to be hot today and we are barely going fast enough to cool ourselves."

Wordlessly, he handed her a skin of water from which she drank eagerly, letting some of it spill down her throat. "Few things taste as good as water on a hot day," she said as she returned the skin. "Can't we go faster now and go slowly during the full heat of the day?" She asked.

Glendon held his horse back and pulled closer to Bridget. "My lord is a poor rider—always has been. No one will ride faster than Vortimer…wouldn't be right."

"Then he requires a horse as lame as himself?"

Glendon's cordial expression went stonily cold as he straightened up, eyes forward.

Well, it's true isn't it? A soldier has to be a horseman! I wonder what Uncle Glamorgan would think if he saw Vortimer riding like a ninny?

She rode in silence, recognizing the familiar trees and hills, knowing the Wythe would be just beyond those hills ahead. Becoming excited at the thought she nudged Alexander next to Vortimer. "The river is just beyond that rise," she pointed.

"And that would be the Wythe?"

"Yes. During the Spring floods we had a devil of a time trying to cross it but it should be much easier now."

They rode side by side silently. Bridget, filled with anticipation, only just managed to keep Alexander under control. She wanted to gallop, race and let the heaving, galloping hulk of Alexander overwhelm her! Fill her body with speed and graceful force! Was there anything better than sitting atop a mount and racing the wind? Letting the horse do what they did best—charge in mindless abandon to who knew what destiny…no, there was no sensation quite like it. Heaving a not very discreet sigh of regret, Bridget acquiesced to Vortimer's plodding.

The Wythe, no longer swollen with the winter melt and the Spring rains, coddled and murmured gently, beckoning the riders. Vortimer stopped at the edge, his face solemn. He waited for the column of men to line up along the shore. There must have been two hundred of them waiting patiently for their leader who took his horse into the middle of the river, turned and faced them.

"Men," he cried, "this is what we have come for! On the other bank is what we will bleed, fight and perhaps die for! Are you with me?"

Two hundred voices shouted their approval, four hundred arms were raised in triumph. The young leader stayed in the stream and rode up and down, looking each man in the eye and nodding, getting individual as well as group confirmation.

"This is what he does best, milady," Glendon said to Bridget, "getting the men spirited!"

Yes, he does have something in his manner, doesn't he? He doesn't bellow or have spit fl, yet I do believe he was heard by all the assembly. And his voice is soft, almost as if he were in an intimate conversation.

"Yes, I can see that," she whispered to his lieutenant. "He does have a presence, doesn't he?"

Completing his inspection, Vortimer led the way as they crossed the Wythe and scrambled up the steep bank. Coming upon the old encampment that Bridget had used with her father, they decided to spend the night. Unlike the last time, these men slept in smaller tents, the largest holding only two men. Bridget looked for Glendon who came up with her pack animal in tow.

"Don't fret, milady! We'll have you set up straight away!" Looking about, his eyes narrowed, he discerned a site suitable for the intended wife of his lord. "Ah, there!" He cried. It was not far from where Bridget had originally spent the night with her two ladies. Bellowing, Glendon stopped two young men from pitching their tents and had them begin work on Bridget's.

For someone who promised not to make a nuisance of herself, I am being quite the pest—intruding on the work of these two soldiers.

Bridget looked about absently, not wanting to watch the men working for her benefit and comfort. She saw the picket line being arranged, fires were being started and some of the horses were already tethered to one of several rope hitches. She did not see Vortimer.

"All done, milady," said one of the men who was already clambering back to finish his own work.

Bridget dismounted and stretched gratefully. The next step of business would be Alexander. Running her hands along the thick neck, she kissed him playfully and began to remove the saddle, blankets and tack with practiced skill. She led him over to the closest of the hitches and fastened him there, allowing enough slack so that he could eat the hay and oats already lying on the ground. One of the soldiers gave Alexander an approving glance and smiled sheepishly at Bridget who smiled back.

At least they recognize a good horse, a fine horse!

Flipping back the tent opening, Bridget despaired at the sparseness: a narrow low cot with one thin blanket, candle and holder, plate, cup and a small bowl. She sat on the pallet, her head touching the side of the tent. Bridget had a sudden overwhelming desire for the comforts of the tent she had shared with her ladies!

I never knew they could travel so, so...miserably! I am determined to see this venture through, regardless of the inconveniences! I will sleep in mud if I have to!

Her face set, Bridget kicked off her boots and stretched out; she at once appreciated what hardships these men, her men, had to endure.

What a strange and marvelous day it has been! All these soldiers, a small army, and *me the only woman! Coming here to inspect my dowry, my land! Odd, I feel proud of this land though I know nothing of it, really. It is as though the land and I reflect each other. Will we meet the approval of Vortimer? What am I thinking? I do not require his approval at all!*

"Milady?" She heard Glendon outside her tent.

To invite him in would invite unwarranted rumors, she knew. She sat up stiffly and pulled on her boots. "Just a moment."

He waited patiently as Bridget, bent over, came out.

"Yes, Glendon?"

"My lord wishes to see you, lady."

Together they turned and strode between the rows of tents towards the tent of Vortimer; about four times as large as the others, his tent commanded a full view of the encampment—two guards announced their approaching.

Vortimer, in spite of his height, did not have to bend out of his tent.

"Ah, my lady, good evening," he said cordially.

"Good evening, lord."

"I have been advised that your quarters are fitting only for a soldier. Consider my camp yours for the remainder of our journey."

"Absolutey not! I have…"

Vortimer lost his smile and became maddeningly blank. "It bears no further discussion. Even now your things are being brought over." He said calmly.

"I told you," she balled her fists and put them on her hips, "that I require no special treatment, my lord!"

"And I told you there is nothing further to discuss." With that he slung a large bag over his left shoulder, turned, and with Glendon by his side, headed towards Bridget's old tent.

Her fists still on her hips, Bridget glowered at the retreating pair.

How dare he make a spectacle of me? How dare he order me about like some commoner?

She flung open the tent's flap angrily, too mad to immediately appreciate the finer creature comforts: she could stand without stooping, two cots, two chairs with a rough table and a brazier.

The audacity of him! Does he think I require this coddling? Trying to make himself appear so solicitous in front of his men.

She sat down hard on the cot's edge, noticing the thicker blankets.

"Milady?"

"What?" She snapped.

"I have your things here." The disembodied voice said bluntly.

"Leave them there…I will bring them in myself."

"As you wish, milady."

Limping heavily, Vortimer agonized silently over his leg as he and Glendon headed towards Bridget's former shelter.

Damn her and damn Varduc for suggesting she be treated with benevolence! She almost spat at me! What did I do wrong? Anyone, anyone else would be grateful for what I did—but not her! What is wrong with her? Perhaps Varduc was wrong and meant her sister! Tonight Glendon and I have to plan how to scout this new place and I do not need to trouble myself over how well she sleeps!

Glendon, aware of his lord's agitation, pointed out several landmarks, remarking how well the encampment had been set up.

"If they were Romans we'd have a trench with ramparts surrounding us." Vortimer growled.

Glendon knew he had been silenced.

The two men surveyed the small army; Vortimer kept his own counsel as Glendon ruminated aloud about the day and the land.

"Have Gwaldner's men here after dinner. I want to go study that map and the land."

"Might be hard to do, lord. You left that chart in your tent with milady."

"Then after dinner you will go to her tent and obtain the map from her and bring it here. I cannot foresee any difficulty from her, can you Glendon? Now, let me go and rest a while. I know we are miles from any enemies but I still want double guards posted…keeps them wary. And make sure she gets dinner."

"Bridget, my lord?"

"Do you know of any other 'she' in camp or have you secreted a companion?"

"Nay, my lord."

"Very well, then, have dinner, the map and those two guides brought here later."

Glendon bowed as Vortimer whipped back the tent flap and sprawled himself on the thin cot, weary from the day and from trying to dampen the excitement he felt building within. This new land, his new land, held so much promise with its expansive fields and thick forests!

"And all I have to do," he muttered as he lay on the cot, "all I have to do is defeat the Vikings." He closed his eyes and fell into a dreamless sleep.

Glendon inspected the men, prepared the sentry schedule and made arrangements to have his tent placed next to Vortimer's. He located the tents of Maldwyn and Astorious, and pointed out the camps of Bridget and Vortimer.

"Now, you will go to her tent after we sup and fetch the map and bring it over to his lord, there." He pointed.

The two young men nodded as Glendon smiled, congratulating himself on his ingenuity in avoiding stirring up Bridget's nest.

The evening settled slowly at this time of year, the air cooled and the evening birds began their lonesome melodies. The smoke of fresh roasted game blanketed the band as the fields and gentle hills became honey-hued from the low sun.

Having had her supper, Bridget retired to her tent, content to let the shadows drag her off to sleep after such an irritating day: the slow pace, Vortimer's indifference, his condescending attitude—all these things upset her, and more.

This is like some impossible dream! My father, the land, the invaders, this marriage. It doesn't seem real, I feel as if I am only an actor in some very bad play. Impossible dream…I haven't dreamt of The Man for some time now, still, I feel his shadow. I should be grateful for that and now perhaps I have cursed myself for thinking of him! Maybe if I…

"Milady? Milady? It is me, Astorious with Maldwyn, vassals of your uncle Glamorgan. Are you yet awake?" He asked from outside the entrance.

Bridget groaned inwardly as she sat on the cot. "Yes," she said. "What is it?"

"My lord Vortimer needs the map that is in your tent. It is in the leather pouch on the table, I am told."

"And?"

"We are to bring it to him, milady."

Bridget whipped open the tent flap so furiously it startled the two of them.

"He dares give me this tent and then he sends two men over to ask for something he has forgotten? Is this what you're after?" She spat as she waved the rolled up document.

"Yes, milady. We are to…"

"You are to do nothing of the kind! This is my tent, my map and my land! You two will follow me to Vortimer—and fetch the table and two stools, I doubt he had the forethought for that."

Bridget clutched the map and walked steadfastly towards Vortimer's tent, not bothering to look back at the two who were getting the equipment. She looked about, immediately impressed by the ordered symmetry of the camp but did not slow her pace. Nearing the tent, she saw his lieutenant standing outside, whispering to Vortimer who was inside. As she came closer, Vortimer himself appeared, the two men waited for her to come closer.

"My lady, there was no need for you to come," said Vortimer. "The map was all we needed."

"My lord," said Bridget hardly bowing, "you ripped me from my very comfortable tent which you are now inhabiting and then disturb me for something that is in the tent which you vacated! How much can one endure? And you need more than the map, you need someone to interpret it."

Vortimer chose to ignore the remark about the tents, only caring about the map in her possession. "I thank you for bringing it so quickly," he noticed the two men carrying the stools and table, "and the furniture."

"It is nothing."

Glendon set up the table and chairs and brought over a lantern, Bridget handed the map to Vortimer who bowed his head and then spread it on the table.

The five of them looked down at it, each getting their own bearing from the river and sketched landmarks.

"We are here," Vortimer pointed.

Bridget, before anyone could agree or disagree, said "No, we are here," and tapped her finger an inch from Vortimer's.

"How so?"

"Here is the river," she drew her finger along it, "and here the rise before we crossed. Here," she pointed at inverted 'v', "is that hill over there beyond the camp."

Vortimer sat and beckoned Bridget to do likewise.

"I see the map better standing, lord."

"As you wish."

"What," he asked, "is this here?"

"When we came here it was very boggy but that was during the rains. It might be easily passable now though I doubt it."

"How so?"

"This river here," she pointed, "and this one here, shows me that the area between them is low and subject to flooding. And the map is incomplete as it does not show the rivulets." She impressed them in the map with her fingernail.

Vortimer looked up at Maldwyn who was shifting from foot to foot. "Does my lady speak correctly?"

Bridget felt herself warm when he said 'my lady' and looked over at Maldwyn who was clearly uncomfortable.

"My lord, your lady speaks correctly," he stammered.

"And why wasn't this indicated?" His voice rising ever so slightly.

Is his temper being stirred this quickly? Or is he just annoyed? What could he expect from this coarse youth?

"We did not think it important when we were here last, lord. The map was only intended for general directions."

"Tell me," Vortimer now looked over to Astorious, "how many campaigns have you endured, both of you?"

"None, lord," he replied quietly.

"How many battles have you planned? Which are the quickest routes between here," he jammed his index finger at one point on the map, "and here!"

Neither man said a word as Vortimer's tone was more an accusation than a question.

Sitting back on his stool, Vortimer rolled up the map quietly and handed it to Glendon who was at attention next to him. "Take as many men as you need, the smartest ones, not necessarily those that can read or write, and break them off in pairs. Tomorrow they will disperse along the length of the river and then head north. I want them to draw and show any old roads, lakes and rivers. I want to see forests and some indication as to how thick they are. I need easily discernible landmarks. I need to see hills and swamps, everything! We will wait for them at the land's end. These two here," he waved his hand dismissively towards Maldwyn and Astorious, "will remain as our guides."

The two young men bowed hurriedly and retreated towards the main camp. Glendon stayed on a bit to go over the particulars as Bridget stood mutely. When Glendon at last left, Vortimer stood and insisted that Bridget take his stool as he went to fetch the other for himself. Returning and smiling, he sat down across from her.

"Thank you for correcting what could have been a time-consuming problem," he muttered. "You will, of course, stay here and eat with me. Would you care for something to drink?"

"Wine, please," Bridget replied, not at all sure if she wanted to accept his gratitude or company.

"I regret that we have no wine. We brought only necessities and wine is an extravagance and distraction a moving army can ill afford. Water will have to do, for now."

He waved over a nearby guard and sent him off to fetch food and drink. Bridget and Vortimer sat in an uncomfortable silence, their eyes barely making contact. "It is a beautiful evening, milady." Said Vortimer. "When were you here last?"

Bridget looked over the encampment, appreciating the straight rows of tents and the uniformity of the fires—it implied an orderliness and in order there was safety.

Order...safety. Haven't had much of that in my life lately! What does he want me to talk about? Look at him, sitting there so confidently! He knows nothing about me, nothing!

"Early Spring, my lord. Good weather going, terrible returning. The river was fast and fat from the rain and melt. Nothing so nice as now."

Vortimer looked at her keenly, nodding encouragement.

He does have the grayest eyes I have ever seen—beautiful if they didn't look so sad.

Bridget felt a sudden urge to comfort Vortimer, a feeling that was awkward, unexpected and utterly impossible.

Where did that come from? Why? I do not love this man and I am certain he only sees me an obligation, a nuisance to be endured in exchange for this land! Damn him and my father! What would Celestine do if she were in my position right now?

"I thought we were going to eat? Where is your man? Is this an example of discipline? Wine, at the very least, should have been provided."

Vortimer stiffened, surprised at the rebuke when Bridget seemed to have softened. With an equanimity from some unknown place within, he raised one eyebrow and smiled, holding back the riot of anger she had suddenly whipped up.

"Forgive me, my lady, the fault is totally mine and my men are not to be blamed. First, there has been no real discipline in any army since the days of Caesar when he had an empire to control. If this were a Roman camp we would be thirty thousand strong with a deep trench and ramparts encircling us. We would have makeshift roads, a command center and pens for the animals. His armies did that each and every night they camped."

Varduc, you bastard! Is she really the treasure and asset you spoke of? How much of her insolence should be endured? What if the men heard her?

"Second," he continued, "my men have been on a hard march ever since, you know, our betrothal was planned and fatigue, worsened by their drinking last night, has peaked. A commander realizes this and takes appropriate measures to ensure they get some relief."

"Third, very few knew you were coming and as I told you last night, no special considerations would be given, which you accepted, demanded actually." Then, in spite of his better judgement, "I should have anticipated your frailty, I apologize."

Frailty! Frailty! I'll rip his ears from his skull! I'll wipe that . . .

At that moment two men came from around the tent; one carried a platter heaped with steaming pile of beans and some newly snared roasted rabbit; the other with a flagon of water and two goblets. They wordlessly placed them on the table, wordlessly left as Vortimer and Bridget glowered at each other.

My, but her eyes do fire up! Well, she insisted upon coming.

Vortimer snatched the rabbit and split it, proffering Bridget half. Her eyes still locked upon his, Bridget took her portion and began pulling the hot meat from the bones with her teeth as Vortimer poured the water. They ate and drank in silence, the campfires brightening as the late afternoon melted into evening, the evening clouds painted in impossible pinks and purples. A silence fell upon the encampment and an uneasy truce arose between Vortimer and Bridget as they ate, scooping the spiced beans up with their fingers.

"Will we reach the sea tomorrow?" He asked finally.

"Depends on how fast we ride and whether you want to scout the land more fully. Thank you for dinner and…your company," she replied at last.

"It is I who am grateful for your pointing out the problems with the map. The land can be studied more later; tomorrow we will ride," he stood, indicating the dinner was over.

Bridget stood uneasily, nodded slightly and headed towards her tent.

"Do you need someone to take you back?"

"I am quite capable, my lord," she said.

Vortimer watched the retreating figure of Bridget thread her way among the tents until the gloom at last enveloped her.

Quite capable I am sure.

Vortimer went into his tent and reclined, his hands clasped behind his head.

Her eyes did fire up quick enough! Good observations about the terrain, too, but how quickly her demeanor changed! What was that all about?

He began to fall asleep, wondering just how deep her fury ran.

Bridget lay on her cot, the small oil lamp sputtering, making the shadows wax and wane.

Order is what is needed. Order in my life. I can't stand this chaos, this being blown about like a feather, subject to the whim of the wind. I am Bridget, not the pale, petty women he is familiar with! How many has he been with? Does he have any bastards? Of course he does! The question should be how many! Forget him for now, forever!

The tormented woman began to list once more all that had happened, attempting to put them in some structure, to classify and assign importance.

The marriage, this marriage to Vortimer! The duplicity of my father and my new relationship with Celestine—thank God! My original namesake, a goddess and not a saint of the church. And what of my hopes for the convent? Gone, now, forever?

She twisted to her side.

Becoming pregnant? Well, I believe Celsestine and I have that well in hand. The Vikings?

Not yet a problem; they are as real as, as real as…the Hooded Man.

She sat up quickly, her heart suddenly racing as she looked about the tent.

Where has he been? I haven't dreamt of him for so long, not since learning of my betrothal! Is he gone now?

She lay back down, wondering if she should extinguish the lamp, lest the entire camp think she was afraid of the dark. She puffed it out and lay back down.

Why did I let myself even think of him? Better to dwell on the real things. There are Gwenthe and Mathilde, how I miss hearing their arguments! And Peter, lovely Peter, keeping everything in order. I haven't prayed in so long, either.

She came about and dropped to her knees, resting her elbows on the cot…but though the words came, her heart was not in it—she felt abandoned in the dark. Not moving, she heard the muted camp sounds: noises of horse and men, preparing for vigilant sleep. She climbed back into bed, reconciled to the notion that sleep would not come.

And who was that odd man? Varduc? How was it he made me feel so…safe? Safety. Order. Isn't this what I am trying to obtain? I cannot control my father, his vassals nor the Vikings. I will do what I can to learn about Varduc and my namesake. The only thing I have power over is my relationship with Vortimer and in that I still feel so inadequate. The Hooded Man be damned! He is only a dream!

A dream that returned with a vengeance, as if all the pent-up horrors had been waiting for this particular night to return. Bridget fretted and moaned but could not escape from the sleep that was torturing her! He was there again, his long cape just brushing the ground that was red with blood—again he displayed his reddened hands and began wringing them, working the blood into his pores…and scratching, the sound of nails scratching—she woke with a start to the sound of someone scratching her tent.

"Are you awake, milady? Are you awake? Starting to break camp!"

She gathered her thoughts swiftly, the emotions of the dream still lingered and she felt a fine bath of sweat beneath her clothes.

"Yes…yes! I am quite awake," she muttered in the darkness.

"Very well, milady."

Catching her breath, Bridget went to her knees, clasped her hands in front of her and tried to pray but the words were as hollow as her enthusiasm—the closeness she once felt with God was no longer.

My God, my Christ, I need you now! Watch over and protect me now and in all the days to come.

Bridget stood, inhaling the early morning air, trying to gather her wits under control once more.

A brand new day, unlike any other that has preceded it! I must make something of that!

She pulled on her boots and walked outside to see the camp's occupants busily breaking down and folding tents, scurrying about for the horses. She felt a sense of urgency and anticipation in their activity—there would be no breakfast this morning. Vortimer had said they would ride today and so it would be!

Bridget spied Glendon riding towards her, the horizon barely light.

"Morning, milady!" he boomed. "Today will be a good day, a great day! My men are fetching your horse and will take care of the tent. My lord offers his respects and desires to know if you need anything. He also requests that you ride in the front with us."

Bridget thought for a moment, briefly overwhelmed by the heartiness of Glendon's booming voice.

"I have only to finish my toilet, sir. And what would I desire? A skin of wine would be nice."

Glendon bellowed with laughter, "As you wish, milady!" and rode off towards the far end of the camp.

Bridget returned to the confines of the tent, pulled down her tights, squatted and voided—she was now ready to face the day, food or no.

Outside once more, she headed towards the horses, spying a man who was leading Alexander towards her. Wordlessly, she took the reins and slung herself into the saddle. "Yes, dear Alexander," she whispered into his cocked ear, "today you and I shall ride." She felt utterly at home and comfortable once more, in control of a great and powerful horse—the terrors of the Hooded Man had all but vanished. She headed towards Vortimer's campsite, wishing she had time to brush her hair that fell in tangles.

Vortimer was already mounted, barking orders when he saw Bridget approach.

"Good morning, milady." He smiled. "Did you sleep well?"

"Tolerable, my lord. I was thinking…"

"Good! I hope to reach the sea by the end of the day. Are you ready? I trust your instinct more than our two guides. Glendon will ride with us, the rest can follow—lead on."

Disgruntled that she was not able to complete her thoughts, she felt warmly complimented by his trust in her.

176

"Ready, then? Forward!"

She wheeled Alexander around and set off in a quick canter, Glendon and Vortimer flanking her.

It was going to be a day unlike any other; the damp air was already beginning to dry as the sun rose on their right, the sky painted red and gold. They rode wordlessly as they scared up birds and rabbits. Bridget surprised herself by the familiarity of the landscape, as if she had lived here her whole life, and she loved it. Fields and meadows, dark stands of trees and scraggly rocks—all these things flooded back, the only difference, she realized suddenly, was that they belonged to her! All of it! She withheld the urge to cry out joyously and just kept riding, looking side to side at her escorts who rode stoically, their eyes taking it all in. Vortimer, however, looked to be in some pain.

"Should we slow down and allow the others to catch up?" She asked.

"Ride on. They will catch up when we stop to water the horses."

It was a comfortable pace, the kind that tired neither horse nor rider. Bridget felt as though she could go on forever, the air caressing her face as the sun now began to warm her back. They splashed through small steams, no one wanting to stop just yet.

It's true what they say about her; she rides like a man—better than most. And she seems so…happy!

Vortimer observed Bridget's demeanor and determined to remember it, just as he was making a soldier's appraisal of the land; his mind attuned to troop placements and vantage points. His right leg was an agony, something about the riding position tore the tendons holding his knee—he had to stop.

"There," he pointed at the grove next to a broad stream, "we can stop, rest and allow the others to catch up."

"But my lord," Bridget protested, "just over that ridge is the most lovely…"

"We will stop here, refresh the horses and ourselves and await the others." He replied curtly.

Bridget turned and was about to spit out a retort when she noticed the sweat on Vortimer's brow and the strange way his lips twisted. She dismounted and allowed Alexander to go to the stream as she watched Vortimer get off his horse with a grimace.

He is in pain! A lot of pain! Look how he holds the reins for support as he leads the horse to water! How did he injure himself? An old battle wound? Did he have it from birth? A pity that one so strong should have to hobble like that. Perhaps this is the perfect place to rest, besides I am hungry and thirsty as well.

Glendon produced a sack and offered some dried fruits to Vortimer and Bridget who gobbled them greedily. Together they knelt on the bank and drank the cold water with cupped hands.

There is nothing weak about this one! Look how she wanted to ride some more! And she eats and drinks like one of my men, a good thing—there will be tough times ahead. Maybe Varduc was right. I am so glad to be off that damn beast! At least I can stretch and walk a little. It is too shady here, my leg needs warmth.

"What is it that is just over that ridge, Bridget?"

That is the first time he has called me by my name! Why does that make me feel so silly and my face is flushing!

Without turning to face him, she pointed up the sun-bathed hill, "A beautiful view amongst so many that it stands out in my mind," she hesitated, "Vortimer."

"Then let's go take a look, the walk will do us and the horses some good."

Together, all three crossed the stream and trudged up the grassy slope. Vortimer limping heavily with Bridget on his left, Glendon on his right. The vista before them was that of high grass waving rhythmically to the gentle breeze. Shadows from the high clouds raced across the undulating expanse. Vortimer stopped and gazed in wonderment at the gentle majesty before him.

"Bona terra," he whispered, "bona terra."

Why, that is the same thing I said when I first saw this place! Could it be that he has soul enough to appreciate good ground.

Unthinking, she reached for his hand and whispered 'bona terra'.

Glendon, two arms away only heard, 'bone tear'. "Odd name for land," he thought, "but I like it!"

Vortimer clasped Bridget's hand within his own, still soaking in the beauty and the serenity, he stood transfixed—he had never seen anything so peaceful. He might have stayed there for hours but he soon heard the approaching army shouting behind them in the distance. His reverie vanished like some dying spark and he unconsciously released her hand and turned towards the approaching column. With some remorse he said to no one in particular, "Time to be on with it," and began down the hill.

He held my hand! Why did he do that? No, it was I who took his—but he did hold it! How striking that we should share the same feeling! Celestine would be furious if she knew what I did but I couldn't help it! It just seemed the proper and right thing to do—but no harm will come from it!

The small band met up with the larger one and Glendon cursed them roundly for their tardiness but allowed all to pause and refresh themselves while telling this one or the other that the name of the new land, their new home, was 'Bone Tear.' To a man they thought it a peculiar name, to a man, they liked it immensely!

"Is it much further, Bridget?" Vortimer asked.

"No, lord. We shall be by the great sea this evening if we hurry."

Vortimer paced among his men, talking to this one or that, his aggravated limp only a shadow of what it was before. Singly and in pairs the men mounted, waiting only for Bridget and Vortimer to lead. The young lord stood by as Bridget mounted Alexander easily; his bad leg forced him to push up with his arms before he could swing it over and sit in the saddle.

Vortimer smiled slightly at Bridget, "Lead on."

Bridget dug her heels into Alexander who responded by dashing up the hillside and was almost to the top before the men below began to follow. Laughing and shouting now, the army raced across the great field, chasing the woman on the large white horse who was leading them to the salt ocean just beyond the horizon.

The band eventually slowed to a more reasonable rate, Bridget with Vortimer and Glendon leading the column of warriors who were chattering like children about Bone Tear. The wind blew gently from the north and as they rode on, Bridget thought she could already smell some salt on the air.

"You ride well, very well." Remarked Vortimer in an offhanded manner.

"Thank you, lord. Riding has been my special joy, ever since I was a child."

"Really? I regret that I am not much of a horseman—my leg makes it difficult."

Believing that Vortimer's injury may have been caused by a horse, Bridget related how she broke her arm and tried to keep it a secret; the story brought a laugh from both men. They rode in silence for the most part, as if talking would impede them. The sun was closer to setting than its zenith when the air took a chilly turn; the shrubs look tired. A solitary gull floated above them, casting a curious eye and then not finding them interesting, sailed off. The air was heavy with sea smell now and Bridget shuddered as she recalled the thunderous winds of her last visit.

"There," she pointed, "just over that ridge."

The limitless blue sea shocked them, as it always did to those confined to the land, with its emptiness. The moment was not lost on Vortimer who shouted, "From these beaches before us, to the river we left behind, is ours!"

A resounding cheer followed and Bridget heard him mutter, "And none will take it from us."

The men broke quickly, setting up camp and tethering the horses. Vortimer, with the thinnest of smiles, asked Bridget to join him for dinner.

"Of course, my lord," she replied as he went off, leaving her to watch as her tent was pitched. She dismounted and allowed Alexander to be taken by a young man who bubbled his admiration for such a fine animal. Waiting listlessly, Bridget felt a familiar stirring.

It is this place, isn't it? I remember the same feeling from the last time I was here. I feel as though my feet are rooting to the earth's core—there is a stability here that I feel no where else.

The young woman shivered involuntarily, eyes closed, hoping no one would notice and not caring if anyone did. For a moment there was no other place, no other worlds, only here and now. A sense of fullness rushed through Bridget as she inhaled deeply, her lungs not capable of sucking in all she desired…she felt whole, she felt safe, she felt…home. Startled by the insight, she opened her eyes once more, the reverie stretched, leaving the residual feelings behind. In less time than she thought possible, she was inside Vortimer's tent, so giddy with her discovery that it took a conscious effort to stay motionless on the thin cot.

Good ground. Bona terra. I heard him say it!

She repressed a giggle.

When do we eat? What will we have? I am famished.

She lay there, smelling the sundry campfires as her nostrils flared, hoping to discover some scent of roast meat.

"My lady?" A disembodied voice from outside her tent.

"Yes?"

"My lord wishes me to escort you to his tent for supper."

Feeling uncharacteristically confident, Bridget emerged with a grin on her face, much to the relief of the young man who had heard some disquieting stories about the moods of his mistress.

"Lead on, sir."

Vortimer spied Bridget from his table as Glendon reviewed the day.

No, not just regal, something more. She has the air—there is something about the way she walks; she walks just as she rides…commanding.

Vortimer felt foolish for not having noticed it before, he who prided himself on observation. He had never expected a woman to have it.

Her sister, Celestine, has a haughty look but lacks the air of confidence that Bridget exhales from each pore! Interesting.

The prospect of Bridget leading his men sparked through his brain and just as quickly left.

"My lords."

Vortimer and Glendon stood as Bridget took the seat to Vortimer's right.

"The men snared some pheasant way back; I hope that meets with your approval?"

"Yes, indeed!" She enthused, delighting in the warm evening, the setting sun and the prospect of a full belly. For a slender moment Bridget thought she hadn't felt this happy since she first took Alexander over a jump.

She listened intently as Vortimer spoke to Glendon.

"The men have ridden hard these several weeks, I know that. I also know that they are infected with the boredom of routine, the bane of any commander. Too, the horses have done all the physical work—this would never happen with Caesar! His armies would march twenty-five, thirty miles a day before they set up camp—horses have given us mobility and speed but at what cost? Tomorrow I want to see a game! Let them exhaust themselves and release some of their energy."

Consisting of mostly youngish men, Vortimer appreciated the need for a change; it kept them fresh—it also allowed for the settling of minor differences that naturally develop amongst warriors living and fighting together.

"Might be bloody, lord."

"So long as they don't kill each other."

Glendon let out a laugh and smiled at Bridget. "It isn't healthy for young blood not to do anything, milady."

"I understand." She replied.

"Tomorrow I will have the squad leaders organize a game of ball."

"You mean where they go about kicking an inflated pig's bladder? I have seen that at fairs."

"Not like this, milady!" Vortimer laughed. "Nothing like this!"

He should really smile more; why must he always hide that and look so grim? Even his eyes lighten!

The roasted birds were brought shortly and the three ate in silence, grunting with each satisfying mouthful. When done, Vortimer tossed the carcass into the fire, an easy grin on his face. "Who," he asked Glendon, "is our best rider, our fastest?"

"Albin." He replied without hesitation.

"Do you have any gold with you?"

"Some, my lord. Why?"

Looking over at Bridget and back again at Glendon, he said, "I will wager one gold piece that my lady can best him."

Bridget choked on the water she was drinking.

"A gold piece, my lord?"

"Yes. One gold piece that my lady can beat our best rider. You can set up the course and the men can watch after the game. Make sure his horse is healthy, watered and well fed. I will not abide any excuses."

Glendon pursed his lips and stuck out his hand to seal the bet with Vortimer.

"A gold piece?" Bridget protested. "I believe I can ride well and Alexander is the finest horse but I have never raced before!"

"Never competed? Why not?"

"I was never asked, my lord."

"Do you want to race or should I just hand over the gold to Glendon right now?"

"I will race, my lord," she said with an edge in her voice, "and win."

"I know you will, Bridget. I never gamble when I think I might lose."

"The victor will get a special prize." Glendon stated, not overly awed by Bridget's posturing.

"Excellent! Then I suggest my lady retire and rest while you and I go over some plans. Besides, night is falling."

They all stood, Bridget's legs feeling wobbly over what had just transpired—she said her goodnights and headed numbly towards her tent.

Race! He wants me to race and he is wagering on me to win! Me to win! I have never raced before but he knows that and still he is betting on me to win! What if I don't? What will he think of me then? No, defeat is out of the question!

Who is this Albin? Which horse is his? What will the course be like? Is Alexander ready for it?

Even before she realized it, she was in front of her tent and going in, lighting the small lamp as sleep was impossible.

I can do this thing; I am Bridget, princess.

Over and over she repeated this to herself, willing herself into a tranquility she should not have felt, allowing the power of this particular bit of land to flow around and into her being. Her body slowly relaxed, her breathing deepened as

182

the race, Vortimer, everything drifted into someplace far away—all that was, was now. Sleep, elusive earlier, enveloped her—and it was dreamless.

Bridget was startled awake the following morning by the clamoring of the camp. She rubbed the sleep from her eyes and stepped out, the sun already well above the horizon. The soldiers nearest her tent were eating hurriedly; she saw Vortimer outside his tent and rather than wait for an invitation, decided to walk over.

"Good morning, my lady." Vortimer bowed slightly and indicated a place for her to sit at the table.

"What is all the commotion this morning?" She asked.

"The men are getting ready for the game...and the race."

Oh, no! Am I that dense to have forgotten all about that? How could I have?

At once her stomach tied itself into a tight knot and she declined the eggs and stale bread, preferring to watch Vortimer eat as she sipped water.

"I think the men are all prepared, lord." Said Glendon coming over, paying his respects to Bridget. "This will be unlike any game you have seen before, milady."

Motioning Vortimer and Bridget up, Glendon swept his hand towards a large expanse, more hilly than flat, more rock than grass. "The hills and depressions will make the game more difficult and more interesting, I think."

They watched as two masses of men, about one hundred and fifty to a side, Bridget reckoned, took to the plain. The man who carried the bladder stood roughly between the opposing groups, separated by about two hundred yards.

"Ready?" He shouted to those on his right. A large cry indicated they were.

"Ready?" He shouted to those on his left. They were ready, too.

He flung the well-worn ball up into the air and scampered away as the opposing groups charged. After two minutes Bridget determined that what rules there were, were few: no weapons, biting or kicking. The tumbling mass of bodies hadn't the slightest organization, Bridget didn't even know what the boundaries were and neither, it seemed, did the combatants. At one point Bridget noticed several older men who were not taking part. Seeing her gaze, Vortimer explained that they were squad leaders, older men who did not take part in such pursuits but led in battle.

"And who is that one over there?" She pointed to the man who had stated the game.

"That's Albin, the man you will race against. I forbid him to take part as I do not want to hear that he lost because of some minor injury or fatigue."

"Oh," was all Bridget could muster.

The contest continued without break, the men chasing and kicking after the ball—there were more bloody noses than not, some limped but carried on defiantly as the sun rose, others puked from exhaustion and then swiftly rejoined their mates.

Glendon was right, I have never seen such bedlam! And they seem to be enjoying this madness!

First by ones, then by twos, men began dropping to all fours, panting with weakness as their squad leaders berated them to get back into the fray which they did gamely—but without the ferocity they displayed earlier—no one ran any more, no one could.

"Time," Vortimer remarked to Glendon.

"Time!" he bellowed.

The men found it easier to collapse than to sit.

"Glendon?"

"Fair, lord, fair. A bit more of sweat and they will be back to standard."

"Very well. Let them rest and drink, see if there are any serious injuries. After that I want you to lay the race."

Glendon bowed hurriedly and immediately began hurling insults at the sprawled bodies as he walked towards them.

The race! For a moment there I had all but forgotten the race. I must go see to Alexander, I have to dress properly!

"My lord," she turned to Vortimer, "I must return to my tent to get ready."

"Of course, as you wish."

Bridget felt her heart pounding with excitement as she flew to her quarters. There, she tore through her things, determined to find the most comfortable, most lucky clothes—she hadn't brought much with her, so she decided to wear the most comfortable tights, tunic and boots she had.

And this shawl he gave me—I will wear it as an emblem—it will be my banner.

She took the stiff fabric and placed it over her neck, letting the ends dangle between her arms. She left the tent and strode over to the horses, Alexander recognized her immediately and pointed his ears quizzically. She ran her hands slowly, gently over his muzzle, kissing him quickly on his nose and whispering excitedly—how she loved him!

Alexander possessed the animal's sense that something was different today by the way his mistress stroked his flank and whispered. At once, his great heart beat more quickly, feeding off the excitement so evident in Bridget—he began to whinny and strain at his tether.

"Soon," she whispered. "Very soon. Save your strength for now, let it build."

A young man came to help her with the tack but Bridget shooed him away, always preferring to do it herself—it allowed time for her to speak with and examine Alexander. She slung on the saddle and adjusted the reins, her heart feverish with anticipation. Out of the corner of her eye she spied a man doing the same thing to a great chestnut-colored stallion—she turned so as to keep horse and rider out of vision, out of mind.

"A race, Alexander! A race! You and I with hundreds watching!"

She laughed with excitement, feeling foolish but supremely happy with herself. Unable to delay any further, she decided to walk the horse over to Vortimer, rather than ride him, letting the anticipation intoxicate her and Alexander. He watched as she headed towards him, pleased that she had worn the shawl but determined not to make an issue of it.

I have never seen her smile so much and the gleam in her eyes is full of mischief, not anger. . . she is pretty, actually.

As Bridget neared she saw his troops, now somewhat refreshed, betting loudly and earnestly—she decided it best not to listen on whom they were betting.

"A fine animal, Bridget—superb. You take good care of him, don't you?"

"Yes, my lord, I do. We take care of one another."

Alexander began bobbing his head which caused Bridget to laugh suddenly. "See? He even understands me!"

"I don't doubt it. Your adversary is my finest horseman. He, too, loves his horse and would probably sleep with it if he could. I am not a horseman and make no pretense about it. I do, however, appreciate talent in fields where I have none. The men are betting against you because they are blind. I am allowing Glendon to determine the course because I do not want to be accused of favoritism when you win. Is that understood? You will win. One thing further, races are not necessarily won by the most swift."

Bridget threw her leg up and over and mounted Alexander in one fluid motion.

"And if I don't win, will you be disappointed?"

"I shall have lost a gold piece, but gained much," he grinned.

"Such faith deserves resolve," she smiled back. "I feel unbeatable here."

There! I said it! Something about this place, this land…I feed off it somehow. I am invincible here!

Bridget felt, rather than heard, Albin approach on his steed. Turning, she saw a young man on a long-legged, powerful horse—the sun made his coat shine like fresh-beaten copper.

"My lady, my lord," he bowed.

Bridget leaned her mouth close to Alexander's ear. "He is nothing," she whispered encouragingly, "this day is ours."

"A beautiful looking horse, my lady. You take good care of him and he appreciates it, I can tell."

Uncertain as to what to say, Bridget nodded and smiled. It was then that Glendon thundered up on his panting horse.

"Are the contestants ready to review the course?"

They nodded.

"Very well, follow me then."

Bridget's brain was in a fog as they rode off, feeling the eyes of the shouting spectators on her—feeling almost freakish. She sat taller, eyes straight, trying desperately to slow her pounding pulse.

Why did he have me race now? Why has he done this? To belittle me in front of his men? What a cowardly thing to do!

But in her heart, she knew better. She no longer heard the mob or felt their gleaming gazes—she only knew that Vortimer was looking at her retreating figure.

Varduc was correct. There is something of steel in her! Look how she focuses on the terrain, not even acknowledging Albin there beside her.

Vortimer, in spite of Bridget's size, volatile flareups and peculiar temperment, felt a distinct pride as he watched her round the course.

Bridget was heeding the circuit now, noting that Glendon had two jumps prepared from thickets on the treeless field—there were two streams, three sharp turns and only one long straightaway.

"There you have it," cried Glendon. "Nothing fancy here—just speed and strength. You go around twice and the first one to pass me the second time, wins. Any questions? Good. Then we shall start by lord."

Albin rode easily, calm and confident—raising his hands and waving to his comrades who were yelling encouragement as they lined the perimeter of the course.

Bridget felt her heart tripping madly and hoped, prayed it didn't show. Alexander, skittish at the presence of the other horse, was behaving badly, aching to run. The keen eyes of the spectators could not fail to notice the anxiety of horse and rider—surely this was no place for a woman! Bridget happened to look towards the crowd and noticed Maldwyn and Astorious, the two men she once flew from as they guarded her—they were busily betting with their new comrades; Bridget hoped they would bet on her!

As they came by Vortimer he motioned for Albin to come over.

"Have you ever lost a race, Albin?"

"Once, lord, many years ago."

"Good, don't make a habit of it. Go out to win."

This little bit of encouragement satisfied Albin who was initially unsure as to what he was supposed to do—lose graciously or win soundly—he would win but allow Bridget to retain some degree of respect by not winning by too large a margin.

Why did Vortimer call him over there? Last minute instructions? Has he told him to let me win? I don't need his intrusion! Vortimer, why have you put me in this damn race? A race, by God, I will win! What did he mean that it is not always won by the most swift?

Bridget consciously made herself relax, cooing into Alexander's ear helped her as much as the horse. Albin flanked the other side of Glendon who was waiting patiently.

"Good luck to the both of you—a special reward goes to the winner. Ready?"

Both riders nodded—Glendon raised his right fist and brought it down quickly—the race had begun.

Alexander fairly jumped from the start, Bridget a bit surprised by his acceleration, held the reins tightly, and settled her upper body against the horse's left neck, her arms pumping in unison with each thundering stride. The line of spectators was an inconsequential blur as she and Alexander pounded along this first part of the course. She looked up and saw the great chestnut—matching Alexander's stride, his great body almost within arm's reach as they came to the first turn, a long one to the left. Bridget leaned inwards and coaxed Alexander with her knees, she was wild with joy as the air whipped through her hair, the shawl flying straight back. Her eyes watered from excitement and the rushing wind.

Vortimer watched from a distance, amazed how Bridget and Alexander melded into one rushing, powerful entity. Albin, on the other hand, was attempting to ride his mount.

I am surprised the others don't notice.

The line flattened and then dipped into a shallow gully followed by a short, steep hill—Bridget shifted her weight accordingly, giving Alexander whatever encouragement he needed. It was a short run to the first jump and Alexander had not come into full stride and took it poorly—she saw Albin pull ahead...not by much, but still...

'Not necessarily won by the most swift'. Is that what Vortimer said?

They headed into the next turn, sharp to the right. Bridget held Alexander back by the lightest of pressure and positioned him on Albin's right quarter. As they headed into the turn proper she shouted, "Fly, Alexander! Fly!"

The great horse responded with a bolt of energy that surprised even Bridget.

He knows! Alexander knows he is in a race and loves it!

Indeed, those who saw his spurt of speed marveled at the horse ridden by the spirited woman who laughed and cried as she guided him along, pulling ahead of Albin on his right as he took the turn too wide. Bridget did not bother to look back; she knew, she knew as certain as breath, that the race was hers for the winning...or losing. Up and down two gentle hills and then crashing through a small brook, the water exploded from Alexander's hooves as horse and rider were past the spray before it could wet them. Alexander was in full stride as they took the next jump, landing lightly and accelerating immediately. Bridget knew Alexander had a mind of his own but held him back gently as they headed down the last long straightaway, wanting to conserve his energy for the final circuit. Somewhere she noticed Glendon but it didn't matter, not really; nothing mattered except for this moment.

Bridget heard her pursuer behind her and began to formulate how she would take each remaining jump and turn. For the first jump she kept Alexander in shorter stride, making the jump slowly but with a measured cadence that made for a swifter recovery—that was all there was. She never thought she would do it, but she allowed Alexander to ease up during the last part of the race, not wanting to shame Vortimer's man in front of his comrades.

She looked over as Glendon dropped his arm, pointing to her as the winner. Bridget threw up both arms as she allowed Alexander to slow down. She felt weak, tired and thoroughly exhilarated as the sweat began pouring from her body. Several of the spectators came over and offered to help her down which she refused. Triumphant, she rode up to Vortimer who was smiling whimsically.

"Lord?"

"I told you, you would win."

Glendon rode over, a wine skin in his hand.

"My lady, the other night you had a desire for some wine. Well, here amongst this rabble I was able to procure this! I cannot vouch for its..."

Bridget was already squirting the warm liquid into her mouth before he could finish. This last bit of bravado brought a rousing cry from the men who were crowding all around horse and rider now. Bridget allowed herself another mouthful and then tossed the skin to Albin who was close by.

"A fine race, sir! And a fine horse!"

Albin laughed gently, still not really believing that he had lost to this woman. Bridget dismounted and allowed Alexander to be cooled and watered as the tension of the race seeped from her bones. The entire camp began to get some order and night fires were being lit as the men recalled the day's events loudly.

"Are you tired?" Vortimer asked.

"No, well, not yet," Bridget laughed.

"Tonight you will rest after dinner. My scouts have returned from surveying the land and we will decide where to build our fortress and tomorrow we will leave to return to your father."

"My father?"

"Have you forgotten? We do have a marriage to attend."

CHAPTER NINE

Where the hell is she and what is she doing now? I should never have let Bridget go on this fool's journey! And she had the stupidity to hold his hand at the table that evening! She should not be allowed to drink so much, my dear sister.

For what seemed to be the thousandth time, Celestine cursed her father, her husband and Bridget—if it were in her power, Vortimer would be castrated.

The lame bastard! His leg is probably the only thing that doesn't work! How ironic that I should have a perfectly wealthy and healthy husband who cannot plant the seed while she gets some lame cocksman. It just isn't fair! And who is that creature in his court? Marduc? No, Varduc! He frightens me—perhaps he could meet with an accident, some bad food? Will Calgwyn have the remedy prepared in time? I will have to have some place to secret it—her toilet would be best, I think.

Lying on Bridget's bed, Celestine's brain plotted possibilities as she and the court awaited Bridget's return and nuptials. The simplest thing as a wedding had also gone awry because of that damned Varduc. The encounter between him and the priest was painful to remember. They had been in her father's small chapel when Varduc declared that it was inappropriate for his master and new mistress.

"What?" Declared Father Junius. "This is a house of God."

"I am sorry to disagree with you, sir," said Varduc. "This is not a house of God and quite frankly, if I were God I would not choose to live here. This is a house of man, built by men with some simple stones and timbers."

"This is where we pray to our God, unbeliever!" He declared with all the righteous indignation he could muster.

"A pity," said Varduc. "I would think that having the ceremony in God's house would be so much more meaningful, don't you?"

"Of course." Father Junius huffed.

"Tell me then, which is greater, the grandest edifice of Man or the simplest creation of Him? Was there not something in your book about a tower and a prideful people?"

Not being all that familiar with scripture and barely able to read, the priest rolled his eyes upwards and thought quickly. "No undertaking of Man can be so excellent as that which He has created by thinking its existence."

"Exactly!" Cried Varduc, slapping the priest on the back. "Which is why this marriage should be performed in His palace, away from the trappings of the court. We have some strong agreement, you and I and I think more of you for it. There is a grove, not too far, which is almost Eden-like in its simple beauty— a jewel from God, I think, that will serve your honorable purpose."

"Yes, marriage is an honorable and holy estate."

"Good," said Varduc. "But might I beg just one favor from your worship?"

"And what might that be?"

"I am but a simple man, not wise in many ways, but I do love my young master and I would be in your debt if I might be there with you as they wed."

Junius looked down at the frail figure who looked as though a strong wind would scatter him like so much dust. "Just to be present?"

"Of course! I know my place, indeed I do. This is a ceremony of the church— who am I to interfere in so holy a ritual?" He held his hands up.

"Very well," replied the priest with the greatest of dignity. "Just remember who is in charge here."

"Oh, indeed I will! Indeed I will."

The little creature was fairly bursting with excitement after that! He made himself so helpful, always about and a nuisance. I trust him as much as I could toss one of the Stones. How do I stay close to Bridget? How do I keep her encouraged?

Warm air blew in from the unshuttered window and along with it the smell of manured fields.

"Gwenthe!" Celestine cried out. "Gwenthe, where are you, woman?"

"Coming…coming." She heard the ponderous strides of the large woman punish the creaking floor.

"Yes, my lady." She gasped between breaths.

"Gwenthe, fetch me some water from that table and give it to me—I am quite thirsty and the dust from this dreadful place has parched my throat."

Bridget's maid dutifully poured the water into a small goblet and walked the four paces to Celestine who was now sitting in her mistress's own bed.

"Has my woman, Calgwyn, arrived yet?"

"No." Said Gwenthe, flushed from exertion and anger.

"Well, you may go. Take this goblet and return it there. I want her brought to me the moment she arrives, is that clear? No matter the time or with whom I am speaking, understood?"

"Very clear, milady." She backed her bulk out the door, refusing any hint of a bow.

Old sow!

Celestine laid back and began reviewing all that had happened, trying to formulate some plan of action—but there was nothing to do but wait and anticipate the actions and reactions of all involved. All she could do, she decided, was to gather up as much information as she could and stay as close to Bridget and Vortimer as possible.

The one thing, the only thing that matters is her becoming pregnant or worse, falling in love. Pfft! Love! What does that have to do with anything? Bridget is such a fool. Where is Calgwyn and what is she doing? We need her elixir!

A sudden increase in the din from the courtyard below led Celestine to look from the window—below she saw several people on horseback, Bridget among them!

Damn! Damn! Damn! Why didn't someone tell me they were coming!

Without thinking she began to straighten her dress and ran her fingers swiftly through her hair. She practiced a few smiles and, satisfied she radiated sublime harmony, headed towards the large hall where she found Mathilde and Gwenthe waiting.

"Your mistress, my sister, will need refreshment after her long journey. Have food and wine brought to her room for the both of us."

Gwenthe, tired of the stairs, hustled the excited Mathilde to the kitchen who just as quickly returned with Bridget in tow.

Look at her! She looks as dark as a peasant—and her hair! Why does she look so happy? And she continues to wear that shawl given her by Vortimer!

"Sister, dear poppet, I am so glad that you are home!" Celestine rushed over and hugged Bridget tightly, desperately wanting to whisper "intact?" but feared she might be over heard.

"Celestine," bubbled Bridget, "it is so good to be back!" I cannot wait to bathe and get out of these clothes and sleep in a decent bed."

Celestine looked about swiftly. "And where is Vortimer?"

"He had to see father, but enough of all that! Gwenthe," she cried jubilantly, "draw me a bath, if you please!"

Gwenthe's old bones were invigorated by the liveliness of Bridget's voice and flew up the stairs after telling the kitchen to prepare hot water for mistress.

Arm in arm, the sisters went Bridget's chambers...Celestine seething with questions and Bridget dying to tell her of all that had happened.

"I was in a race, Celestine. A horse race against Vortimer's best man and I won!" She at last said in her room.

"Whatever are you talking about, Bridget? You sound like some foolish girl."

"And the land! The land was so beautiful and Vortimer thought so as well! He called it bona terra! Good ground, that's what it is like up there, Celestine! Rich, fertile ground! Miles of it with the most extraordinary rivers and lakes! And the great sea at its end!"

This is not good—fertile ground—best to let her get it all out of her system.

"Some wine, my love?"

"God, yes! And my bath!"

Bridget allowed her sister to oversee the drawing of her bath and the setting of their meal. Celestine helped Bridget strip off her road-soiled clothes and tossed them on the floor to be cleaned. Bridget slipped gingerly and gratefully into the steaming water with a heartfelt sigh. "Is anything so wonderful as a bath?" She asked of no one in particular. Celestine dismissed Gwenthe and Mathilde who desperately wanted to speak with Bridget about her trip. Looking at her recumbent sister, Celestine paced quietly.

"Your trip went well, I take it?"

"Marvelously tiring, but marvelous none the less," she replied dreamily, eyes closed.

"And Vortimer?"

"Fine. Annoying at times but fine. He does have the quickest temper, Celestine! However, he bet on me to win the race—and I did!"

"Perhaps this was some ploy to win your...trust and affection."

"Perhaps, but unlikely. Not according to Glendon, his lieutenant, anyway."

"And he was a gentleman?"

"Oh, yes! Always quite proper is Vortimer."

Celestine mulled this last response and was satisfied that Bridget had not done anything that might require the repair of Calgwyn's elixirs. She handed Bridget a goblet of wine who giggled and recounted the wineskin reward after the race.

"Well, dearest sister, it is time to rest for now, I think. You have had an arduous journey—one that no woman should have been subjected to. I want you to rest and soak and get a good meal inside of you. There is much happening here as well."

"Such as?"

"Your wedding for one thing. That rat-like man of Vortimer has weaseled the priest into having it in a grove!"

"Splendid." Replied Bridget, suddenly recalling her namesake.

"Indeed! What will your friend Mother Maria think?"

"Oh."

"And you haven't forgotten what the wedding obligation entails, have you? 'Celestine', she mimicked Bridget's plea, 'I am going to be married and need your help.'"

"No," said Celestine, as the conjugal liability was rudely rubbed against her nose, "I have not forgotten. When will the ceremony be performed?" She asked listlessly.

"Not until Calgwyn gets here, that is for certain."

"Calgwyn? Your woman with the herbs?"

"If not chaste…" said Celestine.

"Careful." Bridget answered.

Celestine quietly refilled her sister's goblet, encouraging her to drink, relax.

"How many men went with you?"

"A few hundred, most of them remain and are building our fortress, our temporary home."

Celestine cringed inwardly when Bridget said 'our'.

"A fortress? It is not right that you should be made to live so miserably, poppet. It would solve many problems if you stayed here, would it not? Many women of class absolve themselves of staying at their husband's side all the time. He can always send for you after this dreadful business is done."

Bridget thought a moment, "No. That is where I belong, not necessarily by his side but there! There is something, some force…it is so difficult to put into words. Don't laugh at me, but somehow I feel 'powerful' when I am there."

Celestine recalled the dark energies she felt at the Stones but said nothing; encouraging Bridget to drink, talk.

A knock on the door was followed by Mathilde who brought in a tray of cheese, meat and bread. She wanted desperately to kiss her mistress but only smiled in silence, not wanting to stir the whipping tongue of Celestine who dismissed her with a wave of her hand.

Calgwyn? Calgwyn, where are you? Our time is like the tide, nothing can stop for long the forces that are in motion.

Celestine had become quite accomplished in disguising thoughts and feelings with her array of practiced expressions; her face masking her soul, she brought her sister some bits of meat and cheese, which she devoured greedily.

My sister doesn't eat, she feeds. Look at her there, soaking like a lump!

Celestine looked hard, trying to see through a man's eyes. Her breasts were not overly large but proportionate, the nipples pink and erect from the water. True, her hair had some appeal but her face was rather plain when all was said and done and her brows were heavy and dark over her green eyes. Her arms and thighs were thick like a man's. Satisfied that there was nothing overly attractive about her sister, Celestine allowed herself the freedom of a cup of wine and sat next to Bridget who languished in the warm water. Bending over, she kissed Bridget lightly on the mouth. "Everything will be all right, poppet. I swear."

Bridget smiled, comfort seeping into her bones.

A timid knock on the door came before Gwenthe's gasping declaration that Calgwyn had arrived.

"You stay here, poppet. Refresh yourself, have some more wine. I will see to my woman. Everything will be all right. I swear." She repeated.

Bridget lost sense of time and place as she drifted somewhere between consciousness and dreaming—she only surfaced to awareness when the water finally chilled uncomfortably—still, it was difficult to leave its wet caress for the insulting chill of the air in the darkened room. With a grudging effort she pushed herself up and scrambled for something warm to put on.

"Mathilde! Gwenthe!" She shouted.

The two women rushed in, Gwenthe finding a heavy wrap and Mathilde hugging the dripping, shivering body of their mistress. Together they dried Bridget and covered her in a thick robe as they stuffed her beneath some blankets. The shivering passed, Bridget laughed and began to speak excitedly, relating all that had happened on her trip north.

"Was he good, milady? Was he sufficiently sized?" Mathilde asked innocently.

"Would you stop it?" She giggled. "I am a Christian woman."

"And what difference would that be making? You are a woman and he is a man! Does his bad leg extend anywhere else?"

"Stop it! I will hear nothing further, understood?"

"He does have lovely eyes," Mathilde continued as if deaf. "So deep and

195

serious—and his shoulders, my lord!"

"Mathilde, you little tramp, leave our lady be! She is just about getting warmed up and refreshed and you are doing nothing to help her!"

"Right! Right you are!" Hopping off the bed she brought a fresh goblet of wine and lit a candle.

"We missed you so much, milady," stated Gwenthe. "And we are glad to have you back with us."

"And I missed the both of you, dreadfully missed you! I have a question to ask the both of you, a favor."

The two nodded.

"I will be going to live with Vortimer. Our new home will not be so grand as this, there will be difficult times, trying times—you understand?"

They nodded again."I need you by my side but I will not have you there unless you are willing to bear the burden. I could command you there but that is not what we are about, is it? I want you there as my companions." Bridget's eyes began to tear slightly and Mathilde and Gwenthe hugged and kissed her, protesting that there was no where else on earth they wanted to be than at her side…all three began crying, feeling silly as their devotion and love expressed itself in tears.

"Tomorrow will be a busy one, milady," said Gwenthe who began straightening herself as she wiped her moist cheeks with the back of her hand. "You should really try to rest."

"Leave a candle burning for me, then," said Bridget as she began getting comfortable. The two women kissed their mistress on each cheek and closed the door.

Yes. Let the candle burn, my dears. I feel the presence of the Hooded Man here in this place and he frightens me—He was gone when we were away but now, now he is waiting.

Bridget closed her eyes and thought about dreams, the power of the spirits, the Hooded Man. Had she learned anything other than that he scared her? No. Had the apparition harmed her in the dream or in the physical world? Again, no. Had he even threatened her? No, but he exuded horrific dread—is that what frightened her? Analyzing the Hooded Man in this manner imparted a small degree of comfort as she examined the fears up close, peeling them apart. So involved was she with the Hooded Man that she did not even think of Vortimer or the morrow until it was too late and she could think no more s sleep overpowered her.

He was there again, ominous and darkly quiet but, she realized, not intimidating. She tried to examine him but found it difficult to overcome the residual terrors. The coppery smell of blood filled the damp air…he held up his hands for her to look at—turned them—and vanished. The rest of the night was dreamless and pitifully short.

The day began as Gwenthe and Mathilde burst through Bridget's door, barely allowing her time to sit up. Mathilde pushed her into the toilet as Gwenthe set out her food.

"Hurry," they declared. "The sun is already up and there is much to do."

"What?" asked Bridget groggily as she sat and allowed Mathilde to work the knots from her twisted hair with painful tugs.

"Your wedding will be tomorrow, your dress needs to be fitted, your hair prepared, your clothes, our things, need to be packed. Peter has allowed himself the task of organizing the feast—there won't be many guests—so many things!"

The sound of the convent bells floated through the window just then and the two women looked at Bridget who just yawned and said, "Why bother? We are too busy right now. Besides, I will see the priest tomorrow."

"You will also see your friend, the abbess," said Mathilde. "I understand that she insisted on being present at the wedding."

I would have made a good nun, a devoted lover and follower of Jesus but He did not hear my prayer a lifetime ago. I am on a different path now—but she was a good friend and a nice woman—I will ask her blessing.

Two seamstresses came in without knocking and began stripping and dressing Bridget who felt calmly detached, grateful that others were making the decisions. Made from silk and linen, her gown was two shades of beige and fawn. Simply cut, it covered her shoulders, arms and hips as it offered up her breasts for examination. The two women tugged this way and that as their fingers fritted and marked the fabric. Satisfied, they removed it quickly and bundled it off, leaving Bridget to dress in her regular clothes.

"What is Vortimer doing today? Where is he?"

"I don't know, milady—but it is bad luck to see him on the eve of your wedding. Your sister is carrying on so and will be here shortly. Some of the lords and ladies are here as well and they have gifts!"

"Then what am I to do today?"

"Do? Lady, tomorrow you will be wed, there will be a feast after which you will go to bed with your new husband. The next morning you and he, along with

Mathilde and myself, will head north. Everything you cherish needs to be packed, all that you need will have to be trundled onto carts and transported to your new home!"

Struck by the finality of it all Bridget took a calming breath and said, "Let us begin. All my clothes, the great chest and the lesser must come. I do not care what my father says, I must have these carpets and my bath. That crucifix over there," she pointed, "and whatever I may have in my toilet. Have I left anything out?"

"Well, milady, you have," snickered Mathilde.

"Yes?"

"Your bed, milady."

"Yes, of course, my bed…and all the linens."

"Of course,…but we can't begin taking it apart until the morning after next."

Bridget hesitated for a moment, realizing that first she and Vortimer must sleep in it the night of the wedding—tomorrow night! This would be her last day as a virgin! Shuddering, she began rifling aimlessly through her chest of clothes hoping that the mindless activity would occupy her thoughts—it didn't.

My last night sleeping alone; my next to last night sleeping here! So many endings.

Her hands ran over hosiery, tunics and gloves—each article had a particular event associated with it; a pair of fine, soft boots, her favorite, given to her by Uncle Glamorgan one Christmas brought a flood of warming, innocent memories—life itself had been sheltered and comforting—she felt her eyes begin to well up but held then in check.

I am the Princess Bridget! I am the Princess Bridget! I thrashed the thieving steward with my bare hands! I was mistress of my father's castle and will soon be the mistress of my own. No man rides better than me and no man will own me! I am no sniveling child—I will do this.

"Keep these boots aside, I will wear them on my ride home."

Gwenthe and Mathilde looked at each other quickly when Bridget said "home" but continued packing without interruption.

"I need some wine. Mathilde, would you go to the kitchen and get me a flagon?"

"A bit early for that, milady. Perhaps you might like some…"

"Your mistress has asked for wine," said Celestine who walked in abruptly, "not your insolence, trollop. Fetch it now and be smart about it."

Lowering her eyes, Mathilde scurried out of the room.

"Packing your things I see," as she kissed Bridget on each cheek. "How do you feel, poppet?"

"Honestly? I feel resigned but determined. I am nervous but who wouldn't be in my situation. Gwenthe," she said, "don't pack Vortimer's shawl. I will wear it tomorrow."

"Poppet, it doesn't go with anything you will be wearing," Celestine protested.

"It will go with me, and that is enough."

Not accustomed to Bridget's sudden obstinacy, Celestine ignored it as she placed the basket she was carrying on the bed—Bridget heard bottles click together.

"Si non caste," said Celestine.

If not chaste

"Tanem caute," Bridget replied.

Then careful

Mathilde appeared at that moment with two goblets and a pitcher filled to the brim with wine. "None for me, Bridget, perhaps later. Go on, perhaps it will cool your nerves."

Bridget laughed, "It is not my nerves, it's my stomach that is tied in knots!"

"This," she waved her hand about the room, "can be done later. We need some time alone. You two may go now."

Gwenthe and Mathilde looked at Bridget who nodded for them to leave. She sipped from her goblet, savoring its flavor. "Well, here we are Celestine. Or rather, here I am just waiting for the morrow," she glanced at the basket.

"There, there, my dear Bridget. It won't be that bad. The most difficult part will be keeping your wits about you and I am confident that you can do that. Do you remember all that we discussed?"

"Perfectly! Your directions have been foremost in my brain."

"Good. Now sit here by me on the bed and let us see what Calgwyn has concocted for you."

Bridget sat as Celestine removed three bottles filled with a dark liquid, the tops sealed with wax.

"I am told that you need only drink a mouthful and that it should be done within a few hours of...mating." Celestine said. "Calgwyn says it does not taste badly and that, you know, there will be some bleeding the following day."

Bridget took one of the bottles, held it with both hands and peered closely. "And this will prevent a child?"

"There is no guarantee but I understand it lessens the chances dramatically."

"Have you used it, Celestine? You have had no child."

"Yes, I have poppet," she lied casually.

Bridget stood suddenly, "I must go to my toilet!"

"What is the matter, sister?"

"Nothing. Just a moment." Bridget hurried from the bed into her private room which contained a low table, water pitched, basin, chamber pot, stool and returned a few minutes later.

"It appears that the elixir works better than we had dreamed, Celestine. It is my time."

"What! Really! Such timing can only be a gift, a portent! That your monthly flow has begun on the eve of your wedding is…it cannot be chance…destiny." Celestine exclaimed with dramatic flourish.

"I suppose it was not my stomach that was nervous after all," said Bridget.

"No matter, poppet. He will not have the insolence to attempt anything at this time—no man would. However, it is a very convenient happenstance, is it not? Proof of your virginity will be found on the stained sheets and the rabble will believe that you and Vortimer have behaved like newlyweds," she clucked. "However, a word of caution! Wear your wadding tightly and do not let your women know under any circumstances! Hide them, burn them, anything!"

Bridget sipped her wine, listening carefully, knowing that so much depended on what she was learning from Celestine. "What of the bottles?"

"Well, they will not be necessary for at least a week. Wrap them yourself in some soft cloth, something that you can get too easily and quickly. When they are unpacked you must be there personally to safeguard them."

Bridget listened, excited to be the central player in so grand a conspiracy. She refilled her goblet. "I am hungry. This time of month always makes me hungry! And I feel so restless! Like I could burst! I just want this over and done with."

"Waiting, anticipating is the most difficult thing," Celestine agreed.

"I would love to go riding right now." Bridget continued. "And just keep on riding and never look back! Go some place where no one knows me!"

They listened to the muted comings and goings of people within and without the castle, allowing a comfortable silence to blossom.

"You know," Bridget said at last, "what I regret the most?"

Celestine arched her brow.

"That we never spent more time together in sisterly union, like this. It took this tragedy to bring us together and that is so sad!" Bridget wiped a small tear from the corner of her eye and took another gulp of wine. ""Why is it that we discover our true friends only during times of difficulty? Oh, Celestine, I am only trying to tell you I love you and will be forever obliged to you! You cannot begin to imagine how comforting your presence and counsel have been!"

"Oh, sister," said Celestine who hugged Bridget and placed her wet cheek against her shoulder. For the briefest of moments Celestine felt a surge of pity and remorse, which she squashed as she would some inconvenient insect.

Is this not perfect? Dear poppet, you and I will be so close, you have no inkling. You do become so maudlin after a few cups! Ah, well, what is it they say "In wine, truth"? Then I must never drink, eh?

"There, my love," as she rocked her gently. "I am your older sister, it is my duty towards you, an obligation I accept with love." She smiled at Bridget who was now blubbering. "Why don't I get us some food?"

Bridget nodded as she went to wash her face. Celestine summoned Mathilde and had a platter of cheese and meats brought up.

When Bridget came out, her eyes reddened but with a dry face, they ate—Celestine nibbling as Bridget filled her mouth so rapidly that chewing was a chore. The room began to darken and Celestine lit two candles. Together they laughed and spoke of their girlhood days, the time before they graduated to womanhood. Bridget did not want the moment to end, preferring that the evening would go on forever, vainly attempting to halt time and the approaching tomorrow.

"I must go to Theodorus," said Celestine finally. "Father has given us a room in the castle this time. I am sure that the men have been in their cups all night."

"Vortimer, too?"

"Of course."

Bridget clutched Celestine's hand as they headed towards the door, not wanting to be alone.

"Never mind, Bridget. All will be well. Is your padding secured?"

"Yes."

"Do you want one of your women to sleep with you?"

Bridget thought for a moment and decided against it. She was not some child afraid of the dark. They kissed one last time and Bridget closed the door—alone. Taking the remainder of the wine, she reinforced the woolen swath between her legs and slipped the three bottles of dark liquid into boots that had already been bundled. Extinguishing one of the candles she laid in bed, certain she would not sleep.

The Hooded Man did not visit her that night. Instead her dreams were filled with confusing images of strangers in stranger places and disjointed emotions. It was still dark when her women entered with the seamstresses. Bridget sprung from the bed, cleaned herself between her legs, stuffed the sodden cloth beneath a corner of carpet and replaced it with another. Washing her face with tepid water, Bridget refused to think.

She allowed the solemn Mathilde to brush her hair. Gwenthe fastened the heavy crucifix around her neck, the cold metal lying between her breasts. Bridget accepted their ministrations stoically. Standing now, Mathilde placed the gilded scarf behind her neck and adjusted its length just so.

"You do look beautiful, milady! An angel!"

Oddly, Bridget felt the same way. Unaccustomed to being in finery and pampered, she felt special.

Just as I should be! I am a princess after all on my wedding day! I feel exactly the way I felt before that race against Albin. I cannot believe I feel so nervous! I mean, there is nothing to this, after all!

A sharp knock on the door momentarily distracted the room's women.

"Who's there?" Cried Gwenthe who just finishing Bridget's hair, having it flowing on the tops of her shoulders.

"Why, a friend of the young mistress, that's who! Varduc, friend to both milady and milord, counselor to him that she will soon wed. I only desire entry on this the most auspicious day of her young life so that…"

Gwenthe threw open the door, stopping the small man in mid-sentence. Bowing quickly to the women around the room, he at last faced Bridget.

"Ah, young mistress," he piped in that peculiar but not unpleasant tone, "the clothes do not do you justice! You are magnificent! Inspiring! My young master will be more in awe of you than he is already! You humble us with your majesterial deportment!"

"Sir," cried Mathilde who was already inching forward, preparing to push Varduc out the door, "You do not belong here in milady's room!"

"Nonsense, sweet girl! As my young mistress is to be wed to my young master I have every right and indeed, an obligation to be here," as he headed towards Bridget who stood mutely by. Standing before her, he bowed deeply, his voice dropping an octave.

"My dear young mistress, permit me, a humble servant, to extend to you this unworthy gift crafted by my own hands."

From beneath his robe he pulled a small wreath that he held gingerly for Bridget's approval. The green-lacquered leaves of holly shone brightly in the dim room. Entwined were white and red berries. "A simple crown, my young mistress, a product of the earth that signifies life, growth and change. It would honor me, your servant, if you would condescend to wear it on this day."

"Peasant women wear this on their wedding day, don't they?" Bridget asked.

"Aye, some do, young mistress."

"I am one with my people, one with my lord, Varduc. You honor me for your thoughtfulness." Bridget stooped and the small man placed the crown on her head.

"My first wedding gift," she giggled, mindful of her first meeting, she was careful not to let any part of her touch Varduc.

"Not to worry," he whispered noticing her awkwardness, "the melding only happens once."

Bridget smiled shyly, embarrassed that he noticed her discomfort.

"And how is my lord this morning?"

"Vortimer? He is excellent! What man would not be having soaring spirits to be married to such as you, young mistress!"

"Shush, little man! You go with your young lord and leave us women here as is proper! Who knows how you managed to get here!" said Gwenthe as she began crowding Varduc out the door with her prodigious bulk.

"Very well! Very well! The mystery of women shall remain so!" He giggled, trying to bow out gracefully and failing as the door slammed him out.

Gwenthe turned to look at Bridget who stood bemusedly. She looked regal, she thought, proud. And the holly crown was the perfect touch, she admitted.

"Gwenthe?"

"Just thinking, milady. Just thinking." She hugged Bridget with her beefy arms, fairly forcing the air from Bridget's lungs, tears of joy and regret streaked her generous cheeks. "I do love milady and will follow her anywhere," she blubbered without shame.

"As do I," said Mathilde who joined the pair. All three hugged and laughed and cried as kisses removed tears. It was some moments before Bridget managed to disengage herself, laughing and crying simultaneously.

"Now look what you have done to me," she cried in mock anger. "I look positively bedraggled!"

Composing themselves, Gwenthe and Mathilde straightened Bridget's clothes, her shawl, crucifix and the crown of holly that radiated a tinge of green over all.

"Let's go, then," said Gwenthe, "and get married."

Bridget found herself entering a state of mental haziness, walking erect she allowed herself to be guided down the steps and through the great hall out the door where a small pony cart waited for her. It was unseemly for a bride's feet to touch the ground as she walked to her wedding and so she was taken to the grove in this fashion. Everywhere along the rutted route the town's people, merchants and peasants with naked children stopped to bow courteously. Bridget, her eyes looking straight ahead as her hands clutched the cart for balance, did manage to see some giggling children who were hiding shyly behind the great skirt of their mother. Smiling, Bridget offered them a wave that made them point excitedly and wave with abandon—Bridget replaced her somber expression with an unabashed grin.

I feel like I am on display but why shouldn't I be?

She began waving and smiling more freely now, determined to enjoy the moment if not for herself then for her people for whom the wedding was all about.

It was a morning of the bluest sky she could remember, the sun was warm and she savored its warmth, wanting to embrace it. Birds called noisily as the cart continued along the troublesome road. Coming up to a wooded area Bridget spied her father and his counselor. Together, Gwaldner and Pardorous walked to the cart that could go no further.

"You look absolutely beautiful, Bridget," said her father as he held her hands and kissed her cheek.

"Indeed you do, Princess," joined Pardorous. "You do us proud! Excuse me for blurting, but you awe us!"

Bridget, erect, placed her hands in the elbows of both men who escorted her into the wooded area along a hard-trodden path. Shaded now, Bridget smelled the wet earth as the trio winded down and down, carefully avoiding any ankle twisting roots that snaked along the ground. The path led to a wide clearing where she saw Vortimer—tall and brooding, wearing a simple tunic of white linen, cinched with finely crafted leather and matching hose, he was freshly shaven and his close-shorn hair glistened.

Varduc and Glendon stood by his side.

Father Junius stood officiously upon a rock beside a small, dark pond and motioned both Bridget and Vortimer to stand before him. Bridget was overcome with a sense of finality and dread but suddenly found herself excited at the prospect of embarking upon a new adventure. Standing to Vortimer's left, she looked into his eyes but he was focused upon the priest.

"Clasp your hands before me," he intoned.

Vortimer turned to Bridget and took both her hands in hers. She took one final look at his hands and certain that they did not belong to the Hooded Man, closed her eyes.

"We are here before God and man to join this man and woman in matrimony. They come here to this place, this place created by He who sees all and whose blessing we invoke. Do any here disagree?"

Bridget at last opened her eyes and locked into Vortimer's that bore intently into hers. She noticed the slightest start of a smile that immediately disappeared but felt his hands squeeze hers the tiniest bit. She squeezed in reply.

"May I have the ring?"

Varduc stepped forward and handed the priest a small gold band.

"With this ring, wrought from gold, we join these two in holy matrimony before man, the Church and before God!"

With the greatest of solemnity he took Bridget's left hand from Vortimer's grasp and attempted to place it on her fourth finger…it would not fit.

No! No! No! It has to fit! It absolutely must!

Bridget was about to begin crying when Vortimer took the ring, placed it on her small finger and whispered softly into her ear, "It is only but a ring, nothing more. I shall get you another."

Bridget felt her heart break slightly as it slid onto her smallest finger.

"This is my hand, lord. That is your ring and it fits just perfectly." she whispered back.

"For what God has wrought, we are grateful. Go forth and be fruitful."

Uncertain as to what was to follow, Vortimer and Bridget were relieved for Varduc's trilling voice, "Splendid! Oh, yes, priest! Splendid! Never has there been such a beautiful pair! My young master with his young mistress! The finest stallion with an unsurpassable mare! Oh, yes!"

The small gathering laughed and came up to hug both Bridget and Vortimer who hugged back in return. They allowed themselves to be led back up the winding path by Varduc who had them step over a broom. "Just a formality, nothing more." Together now and holding hands, they stepped into the waiting cart and headed back towards the castle. The rutted track was lined with more people than before. The elders bowed as their youngsters gamboled, flinging flowers and seeds at the pair. Bridget laughed at the intense merriment, free from the uncertainty that had been but was now no more.

The gates of the castle were open wide for the small cart that bore the newlyweds who then entered the hall where they were met by a raucous thunder of clapping and cheering. Peter, Bridget's steward, dressed in his finest, bowed deeply and gravely, oblivious to the frivolous urgings of the guests. "My lord, my lady, permit me to seat you at the table of honor."

Bridget looked about quickly, relieved to see that new, recently dampened straw covered the floor. Peter had buckets of water placed conspicuously throughout the hall; fire, always a threat, was more so now that the congregation was awash with ale and wines.

"Peter you have done magnificently. Peter, I shall miss you."

"And I will miss you as well, milady." He said as he escorted husband and wife to a single small table on the raised stage.

A chorus of shouts and stamping of feet shook the hall as Bridget and Vortimer stood lamely, looking at the assembled guests who were demanding they kiss; some of the more drunken were demanding much more. Vortimer kissed Bridget hurriedly on the cheek and the couple sat down.

Has there ever been such an embarrassment of people ever assembled together? And these are my father's people! What must Vortimer think? I feel absolutely, positively miserable. What could be worse?

Bridget looked around rapidly and uttered a quiet prayer of gratitude that the minstrel who was at their betrothal was happily absent. Looking about now she spied her abbess sitting with quiet dignity at the fore table, a goblet of wine before her. Their glances touched and both smiled, Bridget immensely relieved, hoping that some part of her stable past would act as an anchor in the current maelstrom. Over to the other side she saw Celestine sitting with her husband and a few of the other nobles; Bridget waved timidly and Celestine graced her with a radiant, encouraging smile. King Gwaldner took this moment to stride into the hall, his face beaming. The assembly stood and quieted down as he made his way to the platform where Vortimer and Bridget now stood.

"Friends," he said, turning to the crowd, "We are here today to celebrate the marriage of my daughter Bridget to Vortimer, my new son-in-law!" A wave of applause and shouts followed. Turning to Vortimer, he said, "I believe we have some business, young man."

Vortimer nodded dumbly, stepped down and knelt before his king, whatever rustling and noise existed, now ceased.

"I, Vortimer, holder of the land north of the Wythe, am your man, beholden to you, to bear you in faith of life against all your enemies, against all men who desire you ill. I swear this freely and with an open heart before all here this day."

Gwaldner looked slowly around the room, his face grave. "Whomever bruises this young man, wounds me. Whomever helps him, earns my faith and my love." He held out his hands to Vortimer who took them in his and kissed them. It was as if a dam for noise had been breached, so great was shouting that fine lines of dust drifted from the rafters and candles flickered. Pulling Vortimer to his feet, king and vassal embraced and kissed. A small band of musicians, previously hidden behind a partition, broke out in merry song as Vortimer joined Bridget.

"Did you spend last night memorizing that?"

"Last night? All week!"

Servants appeared and began bringing out trays of chicken, pork and lamb. Flagons of wine and ale were emptied and immediately replenished as the excitement broke out in earnest now.

Sister Maria, the abbess, seemingly oblivious to the rabble, suddenly found the oddest looking man she had ever seen sitting next to her.

"A fine and beautiful woman and a lovely bride! Wouldn't you agree? Not fitting, I suppose, for my young master there, but such is life!" he chirped into her bent ear.

Turning to face him squarely, she could not help but smile at the funny, little man with the most compelling countenance she had ever seen. "Your master is a fine and handsome man, sir. I only pray he does credit towards my Bridget, a girl whom I have cherished and whose presence I have missed at chapel."

"You rebuke me, good woman! I may be old but I can hear it in your voice, a voice that bathes me like some sonorous balm! My young master has nothing but the greatest respect for you and the church, trust me."

"And you would be?"

"Varduc, dear abbess, counselor to the young man sitting there with Bridget. Shall we go pay our respects?"

"I really do not think this is the proper time to do so," she replied.

young master," said Varduc, "to allow the peasants one season of hunting. Let them stock up on all the meat they can." Vortimer was uncertain, knowing that the land and all it contained essentially belonged to him and that by right no one was allowed to hunt game there—still, these would be people risking their all on a promise. He finally agreed that it would be a good idea, but only for this one season.

The night before the wedding was the first he could recall that he did not fall asleep immediately. It wasn't just Bridget and all the warnings that Varduc had given, nor was it the sure threat of the Vikings that kept him tossing in fits and starts—it was the land. The unexpected stewardship of a rich land was something he had never dreamed of, being content with the stipends and rewards that came from successful campaigns. But this, this was something enormous and not in his control. He would have someplace to return to, a home. Varduc assured him in private that Bridget and only Bridget, could help him. All these things kept flying through his head as the sky darkened outside the hall.

The revelers were becoming unarousable and the breathless dancers were slow to respond to the exhausted musicians. Bridget joined Vortimer, her face and breasts shone with sweat. In spite of it all, she looked as though she could continue till dawn. Varduc approached their table and whispered just loudly enough for them to hear, "Now, young masters, it is time to make your escape. Go to bed and sleep. Tomorrow we begin a great work."

No! Is it that time already! I am not prepared, I really am not!

Still, she did not resist when Vortimer grabbed her hand and led her away from the table towards the stairs that led to her room. All that had happened in the years before now meant nothing to her.

A single candle was lit on the dresser, its flame steady and true. She wanted to snuff it, to be in total darkness but knew that this would be something only a child would do.

"I must change by myself, lord. I…I am a virgin and I have…"

"Why don't you change in your room," he said quietly, "if that would make you feel more at ease."

She almost cried from gratitude but instead hurried to her toilet, closing the door quietly. Forgetting the candle in her excitement to undress in solitude, Bridget found herself in inky blackness, alone with just the tripping of her heart. She took two deep breaths, removed her shawl, folded it gently and placed it on the floor. Unclasping the crucifix, she let it fall to the floor. Her hands trembling, she began to undo the gown that was damp and stuck with sweat and stepped out of it. She felt around for the basin of water and splashed some water on her face. Feeling better, she stood and at last removed the sodden pad between her legs and wrapped it in a small cloth. Opening the door slightly, she was able to see the dimly lit bed with Vortimer beneath the covers.

I am the Princess Bridget.

She walked quickly to the edge of the bed, once again forgetting to blow out the candle, and hastily went beneath the thin blanket, making sure not to touch any part of her husband. Lying in silence for a moment, Vortimer turned on his side and propped his head up with his bent arm.

"You are very beautiful, Bridget, and a marvelous woman. I am proud to be your husband."

This is not what I expected! What is the matter with me? Does he find me that ugly?

"Thank you for that, lord."

"It is only the truth."

"Vortimer, I have never been with a man, you know that. And I, I am not wise or experienced and I…"

"Bridget," he said gently, "I have never been with you before, either. Consider me your virgin."

So unexpected and so gentle was his reply that Bridget began to giggle warmly, the giggle grew into a laugh that was followed by uncontrolled tears of happiness. Her laughter was infectious and soon Vortimer began laughing as well. Gwenthe and Mathilde, crouched outside the bedroom door did not know what to make of this at all.

Still lying flat on her back, she wiped the tears from her eyes and composed herself.

"There is one other thing, lord."

"Yes?"

"It is my time of the month to bleed. It is something I have no control over and I…"

Overcome with relief with this news, Vortimer did not hear the rest. It was the perfect, the only reason he could have for not consummating the marriage. Varduc had warned him against imposing his will on her and never having been with a virgin or a wife had placed him in mental turmoil.

"It is not the end of the earth, Bridget, is it?"

"No," she replied, "I suppose not. But I only wanted to, you know, please you."

She turned and propped herself on her elbow, gazing into his face that was half in shadow.

"This is pleasing me," he said as he kissed her gently on the lips.

Even though Bridget did not respond, he felt himself stiffen—something that could not be helped. He inched his hips back, not wanting to alarm her, not now.

"Why were you so quiet tonight?"

"Just so many things going on and too rapidly. I am a man who is used to some control in his life although I now believe that I have deluded myself all these years."

"I have felt the same way as well," she replied. "All I ever wanted to do was join the convent or be sent away to some great court. Is that being childish, silly?"

"No more than any others."

"Have you traveled, Vortimer? You must have! What was the grandest thing you ever saw?"

He thought for a moment, started to speak, stopped and closed his eyes. "The pyramids of Egypt, elephants, Leviathan, men black as ash, monkeys, mountains so high they are forever covered in snow and a library filled with scrolls from floor to ceiling."

"I have heard of the pyramids from my tutor. What are they? And what is an elephant?"

How do I describe to you, Bridget, the grandeur and the majesty of the Pyramids? You look at them and gaze in wonderment at their majestical size and beauty. What can I give you to even compare them to? And an elephant. That wondrous beast with the trunk that could crush the living air from your lungs, how do I tell you of that or of his massive legs? How do I explain these things? And the mighty Leviathan that cruises the black waters and blasts steam from a hole in the top of his head, how?

Hesitatingly, in the darkened room, his head propped on his elbow, Vortimer tried to describe all that he had seen. Slowly at first and then with increasing confidence he not only attempted to describe these things, but to impart their emotional impact as well. Bridget stopped him frequently, asking for details or scolding him for making these things up. Vortimer felt his erection subside as he and Bridget spoke.

She has a keen mind, this one! There is still something else about her, however, something very deep.

And so the night continued, each sharing some small part of their lives. Years later it would be a matter of contention between them as to who fell asleep first.

The sky was hardly light in the east when Mathilde and Gwenthe knocked timidly on the bedroom door. Vortimer was the first to awaken and had them enter.

"My lord!" said Mathilde who looked at Vortimer's muscular shoulders as he sat up in bed.

"Yes. You must be Mathilde and that woman behind you is Gwenthe. Am I right so far?"

"Oh, you be more than right, my lord!"

Gwenthe was muttering under her breath as she set up a basin of warm water.

"There's food waiting for the both of you downstairs, my lord," Gwenthe said dryly, not gazing at Vortimer directly.

"Thank you both."

With that, Gwenthe tugged Mathilde's sleeve and led her out the door.

Vortimer stretched and gently shook Bridget's shoulder. He shook a bit harder, whispering loudly.

"Yes. Yes!"

Oh my! We fell asleep and nothing, nothing happened! Oh, how wonderful! Oh, I must look terrible and I am naked and he is here and I feel the blood between my legs!

"Close your eyes."

"What?"

"Just close your eyes."

She watched and when they were closed, scurried from the bed to her toilet. "You can get dressed in there!" She yelled from behind the door. "I will meet you in the hall."

"You are my wife," he said with no trace of humor. "We shall go down together as man and wife."

Bridget thought rapidly. "Then hand me my things while I clean up."

She listened as Vortimer rose from the bed and plodded heavily on the carpets. She heard some rustling and finally the door opened with his fist full of her clothes stuck through.

"Thank you."

Treat her as you did that little bird, isn't that what Varduc warned? Still, she is my wife, after all! What is a man supposed to do? Yet the sheets show that is her time, couldn't she have worn something?

Shrugging, Vortimer splashed the tepid water on his face and wonderer if he would ever become accustomed to such luxury as a real bed. Bridget called for a damp cloth, which he fetched and handed through the door. Bridget wiped the blood from her thighs and fixed the woolen pad as she pulled on her tights.

What am I worried about? Why should I really care what he thinks of the way I look? But that was nice last night…he must draw me a sketch of the elephant! Better, I will ask his lieutenant to see if he was lying! And people all black! How absurd!

Tugging on her tunic and boots, Bridget finally entered the room and went to the basin to rinse her face and clean her eyes.

He is tall! And his shoulders so broad. Is this how marriages begin? I didn't dream of the Hooded Man, so that is a good sign. What will the day be like? Is everything packed? What else do I need?

"Shall we go?" He asked. But it did not sound like a question to Bridget who dried her face quickly.

The hall still had remnants of the prior evening's celebrants sleeping in quiet corners with their dogs . The couple found the king, his counselor and Varduc sitting and eating."You will be leaving soon," said her father to Vortimer. "You have much to do and little time, I know. However, I will do all that I can and will be sending what you need. If something unforeseen happens, send a messenger. You have my daughter now, Vortimer and a land that only promises bounty. I am forgiving one year's tribute for your labors, you will need that for the winter."

"Your lord is gracious," replied Vortimer. "Your lord is also correct in that we have much to do and little time. Ready, Bridget?"

"I am always ready, Vortimer." She replied curtly.

Standing, they each hugged one another and the next moment she found herself on Alexander and headed out the gates. They rode so hard that conversation was only possible when they stopped to water the horses and even then it was for the briefest of moments. They took a slightly different route this time, Vortimer wanting to see more of Bone Tear.

Where are all my things? When will Gwenthe and Mathilde follow? My pad is sodden and I can't stand it! Too many questions and no answers! Is this it, then? That was my wedding? Vortimer is my husband?

All these and more occupied Bridget's consciousness so intensely that she found no joy in riding. It was not until the sun touched the horizon that they slowed to make camp. They were a small band, maybe fifty, she guessed. The tents and fires were set with military efficiency.

"What's the matter?" She asked, noticing Vortimer wincing with each step.

"This damned leg, Bridget! This cursed leg! Riding is difficult for me, that's all. It will pass. They ate that night with the rest of the troops. Bridget beginning to recognize faces and associating names to them. She found them funny, actually, with their grave ways that eventually gave way to a familiar yet respectful rapport. She listened as Vortimer spoke with them, answering and asking questions thoughtfully and in a voice she had to strain to hear.

That is how he does it! Look at him, he knows them each by name, places a hand on a shoulder or looks directly in their eyes. He doesn't laugh but always looks so grave.

She took the time to look at his face again, forgetting for the moment the way he limped. His eyes with deep intensity and his mouth opening only to speak and then quietly, factually. He was not above partaking from any cup or scrap of food that was offered. And though he joined their banter and shared their food, Bridget could not help but notice his reserve and commanding air that was so apparent in his bearing that it seemed to envelope him in an invisible cloud.

He never laughs, not really. Not from his belly. Look at how all the men follow him with their faces as he walks about; as if they were expecting some blessing or special attention. They hang on each word he speaks as if it were from God Himself!

She tried to imagine herself as one of the men, a soldier, but found it impossible. As a woman who happened to be his wife, however, she was successful.

He is not unhandsome and I much like the shorter hair. He carries himself well and is deliberate in his manner and countenance, yet there is some deep tension there, very deep, I can feel it. He is not like father nor like uncle Glamorgan—much different, my husband. Yet I can see how the men like him, admire him, even! He is confident or at least pretends to be.

All at once she thought of edge of the earth that met the open sea.

Others are like the waves that crash and make a fearful noise and then are gone; Vortimer is the current, the deep, hidden movement, powerful and relentless.

She surprised herself with this insight and consciously resolved to think no more on the matter.

The fires grew brighter now and once more Bridget knew it would be time for bed…with him. The men began drifting off to their respective posts as Vortimer wordlessly took her hand and headed towards their tent. Their two cots were placed side by side; they stripped silently and swiftly in the tent's gloom.

Vortimer stretched out and placed his arm so that Bridget might use it as a pillow—she lay on her side with her cheek pressed against the thick upper part.

"I am so very tired," she said. "You?"

"Riding tires me, yes. It doesn't tire you, does it? Staying on for too long aggravates my leg."

What of his leg? Was he born that way? I haven't even seen it. I wonder if it terribly scarred?

"May I ask you a question?" she asked quietly, unsure as to what exactly to ask and how.

"I'm sorry, Bridget, but I am tired and the story behind my leg is long and venomous; a topic that would undoubtedly keep me awake. Another time."

What am I, a child to be dismissed like that?

She turned on her left side, foregoing whatever support Vortimer's arm provided.

Vortimer let out a sigh and rolled onto his right, making sure that no part of their bodies touched. Bridget waited for him to offer some explanation, some apology but all she heard was his deepening breathing and the muffled sounds of the night. She was just beginning to drift off when she felt Vortimer's legs and arms began to twitch in small, spasmodic fits. Bridget rolled over to observe what she thought would be a comical entertainment, something to tease him about in the morning.

The only light that seeped into the tent was from the outside fires but it was enough to show the grimace on his face. His lips parted slightly as he uttered low moans and cries. Bridget listened as hard as she could but try as she might, could discern nothing intelligible from the mournful sounds. His arm movements were not random, she noticed, but more like defensive motions, as if fighting some invisible opponent. The scene repulsed yet entranced her in some obscene way, as if she was learning some secret he wanted hidden, buried.

The combative movements gave way to softer gestures as his cries diminished and eventually ceased. She looked at him now, his features yet unsoftened by sleep. Bridget began to feel a stirring in her that was as surprising as it was deep—a flood of pity welled up inside her and made its way out of her body in the form of silent tears that she did not wipe away. Her heart suddenly ached for a pain that was not her own.

Did I do this by mentioning his leg? Am I responsible for this bitter dream? Does it matter? I did nothing to intentionally hurt him. Vortimer, you are not the man you pretend to be are you?

She took her index finger and gently drew it over his brows, being careful not to awaken him. She moved closer and gently placed her head between his chest and shoulder, listening to his heart beating as her head rose and fell on each breath. In imperceptible degrees she began to nod off, feeling somehow secure knowing that she was in some way, protecting, healing him.

Vortimer awoke with a start, as soldiers do, finding Bridget snuggled close against him. An immediate erection ensued and he closed his eyes and laid his head back down in the dark.

What was it we were talking about last night? She seemed angered by something yet here she is by my side. Varduc, where the hell are you? I want her! The way she moves, her confidence and manner, her willingness to come up here! The smell of her hair and the touch of her skin against mine…lying down we are just the right height, she and I.

He listened to the sounds outside, recognizing the movements of the posted guards. Immediately and against his wishes, his brain began formulating plans for the day. When they would arrive at the fortress, examination of its progress, scouting and manpower estimates, supplies or lack thereof.

Enough! Let me just lie here. Let me breathe the foggy air.

Ironically, the more he allowed himself to forget stratagems, the more intense his erection became till it became a throbbing pain. He laughed to himself, amazed by his current circumstances yet cautiously happy.

Happiness? Me? These two things have never met before, I think. Damn, but she feels good next to me! As if her skin was fused with mine.

Putting Varduc's warnings aside, Vortimer moved so very carefully and extricated himself from Bridget's nocturnal embrace. He propped his head on his crooked arm and looked at her face in peaceful repose. He kissed her forehead, her nose and her lips with the gentleness of a youth. Bridget stirred slowly and he kissed her again on the mouth. Her eyes closed, Bridget was suddenly wracked by so many emotions that coursed through her.

Vortimer is kissing me! My husband! My! Oh, my!

Forgetting all of Celestine's prohibitions, Bridget's tongue danced with Vortimer's, unmindful of the way her body responded independent of her own thoughts.

So gentle, he is so very gentle! And soft and he tastes good.

She felt her nipples blossom.

He pulled away as she opened her eyes.

"Good morning."

"Good morning," she replied, somewhat breathlessly.

How did that happen? What happened? I cannot believe the way I feel—I never knew a kiss could do that! Why did he stop? Oh, why did he stop! No! Celestine warned me…be careful! Careful, don't let on.

"You had a dream last night, Vortimer. You were talking in your sleep."

"Really? I don't recall any. What did I say?"

"Oh, nothing I could make out. Gibberish."

He laughed that small laugh that Bridget found so fascinating and boyish.

Celestine, this would be so easy if Vortimer was not who he is!

"We will arrive today, around noon, I think," he said, his gray eyes looking into hers, the memory of that sudden kiss still affecting the erection that he tried unsuccessfully to will down. "I hope you won't be disappointed."

"How so?"

"This is a fortress, an outpost. The conveniences will be few and the days hard."

"And do you think I am not a capable woman, Vortimer? Is that what you believe? This, all this, is my dowry to you!"

Bridget felt her ire rising.

"This is now ours! You said it yourself, 'good ground'. This good ground is where my home is. I know what you have to do, husband, I do. You must keep it! Defend it! I will do all in my power to help you. On that you may wager safely. Tell me truth?"

"Truth?"

"Yes, truth. Did you arrange for me to win that horse race?"

"I know that we barely know one another but know this: if I tell you something, it is in truth. I knew, or was fairly certain you would win. No, I did not arrange anything. The men would have found out about it eventually and that would have diminished you in their eyes more than losing."

"And how is it that you want them to see me?"

"As Vortimer's wife. Come, the sky is getting lighter and we must get moving."

Standing quickly, he turned his back to hide what was painfully obvious to him and he quickly dressed, listening to her do the same.

True to his estimate they arrived at the hottest part of the day, their bodies slicked with sweat. Even from a distance Bridget saw that the backs of the soldiers who were now constructing the fortress were red as holly berries, up close she saw they were wet with broken blisters—yet they worked without complaint. The camp looked pitifully meager, long timbers being planted deep into trenches and then lashed together and braced. It would take some time for real carpenters and smiths to arrive and strengthen the walls—but for now it was home.

Greetings were shouted back and forth between the new arrivals and the toilers as Vortimer sought Glendon.

This is no place for Bridget, I don't care what she thinks! It is too mean, too base.

"Vortimer?" she asked as they began to dismount.

"Yes."

"Are the boundaries for this building truly set?"

"No, not yet."

"Good," she said as she looked about with a critical eye. "Make it larger. This is home."

"It is a fortress."

"If you want to instill a faith in your men, vassals and peasants show them that you intend to remain for more than just a campaign."

Vortimer looked at her dourly, recalling Varduc's caution.

"I can feel it, Vortimer, I can," she said stubbornly.

"It will mean that our own dwelling will take longer to prepare," he replied.

"This," she cast her arm around, "is our dwelling, our home. Our residence is of no consequence to me."

"We will be living there," he pointed to a barely completed shed.

"It is sufficient, husband."

"Good, now let me find Glendon. Tether Alexander and I will return as soon as I can."

Bridget walked over the muddy earth to what would be their hall, Vortimer's Hall, and walked in. Just one story now, the sun shone through the gaps of the roofing planks. About half the size of her father's, Bridget did not see what was but what it could become.

The kitchen will be there and over there the throne. I want two sets of stairs leading upstairs. My God, but it is hot!

Without any windows, the airless room was as humid as a hot mist and sweat began to seep from her pores.

I think we should be better off in the tent for the next few nights. I can have my things unpacked here, though. When will Gwenthe and Mathilde get here? What will they think? So much to do! Too much to do! Order, I need a plan. First, I need to get out of this oven, my clothes are sticking.

Stepping outside, Bridget breathed in long and hard, determined to begin her duties as mistress of the castle. Walking around the hall's perimeter she was struck by how ramshackle it looked as compared to her father's. The memory of her father brought an unexpected rush of anger.

This is his doing! Not mine, not Vortimer's. I'll show him. I'll show him just what I can do! It may be mean and poor now but wait, wait till we finish! They'll all be begging to come here! We will have the richest of carpets and paintings and Celestine...

The thought of her sister brought her back to reality as harshly as stubbing her toe.

Celestine! Celestine! How I wish you were here. No, not really. It all looks so vile, nothing that you are used to! I need you for advice! There are so many things happening and too quickly. I need a plan. Isn't that what she would do? She is so practical. I need some wine—well, forget that for now, some ale would do. The bottles of that drink made by her woman! I have to get that! I will stop bleeding soon and Vortimer will demand what he thinks is his! What will that be like? And we cannot do it in the hall—the tent is preferable.

Her mind jumping from one thing to the next, Bridget tromped through the mud, picturing how the final project would look. Attempting to determine what it was she would have to do to make the idea of Bona Terra a reality.

We need a census! Anyone living on our grounds has to be accounted for and taxed! How much? Enough to support us and the army and to build and purchase arms and....and finery. No! That cannot be! We have other things to consider—the Vikings. Let's take care of them first.

She continued walking around the perimeter of the fort, finally noticing how it had been placed on rise that allowed for an excellent view of the surrounding lowlands. In her mind's eye she placed it on the map and appreciated how Vortimer chose it, not for its views but for its strategic placement.

A smart man, my husband.

As she patrolled she was pleased to note how the laborers, her laborers, stopped to nod their head in respect, some saying, milady. Bridget took time to watch and ask questions as to what their names were and what it was their toil was accomplishing. Eager to curry favor with their new mistress and to take a moment respite, they were more than happy to answer her questions until a sizable group surrounded her. She was taller than most and was happily speaking with them until she heard the thundering voice of Glendon curse them back to work.

"My lady," he bowed rapidly, "work cannot cease until dark!"

"Of course, I merely wanted to learn what was going on with my new home. Besides, I do not yet know these men, their names and such."

"Do not become familiar with them," said Vortimer who came upon them suddenly. "It is not wise."

"And why is that?

He looked at her sternly, at first, then softened. "These men fight, possibly die. Would you send someone familiar into such? How many times could you bear having your heart break, having all these 'friends' die? Too, there is the matter of their place. Look where they are, Bridget. They belong there, sweating and working."

"My lord, I was merely…"

"With all due respect to you and my counselor, Varduc, the subject bears no further discussion."

Bridget felt her spine stiffen. "Well," she replied archly, "this may be one of many topics that will not bear discussion."

Glendon left hurriedly to oversee some work, not wanting to be privy to a battle he thought would be grand. He knew Vortimer since his youth and knew him as well as any man could know another. Bridget, he judged, was more iron than silk—if he didn't know better he'd say she had balls.

"As you wish, Bridget. Now tell me, what do you think of the fortress? I am having it enlarged as you suggested—the idea makes sense."

What? First he insults me with his dismissive action as though I was a child and now he coddles me? What does he think I am?

Bridget was put off balance by Vortimer's refusal to engage in further argument and it took her a moment to collect her thoughts.

"It's not much to look at," she said finally, 'because there's nothing to really look at," she laughed. "I was inside where our hall will be and I think it would be better off in the tent for tonight or for even a few nights."

"Look there."

Bridget turned and saw a thin caravan of carts, some drawn by horses or oxen, others by men. They were coming for the promise of land, most of them. Then there were those who skirted the boundaries of law too often and for them it was strongly suggested they may have a longer life if they started afresh. Whatever their reasons, they were coming.

"Glendon will sup with us tonight. We have to make plans for these people, specific plans. I want to know their trades, and number. I need to know where they come from and we need to know where they will be living."

"I can do that," she replied.

The two of them began walking about the hillocks, pointing out possible fertile lands, water sources, defensive positions and the general ideal location of their home. Bridget noted that the more Vortimer talked excitedly, the less he limped. She thought he became like a little boy, excited with some new toy and this perplexed her to no end but she had learned that she could learn more by listening than talking—she was a marvelous listener.

Dinner was outside the ramshackle building that would later serve as their quarters. There was fresh meat and goblets of wine that Glendon had some how managed to appropriate. The talk that night was all business—Vortimer would oversee the construction of their castle and its defensives with Glendon, several handpicked men would accompany Bridget and begin a survey of the arrivals. The peasants would be scattered according to their family ties. Construction would begin on a mill, silos for storages would have to be built as would a place for smiths and joiners and carpenters and the other tradesmen that would be necessary if Bona Terra would thrive. The talk became excited and heated and Bridget watched Vortimer so closely, his eyes, his facial changes and the tone of his voice that gave lie to his normally expressionless face.

Who are you, my disturbing husband? The pitiful boy who cries in the night? The valiant soldier? The stern lord? Who are you? Will I be enough for you? Can we do this thing, you and I? Do you not find me attractive in some way? You haven't even touched me and I am sorry that I am not as pretty as those you must have had before but I am your wife!

It was fully dark when Glendon took his leave, Vortimer and Bridget sat silently by the fire, gazing into the flames, lost in their thoughts.

"I like this place, Vortimer."

"As do I." And he reached out and held her hand, continuing his look into the fire. Together, holding hands, they looked into the flames, their thoughts locked upon some hidden purpose as the flames flickered and waved till at last they diminished into undulating waves of coals. As of one mind they retired to their nearby tent.

As they began to remove their clothes in the semi-darkness Bridget turned. "Vortimer, I wish to see you, all of you. Your leg, your chest...you. I am still bleeding but we are man and wife and I want to see you." She didn't know why she said that, exactly, maybe it was the wine, but the past few days had set her mind on a course that was new and frightening and this, like the old steward, had to be faced.

Vortimer looked at her silently with his maddeningly expressionless face. He took off his tunic and she saw the muscles of his shoulders ripple in the dim light—his chest was hairy but not extravagantly so and his belly was flat. He looked into her eyes as he pulled down his tights and stood before her as she sat on the cot. His torso was long, she noted, and trim, power dwelled in the deep chest. His staff hung down, neither extravagant nor small—it just was. His left leg was finely muscled and she saw just as in his shoulders that the muscles rippled with each movement, like corded ropes beneath his skin. Vortimer stood mutely as Bridget examined his right leg where a scar ran from hip to knee, the leg a quarter less than the left but what sinew remained looked as taut as a bowstring. Without bidding he turned and Bridget was able to examine him without his eyes peering into hers—the deep shoulders, his muscular flanks and buttocks and calves.

He turned deliberately, knelt before her and took her chin into his hand and placed his lips upon hers, their lips finally meeting. It was a slow, soft kiss and Bridget was shocked, thrilled by the unexpected sensations that out of nowhere, began charging through her body. She kept her eyes closed and allowed Vortimer's mouth to control hers—she inhaled his breath and savored its taste. Without thought, Bridget's tongue began to make demands of its own, seeking Vortimer's. All the while, it remained the most gentle of kisses, complete and entire, it sought nothing else. They would remember it all their lives.

Mathilde was right all along! And if Mathilde was right then what of my sister?

Some how the kiss ended mutually yet they faces continued to touch—nose, cheek and chin.

"I am not yet ready," she whispered.

Vortimer, ever mindful of Varduc's counsel, sighed and laughed awkwardly. "You may not be but I am."

Bridget looked down.

All that from a kiss?

"Oh, my!" She giggled.

What a stupid thing to say! Oh, I feel like such an ass! What must he think of me?

To her immense relief, Vortimer began laughing and continued for so long that Bridget also began laughing till at last tears began. The passion that had been thick and heavy dissipated and was replaced with a feeling of comfortability when they at last retired for the night, neither falling asleep as quickly as they were accustomed.

The day began decisively. Vortimer rode with Glendon and several others to survey the fields and woods, determining battle strategy. Bridget had the onerous task of taking a census. Accompanied by three men, none of whom could read or write, Bridget rode Alexander into the magnificent confusion of the newcomers. Pigs, naked children, goats, and chickens scattered grudgingly as they rode into what Bridget decided was little more than a sewer with people.

At least the oxen and horses are tethered.

Mindful only of the shawl that Vortimer had given her, Bridget trudged through the excrement and commanded a table and chair to be found—it would be easier if they came to her and they did. The eldest male of each family reported cap in hand and stuttering reported their number, ages, possessions and skills, if any. Simple peasants most of them, they were directed as to how much land they could cultivate—where was their decision. Their faces registered disbelief when told they could hunt game without penalty. Bridget wrote "salt' in the margin— they'd need it to preserve the meat. By far, they were mostly families—brothers with wives and children or fathers with several children along with any elderly.

Bridget's hand began to ache from all the writing and she had some ale and a piece of hard cheese brought to her—she would stop only because of darkness. Her guards, though illiterate, were large and forceful as they bullied the crowds into order and once cataloged, to vacate immediately.

Vortimer chose them more wisely than I would have. Is that how his mind works? Get the task done with a minimum of manpower? What is his mind? What is he doing now? Where is the cart with my things, my drinks prepared by Calgwyn? Today is the last of my flow, I fear. That kiss!

Bridget closed her eyes, briefly allowing the memory of last night to soak in, replacing the surrounding smell of piss and shit with the memory of Vortimer's moist breath. She shook her right hand vigorously to relieve the stiffness and began once more; grateful that night was approaching.

When at last it became too dark, she stood stiffly, motioned for her escorts and with unaccustomed awkwardness, mounted Alexander, grateful that her muscles had not fully cramped. The ride back to the fortress was spent bending and twisting her torso, working out the kinks. More tired than she thought possible, she rode directly to her tent where she found Vortimer seated with Glendon before a fire with skewers of grease-dripping meat hung over it;

Bridget felt and heard her stomach. She dismounted wordlessly and handed Alexander to one of her burly guards.

Vortimer stood and clasped her hands, noting the bedraggled look on his wife's face. He moved forward as if to kiss her but stopped, contenting himself with holding her hand and leading her to a seat.

"Tired, Bridget? How did your day go? Hungry?"

"Brutally tired and tiresome was my day. Hungry? No, famished!"

Glendon gingerly picked one of the skewers and handed it to Bridget who chewed into the venison greedily. Vortimer arched an eyebrow and handed her a glass of wine, which she downed in two gulps, barely taking a breath.

"I think, Glendon, that this means we are at last able to eat," chuckled Vortimer.

"Aye, lord!"

Together all three ate, Bridget making the most noise, unmindful of the grease that dripped down her chin but careful to preserve the cleanliness of her shawl. "I shouldn't wear your gift all the time, Vortimer, but I do love it!"

"I think you should wear it all the time," he replied, "except when eating."

Together the trio began laughing quietly, then loudly, then uncontrollably. Bridget, her mouth full, found herself almost choking as tears of joy trickled down her cheeks, Vortimer laughed so hard that his sides ached—Glendon failed dismally at maintaining any distance and joined the couple in their merriment. When at last the laughing had subsided to intermittent chuckles, Vortimer asked Bridget as to what she had learned that day. Her immediate hunger calmed, she recounted the census and all that she had discovered, promising to continue tomorrow. Vortimer then detailed all that he and Glendon had observed, attempting to describe the lay of the land to Bridget. Bellies full and bodies weary, they stared thoughtlessly into the shrinking fire, inwardly content that their labors had been worthy. When the fire was finally no more than glowing coals and they were more in darkness than light, Vortimer reached over and squeezed Bridget's hand softly, observing that the next day would be arduous as well.

They stripped silently in the darkened tent and gratefully slid beneath the thin cover.

"You did well today, Bridget."

Bridget's spirit lifted at his praise, happy that her efforts had been appreciated.

"We did well today," she replied.

Mumbling, Vortimer turned onto his right side, placed his left arm across Bridget's body and kissed her cheek, then her lips.

"Soon, my lord," Bridget apologized as she turned onto her right side.

Where is the cart with my things? The bottles that Celestine had made for me, I need them! How much longer can I delay the inevitable. I can feel it hard against me! But his touch is so gentle and his manner so tolerant.

Bridget hurriedly began to recall all that Celestine had taught but it seemed so inadequate, so far in the past as to be useless—he was here naked beside her right now! She said a quick and fervent prayer to no one in particular that her possessions, her bottles, would arrive in the morning. She moved her hips ever so slightly away from Vortimer's stiffness and breathed a silent sigh of relief.

It had better come tomorrow.

His arm possessing her hip, Bridget drifted into an uneasy sleep.

The following morning was much like the one before except that Vortimer noticed a certain edginess in Bridget's demeanor, but as she said nothing was wrong he ascribed it to a woman's thing. Once again the pair went their separate ways—Vortimer to scout the land, Bridget to continue the census.

Even her bullying escorts noticed the change in Bridget's behavior—distracted and curt—wisely, they did not attempt any conversation, knowing how lords and particularly ladies, could become haughty.

Once again they rode into the cesspool that was the encampment, the smell more rank than the day before. Once again Bridget sat grimly down and began cataloging with cold determination, glancing often to see if there were any new arrivals. It was not until noon that she required a respite, her hand and eyes weary from writing endless family details that all began to sound the same; that more than anything else tired her to death. The longer she sat and wrote, the more agitated she became, looking feverishly for the arrival of her belongings.

It was just shortly after she began her break that the din of the encampment notched up an octave—frantic for Calgwyn's elixirs, Bridget's senses were stretched to their limits, as if will alone could make things happen. Turning and then running towards the new tumult, Bridget spied a procession coming along the rough trail, not just a procession but a retinue, a line of soldiers carrying the banners of her father and Vortimer—they were here! Bridget let out a yelp and forgetting her rank, ran towards the approaching column. She began to recognize familiar faces of her father's retinue who saluted her respectfully, pointing to the rear when she asked about her belongings. There, bringing up the rear, were three large carts and Mathilde and Gwenthe.

She ran towards them, her body and spirit delirious with joy and relief. She found her two servants sitting dourly on the rear of a cart but that changed the moment they saw their mistress. Together they leapt off and began laughing and hugging Bridget who hugged them back.

"Thank God you are here! Thank God!" was all Bridget could say. When her initial excitement had abated she began to objectively and swiftly tell her two women what had to be done.

"Come with me! We have little time to talk now but I promise that tomorrow we will laugh, just as before!"

Following Bridget, the pair stepped gingerly into the quagmire of the encampment. Bridget motioned to one of her escorts. "These are my women and need to be taken to the fort, do you understand? Those carts there have my things and you will say to whomever is in charge that Bridget commands that at least two men begin unloading them and placing them in an orderly fashion in the hall—Vortimer would wish it so! Do you understand?"

He nodded.

"My bed is to be assembled and my ladies will help to prepare it—they may sleep in the tent of my lord tonight. Do you understand?"

This time he grunted and nodded.

Bridget turned to the breathless Gwenthe and Mathilde and grasped their hands. "There is so much happening, you have no idea! So much to do and time flies! I promise that you will sleep well tonight but you must do one thing. Wrapped in a yellow blanket are some boots with three bottles inside. You must take the boots and place them in the corner furthest from the bed. Can you do that? It is more important than I can tell you. You have to remember and you must do this!"

The two women were taken aback by the urgency in Bridget's voice but they agreed that it would be done one way or another.

Satisfied, Bridget allowed her escort to take charge of the carts and her women were bundled roughly back into the carts that were coaxed that much more swiftly towards the castle. Bridget let out a sigh of relief as she waved to the departing figures of Gwenthe and Mathilde.

For the rest of the afternoon Bridget's hand fairly flew across the pages as family after bedraggled family had their names and histories listed in Bridget's thickening catalog. For her part, Bridget thought that the more quickly she worked the sooner she could leave. After a few hours she decided that she had done enough, though it was not nearly as dark as it had been the day before, she motioned to her men that it was time to leave.

Still light, she went directly to the structure that would one day house the hall. It was a hive of activity as laborers struggled with timbers and planks. The interior was filled with choking dust but some men were spreading dampened hay to keep it down. Mathilde and Gwenthe were going about the business of making at least a small portion of it fit for Bridget's sleeping quarters—the bed was already assembled and the mattress being aired and fluffed.

"Gwenthe, did you find those bottles?"

"Yes, milady, but with all this commotion and mucking about I thought it best to put them there in the lower drawer of your cabinet," she pointed. The room, in addition to being stifling, was still dark as windows had not yet been cut—but Bridget saw the tall, dark chest sitting in a corner. She pulled on the heavy drawer to find the bottles safely nestled among her linens.

"Excellent, Gwenthe! Excellent! You have saved me!"

Bridget fairly ran with excitement from the room as Mathilde and Gwenthe shared puzzled looks.

The bottles are in place. I know I can get to them easily enough as they have placed the chest facing one of the walls—to give me privacy from Vortimer in the bed. Yes, I can do this!

Free from the sweltering interior, Bridget breathed deeply and looked about—Vortimer should be returning soon as dusk was just beginning to unfurl itself from the east. She went to Vortimer's tent and washed her face with some tepid water. It felt so refreshing that she did her arms and neck as well.

She knew her hair was thick with knots so she tried running her fingers through it but soon gave up.

She lay down on her cot, closed her eyes and tried to empty her mind, preferring the smells and sounds of outside to fill it. She was just beginning to doze as Vortimer drew back the tent flap.

"Oh! You startled me! I was more tired that I supposed," she said as she sat up quickly

"You've been working hard; we've all been working hard. Our food is ready, come."

It was full dark and she realized that the clamoring of earlier had blessedly ceased and was replaced by the night sounds of trilling insects and the whinnies of distant horses. Fires of various sizes dotted nearby and way off in the distance she spied the flickering of similar flames.

"Look," she said to Vortimer, "our people are out there now."

He followed her gaze and stared quietly for a moment, soaking up the tranquility of the moment as he squeezed her hand.

Dinner was quiet. Glendon and Vortimer described several streams and lakes thick with fish. Bridget reviewed the number of families now filling Bone Tear. She mentioned nonchalantly that her ladies and things had arrived and would Vortimer mind if Gwenthe and Mathilde slept in his tent for the time being. He acquiesced easily as he was in a peaceful mood this evening.

"Tomorrow we begin again what we did today," he finally declared. "Let's rest these weary bones."

"First allow me to usher my ladies to the tent, my lord. So that we may sleep in the privacy of our quarters."

She went to the hall to find Gwenthe and Mathilde still inside, working by two small candles.

"Come you two! You are tired and famished. You may sleep in our tent tonight and continue with this in the morning!" She clutched their hands and led them towards the tent. They bowed hurriedly to Vortimer, thanking him for his kindness.

Bridget took Vortimer's hand in hers and began leading him towards the hall, the inside faintly illuminated with the flickering candles.

"Wait here for a moment and let me prepare, please," she said as she left Vortimer standing by the entrance.

He stood mutely, his mind and body a jumble of emotions. That he wanted Bridget was a certainty. Just the scent of her lying there in bed next to him made him up. He recalled the night they had kissed and how his erection was so hard it became ached—the same as when they innocently touched. The sensation, the need to be inside her and to fill her was maddening. Still, Varduc's warnings were etched into his brain. Every word and action about and towards her were spoken with forethought. They were honest and forthright but Vortimer was determined to say nothing detrimental. The new work of the fortress was a blessing in that it occupied his mind with stratagems and momentarily made him forget his hunger for a time. And she was a virgin.

Vortimer had had many women in the past, perhaps fathered a child or two, he was not certain. Women were attracted to his easy manner that was both respectful and confident and they were eager to give him their warm solace—

but none had been virgins. Oh, he had boasted about having a virgin with his men on those nights when lies and truth became mixed with too much wine but the truth was much plainer.

I will treat her as kindly and gently as she will permit. That is all I can do! She is my wife, after all and a man has his duty, his obligation and his right to her.

He let out a deep breath, tried to ignore his already pulsating penis and then walked in slowly. Bridget had extinguished one of the candles so that now there was just one several feet from the bed. She was under a thin cover that was pulled up to her chin and her eyes were staring into Vortimer's as he walked to the side of the bed and began peeling off his clothes, his back towards her. He gingerly slid under the covers and lay there for a moment.

"Vortimer, I am a virgin."

"I remember."

Then, as if from nowhere he said, "So am I."

Bridget did not expect this and suddenly started to giggle at the thought, she tried to stifle it with the gravity of her situation and that made her laugh all the more, till tears began rolling down her cheeks. Vortimer smiled with relief that his little unintended joke had pleased her. He turned towards Bridget and when she finally stopped laughing, kissed her mouth softly. She allowed his lips and the tip of his tongue to caress hers, wanting to respond but hesitant. She felt as though she was gently melting inside and the warm room suddenly became much hotter, unbearably so. She did not protest when Vortimer pulled the sheet down to her hips, instead a soft moan came.

Her eyes were closed as her mouth began to respond to his probing tongue—sucking his lip, licking his mouth softly, sometimes with an intensity that surprised her. Her breathing deepened and became coarser as her entire body began to throb internally—he was maddeningly slow! He moved closer to her and laid his chest across hers as she shuddered—their mouths never ceasing. She felt his staff along her thigh but gave it no thought, what was happening to her was beyond thought and fear and Celestine. The universe she had known had suddenly ceased, every known and unknown thing was now pumping through her veins, stiffening her nipples that were pressed by his chest. She took her right arm and held him closer, wanting to force his body into hers.

Their breathing was now more animal than human as Vortimer placed his body fully on top of hers—she opened her legs to accommodate his hips—they both moaned as Vortimer propped himself up on his arms. Bridget opened her eyes to see his face, bathed in shadow and soft light, she caressed his shoulders as he began inching upwards towards her opened lips. He reached down for a moment and Bridget felt those other wet lips part and she spasmed sharply which pushed it in further.

She waited with her whole being as she felt a sudden pressure and then pain down there; she winced and bit her lower lip but then he eased back slightly and she recaptured her breath. Slowly, very slowly, she felt the pressure begin again, this time without thinking she thrust up her hips to meet his and gave a sharp cry as the pain stabbed through her. Still, she held her hips up, gasping as she did so—her strong fingers dug into his shoulders. She allowed her hips to fall back gently as the pain diminished—she felt very wet.

Their bodies were sweat covered as they remained motionless, both with their eyes closed. Vortimer began a slow but insistent pumping. It didn't hurt as badly as before but the pain was still there and drew her away from the other wonderful things she was feeling. She opened her eyes to see his face as he rhythmically pushed inside. By small degrees he increased the tempo and strength of each thrust—grunting from the exertion. Faster now, much faster and harder. He arched backward and let out a deep, soft cry as his body shuddered. Bridget felt a liquid warmth fill her. Not unpleasing but was this it? She felt as though there was something terribly wrong, missing. She felt guilty that her ignorance and inexperience had caused this failure—but she said nothing as Vortimer gently lifted himself off her and fell over on his back. She felt a warm stickiness on her inner thighs and told him she'd be right back.

He watched as she wobbled on weak legs to behind the dresser, his breaths coming in deep gulps, sweat beading his face and chest even though he was now finished. He heard her open a drawer and then a little while later heard it close. She sneezed once, twice, three times. His eyes only reopened after he felt her climb back into the bed.

"Are you all right?" he asked.

"Yes, fine. A little sore and some bleeding."

"Oh," was all he could say and he suddenly felt so much the fool. "Bridget, I didn't mean to…"

"I know," she whispered, "I know."

Vortimer felt a sudden exhaustion fall upon him and all he wanted to do was go to sleep but Varduc's trilling misgivings kept him awake until Bridget should fall asleep first.

"Was I, was I…satisfactory?"

"Bridget, you were more than satisfactory, you were wonderful! You were frightened and there was pain and there was blood. You are my wife and you are extraordinary, I swear."

"I have never been frightened in my life."

"I have," he replied, "many times."

She thought for a moment and laid on her side to face him. "Kiss me here," she pointed to her neck. He kissed it softly.

"Now kiss me here," she placed her finger on her chin. He did as he was bid.

"Here," she offered her shoulder and he kissed that slowly as well, feeling himself begin to stiffen once more.

"Now here," she placed her finger between her breasts. He was placing his lips there when she shifted, placing her nipple before his mouth. He kissed it, licked it and sucked it softly.

Bridget thought that the second time was much better than the first.

After the third time she was certain of one thing, Celestine was horribly wrong.

CHAPTER TEN

Celestine hurled the heavy brass bowl against the wall. Failing to break it, she began sweeping her arms across the tables and chests, receiving satisfaction from the crash and crack of glass. She spied Bridget's latest letter on the bed and shredded it to tatters, each rip accompanied with spittle and a grunt.

Send more bottles! Send more bottles! What is Bridget doing up there? The bitch is in heat! Didn't she remember a damn thing I taught her? What if she becomes pregnant? What will she do then? What will I do?

A gentle throbbing began deep in her temples, which she began to massage with her fingers, fearful of the bursting pain she knew would follow.

"Calgwyn!" She bellowed. "Calgwyn!"

She lay on the bed, shutting her eyes, as the light became an agony. Still, the letter's contents continued to roar through her pounding head.

She sounds so damn happy there, the both of them! Telling me how wonderful Vortimer is, the progress of the castle, the richness of the land. Next the little slut will tell me she is falling in love!

"Calgwyn! Someone get me Calgwyn!"

She heard feet scurrying over the hall leading to her room and a breathless Calgwyn entered. Her lot had changed remarkably since coming to the castle as Celestine's woman. Her clothes, once rags, were now made from the discards of her mistress. Freed from the drudgery of fieldwork and privy to the kitchen, Calgwyn's frame had gone from angular to softly rounded.

"Calgwyn, my skull is not yet in its full misery. Close the shutters and prepare me some of your tea."

Calgwyn bowed out, her feet crunching the glass shards strewn on the floor. Celestine laid back and tried to breathe lightly.

This is Bridget's fault, all of it. I was never this wretched in my life! She created this brain spasm—her and Vortimer! I have sat long enough and waited and waited but now I must do something!

She could feel each heartbeat rip through her skull and let out a small moan; each pulsation deepening her hatred of Bridget and Vortimer. Slivers of agony were lancing behind her eyes and yet she was beginning to formulate a plan. The details would be impossible to consider at this exact moment but one thing was certain—she would visit The Stones on the morrow.

Calgwyn's elixir made it possible. She endured the ride as best she could on the following morning, the pain present but tolerable. Celestine left the cart and guards as she picked her way through the sharp growth that snagged and tore at her dress.

Here it is high summer, yet the oaks have sickly, thin leaves and the oddest twisted and stumped branches. No bird song, no birds at all.

A stiff wind scraped the upper limbs together yet Celestine did not feel it close to the ground where she stumbled and swore.

A wind that sways the trees but does not cool, no birds, misshapen oaks—let the rabble avoid this power—I am made of sterner stuff.

She finally tripped into the eerie clearing and paused, cooling and clearing her mind—willing herself to become receptive. She walked the perimeter of the circle, running her hands over each rough stone, feeling the power—all was silent as she trod the ankle-high grass and then paraded to the center. Celestine had no inkling as to the how or why of her ability to receive communion in the circle. That it was so was sufficient and she felt both blessed and beholding for the gift.

Her head no longer pained, her shoulders slumped as she stood weakly and after a time began to hear the whispers, many whispers—each with a different voice but with the same insistent message. Her body rocked gently as she nodded her head, a thin smile on her face. The persuasive voices grew stronger rather than louder, vibrating in rhythm to Celestine's tripping heart. She dropped to her knees, ready.

Pulling her dress up to her waist with her left hand, she placed her right between her legs and began rubbing and stroking her soft hair and pliant lips, letting a finger slide between them, finding her wet heat. She laid fully on her belly, legs spread and began grinding her hips against the earth, groaning with each thrust as the rough earth rubbed against her. She pushed up on her arms and continued rocking, rocking harder and positioning her pelvis just the right way so that the lips spread, allowing the full pleasure to assault her. Celestine continued her gyrations, savoring each lascivious sensation with a gasp; sweat streaked her face. She changed the rhythms and strength of her thrusting according to the voices that stroked the wetness between her thighs. The crescendo ebbed and flowed, higher and closer, always closer—her breathing became sporadic, her hips began to pound the ground unceasingly until, at last, she let out one long cry, shuddered and lay limp. Small spasms wracked through her weakened body, jamming her swollen mound against an irregularity on the ground. It was not until many minutes later that Celestine felt her exposed buttocks being warmed by the sun.

Her menstrual blood flowed and mingled with the juices she had created, baptizing the dirt—she smelled her musk and smiled. She knew what to do now. Celestine stood unsteadily and rather than letting her dress fall, continued to hold it up. She walked confidently to the nearest stone, ran her free hand over it and rested her cheek against its cool surface, waiting for the right time. At last she faced the rough rock, kissed it gently, grasped it and began to rub her pleasure against it, marking a rough corner with her blood, heedless of the pain because now there was only pleasure. She marked each of the Stones in the same fashion and when they were all done, she giggled like a mischievous, young girl. Oh, she now knew what to do; it was only a matter of taking advantage of the opportunities promised by the voices.

She pulled down her dress and brushed herself off, humming a song as she headed back towards the awaiting carriage. Celestine did not mind the rough jostling back as her thoughts drifted between her legs and what to do with Bridget. Without a word she went to her room when they arrived, anxious now to clean her thighs and straighten her garb. Satisfied with her appearance, she summoned Calgwyn.

"Yes, milady?"

"We shall be going to visit my sister. Pack some of your things, most important are your roots and such."

"For how long, milady? My husband..."

"Ah, your husband, of course! He still lives with the pigs and chickens, no? You are always free to follow your own mind, my dear, always. I am certain that I could find another with your talents if I had to."

Calgwyn's decision took less than two heartbeats; she left to pack her things.

* * *

Vortimer brooded in his hall, content to be alone with his troubling thoughts for the moment. The construction of the fortress had come more swiftly and grander than he had planned. Experienced carpenters and smiths had shored up the timbers and made the walls and ceilings square and sturdy. His vassals worked unceasingly in his fields and the earth was rich. His wife was becoming more indispensable each day as she handled the administrative duties for which he was never groomed. Bridget's fingers were forever smudged with the ink of her numerous journals that listed everyone and everything north of the Wythe—livestock, people, barrels, men of trades and crafts—and she was the best damned mapmaker he had ever seen! Still, he fretted, knowing that his moment for testing was nearing.

He was startled from his dark thoughts by Varduc who sat next to him unceremoniously.

"Why so troubled, young master? I see black clouds tumbling about your head when there should be blue skies! Isn't everything wonderful? Isn't this the most marvelous place to be? The land, your people, your wife—everything is just as it should be."

Vortimer remained silent and started to get up when Varduc shot out his hand and held on to his master's arm.

"Sit, young master. You can hide from me for just so long but from your thoughts, never! What troubles you so?"

Vortimer sat for a moment and locked eyes with his odd counselor. "The Northmen trouble me, what else. They will be coming and soon! I do not know if we have the men to defeat them. I do not know if I have the ability to kill them."

"Haven't you wondered," replied Varduc, "at the sufficiency of rain we have had this year? Not too much or too little? Just the right amount to nourish the fields and fill the streams."

"I talk about life and death and you talk about the crops!"

"The crops are life and death also, young master. Perhaps more so."

"I am tired of your damn riddles! You are my counselor, counsel and be done."

"I have known you these many years and yet you whine about the same things!" He replied heatedly. "I am tired of your doubts and fears."

"A good commander knows his weaknesses," said Vortimer.

"A wise commander knows his strengths," Varduc retorted.

"You speak to me of strengths? What do you know of formations? Armaments? The Vikings? Why, if Alexander or Caesar…"

Varduc slapped his hand loudly on the table, his boyish face twisted with anger. "You are not Caesar! You are not Alexander! You are Vortimer, leader of a band of talented scoundrels and cutthroats. Leader of men who crave the blood and riches of their enemy. You are Vortimer, the Iron Dog!"

"The 'Iron Dog'?"

"Yes," said Varduc whimsically, "that is what some call you."

"The Iron Dog?"

"Yes, have you gone deaf as well as stupid? They call you that because of your tenacity, your unwillingness or inability to let go once your jaws are locked onto your opponent."

Vortimer sat for a moment, waiting to see if Varduc betrayed some indication of a joke at his expense. When he did not, the young man with the gray, cloudy eyes sat back. "I need to know how to beat them."

"The answer, young master, is all about you—it is in the skies above your head and the dirt beneath your boots."

"I believe I have asked a simple question."

"I believe I have answered it, young master."

Varduc stood triumphantly, bowed and scurried the length of the hall, leaving the perplexed Vortimer just as he had found him—brooding.

Damn fool! What kind of man am I to have such as Varduc counsel? I seek answers and he speaks in riddles! No wonder the Christ church is making his kind scarce. Why does he always do this? True, he is wise but why must he muddy the waters? Look what he has done! I was trying to concentrate on the Vikings and he has unsettled my thinking!

Shaking his head, Vortimer limped out the dusty hall. The sun was full up and from his high vantage point he watched as people bustled within and without the fortress walls. He didn't know the machinations of commerce and for now pretended that he didn't care—there were meatier issues just over the north horizon. He walked gingerly down the slope to the courtyard, barely acknowledging the salutes and bows. Vortimer knew he needed room and peace to think and Bone Tear had miles of meadows, forests in which to do so.

By rights, Glendon should have been with him but Vortimer, as usual, preferred to keep his fears unshared, hiding them behind his eyes. The merciless scavenger of doubt pecked and scratched as he headed towards a hill thick with trees. The mere act of walking acted as a balm for his spirit and though he did not consciously register it, the brightness of the day did much to keep him from outright despair. He sat beneath a suitable oak, glad to be free from the clamoring of the fortress and alone with his thoughts.

How many of them? How many of us? Where is the most advantageous place to battle?

Will they fight as a mob or will they plan with feints and surprises? How should we react? Will Gwaldner provide the men he promised? What if he doesn't? Do we use our own peasants?

And then his most secret terror shouldered the others aside.

Will I be killed? Mutilated? What does dying feel like?

He tossed those thoughts aside, willing himself to focus on the problem and its solution. A commander could not allow himself to dwell on personal fears, ever. Vortimer had two possible outcomes: victory or defeat—it was ultimately perplexing in its simplicity. He plucked a sprig of grass and threw it.

"Simple."

From across the bright, rolling hills he saw a tall figure on a white horse approaching the fortress. Even at this great distance, Vortimer recognized the way Bridget carried herself while riding—she could be riding a nag and still he knew he'd recognize that strong bearing. He allowed himself the luxury of thinking about her. How the weeks since the wedding had been one revelation after another! Bridget, he had come to accept, was many things: humorous, serious, willful to the point of obstinacy, strong, intuitive and, he had to admit it, an exhausting lover. She was another reason he could not let himself fail—she had blind faith in his ability. One night she told him she "felt" their victory—and that made it reality.

He watched as she stopped by the gates to speak with two men who pointed towards the hill where he sat. He knew he could not avoid her, much as he wanted. This was no time for a woman no matter how competent. Dismally, he watched as she approached, knowing he could not escape her boundless, annoying optimism. Vortimer's spirits sunk yet lower.

"Ah, my husband! Here you are!" Bridget cried as she unhorsed fluidly. Vortimer averting her eyes, did not attempt to rise.

"What is it, Vortimer?" Bridget said as she sat down heavily.

"Nothing."

"Nothing? Come, I know you better than you know yourself. I can tell when you are troubled by something."

"Then you would also know that I prefer to be with my own thoughts."

"And what are those thoughts?" she asked, ignoring him.

"Can't you just let me be? Don't you have chickens to count or something very important to do?"

I will ignore his insult. I know this man and what perplexes him. He is so transparent!

"The only important thing right now is my lord and husband. Tell me, your wife and helpmate, what saddens those eyes?"

Vortimer closed his eyes, took a deep breath and whispered, "The Vikings."

"And?" she asked.

"What more could there possibly be?" He replied with restrained sarcasm.

Determined to ignore her husband's rebuff, Bridget instead took hold of his hand.

"And what are your thoughts?"

Vortimer hesitated and then started to recite his misgivings. Bridget allowed him to continue, nodding encouragingly, sensing rather than understanding the logistical problems her husband faced. The longer he continued, the more freely Vortimer exposed his troubles, except the one that dealt with his own mortality. He concluded by mentioning his exasperating meeting with Varduc.

"Above your head and beneath your boots?"

"Not much help, eh?"

"But he is wise and he is your counselor. Let's walk."

"Walk?"

"Yes," she replied firmly, "I have this sense of something."

Vortimer felt secretly relieved to have confessed to Bridget, as the terrible burden he had struggled to carry alone were now also borne by her. Unaccustomed to being this intimate, he found himself wanting to make love with her right there in the rough grass—but all he saw was Bridget's retreating back

Is this what Varduc meant about her? Being someone to speak with and share my troubles? I could have done the same with Glendon. Still, it would not have been the same—you can't do that with a man.

They walked along the fringe of the wooded hill in the sunshine, Alexander dutifully following. Wordless, they kept their own counsel for a mile, till Bridget finally glanced up. "Look."

Vortimer followed her gaze and saw three, no, four sparrows flying madly about a crow. Each of the smaller birds harassed the retreating bird from all angles. They were small and fast; the crow could only fly in a slow, straight line—turning its head to protest loudly. The sparrows were relentless in their attack. Driving their small bodies and beaks into the crow, it was forced to stop beating its large wings to defend itself and would then falter in midair. The sparrows did not cease until the much larger black bird had been driven off. Vortimer focused on the sparrows—quick, attacking from all angles—size meant nothing, agility was everything.

How many times have I seen this? A score, at least, but for now it is as if I am learning and seeing something for the first time. What is it?

"Look, my lord."

Vortimer glanced down to where Bridget was pointing. There was an open area of sand and earth amidst the grasses, no larger than a tunic and as Vortimer lowered himself he saw ants—hundreds, maybe thousands of the insects engaged in a chaotic melee. Dropping to his knees he looked closer and saw that some were black, others a reddish-brown. He had never before compared ants, they were mostly a nuisance but now he watched closely, intrigued by the carnage in the dust.

The black ants were smaller by far but much quicker, his militaristic eyes saw. It was not uncommon to see a larger ant carry three or four of the blacks on his back, rear up and snap his pincers fruitlessly as his legs and neck were being chewed off. There were many dead of both colors. Entranced, Vortimer watched closely, his eyes unable to watch any single combatant.

Would they scream? Who is the commander? Where is the front? The rear? Are there reinforcements? The air above my head and the dirt beneath my boots.

Vortimer stood and looked about, oblivious to the battleground next to his boots and even to Bridget who stood beside him—he felt the germ of a plan deep within his skull and knew the solution to the Vikings was almost in his grasp.

Damn you, Varduc!

"Come," he grasped Bridget's hand, "let's go back! I have some things to discuss with Glendon and Varduc over dinner."

Leading Alexander by his reins, Bridget marveled at the remarkable change that had washed over her husband—he was even whistling and his limp was barely noticeable.

Bridget made arrangements for dinner that night and at Vortimer's insistence, dismissed all the kitchen help as well as Mathilde and Gwenthe. "We don't want any more ears to hear this than is necessary," he said.

There was scant ceremony but courtesy a plenty when both Glendon and Varduc arrived. The table had been set with meats and generous flagons of wine. For the first time Bridget was to observe how Vortimer and his two most trusted men analyzed important matters.

Are they going to reminisce all night long? Is this the way it is done? What does it matter to discuss old battles and older comrades? Are we going to have enough wine? Even Vortimer is grinning and Varduc's voice changes pitch with each sentence. They do seem to be in a good mood, particularly Vortimer. Is this the time to ask? Maybe another goblet of wine would help.

Bridget stood and poured wine for the guests and herself, acknowledging their thanks with a smile and a slight bow.

"Here," said Varduc, "is a toast to my young mistress! She does honor us by her presence."

Bridget felt herself blush as all three raised their cups to her and drank. Not to be outdone, Bridget stood and said, "And here is to the men in my life—may they serve Bone Tear." They laughed robustly as they drained the goblets.

"My lord," Bridget said calmly, "may I ask a question? You three have known each other for years and are such close companions and there is so much I don't know about each of you I feel like some child who must be silent in the presence of his parents."

Vortimer thought for a moment, glanced at his two men, then at Bridget. "Ask, my dear."

"My lord, how did all three of you come to be together? When and where did you meet? What were the circumstances?"

"Varduc could probably tell you how it is we are joined but we'd be here till dawn, so I, my dear wife, will tell all. These two," he waved his hand towards Glendon and Varduc, "will swear that what I tell you is truth."

Vortimer sat back in his chair, getting comfortable.

"I was the youngest of four sons but barely eight years separated me from my eldest brother. Even at an early age I could discern plotting and secret alliances between my older brothers, caused in part by several nobles who loved the possibility of power more than they honored my father. After many years I learned that there was some talk of my being poisoned." Vortimer chuckled. "But that, as you can see, did not happen."

"It was as common then as it is now, that families of rank send their children to be cared for by families of greater station. Ostensibly this was to afford a broader education for the child and expose him more to the world. As I was something of an intelligent child, my father decided to send me off at the age of eight or nine. It was terrible."

Bridget nodded, enraptured not only for the story that was unfolding but because she had never heard her husband speak so much at one time.

"Picture this crying child being torn away from his friends and family. I was not even allowed to take my dog! But Fortune, as it so often does, was smiling on me even though I considered myself the most wretched person in the world at that time. I was taken to the court of Augustinus—a man whose heart was as gentle as his hands were rough!"

Varduc and Glendon nodded in unison.

Odd, that I never imagined Vortimer as a child. To me he always seems so forceful, so permanent—I still cannot imagine him as some young boy. I wonder what he looked like— thin as a reed or fat as a toad?

"Did you cry, then?" Bridget asked.

"As many tears as a young boy could wring from his eyes, even though I knew I was wrong. I did not care."

"Augustinus took a liking to me immediately and to this day I honor his spirit. I went on campaigns, traveled, had tutors and trained for combat."

"Did you know, young mistress," chirped Varduc, "that your husband speaks several languages? A pity he cannot command a pen in the same way he commands his tongue! Why my grandmother..."

"I enjoyed arms training the most," Vortimer continued, ignoring Varduc.

"Life, it seemed, was good with one exception, Augustinus' son. Three years my senior, he tormented me cruelly and obsessively. But what was I to do? Here I was, there at the pleasure of the court, a guest in a great house—was I to complain about the beatings and tauntings? Certainly not. The years slipped by and his petty jealousies softened, whether by indifference or by my growing larger, I don't know."

"Why did he treat you so cruelly, Vortimer? I would have thought he would treat you as a younger brother?"

"Oh, indeed he did, Bridget. He treated me as the younger brother who was favored by his father. I think this jealousy fueled his hatred. Now, where was I?"

"You were getting older."

"Ah, yes! I guess I was about thirteen years old when I met that hulking brute over there." He pointed to Glendon who smiled broadly.

"We were boon friends, Vortimer and I, from the first." Glendon said. "My father was a true vassal of Augustinus and there was hardly a day that we did not share in some way or other."

"Yes," Vortimer said, "we were the closest of friends, still are—but let me continue. It was in the spring of my fourteenth year that I was discovered by Varduc, there. Do you recall the circumstances?"

"Of course, young master. You were lying idly on a bank, letting your feet dangle in the water as you dreamed mighty dreams about that young girl with the fiery hair that you had just met and..."

"I was dreaming no dreams! But tell Bridget how it is you came to be there."

"I was drawn, compelled to go to him, young mistress. I felt some stirring, much like the geese when they know it is time to fly south—something in the earth drew me to this lad. You can imagine my supreme disappointment after finally finding him—stubborn, contentious, brooding. If it were not for me and Glendon he might have become a Christian!" The whole table laughed.

"How old are you, Varduc?" Bridget asked.

The little man squinted for a moment. "I cannot say for certain, young mistress, but I have seen forests grow and die." He said this without the slightest suggestion of humor. "Do you recall the fishing pole, young master," he said, trying to remove the sudden serious turn the conversation had taken.

"Of course! Do you remember, Glendon?"

"Of course!"

"Tell me about the fishing pole, then," Bridget exclaimed.

"Well," said Vortimer, "it was a fine summer's day and I was walking idly about, not a care in the world and thought I would go to this pond and swim. On my way there Varduc stops me and says, 'Heed me well, do not go down to the pond, young master'." Vortimer chuckled at his poor attempt to imitate Varduc's piping voice.

"But like any young man I totally disobeyed him and went on my way and there I found Glendon fishing."

"And?" she asked.

"What else? He wanted to fish, I wanted to swim. Matters of this importance could only be decided by combat!"

"No!"

"Oh, indeed, yes!" said Glendon who was beginning to laugh. "Mortal combat! "Young Vortimer was taller but I was larger across the shoulders and chest—also stronger."

Vortimer nodded in agreement.

"What a fight! I had bloodied his nose, broken it and kept trying to make him surrender. Each time I knocked him down he squirted away like an eel—my arms were getting tired from the trouncing I was giving him!"

"Now that is a bold lie!" cried Vortimer.

"Well, I was beating you, sure enough. But damned if he did not give up! He was like a seething hound, almost crazed! And then he started to go on the attack till at last he finally wore me down! My tunic all bloodied by his dripping nose.

We laid there in the grass, totally spent and do you know what we did then? We started to laugh! We laughed till tears ran down our faces. Then, as my fishing pole had been smashed to kindling, we went swimming."

"After all that?"

"Of course! We were friends." All four laughed at the perfect incongruity.

"What else happened while you there, Vortimer?"

The laughter ceased abruptly as Vortimer's eyes became like wet stones. After a few moments he softened, took a mouthful of wine and said, "My leg, of course. What else?"

"I was seventeen, full of spirit and full of myself, just like any youth. I had friends in and around the court, a man as close to me as any father and the phantom of the Future in front of me. I was going towards the courtyard where we would have our daily fighting lesson with full swords and shields. Not much of a lesson, really. We made a lot of noise as we clamored and banged as loudly as possible to impress the ladies who might be watching—it is something young men do."

"Anyway, I was going there and Varduc appeared out of no where and again said, 'Heed me, young master, do not go to the courtyard this day'. I had forgotten his warning about the time with the fishing pole and so ignored him again."

"They had already begun the exercise when I picked up my sword and shield, looking for an opponent to 'dance' with. That's what we called it because each blow was aimed not at a vulnerable body part but at the shield, instead. No one got hurt, a lot of noise was made and the ladies loved it! So, who comes along but the son of Augustinus and we begin our practiced parrying. Lunges, blocks and thrusts, shields crashing together! I struck a downward blow on his shield that carried me down slightly to the left. I raised my shield to meet his blow…instead his sword ripped me from hip to knee. I looked down at this enormous wound, blood everywhere and then looked up at him. He had a smile, I swear, he had a smile on that face of his! Then, I simply fainted. I will never forget that man or his face, Augustus be damned!"

"Augustus?" Bridget asked.

"Yes, the son of Augustinus was Augustus."

No! It can't be! There must be some cruel coincidence here. Certainly the man who almost killed Vortimer could not possibly be the man the church wanted me to marry. Augustus is a common name, after all.

The table sat silently till Glendon cleared his throat. "The old man was beside himself with anger and rage and packed Augustus, who swore it was a mistake, off to Italy the following morning. For weeks my lord sat at Vortimer's bed, neither eating nor sleeping. Caring for Vortimer as much as any father for his natural son. By rights, Vortimer should have died several times. There was the loss of blood, the fevers and the doctors to overcome. Varduc had us bathe the wound with seawater three times a day and prepared all his brews and poultices. We never left his bedside, cleaning him, praying for him."

"I knew, young mistress, that he was not going to die, at least not at that time. Otherwise I would not have been called to him as I was. How he survived such a wound is just as mysterious as to why he received it—all things serve some purpose that may forever remain hidden from our ken." Varduc added.

The evening had been growing long but so enthralled was Bridget by the lively stories that she put off lighting the candles until now.

Holding up his goblet for her to fill, Vortimer solemnly toasted the room. "What is done cannot be undone. We go on!"

He turned and smiled somewhat sheepishly at Bridget, "Does that answer your query?"

"Most totally, lord. I toast the companions who have saved your life."

"Now," said Vortimer brusquely, "we have the future of Bone Tear to consider. As I was thinking about our position I was reminded of a story about Alexander. His troops had been brought by ships to fight against an army that vastly outnumbered them. Do you know what the madman did? He torched the ships, making it impossible for his men to even think of retreat! They would either be victorious or die. I find that we are much in the same situation. We cannot lose to the Vikings nor can we retreat. Should they drive us from here I believe that we would fall to the butchery of our allies to the south."

"But my father promised you the aid of Glamorgan," Bridget protested.

"Yes, and if our combined forces cannot withstand the invaders we will retreat into the waiting maws of the others. They know easy prey when they smell it. Our only course is victory."

Vortimer's cold assessment silenced the room—he saw that Bridget had paled and Glendon's was minus his usual grin. Varduc, however, had a knowing glint in his eye.

"So, what do you propose to do, young master?" he asked.

"We will use our peasants in the battle."

"Vortimer," Glendon protested, "how worthwhile is that and what will it accomplish? How many times have we used them in other engagements and to what purpose? They do one of two things to the enemy: anger them because they have been insulted by our use of untrained men or else they get their blood warmed by slaughtering these sheep! No, I can't see any purpose in using farmers."

It had been a common practice to use peasants to bolster flagging armies, allowing the real soldiers to gain a few precious moments on the battlefield to use their skill. Poorly armed, often with pitchforks or hoes, and with meager protection, they were universally slaughtered. Any survivors were either cowards, lucky or able to hide beneath a dead comrade, feigning their own death.

"We are going to do this differently, Glendon, trust me. We are going to train them."

"Lord, I will follow you anywhere, offer my life for yours, but train them? How many years has it taken us to use our swords and shields well? Besides, training takes time and they have work to do each day! And who will do it? How do we get them here?"

"I am not seeking you to lay down your life for mine, not yet," Vortimer stated flatly. "What I am telling you is this: we are going to give them pikes to fight with and the training with it. They already use staves for their own purposes so they have some familiarity with a pole weapon and we won't have to supply or train them how to use a shield properly."

The pike, or bill, was a stout length of oak about half the diameter of a forearm and as tall as a man with a metal fitting on one end that consisted of a either a small axe head or hook at its base with an elongated, sharp point that could puncture leather and flesh.

Glendon thought about it for a moment. "And the training?"

"Take each of your men and tell them to go to each village and choose a man of suitable age. That man is going to train his personal cohort in the use of the pike—the better the training, the better his chance of living. Too, I want them to fight as a team and what better way than by this? The exercises are to be done each Sunday when they are not required to work our fields."

The table sat silently for a moment, letting the enormity of what Vortimer was suggesting, sink in. Training the peasants to fight was one thing, but to arm them as well!

"Let each man supply his own food and drink. The farmers are thin enough as it is and I want them as strong as possible for this fight, understood? Any man taking food from a peasant is stealing from me and will be dealt with accordingly."

Glendon muttered.

"Think of it this way, Glendon," suggested Vortimer. "The peasant will, for one day, be your ally. You need him strong and you need him to trust in your own skills. You will fight not as individuals but as a team, a pair of killers."

Glendon smiled a little at this, the thought of killing the enemy was always pleasing.

"The pike, you say?"

"Yes, we can produce them easily and in sufficient number. As it is a two-handed weapon they won't require shields or training with that. Think of it! As you frontally deal with the enemy, your little farmer is harassing him from the side or rear—plunging the spike into his uncovered back or neck or pulling him down with the hook so that you might deal the killing blow."

Glendon closed his eyes, allowing the skirmish to play out in his mind.

"Might work...after a fashion. Certainly different, I grant you that."

Arming the peasants? What sort of madness is my husband thinking? And training them as well? This will not sit well with my father! We can't allow rabble to carry weapons! The entire idea is just absurd!

"We will also need a count of the weapons," Vortimer continued, "and collect them afterwards. Bridget can handle that aspect of the battle."

She felt herself flush with pride that Vortimer was making her a part of his battle scheme—but there was to be more.

Clearing the table of food, Vortimer produced the map of Bone Tear that Bridget had drawn up. There, in the darkening room and to the amazement of those who watched, Vortimer laid out his battle plan, his finger jabbing the map at several strategic places. Bridget deciphered her curious markings to the group, describing what the land was like at each point.

"Well?" He asked finally.

Varduc straightened his diminutive frame and cleared his throat. "I have had a bit too much to drink, young master, but as I see it, neither Alexander nor Caesar have ever had such a plan."

"Then you agree?"

"I agree that it is a bold plan, innovative, certainly. As to its success, well, that is always in the hands of the gods. For my own part, I will admit to its brilliance.

today—I have some ideas and you know the lay of the land better than anyone."

"You flatter me."

"I do not flatter, Bridget. That is not part of my makeup, I use you for the valuable person you are. Hurry, now. I will get Glendon before he takes off; and bring your map!"

Bridget set hurriedly about to change into riding gear as Vortimer went off in search Glendon.

What is this all about? He seems like a man possessed! Why does a man smile and become alive with a task? Or is it as Vortimer suggested? That having a direction, no matter where, is better than nothing? Why is my life so chaotic? For that matter, why is life so full of turns? All I wanted to be was a follower of the Christ and now look at me! Being part of a battle plan!

She stopped abruptly, aware once more of the possibility of Vortimer's death. His ideas were innovative, no doubt, and sure to succeed but what of the consequences? She pulled up her boots and like Vortimer, placed the possibility of death where it belonged.

The trio rode swiftly that morning, Vortimer hoping to get this part of his stratagem behind him. They rode to where the land met the north ocean, subdued in the lulling summer heat. Dismounting, Vortimer called for the chart and pointed to three places. "They will land here, here, or here. These are the only safe harbors for their long boats. Glendon, after Lugsasadh I will want two lookouts placed by each of these three beaches, understood? And they must be able to count!"

Glendon nodded.

"As soon as they see a sail on the horizon they are to ride like the wind back to the fortress where we will have the archers ready to go at a moments notice. Do you understand?"

"Yes, lord."

"Archers?" asked Bridget.

"Yes, they will do their work at night. Now, regardless of which beach they choose, we must have our confrontation here!" He pointed at the map.

The area was suitable for a battle, Bridget knew already. With swamps on both sides, the Vikings would choose the quickest route to their quarry.

"What do you think, Glendon?"

"After weeks at sea, I think they'd want to get this over as quickly as possible. I heard they have used this way before."

"Good, then let's go see the actual lay of the land! Bridget, keep a keen eye. We'll need it."

Can't we just stay here for a moment? I do love this place! The sky, land and water— together. And it is just a perfect day to sit here, have some wine and something to eat. I know just how tempestuous it can be here! His leg doesn't seem to be bothering him much today— could the Augustus I might have married been the one who wounded my husband?

"I think it best that we let the horses rest, Vortimer. They have ridden hard and not being soldiers, are unaware of the urgency."

"Perhaps you're right. You do know your horses, I grant you that. We'll let them graze for a bit, besides, it doesn't darken till later and the day is beautiful! A pity we had to spend it doing this."

Vortimer and Glendon allowed Bridget the most comfortable place to sit while they lay on their backs. Votimer, gazing up at the thick, white clouds, shared the rest of his battle plan. He did not ask for comments or suggestions, he simply uttered his thoughts. Bridget did not know if this sort of thinking was new or old and listened dumbly; Glendon attended in amazement.

"Well," Vortimer said at last, "it is time to see exactly where the killing will be done."

He stood and stretched while Glendon fetched the horses. Bridget stood as well, still unsure as to what it was she had just heard but knew it was unique in some way.

Once again they drove their animals with abandon but Bridget didn't care— Alexander was more than up to the task, his great lungs bellowing as his hooves thundered across the hard ground. They came at last to a large meadow that was thick with waist high wild grasses.

"They will be where we are now," Vortimer said. "We will be there." He pointed to an opposite rise several hundred yards away.

"They will begin walking slowly towards us," Vortimer said as he rode forward, Bridget trying to visualize the scene as her husband described it. "We will be doing the same. About here," he turned to Glendon, "they will begin to quicken the pace." He rode several yards further. "Here I want wasp nests placed along in a line from here to there," he pointed. "The beekeepers should have no problem removing the nests from the trees as it will be cooler and the little bastards are slower, no? But we'll waken them and give them some Viking blood to taste." He chuckled.

He rode forward some more till he was a bit more than half way to the hill where he and his men would be assembled.

"Glendon, get a company of men and dig a trench wide enough that a man can't jump it and as high as his head. Take all the men you need. The difficult thing is this: scattering the dirt so that there is no indication that it was even dug. The grass will be higher then and will hide it, still, it might do well to cover it over."

"Yes, lord. It will be done."

"I know it will."

This is his plan, then? To harass the enemy at night when they come ashore with hidden archers shooting into their camps and then this field with wasps and a trench to impede and confuse them before they are mown down?

Bridget found herself smiling faintly at the audacity of the plan, not knowing whether anything like this had been tried before. She watched Glendon throughout, trying to read his face and discern his reaction but the hulking man was like Vortimer in that his expression said nothing, hid everything.

"I think we have had a long day," he said to no one in particular, "and my leg is on fire. Let's get back before it is too dark and we lose our way."

Indeed, the sun was lowering earlier each day and whenever they stopped upon a prominence they could spy the flickering fires of the peasants in the distance that increased in number and brightness as they neared the fortress. Wearied, but refusing to complain, Bridget was silently glad when they at last rode through the gates, giving the horses to the men who greeted them. Vortimer gave last instructions to Glendon who acknowledged them with a grunt. Done, he and Bridget headed towards their quarters which seemed to forever be changing minutely each day—now they had some rough hewn steps leading towards it.

"My lord! My lady!" cried Gwenthe. "Mathilde, get them something from the kitchen! Here, sit!"

Bridget and Vortimer allowed Gwenthe to fuss over them at the table as Mathilde brought coarse bread that they soaked in bowls of steaming barley soup. Neither could contain their hunger and few words were spoken as they filled their bellies. When at last they were done, Gwenthe cleared her throat and stood sheepishly.

"A messenger came today," she said, looking at Bridget. "Your sister will be arriving here tomorrow or the next."

"My sister? How wonderful! What on earth for? Gwenthe, you must prepare her a room! You know how she can be."

"Yes, milady."

Her sister, here? Now? I trust that woman as much as I trust . . . one of those wasps! Still, she is Bridget's sister and there is nothing that can be done about that. I suppose it will be a nice diversion for Bridget to see her family again. Still, I'd rather Celestine was somewhere else, far away.

"To what do we owe the pleasure of your sister's company?"

"Is it wrong for her to visit? She is my sister, after all! Besides, you have all your comrades and who do I have?"

"Gwenthe and Mathilde."

"That is not the same and you know it!" Bridget snapped.

"I only asked why your sister has chosen now, this time, to visit?"

"Perhaps she comes because she loves me," she lied.

Oh, husband! If you only knew why she is coming here! No doubt to scold me severely and I deserve it, of course.

"Well," said Vortimer glumly, "we haven't the finery or amusements to entertain her. She must know what we are about here! We have no time for polite diversions!"

"She is my sister, lord, and I will find the time to make her feel welcome even if you cannot!"

"Bridget, this is insane! She is your sister, your problem!"

"My sister is not a problem, lord!" Bridget said aggressively. "She will be our guest and I will make her feel welcome in spite of you."

"Then offer her my compliments but I have other, more pressing matters at the moment and so do you! Don't forget the pikes and send the beekeepers to me. I am tired and it has been a long day and I am going to bed."

He stood abruptly, nodded to Gwenthe and Mathilde who observed the spat from a dark corner, and limped towards the steps that led to his room.

"I shall be up shortly," Bridget mumbled to his retreating back.

How did this happen? How could this all happen so quickly and out of control? Just a few hours ago I was worried about his life and now I am so mad at him I could spit!

Bridget smacked her palm so loudly on the table that Gwenthe and Mathilde jumped.

How could he do this to me? He is too exasperating! I would have done anything to keep him safe and free from harm! All I wanted was some small show of respect for my sister and he treats her as though she were some common trollop! 'My problem', he says! She is my sister and it has been she who has kept my belly free from a child. It was she who taught me how to behave with a man, though she was much mistaken about it not being pleasurable. Still, I know how to cool Vortimer's passion, just like tonight!

Bridget became acutely saddened by their dinner conversation. Things had been going so well for such a long time that this sudden argument caught her by surpise; her temper was like the roiling water in a covered cauldron, just wanting to scald a fool.

Vortimer, she is only my sister! I will perform my duties and keep Celestine as far from your affairs as possible, but you must put on some airs of civility, at least. Her husband is the wealthiest in these parts and the time may come when we may need his assistance. I will appeal to his political, rational side, then. Everything will be all right.

Calling over her two women, Bridget indicated where Celestine's quarters would be set up Seeing the expressions on both, she apologized for the inconvenience and difficulty Celestine was certain to cause but promised to keep her occupied as much as possible. Sitting alone at the table, Bridget wondered why Celestine was actually coming and why it had perturbed Vortimer so much? Unable to come up with a satisfactory answer, Bridget finally went up to their room where she found Vortimer lying beneath a thin cover, his back to her. Bridget dropped her garments and slid silently next to him, draping her arm over his shoulder and molding her body to his. Vortimer did not stir nor did he close his eyes, sleep would come much later.

Their day began, as always, before dawn. They kissed each other rather hurriedly, Bridget thought, but at least they had kissed. They washed quickly, dressed and went downstairs where a breakfast of eggs and bread was already waiting.

"Don't forget about those pikes, Bridget. I have several types, different variations, give them to the smith and have fifty of each made."

"Of course, and I will send the beekeepers to you as quickly as possible, though it may be difficult to locate them."

"Well, that goes without saying, of course. For now, though, no word of what is planned, understood?" He hesitated a moment. "Do you think it a good plan, Bridget? Answer me honestly."

"I always will answer you honestly and true, husband, for that is the basis of a firm understanding, is it not? I know nothing of battles and warfare, I admit. With that in mind, I think your ideas are extraordinary, perhaps brilliant."

"Varduc gave them to me. Rather he led me to them."

Yes, and I must see Varduc, my husband. He and I have much to discuss.

"I am off to see that Glendon is arranging for the digging of the trench and the training of the peasants—there should be some sport in that!"

"How so?"

Vortimer walked over to the main door and shouted for someone to bring him a pike immediately. Within the space of a few moments he returned with the weapon. It was wicked looking; someone seeing it for the first time would have no doubt that such an instrument was made only for killing and maiming. Even a sword could be used for some peaceful purpose, such as cutting down a tree, but not a pike. From its iron tip to the evil looking hook located a foot below it, the pike was a formidable weapon in skilled hands—ironically, those proficient in its use dealt more death blows with the blunt end of the oaken shaft. The tip was honed to a fine, strong point that with enough force could pierce through the iron links of mail or leather to the softer muscles and organs beneath. While it did not always penetrate deeply enough to deliver a fatal wound to heart or lungs, it was admirably suited to puncture muscle and cause extensive bleeding.

Care had to be taken with the hook. If it impaled someone high on the torso or thigh, it was possible that it could be ripped from the hands of the attacker with a forceful surge. It was always best to hook below the knees or elbows and thus pull the enemy to the ground where he might be easier prey. Hooking and then ripping a man through his throat was almost always lethal and it was shocking as to just how far the blood exploded from the wound.

Vortimer explained all this to Bridget graphically, using his own body as a model. She shivered inwardly, chilled at the thought that so gruesome a weapon could end her husband's life—yet she maintained an expression of profound interest, determined not to let the tears of fear drip down her face.

"Don't forget, and this is important, we need a complete count of every pike made. After the battle they are to be returned or at least accounted for. It'd do us no good to have these in the hands of the peasants, not at all!"

"Of course, Vortimer."

And I must find Varduc as well.

"I am off to find Glendon. I am not sure when I will be back."

"Dinner will be here for you as will I, my lord"

He looked at her closely, as if trying to find what thoughts were scurrying behind her green eyes. He kissed her lips gently. "Be well," he whispered.

255

"Be well," she replied in kind.

Waiting till Vortimer was well without the door, Bridget summoned Gwenthe and Mathilde, giving specific instructions as to how Celestine's room was to prepared. "I have other duties to attend to at the moment, so I will leave you two to be about it. If you should see Varduc, tell him I must see him immediately."

"That strange little man?" Matilde squealed.

"Strange perhaps, but utterly essential at the moment. Fetch me down my census, I have some things to look up. Then you two can begin preparing Celestine's quarters. Tell cook we will need the finest fare. Oh, and make sure Celestine has a tub in her room!"

Handing Bridget the sheaf of papers she requested, Mathilde and Gwenthe disappeared upstairs where they would argue about everything under the sun— particularly the peevish Celestine.

Bridget began thumbing over the pages, making mental notes of the beekeepers and their families and where each might generally be found. She would locate them this very day.

Satisfied, she headed out and down towards the stables where she and two escorts, the same who had been with her when she first made her census, had Alexander saddled. In a rough sack she had the pikes given her by Vortimer. It was not difficult to find the smith, she only had to look for plumes of thick smoke that smudged the clear sky of the morning. The din of hot metal being hammered and the rasping bellows was only exceeded by the chorus of cursing that sprung from the sweaty master as he verbally flayed his apprentices.

"Watch your tongue, master smith," said her first guard, "Lady Bridget has some business."

Bare to the waist, sweat-covered, he wore an oily leather apron. "Pardon me, missus," he bowed, "but there's some that don' unnerstan' lessen you speaks to 'em like they ought."

"Indeed, master smith! I have a commission for you from our lord."

She handed the man the pikes without dismounting. He examined them closely, remarking on their poor workmanship. "See this one!" He held it up. "I knew the man who fashioned this trash! And he calls himself a master, the bastard! Ha!"

"My husband is certain you can do better. There are five varieties here, we shall need one hundred of each. Can you do it?"

"Course I can do it but when will you be needing 'em?"

"The question is this, master smith, how long do you want to stay in our favor?"

"Aye, milady, I unnerstan'. We'll begin immediately."

"And should we come by some night and see your fires doused we will assume the job is completed, then?"

He hesitated a moment till he finally understood. "Night and day till the job is done."

"My lord will be pleased if you would deliver each day's work directly to me, is that understood?"

"Yes, missus. The longer we stay here talkin' the less time I have! I'll have 'em for you starting tomorrow."

He turned and yelled for his men to stop what they were doing for he was going to show them how a real craftsman fashioned a pike and by God, they would, too!

Satisfied with the first part of her assignment, Bridget's next task was more enjoyable as she was able to ride away from the confines of the fortress and into the fields and through the clusters of hovels. After two hours of questioning countless tenants she was able to learn the approximate location of only two of the beekeepers. Though it was a random search, it enabled her to see just how well or poorly the people fared, the conditions of their shacks and the size of the fields.

We could do with more people here, that's a fact. Maybe after we defeat the Vikings we will have more. More people, greater harvests, more wealth, more power, greater security.

She began to visualize Bone Tear as a thriving, powerful kingdom, greater than her father's, greater than anyone's! Countless courts would curry the favor of both she and Vortimer.

Vortimer! How did I get so angry with you last night? And why? Celestine! How silly it was of you to be so upset by her coming here. I know the real reason, she is wondering why you and I are making love so often! Oh, it has been like nothing I could have imagined, my husband. You are not like the dolts she spoke of! You are gentle for a man who is so powerful, and caring as well. I could lose myself in your arms and running my hands over your shoulders when you are inside me is a delight I never dreamt. How is it that one who has seen so much blood and death could also possess such a gentle and overwhelming passion? And your eyes, your grey eyes become so intense at the final moment!

Bridget felt herself grow warm with the memory of Vortimer inside of her and it was difficult to leave that feeling to deal with the matter at hand, the Vikings. Her wistful expression became grim. She urged Alexander on. It was well past noon before she located two of the three. She ordered them to present themselves to Vortimer within the next three days as he had urgent business to discuss with them. She also told them to find the third and bring him along as well. Satisfied that she had carried out her mission successfully, she headed back to the fortress—there was one last thing to do, find Varduc. She passed the smith on her way and dutifully noted an increased clamoring from within that was only surpassed by the master who was merrily heaping generous portions of abuse upon his hapless apprentices.

Though tired, she removed Alexander's tack herself and toweled him down, whispering in his ear that he was the greatest horse in the kingdom. She took a small carrot from one of the stable boys and gave it to him before he was led away.

Bridget walked up the steep steps and stopped halfway, allowing the midday breeze to blow through her hair and cool her skin. It was a grand view, she thought, beautiful, actually.

Bona Terra…Bone Tear…how fitting.

Gwenthe and Mathilde were waiting for her in the hall and proceeded to bring Bridget something to eat and drink.

"That strange man, Varduc, is upstairs in the private room. I didn't want him to be up there but he is your husband's counselor and he does have a thing with words to get his own way."

"It is all right, Mathilde. I will go see him now. Has anyone heard from Vortimer or my sister?"

"No, milady."

"See that Varduc and I are not disturbed. It is getting late so Celestine probably won't be here until tomorrow. Is her room ready?"

"Aye."

Bridget found Varduc staring out the window, his pallor accentuated by the strong light. Without turning he said, "Good day, young mistress. Yes, you are quite correct in observing that this is fertile ground. A pity that blood and bone must be sacrificed to keep it so. I saw you down there on the steps, gazing at the fields and beyond."

"You read my thoughts?"

"No, I just observed a beautiful young woman looking at a magnificent vista. What else would she be thinking?"

Bridget sat. "Then you know why I wanted to see you?"

Varduc grasped the window's edge and inhaled heavily. "Of course," he sighed,"Vortimer"

"Then you can read minds!"

"No, young mistress. I simply asked myself why you should want to see me so urgently after the plans for battle were discussed and the blood drained from your face."

"It was that obvious?"

"Only to those attuned to observe, young mistress. Now, get on with it and ask me what I cannot give."

"I want Vortimer to live. I want his life spared. I want him safe from hurt," she whispered huskily.

He waited a few moments before responding, still looking out at the land below, "Why?"

Of all the things Varduc could have said, this was the most unexpected and uncomfortable and Bridget felt herself become flustered.

Why, indeed!

"Because he is a good and brave man, and he is my husband and your close friend."

"He is as close to me as if he was my own, young mistress, perhaps closer," Varduc turned to face her, "**and** I love him."

Bridget's discomfort pushed her to react the only way she knew, "I will not bandy words with you. My reasons are my own! Can you, will you keep him safe or not?"

Varduc responded with a smile and sat across from Bridget. "Some people cannot recognize truth because it frightens them, it goes against everything they have ever believed, young mistress—I am not one of those people, however, so I will tell you the truth. I cannot promise you that his life will be spared; I cannot swear to his safety." He laughed unexpectedly, "I cannot even promise that this battle will be won!"

"What? What kind of wizard are you?"

Varduc started laughing uncontrollably and this perplexed Bridget even more.

"Wizard? Me? What fairy tales have you been taught?"

"Well, then, what are you? What kind of man reads minds and sees forests grow if not a wizard?"

"Young mistress, I am a very old man who has had the good fortune to be blessed by the goddess whom I serve in my own humble way. She has given me certain gifts which I use wisely and sparingly. She has not cursed me with the knowledge of the future. Being a seer would drive one mad with frustration, I imagine. The strange, diminutive man you see before you is the last of my kind, I believe. Though I have had some intimations of one greater than I who has yet to be born."

"Will he live or die?" Bridger persisted.

"Oh, he will most certainly die, young mistress! Me, you, anyone, anything that lives will die. Even your Christ died! Would you put him above the son of your God?"

Bridget felt a black anger being born deep within, much like the time with the dishonest steward. Her shoulders stiffened as her hands unconsciously fisted and relaxed, fisted and relaxed.

"Forgive me, young mistress, please forgive this foolish and philosophical old man," he giggled. "You come to me scared and concerned and I am trying to teach you a thing of Life and Death. Just hear me out."

Bridget closed her eyes and willed herself to relax as Varduc's whistling voice washed through her.

"Vortimer, the Iron Dog, is a battler and warrior. Some day he may become a leader who allows others to risk death but that time is not yet. No one knows the number of his days. Some die before they have even taken three breathes, others, like me, die old and feeble. Which is best? I have tried to discover but still do not know, young mistress." He hesitated a moment. "What I can do is to try to maintain his safety and one thing further though I hesitate, it depends upon what you are willing to sacrifice."

"Depends on what, what? What sacrifice do I have to make?"

"Nothing quite so dramatic as blood being spilt, the goddess is not interested in some dead chicken or lamb—she demands more!"

"What?"

"Lughnasadh is approaching rapidly. If, on that day, the proper sacrifice is made, I may be able to grant you one boon."

"Lugnasadh?"

"Your priests have changed it to 'loaf mass'. Perhaps you have heard it referred to as Lammas in early August?

"Oh, yes! When we bake bread from the first harvested wheat and bring it to the church. But what is my offering?"

Varduc grimaced. "The feast is so much older and more sacred than what your Christian friends would have you believe, young mistress."

"Yes?"

"It is a remembrance of the death of Lugh's foster-mother, Tailtiu. She died clearing land so that grains and crops could be planted and then harvested so that we all might live. We honor the death of the harvest gods who sacrifice themselves so that we, the children of the Goddess, may put food on the table. It is also a time of jubilation because the gods of the harvest will be renewed once more. So has it been, so it will remain—no matter what your Christians do, the Great Circle continues."

"But what of my sacrifice and renewal? What am I to do so that your boon will be granted?"

"I am an old man and not entirely sure, but I will know, young mistress. More importantly, you will recognize it as well. If it occurs, you will be on the field of battle with Vortimer, closer than his shield. Perhaps that burning rage that is barely hidden behind your eyes may keep him safe from harm."

Bridget hesitated. How could she be on the field with Vortimer? Still, Varduc had a sincerity that could not be dismissed as a riddle, not with something so serious as Vortimer's life. He sat there impassively, sadness draping his usually beaming countenance.

"Do you know why," Varduc asked, "the Vikings are such fierce warriors?"

Bridget shrugged.

"Because they do not fear dying. Life and Death to them is one in the same. They may be savages but they do have an acute wisdom."

Bridget sat back in her chair, drained more by the encounter with Varduc than the hardest ride she ever rode.

"You say you are not a seer, but I feel you see something! You must! Tell me what you see, Varduc, and I swear this will be the end of it!"

He closed his eyes, slumped his shoulders and for a while Bridget thought he might have fallen asleep. The air in the room became thick and dank.

"Hands," he muttered. "I see hands covered in blood, cold blood, very cold."

The hands! He has seen the bloody hands! Has he seen the Hooded Man? Does he know who he is?

He snapped his eyes open.

"Young mistress, I apologize for not being able to give you what you most desire; it is not in my power nor yours. I am very tired and must go now. Besides, Vortimer will be arriving shortly and it would not be wise to let your fear show, something else perhaps, but never fear. Doing that would show that you doubted him. And no soldier, not even the Iron Dog, can abide doubt."

He stood gracefully as he pushed back the chair and headed out the door with no further word.

Feeling herself dismissed, Bridget sat still, digesting all that had been heard but remained unsatisfied. No wonder Vortimer could curse and praise his counselor in the same breath!

Lughnasadh! All this time I thought it was a time just to bring the first baked bread from the new harvest to the church! No wonder the peasants celebrate it so robustly! The gods laid down their lives for them at harvest but will be reborn in the Spring. The Endless Circle.

Bridget recalled how the holiday was celebrated with abandon! There were fairs, jugglers, singers, musicians and athletic contests. It was a glorious time of rest and play before the arduous task of harvest began.

And those great wheels that they set on fire and rolled down the hills—the passage of the sun?

The young woman was suddenly confused. Death and Rebirth, wasn't that what the church taught? God sacrificing Himself for the salvation of humanity. Didn't that belong only to the church? Feeling she was at the edge of some great heresy or about to taste the apple of forbidden knowledge, Bridget retreated.

This is far too complicated for me to understand right now. Perhaps another time, for now I have to get ready for Vortimer and see to Celestine's quarters. What will my sacrifice be on Lammas, I mean Lughnasadh?

Uncharacteristically befuddled by all that she had learned, Bridget summoned her ladies who arrived within moments.

"Show me Celestine's room."

It was larger than the room shared by her and Vortimer with a window that looked like an afterthought and the floor covered with the thinnest of carpets. The bed looked comfortable and clean enough and as requested, a tub sat against a far wall.

"Was the best we could do, milady," said Gwenthe.

"Well, the best is all we can offer, isn't it? I no longer care if she is put out. Bone Tear is in no position to entertain at the moment. That reminds me, Lughnasadh draws near. What have you heard?"

Gwenthe and Mathilde looked at one another, Bridget had never used the old name before. "Oh, they be getting ready," cried Mathilde. "Many is the family that brought their grains from where they left and there is to be ale aplenty. I also know that several of them play instruments but have voices that scratch your ears! But who cares? It will be fun!"

"Well, keep me informed. It is a very important feast and I want to be a part of it. Vortimer should be here shortly and he will be tired and hungry, have a good dinner prepared and ready."

Bridget went down to the hall, having only herself for company.

It is terribly lonely, after all. I have a husband, soldiers and women at my disposal but when all is said and done, I remain alone with only my fears and misgivings for company.

Bridget was not at all pleased with her sister's room and Varduc's 'wisdom' made her uneasy.

Varduc should have lied to me—told me that victory was a certainty and that Vortimer avoided death as easily as he conquered his foes—but that would be a lie he knew I would see right through! No, I am better for hearing his truth.

She sat glumly, wringing her hands unconsciously, barely mindful of the pleasing aromas that were drifting from the kitchen. Bridget's morose thoughts were quickly subdued by Vortimer's entrance into the hall with little preamble— she stood and flung herself into his surprised arms.

"Bridget, I was barely gone half a day," he said jokingly but continued to hold her close.

"I know, I know! I just missed you! Can't a wife miss her husband, after all? Or would you want me to be a lady?"

"I much prefer the Bridget I am holding in my arms than to any other sort. But at the moment I am famished and my leg is on fire. Let's sit and you can tell me about your day while I will tell you what I have discovered."

The table was simply set but the meat was well-seasoned. Bridget recounted her experiences with the smith and beekeepers. "And how did your day go with villagers?"

"As well as could be expected, I suspect. No one was pleased with being forced into military service and who could blame them? Farming may be a brutal existence but it doesn't often lead to a painful death, no? They were pleased about being trained in the use of arms, however. Glendon thought so as well. I think my men will find themselves some worthy allies and they had better treat them as such! But I also discovered something unsettling."

"Lord?"

Vortimer looked about to make sure their conversation was not easily overheard by Gwenthe or Mathilde.

"Did you know that your peasants, our peasants, kill their female children?"

Bridget was about to begin a fiery defense of her people but hesitated for the briefest of moments—there had been rumors but that was ages ago and had long been condemned.

"What makes you think so, Vortimer," she whispered.

"We went through several small villages and a few larger ones, estimating how many households and men would be available to fight. Then it struck me, the boys outnumbered the girls by about three to one! I knew they did this sort of thing back from where I came from but I did not think it was still practiced, did you?"

Bridget suddenly recalled that one night at her father's when she spied a figure running furtively into the forest while carrying a small bundle—the memory sent a sudden chill through her.

"No,' she lied. "I thought these were just tales told to frighten little girls who misbehaved. Why do they do this? What can we do to stop them?"

"They do it to survive. A boy child is stronger and can begin working the fields earlier than his sister. Or he can learn a trade or a craft. The women are seen as being weak, a hindrance rather than a help. How to stop them? I was hoping you might have some better ideas as the previous ones haven't worked. This is something we will have to do in concert once we finish the business that is at hand. Any word on Celestine's arrival?"

"Not yet but I suspect tomorrow."

"It seems to me that things are coming to a head far too quickly but we have no control over time, we just have to use what we do have, wisely."

The rest of the meal was eaten slowly, each attuned to the nuances of the other.

Whatever animosity had existed over Celestine's visit had been smothered by their joint efforts in preparing for the defense of Bone Tear. That night they lay in bed tired but too restless to sleep. The conversation touched upon many things: the peasants, the ferocious smith, how Celestine would regard her accommodations (this made them both laugh) and Lugnasadh.

"Lugnasadh?" said Vortimer. I thought you would have said Lammas in deference to the church. But what is your concern over the holiday?"

"I think it is important, very important for all of us that we make this the finest, largest celebration possible. I realize that our initial crops will be meager but I will have grain sent from my father for us to use. Too, the people need it. Don't ask me how I know, I just do. I have even seen it in your men—we need to sow a sense of loyalty among the peasants—particularly as we are requiring them to bear arms."

Varduc, how could I have doubted your wisdom? This woman, often maddening, has become my greatest asset after all.

"I do not know how these things get arranged but you have my full support to see it gets accomplished. It may even occupy Celestine! Begin tomorrow."

"Is there anything else my lord wishes," she laughed.

"Yes, now that you mention it."

Bridget did not bother with her dwindling supply of Celestine's elixir nor did she bother to squat and sneeze—she knew her cycle was fast upon her. Instead she allowed herself the rare pleasure of just lying in Vortimer's arms afterwards, amazed at how much contentment this simple contact gave.

This is maddening! He can make me so angry so quickly and then there are the times like this when my universe is within his arms. Why is this so? Am I not my own woman?

Bridget buried her cheek against Vortimer's shoulder and thought of all the changes that had come upon her. She was no longer the simple girl who yearned for the cold comfort of the nunnery—the thought brought a smile.

How foolish I was! To think that I might never had moments such as these. What did the abbess say about taking widows into the order? Never! That wicked woman, even suggesting such a thing. Still, it was I who wanted to join. I was a complete fool! I will never be a widow.

Bridget felt Vortimer begin to stir in his sleep and within moments he was battling his nocturnal foes. She listened closely but mostly it was grunts and cries—she felt the sweat seep from his skin as she held him tighter, afraid to waken him, not knowing what it might do. Would he be embarrassed? Grateful? She hated this! It had been so long since the last time, she thought that it was all behind them.

Vortimer's whimpering caused Bridget to weep silently and she clutched him tighter, whispering gently into his ear, desperately trying to take him from the horrible place he was in. Slowly, in small bits, she felt his body relax but this did not stop her tears that spilled generously down her chin. It seemed as though her tremors increased as his subsided. It was long, dark moments before both were quietly lying together.

Bridget was frightened more than anything; that and feeling powerless.

Varduc said I would be in battle next to him, close as his shield. I cannot even protect him from a damn dream. Vortimer, Vortimer! What is it that plagues you? I have never told you of the Hooded Man, have I?

She shivered at the thought of the bloody hands and realized that it had been a long time since she had dreamed of him. Why was that? Was she as terrified and troubled as Vortimer? She did not recall ever soaking her sheets through.

Bridget imagined herself as Vortimer's shield, deflecting swords, spears and arrows—sacrificing herself for him. The image twirled and twisted in the vague interlude before sleep, however imperfect it was.

The following morning began as all their previous mornings—early and bustling. Bridget did not bother to mention Vortimer's dream and if he had any memory of it he hid it. Bridget was more concerned with her monthly flow at the moment and she forewarned Vortimer who nodded sheepishly—as if this was something of a woman that only women should share.

Their meal was hurried and Bridget studied his countenance and mannerisms, wanting to see if she could discern any troubles—she did not. They went their separate ways—he to examine the building of the trench and to see to the training of the peasants. Bridget would check on the pikes and make preparations for Lugnasadh.

She was about to begin making a list of necessary items when a messenger was brought in to announce that her ladyship, Celestine, would be arriving before the noon hour.

Celestine! How could I have forgotten? My brain has too many things going on! Well, nothing can be done regarding my sister. All I can do is to prepare for the feast and to check on the pikes.

Bridget buried herself in her work but felt the tension twist her belly as the sun rose higher. She was trying to figure how many bushels of grain they would need when the doors of the hall opened and Celestine was announced.

Bridget was unprepared for the figure that presented itself as Celestine. While Celestine had always been beautiful, the woman before her was, well, dazzling—Celsestine radiated warmth and light where none had been before. She even smiled generously at Mathilde and Gwenthe who bowed their respects. It was as if a goodness glowed within and spilled out in a smile that charmed all those fortunate enough to behold it. Bridget, a head taller than her sister, felt her shoulders droop and neck bow.

"Bridget! Dear, Bridget!" Celestine came to Bridget in a rush of hugs and kisses given with abandon and joy.

"Celestine! I am so glad you are here. Oh, I really am! I am sorry that our dwelling is not…"

""Hush, you silly goose, my poppet! Where is my brother-in-law, your husband? My, you are quite the woman now, aren't you? Look at you!"

"Oh, Celestine. Stop it."

"Poppet, you really are! I can see it in the way you carry yourself! But enough of this for now. Come, show me to my rooms, let me refresh myself a bit. No, that can wait. Have my things," she waved towards chests that were being stacked by the door, "brought to my room. I really want to talk with you alone for a bit."

Bridget held Celestine's hand as she brought her into her bedroom.

"Ah," said Celsestine as she looked at the bed, "this is where you whore yourself?"

"What?" said Bridget, certain that she had misunderstood.

Celestine's smile was even more radiant and expansive. "Isn't this where you spread your legs for him? Isn't it here in the bed or do you also do it in the stables. Surely I cannot embarrass you poppet! You like having him inside of you, feeling his juice up inside your belly. Is this the same girl who cried how frightened she was?"

Celestine's hand whipped out sharply and slapped Bridget full on the face.

Bridget did not know what was more surprising—Celestine's venomous words or the sting of her hand—she stood motionless, speechless.

Celestine sat on the side of the bed. "What, dear sister, nothing to say? Is your tongue stuck? I'll wager it is busy when you lie here with him. Tell me, how do you use it? Does he like it? It is evident that you are not the silly virgin you led me to believe in. You made a fool of me."

"Stop it! Please," Bridget cried. "It is all wrong. All of it! I didn't know what to do and I was so scared and alone." She started to blubber, the words coming out in pieces. "He is so nice to me and not terrible and there are just so many things and I felt safe in his arms!"

All Bridget's fears, known and unknown, erupted from her heaving chest and vented through her eyes. She dropped to her knees, placed her head on Celestine's and wept uncontrollably.

Bridget, Bridget! Whatever am I to do with you? How can I keep you from having his child if you persist in behaving so like a whore? Where are your brains at, girl? Well, it is obvious that you are not thinking with your brains, my poppet, my tart. Let us assess the damage and see what needs to be done. She and Vortimer actually live here? Well, it is better than a stable, I suppose.

"Dear Bridget, dear Bridget," Celestine hugged her, gently enveloping and rocking her back and forth ever so gently, kissing the back of her head—allowing Bridget's crying to diminish.

Look at you! Your face is all red and blotched. If you ever saw what you looked like, you would never again shed a tear!

"I am sorry I struck you sister. I truly am! Please forgive me! It is just that I have been so worried and concerned for both you and he and I recall how much you feared becoming pregnant. I said some terrible things but I spoke my heart—I cannot apologize for that." Celestine fell to her knees, faced Bridget and rested her cheek on the big girl's shoulder.

'You have done so much to help me, Celestine, and it appears that I have been ungrateful! No, let me apologize! Or let us both not apologize, just hold me and know that nothing has changed and that I still love you."

Celestine laughed weakly. "Oh, a great deal has changed, Bridget, a great deal! You are no longer the timorous virgin. Well, we could not expect that to last forever, could we? The important thing is…" she let the sentence die.

"No, I am not pregnant. I am certain! Even now I am bleeding and I have been careful in doing all that we ever spoke of. It is just that, well, he is very passionate."

Celestine desperately wanted to place her hand between Bridget's legs and smear her menstrual blood to make sure but controlled the sudden compulsion which excited her somehow.

"Of course he is. Now we just have to learn how to control yours, Bridget." Celestine laughed genuinely, stood and pulled Bridget to her feet. "Come, show me to my quarters. Let me get my things unpacked. Where is my brother-in-law?"

Bridget led Celestine to her rooms and was overjoyed with her sister's effusive approval. Bridget noticed Calgwyn, her sister's woman, carefully unpacking Celestine's things, and nodded in recognition. Calgwyn curtsied, noting Bridget's flushed face and ragged appearance.

Bridget left the two of them, went to her own quarters to refresh then the kitchen to make sure the night's meal would be particularly pleasing to Celestine.

Bridget, confused by all that had happened, felt it best to concentrate on one thing at a time and this worked perfectly. Next, she visited the smith, counting the pikes and making arrangements with Vortimer's man to begin their distribution. Satisfied, she returned to the hall, determined to calculate their needs for Lugnasadh.

The day wore on, Bridget ignoring the comings and goings of her home, preferring to forget all the words that had passed between her and Celestine as she tried to concentrate on the tasks before her. It was one thing to have managed her father's castle but this was far beyond running a household. The hours dragged by and Bridget was startled by Celestine's hand on her shoulder.

"Poppet, whatever are you doing? You look positively overwhelmed!"

Bridget shoved her papers away and tried to explain it to her sister who nodded with sympathy and the slightest of smiles that grew the longer Bridget complained.

"Sister, sister," Celestine chided, "there is nothing to fret about. It is all taken care of."

"What do you mean?"

"First, the peasants have been able to hunt game and there is ample salt, no? They won't starve. Second, there were promises of grain and foodstuffs from father's nobles at your wedding—I will see that the promises are kept. Third, for Lammas or any celebration all they need are beer and games and they can supply that themselves."

"Are you certain?"

"My dear, what is a sister for if not to aid her sister? But the smells from your kitchen are enticing and I am not used to traveling this far at all! Shall we eat?"

"I was hoping that we could wait for Vortimer. I know he was desperate to see you again," Bridget lied.

"Oh, milady," cried Mathilde who was coming from the kitchen, "a messenger came earlier and you were so busy. My lord will be in the field tonight with Glendon and he sends his regrets but he will be back tomorrow as early as possible."

"There, you see? Everything settled. We can even sleep together! But for now I would like to eat."

Bridget had dinner served and watched as Celestine ate vigorously, something she had never seen before. Through it all, Celestine told Bridget the latest gossip from the courts and after several goblets of wine, Bridget, eager to keep up her end of the conversation forgot Vortimer's admonition and revealed the battle stratagem to her sister.

"Arming the scum? Training them? That sounds desperate! Well, I know that Lord Glamorgan and his men will be here and if Vortimer is anything like his reputation then I do not foresee any problem. A wonderful dinner, Bridget! You have out done yourself in spite of your mean surroundings! Shall we retire to my room for the evening? We have much to discuss."

Arm in arm, the two women ascended the stairs to the upper chambers. Celestine's woman had everything laid out.

"Now, poppet, let us talk! Such a beautiful view! No wonder you are so enchanted! The sky looks more brilliant here, the fields more lush." She mused.

"I hope you find your quarters comfortable. Everything happened so quickly and we were unsure as to how large to build the fortress. For how long will you be staying?"

Celestine did not answer immediately, preferring to look out the window, the sun bathing her face and adding a glow to her fine hair.

How long? I'd stay as long it took to insure you never have a child but I cannot hover about you all the time, can I? The Stones have promised that I will bear a son, shouldn't I be satisfied with that? Still, I want to make absolutely certain there are no complications, loose threads or brats about! Accidents and diseases happen all the time, such a pity for the children! Too, the battlefield is such a perilous place, poppet! When will they come? Ah, that I could stay as long as it took!

"Is Vortimer's creature about?"

"You mean Varduc?"

"Yes, is that his name? An odd fellow, don't you agree?"

"A bit strange, perhaps," Bridget replied, wondering why Celestine even mentioned him.

"I will only be here a few days, my dear. I have to return as Theodorus is fairly worthless in running our holdings. My woman will remain longer as I have instructed her to prepare enough elixir from your local flora. She can sleep in the kitchen, she doesn't eat much and will be out of the way."

"What do I tell Vortimer?"

"Tell him that she is a gift, that she is preparing recipes to increase your vitality during these hard times! In the meantime, you must reaffirm your original desires both to me and to yourself. I could not bear to see you die from a big belly caused by some silly indiscretion during a moment of weakness, Bridget. No, I could not bear that! You are all I have in the world!"

Seduced by her sister, Bridget was overwhelmed with gratitude.

"I have never known that one person could owe so much to another, Celestine," she knelt next to her and kissed her hand. "I feel my resolve much stronger now, it will never falter."

Raising Bridget to her feet, Celestine hugged her warmly and the pair watched as the shadows lengthened. The sky, once cloudless, became a serene palette of crimsons and purples. The trilling of the night insects increased while the bustlings of humanity diminished. The cooling land spawned a breeze that refreshed them both. Celestine wanted Bridget to sleep with her but she declined. Her flow made her feel uncomfortable, she said, and besides, Celestine always slept late.

Once in her own room, Bridget stripped and changed the padding between her legs, noting how sodden it had become. She had become accustomed to Vortimer lying next to her in bed and sleep came slowly now that he was absent, his scent, however, remained on the bedding.

Bridget woke when it was still dark and spent most of the morning in the hall, going over records and receipts, declining to eat until her sister arose. Celestine did not appear until the sun was well above the horizon and promised to make the day sweltering. Together they ate, Celestine reflecting on her inability to sleep in a strange bed as Bridget yearned for Vortimer to return. In spite of her renewed pledge to Celsestine, she found his presence comforting and somehow his wry smile made her laugh within. That she never wanted a child was true enough and that she would do everything to prevent becoming pregnant was also true; still, there was no reason why she could not miss her husband, was there?

Bridget allowed her conflicting drives to seethe, absently listening to Celestine prattle about new fabrics she was expecting. Bridget was about to leave to check on the smith's progress when Vortimer burst unannounced through the main door. Limping and sweating, he called for some food as he headed toward the two women.

Bridget hugged him warmly, kissing his cheeks as was proper before company.

"Ah, Bridget! So good to be home! I see we have a guest! Celestine," he bowed gently, "we welcome you to our home."

His mouth belies his heart, I can tell! Could he suspect that my sister and I are deceiving him? But it is not a deception, not really.

would not change any thing about you, I swear! But know this, deep in my heart I have reason to believe that all will be well. This is something more than just the fancy of a wife, it is far deeper than that. I feel it when I walk on the ground or when the sun shines on me. I hear it in the winds and smell it in the tall grasses. This is our land, it will be no one else's."

"In truth?"

"Always in truth."

For the first time that she could remember, Vortimer placed his head on her shoulder and his arm over her waist. She felt his breath upon her breast and at once her heart ached to protect him at all costs. She kissed his forehead softly.

Always in truth.

The day began more hectic than usual as Celestine had risen with the sun to get an early start on her journey south. The sisters protested their love and devotion for each other as Vortimer made sure Celestine's carriage, belongings and escort were in order.

"I will not forget to see that the supplies are sent, poppet; and you must not forget your promise! I love you! Send Calgwyn back when she has completed her task."

"And I love you, Celestine. Your words are stronger now than ever before."

"Just one thing further before I leave. Why not let Vortimer take a slut? It is something to consider, dear. The finest women find this perfectly acceptable."

"Perhaps," replied Bridget who was taken aback at the suggestion.

They kissed one last time and Bridget watched till the retinue was out of sight—sickened by the thought of Vortimer with another woman.

Bridget did not think the pace of preparations could become any more feverish but the next few weeks proved her wrong. True to her promise, Celestine had bushels of grain sent and granaries had to be constructed and a miller located. The smith's pikes were distributed daily and Vortimer was relentless in readying his troops, driving them and himself to exhaustion. Each plan, it seemed, had several contingencies that were drilled over and over. Some nights they slept together but lovemaking had become sporadic, not because of Bridget's deceptions but because each was preoccupied with the day's events and the demands of the next.

Bridget watched as Vortimer's demeanor changed. He became short-tempered, even with Gwenthe and Mathilde. Never one to speak without something to say, he spoke even less and Bridget found herself having to pull even the curtest response from him. His nightmares became more frequent and intense and this more than anything else, both frightened and affected her to the point of weeping. The only one who seemed impervious to all that was happening was Varduc.

Desperate for answers and reassurances, Bridget was never able to speak with the bird-like man in private. He was, it seemed, everywhere and nowhere. Either he was at Vortimer's side or Glendon's. Twice she had seen him with the smith as he forged the evil-looking bills which Bridget had to admit were of better quality than the ones she had given him. At other times she saw Varduc wandering aimlessly about, speaking to tradesmen or peasants—it was maddening that he spoke to everyone except her!

The days, though hot were visibly growing shorter as midsummer was long past. The peasants were diligently praying to the goddess for a good harvest as they tended their fields and flocks. A good yield meant food for man and beast during the approaching winter, the alternative was unthinkable—starvation for all. Sacrifices were being made to Lugh even before his feast.

Unfettered by the church, Bridget and Vortimer woke on the appointed day to find that red and white colored ribbons and strips of cloth hung from doorways and posts and waved in the easy morning air. Overnight, it seemed, a great crowd had camped outside the fortress.

"Look at them all!" Bridget exclaimed giddily.

Families dotted the fields beyond the gates and slept in or under their carts or meanly constructed tents. Children ran between smoky fires as the women prepared the morning meal while the men, lean and dark, gathered in small, animated groups. Vendors of cloth, ornaments, leather-goods and iron were optimistically setting up booths as they hawked their wares even before they were displayed. It would be a day free from the sweat of drudgery; it would be a rare day of play, games, races, ale and mischief

Look at them all! Look at them all! These are all our people! Vortimer looks so haggard and worn…we have all been working too hard. I cannot recall the last time he smiled. Where is Varduc? What of the sacrifice I have to make before the day's end? Why haven't I been able to speak with him?

"Would you care to go down there, Bridget?" Vortimer asked quietly.

"What?"

"Do you want to go down there among the people? Maybe purchase some ribbons? I know you have been working tirelessly, we all have been! I also know that you have been without the finer things, as Celestine made clear."

"I would like nothing more than to go down there by your side, Vortimer. Perhaps we can find some sweetcakes?"

Is this happening? Does this mean that he appreciates me and all I have done? But he has toiled and worried more than any of us!

Bridget took more time dressing that morning than usual, having Mathilde brush her hair, something she had not done for weeks, it seemed. She took great care in adjusting the shawl Vortimer had given her so that it could be viewed with better advantage. Vortimer dismissed the entire household staff, including Gwenthe and Mathilde, allowing them all this bit of dalliance.

"Do we walk or ride?" Bridget asked.

"Well, as it appears that everyone has left and I do not care to saddle our horses, I think it best if we walk."

The only commerce they noticed was the smith, everyone else was outside the gates, including Glendon who allowed himself to get caught up in the infectious frivolity. Together the three of them walked and watched the jugglers and musicians. Vortimer was asked to judge a tug-of-war while Bridget was given honey-glazed apples.

"See here! My lady adores my wares! Eat! Get the best right here!" the vendor shouted.

Little giggling children ran up and bowed so ungracefully that they could not help but laugh and ale was in an endless supply. Though not yet noon, most of the men and many of the women were speaking thickly as they tottered along.

"What do you think?" asked Glendon as they walked among the milling throng.

Vortimer thought a moment before answering, looking all about. "These are our people. No better and certainly no worse than many we have seen. They do make a merry bunch!"

"Young master! Young mistress! Lord Glendon! Such a marvelous celebration!" said Varduc who appeared, as usual, from no where.

Varduc, you aggravating, little man! You come at the most inopportune of times! How can I speak to you alone? What is it I must sacrifice and to whom? And you look inebriated!

"Will you be entering the race, young master?" Varduc asked.

"I don't know. When will it be held?"

"Race? What race?" Bridget asked peevishly. "Vortimer, your leg…"

"You have never seen my lord run, milady," said Glendon.

"Thank you, Glendon, but I can answer on my own," Vortimer said."What time is the race, Varduc, and what is the course?"

"It will begin as the sun casts long shadows, young master. Ten times around the perimeter of the gates! Ten times!"

"Very well, then. Fetch me some ill-fitting clothes and a cap too large. We have some hours before the race and I will have to locate a place to change. Come, Bridget, let's find you some ribbons."

"Have you gone mad? Why a foot race? Why not a horse race?"

"A horse race so you could win? Most of them don't own horses and those they do have are used to pull, not run. Come, let us watch the wrestlers over there. Where are some pretty ribbons?"

"Vortimer, I must really..."

"It bears no further discussion," he smiled. "Now, where are those ribbons?"

Bridget stewed with indignation and glowered at the grinning Varduc who seemed oblivious to any argument. The joy that Bridget felt earlier had vanished as dew before the sun.

Why does he have to do this? Where is the merit in it? That damned Varduc! Where did he come from and why did he have to mention the race at all? His leg will be in agony and he will be more crippled! Why must he do this? Well, as it bears no further discussion, it bears no further thought!

Still, Bridget could not shake the feeling of impending calamity and the gayest of cloth and ribbons did nothing to alleviate it. Vortimer and Glendon carried on as if nothing was going to happen and Varduc, well, he had disappeared into the crowd once more. Thirsty from the dust and heat, Bridget began to drink whatever ales were proffered her way and became sullen.

The day wore on and the crowds began ringing the hills surrounding the fortress to get the best view of the coming race.

"Glendon," said Vortimer who had some rags now tucked beneath his arm, "I am going to change over there," he pointed to some vacant carts. "Bridget, have the faith in me I had in you," he chided as he kissed her cheek. "Go with Glendon to the ramparts of the fortress, it will be the best way to see the running."

Bridget did not respond to Vortimer's words or kiss but headed abruptly towards the fortress, Glendon fast behind. The day had begun to cool and both Bridget and Glendon relished the breeze as they looked down on the mob of maybe fifty people gathered together at the race's start.

"Which one is he?" she asked.

"Can't tell, milady. That's the point isn't it? If he ran as Vortimer they'd let him win if they valued their skins. As it is, the Iron Dog will run disguised."

"But he is so tall!"

"I think you will see a stooped beggar running for quite some time. That'll be he."

"How can he run, let alone think he can win?"

"Have faith, milady. Care to wager?"

She ignored him.

There were big bellied men, shirtless youths and girls and women who would be in the race and this delighted the spectators who laughed and shouted drunken encouragement to the participants who were forming a starting line about three deep—and then there was Varduc! Bridget felt her anger rise once more at all this folly.

There was a different quality in his voice; it carried effortlessly and silenced the crowds—even the children quieted.

"We come here to honor Lugh! We come here seeking a bountiful harvest! We come here as Bone Tear!"

The crowd erupted into great shouts of affirmation.

"Ten times around the boundary set is the race. To the winner, this loaf of bread!" He held it over his head and this brought another roar of approval.

"Runners—start!"

Bridget's heart jumped, no matter what she thought, Vortimer was down there somewhere.

As expected, several youths took off like deer being chased by hounds. The rest of the runners ran in a bunch. Bridget and Glendon did not follow the leaders but focused on the pack in the rear. "There he is! There he is!" shouted Bridget as she pointed at a curious old man running tentatively. "I know that's Vortimer!"

"I think you be right, milady!"

Vortimer plodded more than ran, stooped over, his arms swung easily but his limp was painfully evident to Bridget who shook her head.

A curious thing began to happen even before one circuit had been completed. Two of the early leaders were bent over, clutching their sides, gasping for air and this delighted the spectators who shouted in derisive merriment at their anguish yet who took them aside and sat them down to rest. No one paid attention to the last runner who was running next to a big-breasted woman who struggled mightily to keep them from heaving back and forth. Bridget saw Vortimer tell her something and the woman began laughing so hard she stopped running, her face florid and sweat-streaked.

With one circuit completed, Vortimer was last but appeared to be running comfortably in spite of remaining hunched over.

He is the only one wearing a cap! He must be so hot! But he chose to do this!

More runners began to drop as the race continued up and down the rolling hills—Vortimer only passed those who had dropped by the wayside. Though last, he was closer to the leaders now. The runners had run around four times when Bridget remarked to Glendon that Vortimer was standing more erect now, his eyes never wavering from the runner in front of him.

"Iron Dog, milady. Iron Dog."

Bridget felt herself becoming more excited as the runners continued.

Can he actually do this? Can he really finish when so many others have given up?

Six times around now and Vortimer began passing runners who had lost either the legs or the lungs to keep running at the same pace. The crowds were now seriously into the race urging the remaining runners with yells of encouragement that seemed to propel them just that much faster, even Vortimer! He ran through a small group of runners and now only had three runners in front of him.

Bridget began screaming his name and pummeling Glendon's massive shoulders with her fists. "Look at him! Look at Vortimer! Glendon, look at Vortimer!"

"Now you shall see what your husband is all about, milady!" he laughed.

Not accustomed to viewing long distance running events, it was evident even to Bridget that the leading runners were in trouble by the way they gulped in air and swung their arms wildly, steps faltering.

Vortimer took the lead at the beginning of the eighth lap and the crowd went delirious with shouts that this impoverished upstart with the bad leg was now the leader. Several times Vortimer looked back to see where the remaining runners were and whether or not someone had a reserve of energy. Believing no one could threaten his lead, Vortimer flung off his cap and stood to his full height as he stripped off his sodden tunic.

Bridget did not know where the cry began or who started it but once the viewers recognized their lord they began to chant, "Bone Tear! Bone Tear!" The din grew and thundered as Vortimer rounded the course and became recognized by all.

"Bone Tear! Bone Tear!" The cries crashed through the hills and Bridget swore the ramparts vibrated. The crowd shook their fists in the air as Vortimer raised his in salute. "Bone Tear! Bone Tear! Bone Tear!"

Bridget's voiced joined the multitude's and she began weeping with the joy and splendor of it all. "Bone Tear! Bone Tear! Bone Tear!" Every throat and every fist was now one as they shared Vortimer's victory as though it were their own and still they cried out with fierce abandon, filling the evening air. The shouting only deepened as Vortimer began the final lap, waving to the viewers, shouting to them.

Bridget watched, delirious with joy at what she had just witnessed and the fevered passion of the peasants shouting "Bone Tear!" as she clambered down from the ramparts and ran out the gates. Charging like an enraged bull, the crowd surrounding Vortimer parted as Bridget threw herself wildly into his arms, knocking him and herself to the ground. She didn't care, she just kept kissing his face wildly and yelling, "You are a crazy man! You are a crazy man!"

Hands lifted the pair onto their shoulders and continued their shouts of "Bone Tear" as ale and water was sprayed over everyone. Bridget saw Vortimer shouting as well but could not hear him. Round and round they were paraded until they at last were before Varduc who appeared to be the only person not crying out. Varduc patiently waited for the noise to cease. When at last it did, he handed the bread up to Vortimer who took it silently.

He broke off a piece and handed it to Bridget and took another for himself and began to chew. Then he began breaking off more pieces and began flinging them into the crowd who scrambled for them. Once more, "Bone Tear! Bone Tear!" erupted. The couple were carried with great ceremony to the gates before they were allowed to walk on their own and only then did Bridget see just how weakened Vortimer was, in spite of his grin.

He truly is a crazy man! He can barely stand, but the crowd! Has there ever been such a demonstration? Why did you do this? Why?

She asked herself the same questions over and over as they walked silently to their quarters—Vortimer placed his arm around her shoulder for support as they walked the final stairs to their room. Without a word, Bridget helped remove his clothing and had lie in bed as she found a basin of water and a cloth. Slowly and with uncharacteristic gentleness, she began wiping him down with the dampened cloth. All Vortimer could do was sigh, his eyes closed. In the dimming light, Bridget lit a candle and continued washing his glistening body.

"Just one question, my crazy husband: why did you do this madness?"

"For you...for Bone Tear," he whispered.

Bridget stood and began removing her clothes, looking out the window she saw the large, burning wheels being rolled down nearby hills.

"Lie back and do not move," she said as she began kissing his cheek and then his lips. Vortimer began to stir in response. "Do not move," she repeated as she ran her fingertips over his nipples and chest. "Be still."

Bridget continued her gentle caressing and kissing, feeling that somehow something was about to happen this night and it was deep, so very deep. She continued deliberately, savoring each sinew and each moan from Vortimer. She was not trying to tease him, not at all—that would be frivolous and Bridget was not of that mind, not tonight.

She straddled him and placed him inside of her and both moaned in unison. True to her command, Vortimer remained still, allowing Bridget to move to her own rhythms. She would stop every so often and bend over to kiss him, her nipples brushing his chest before she sat up again. It went on and on with varying movements and cadences that Bridget herself could not fathom. It built slowly between the two of them, uniting them. Every cell of every fiber cried out for renewal, for completion of this night, this moment. Bridget cried out and Vortimer gasped when at last it happened—and Bridget remained, slumping slightly onto Vortimer's heaving chest. She did not get up, her body shook with small spasms at times but over time they diminished and then ceased entirely.

She kissed him so very gently on the lips and then once more.

Now, filled by her husband in so many ways Bridget was stabbed by a Truth. *I am the sacrifice.*

CHAPTER ELEVEN

Over the weeks Bridget came to learn the most difficult task of all was waiting. Bone Tear was battle ready. Sentries with the swiftest horses had been posted along the coast; when they weren't working the fields, peasants continued to hone their skills with the pikes. Sick animals had been slaughtered and staked upstream of possible water sources for the marauders. Vortimer's men were edgy and bloody arguments erupted daily. Glendon had to intervene with corporal punishment which lessened the outbursts but did nothing to relieve the exquisite anticipation of the army. The weeks passed, the days shortened and the sun no longer warmed as before.

This heaviness is even affecting me physically. I am tired of feeling ill all the time. The only way to relieve it is the way I most dread! I am heartsick! And Varduc didn't help when he said the Vikings knew we were here! I had hoped that our presence would have surprised them.

Bridget paced in the hall, then outside, then back in. Even riding Alexander seemed pointless as she no longer found it pleasurable. No one was immune from the suffocating air of expectancy; even Varduc was somber and that in itself disturbed Bridget.

We never did discuss the offering the goddess wanted, did we? We both knew what happened that night of Lugnasadh—we saw it in each other's eyes the following day when Vortimer could barely walk. How is it that I will be with Vortimer on the day of battle, little man? The sacrifice was made! No, I do not believe that you are a man at all, not any more.

Why is my sister suspicious about you, Varduc? What has she ever done to you or you to her? Can she sense something I cannot? Well, I am sure she would have warned me. I must answer her last two correspondences and be circumspect regarding me and Vortimer! She must never know what has transpired! She would become enraged! I am so sorry that you and your husband do not share what Vortimer and I do, Celestine.

Thankful to be engaged in some activity, Bridget sharpened her quill and began to write when she heard a confused commotion at the door—her heart skipped two beats.

It is now.

Vortimer and Glendon strode in purposefully, their faces grim.

"Send the archers! Assemble the men and have them muster their peasants—we leave as quickly as possible!" Vortimer said to Glendon.

"It is already being done, lord. The alarms are being sent."

Bridget stood. "How many, Vortimer? How many ships?"

"Forty," he said bitterly, "maybe fifty. This is no raiding party but an assault!" He turned to Glendon, "Send two messengers to Glamorgan! I want at least one to get there if the other should have an accident. They must ride now! And notify the abbess that her services will soon be needed!"

"Where are they landing?" Bridget asked.

Vortimer spread the original map that Bridget made on the table. "Here." He tapped. "Forty to fifty ships, there were so many and so close together that he could not get an accurate count. Well, let's be at it. Our time is come."

"I am going with you, Vortimer."

"You cannot possibly come, Bridget! It is out of the question!"

"You are my husband and my lord. This is my land and my people. I am coming with you. It bears no further discussion."

Vortimer hesitated and looked into her defiant eyes. "Very well. Pack light and leave your women here. You will ride with me at the front of the column. 'No further discussion,' eh?"

Bridget flew to her room, trying to suppress the seething emotions that tore at her. She chose her most worn and comfortable clothes and boots, not forgetting to wear the shawl that Vortimer had given her a lifetime ago. Mathilde and Gwenthe wailed and carried on so that Bridget began to lose her temper. "You two will be fine! We will all be safe! Think of the men out there, instead! When we return we shall have a great feast and I will make you listen to all that has happened, I swear."

"It is just that we love you," blubbered Mathilde.

"And I love the both of you! Which is why we will be coming back! So dry your eyes and be brave! Pray if you must, but I must go!"

The courtyard was a controlled frenzy as soldiers readied their gear and horses while the villagers shouted words of encouragement. Bridget found Vortimer already mounted and holding Alexander's reins.

"Do you remember the first time we rode together, Bridget?"

"Of course! You barely spoke to me!"

"I am much wiser, now I listen!"

How can he go on like this? Even the men are joking and laughing!

"When will we leave?"

"As soon as everyone is mustered. We have some time yet. It is best we go outside the gates, I think."

Side by side they waited and were soon joined by Varduc who was mercifully quiet and by Glendon who was not. The men lined up four columns deep, some stood while others sprawled out on what would otherwise have been a marvelous day—the sun was warm, the air dry and cool. While the regular soldiers looked to be at ease, the peasants were fidgety and their faces anxious. Vortimer rode up to them, asked their names and had them sit to conserve energy. At last the supply wagons appeared and Glendon reported that all was ready.

"Then let us march!" said Vortimer.

A cry went out from the troops when they realized that Bridget was just not seeing them off but was going with them as well! Had any other woman done such a thing? It was a good portent. Many shouted her name as she rode by, asking if she would race Alexander again.

"You are very popular with my men," Vortimer observed wryly.

"And why not? I am a superior woman!" She quipped, forgetting the gravity of the moment.

Though the men marched at double speed, Bridget found the pace annoyingly slow but kept quiet as Vortimer's wrinkled brow indicated he was concentrating on other matters. Full of questions but not wishing to disturb her husband, she rode next to Glendon.

"Why were the archers sent ahead, Glendon? Where are they?"

"Just a little scheme that came into Vortimer's head. He knows they have come a long way in those damned ships and would take a day to disembark and rest before moving on. The archers will be concealed in wooded areas close by and do their work at night! Might not kill anyone but they will keep the camps lively! And men who do not sleep are men who make mistakes, Vikings or not!"

"Isn't that unusual?"

"Very unusual but a grand idea! Stinging them like that at night and avoiding them at the same time."

"I am frightened," she confessed quietly.

Glendon looked at her with his usual grin. "Most of us are but it is too early for that yet! Look at how the leaves have turned, smell the earth and listen to the crickets and wild geese."

"Easy for you to say! You have done this before!"

"No, milady. It is never easy. Make no mistake about that!"

Bridget pulled next to Varduc who sat perched upon a plodding nag. He rode uncomfortably, his bottom slapping the saddle.

"Ah! Would that I had mastered riding these beasts! Even the young master rides better than I!"

"How will I be with Vortimer? The sacrifice has been made—you know it!"

"Yes. You have sacrificed that most precious thing, young mistress. You have sacrificed yourself and the goddess is pleased. Love is not easy, is it? But it is the ultimate force in the universe—it drives the winds, allows for crops to grow, everything! It is the one thing of which I am truly certain. I am also in the way of knowing that my young master loves you as well. Together you make a formidable pair!"

"Yes, I do love Vortimer! With all my heart! But why must we go through this trial?"

Varduc snorted. "Why? Because that is the way of Life! Why should you be different from everyone else?"

"I am not here for a lesson! How will I be with Vortimer?"

"Ah! Right to the point! In that way you are much like your husband! You will see through his eyes and hear with his ears. Your muscles will twitch and your lungs and heart will be as his. I can say no more. Ride next to him. He needs you there as he is now the loneliest of men. Go!"

How like Vortimer not to say anything! Of course I shall ride next to him but why doesn't he share his thoughts? I am his wife, after all. Yes, I know that he loves me though he has not said it. It is in the way he looks at me and his gentleness. That little smile of his that is too infrequent—that is how I know.

They rode together, Vortimer oblivious to his surroundings, stared straight ahead as he swayed gently on his horse. "We will march hard today and camp late so that we may reach the field by noon tomorrow. They are most likely disembarked by now and getting organized. After a wearying voyage they will want to rest one night. Their scouts will have found no resistance and feel secure! It will be a moonless night—perfect for the archers who will be in two groups and on the move after each volley."

Bridget nodded.

285

"The Vikings have few horses, too difficult to transport and will not be mobile. Our bowmen can shoot and ride away at their leisure."

"Then you have it all planned out?"

He laughed softly. "Plans have a way of never going the way we expect."

"What have you not planned for? I was there and you have taken the measure of everything!"

"The south, your father's vassals. I don't trust them. They may use this as an opportunity to rebel with Glamorgan engaged here. Still, that is something I have no control over and haven't the time to worry about right now."

"Are you worried then?"

"No, not really…"

"Well," she responded, "I have faith in the crazy man that won that absurd race."

He smiled at the memory and after a moment said, "I am glad you are here with me."

Bridget smiled inwardly and thought no answer was best. They continued on and to her surprise, Bridget found that she was able to delight in the day. The sun on her back and the cool air gave surprising comfort. The rolling hills were thick with multihued trees and birds of every feather were beginning to cluster. Samhain might be a celebration of Death in the Great Circle, but for now everything was alive and vital. Bridget became acutely aware of the irony that all soldiers shared—the closer they came to death the more alive they felt.

They camped just before sunset and Vortimer with Glendon spent the early evening in idle chatter with the troops—answering questions, relaying jokes—doing their best to set the men at ease. The four of them, Vortimer, Bridget, Glendon and Varduc were the last to eat. They sat round the crackling fire in silence, their breath visible in the chilled air of night as crickets chirped in the thickets, no one willing to share their thoughts.

I should be tired but I am not. How can I think of sleep on a night like this? How do they do it?

Varduc broke the silence. "There is some disarray at their camp."

No one bothered to ask how he came by his knowledge as he would not be able to tell them—he only knew.

"The archers?"

"Yes, young master. They are causing a great deal of confusion."

Vortimer grunted and jabbed a stick into the fire, rattling the coals.

Why don't they speak? There must be hundreds of things on their minds right now yet they stare mutely into the flames!

The fire had dwindled to little more than coals when Vortimer finally asked, "You know what needs to be done when we arrive tomorrow, Glendon?"

"Yes, lord."

"Good, then I suggest we retire and do what the savages will be doing precious little of tonight."

Vortimer's field tent was not much larger than those used by his men. There were two separate cots and except for their boots, would sleep clothed.

"Pull your cot next to mine," she said. "I need you next to me this night."

He pulled it over in the gloom and placed his arm over her protectively as he kissed her cheek lightly.

Vortimer! This is insanity! Can't we just flee? Go somewhere else far away? What is the point in all this if you should be killed or maimed?

Believing the thought might make it so, Bridget discarded the idea quickly and instead thought of whistling arrows piercing the tents that were less than two days away.

"You didn't eat much tonight, Bridget."

"Couldn't. No appetite and my stomach has been disturbed with all that is happening."

"Well, that does happen, true. However, try to sleep."

"How can you sleep at all?"

"Because there is nothing else left to be done. What will happen, will happen. Don't make me regret that you are here."

Bridget lay on her side as Vortimer molded his body to hers, his breathing becoming slow and shallow till at last even she fell into a restless sleep, waking several times during the night, fearful of what lay ahead.

Camp broke quickly in the dark, well before the sky had begun to lighten. Everyone knew that in a few hours they would begin making final preparations for the battle that would make them victorious. Few, if any, dwelt on any other outcome. Vortimer was even more silent than usual and Bridget copied Varduc and Glendon who kept their distance—they would come when summoned.

I remember the first night I saw him and wondered what it was about his eyes, 'old soul eyes'. I see it in his face now, sadness overwhelming everything else—complete and crushing. Oh, Vortimer! That this could be lifted from you! That there was something I could do, my love! My heart aches for your pain and does not know how you bear it.

Wanting to weep, Bridget instead sat taller, determined that for now she would be the wife of the Iron Dog—she knew it was a sham but it was all she could do for now. Bridget focused on the sounds of the men behind her, the cadence of their marching was blessedly lulling and it surprised her when they finally arrived.

How beautiful the meadow is! Bona Terra! How can a place like this be cursed?

Bridget had little time to ponder her thoughts. The earlier gloom was replaced with ordered, frantic activity. Tents were pitched behind the hill where the troops would make their stand. Riders were dispatched in all directions—some to locate the Vikings, others to find Glamorgan's men.

Bridget watched transfixed as Vortimer her husband became Vortimer, the Iron Dog. Pointing this way and that, he directed Glendon and several men on horseback. Carts with tents, food and weapons were hurriedly emptied as the men readied their leather armor—blades were sharpened and glinted brightly in the noonday sun. There was an air of solemn determination now—whatever fears and doubts may have existed before were no longer. Conversations between the men were relaxed and to the point. There were, however, those who stayed apart and in their eyes Bridget saw the cold fire that Vortimer wished he had.

No, my husband, I much prefer yours. Theirs are empty, frightening, full of death. No, I will that those old soul eyes of yours never change so that I might look into them forever.

Bridget, it seemed, was the only one with nothing to do. She dismounted and with Alexander, walked amongst the men just as she had seen Vortimer and Glendon do the night before. They paid their respects with a smile, a tilt of their heads and returned to their weapons. Others wanted to kiss her hand for luck, they said, and Bridget obliged with a smile and words of encouragement. She had become familiar with many faces, knew some by name and in the back of her head wondered if she would ever see or speak with them again.

Looking towards the meadow, thick with waist-high grasses undulating in soft waves, Bridget watched as Vortimer spoke with his lieutenants.

Yes, there is the trench! Barely visible, a dark crease from this vantage point, an irregularity to anyone who didn't know better. You are so clever, Vortimer!

Bridget continued wending her way as she regarded a single cart with three men go midway between the trench and the base of the opposing hillside. Smoke arose from pots in the back. Each beekeeper gingerly grabbed a sack, ran out and gently rolled the contents in the grass. They repeated this several times, sometimes swatting blindly at the air. While their ride there had been marked by care, the return trip was one of abandon.

The sun was well past its zenith when Vortimer finally returned to Bridget, not that he had much time to speak. Messengers continued to report excitedly— Glamorgan had been positioned and waiting just south of the Wythe and would be there by nightfall—the archers had been having success and would continue their harassment during the night before returning. Two riders each carrying something wrapped in cloths whispered to Vortimer who nodded, smiled and pointed towards the upper crest where they dropped their mysterious cargo.

"I think, young mistress, that we should choose your vantage point now while there is still light," said Varduc who appeared at Bridget's side as if from nowhere.

They walked in silence along a ridge to the right of the encampment that would give Bridget an unobstructed view of both hillsides and the meadow between them. "Here is best, young mistress. The men will be able to see you as you sit upon Alexander."

"And Vortimer?"

"Vortimer will have eyes for nothing except what is at hand!"

"And this is how I will be with him?"

"In ways you cannot imagine, young mistress. In ways you cannot imagine."

"Very well. Let me return."

Together they went back to the camp as the sun touched the western horizon. Fires were being lit and now with the enemy so close, sentries were posted. Everything was in order and the army waited expectantly once again. Bridget had hoped that she might spend more time alone with Vortimer but that was not to be.

"What is that strange light in the north?" she pointed.

"That," replied Glendon, "is their fires."

So close! Too close!

It was not much longer when Glamorgan, Uncle Glamorgan appeared. Grim faced, he reported directly to Vortimer who sat him down and brought food and drink himself.

"It was a difficult march but we are here!" The old warrior said gruffly— caught unawares by Bridget's presence. She wanted desperately to fling her arms around this bear of a man but waited—there were far more urgent matters at hand. Vortimer directed Glamorgan to spend the night amidst his own troops and not light any more fires. Before dawn they would position themselves in a heavily wooded area on the left flank.

"We will engage them here," he pointed. "You will wait till we are in the thick of it before you come up behind them—let them keep their attention on us before you begin your assault from the rear."

Glamorgan looked sourly at the chart, glancing furtively at Bridget.

"A good plan," he finally muttered. "The king sends his blessings and awaits word of our victory. Why," he glanced at Bridget, "is she here?"

"Did you ever try to argue with her?"

Glamorgan bellowed, "Yes, I know what you mean!"

He walked over to his little princess, wrapped his thick arms around her and gave a powerful hug. For her all faith in Vortimer, Bridget felt more assured now that Glamorgan, her childhood friend and protector, was here.

"Uncle, I am so glad you have made it here on time!"

"Wouldn't miss a good fight like this," he winked. "But I have things to attend to. We will talk more tomorrow, I swear!" With that, he allowed her to breathe once more as he disappeared into the gloom.

No one had the stomach for food but Varduc insisted they eat, demanded it. The silence around the fire was overwhelming now as they chewed reluctantly.

"Varduc, you will stay by Bridget's side tomorrow. Don't let her do anything foolish."

"Of course, young master. Be assured that we shall remain together."

"Then there is nothing left for us to do except wait for the morrow," said Vortimer who held out his hand for Bridget. Together they removed themselves from the dwindling circle of light to the tent. This close to the enemy, they did not remove their boots as they lay in their cots.

"What are you thinking, lord?" she asked.

"I have thought too much and now that I want to stop my brain won't let me," he complained. "Bridget, in case…"

She put her finger to his lips and then placed hers on them and kissed him tenderly, refusing to let him utter what could never be. They lay in silence and surprisingly fell into a dreamless sleep that was broken only when Vortimer rose and began retching violently. He sat bent over on the side of the cot as he alternately gasped for air between spasmodic fits.

"I know I woke you," he said finally. "Glendon has probably already pissed his pants." He laughed weakly before finding some water and cleaned out his mouth and throat.

"I don't care about Glendon, only you."

Vortimer stood in the darkness and grunted as he slipped into his heavy felt jacket. "It is time, Bridget."

I don't want to hear those words! I do not ever want to hear those words! Can't we just flee and let them take the damn land? How important is it, anyway? We could live far from here and you could show me the pyramids and elephants!

"Yes," she croaked from her dry throat.

They stood outside and glanced at the pink band in the eastern sky. Varduc approached from the darkness as he led Alexander by his bridle but Bridget motioned him away. She held Vortimer's shoulders as she faced him. "Vortimer, I love you," she whispered just before placing her mouth on his. She did not wait to hear his reply, did not want to hear it—instead she turned sharply and walked briskly towards Varduc so Vortimer could not see the tears streaking her cheeks.

The tall grass was cold and wet and a thin fog spread softly over the meadow. Bridget was blind to her surroundings as she wiped her eyes and allowed Varduc to lead.

I am the Princess of Bone Tear! Wife to the Iron Dog and this is not the time for tears!

"Well?" She asked when they arrived at the designated point.

Varduc reached into his robes and produced a vial sealed with wax that he handed to her. "Drink this quickly, young mistress and then mount your steed and wait. You needn't talk to me, all will be as I promised."

She drank the liquid in one gulp and remarked to herself that it was bitter, terribly bitter! She threw one leg over Alexander who looked at her quizzically.

Bitter but also very warming. I feel so lightheaded, giddy. I hope I don't fall off. Numbing as well, but different. I don't feel weak but strong and what are those strange noises and what is the matter with my eyes? Am I going blind! I can no longer see the fields! Or Alexander's head!

She opened her mouth to scream in terror but only croaked.

"Have a suitable breakfast, my lord?" Glendon asked wickedly.

"Have you changed into fresh under garments?" Vortimer replied.

Together they helped each other into their stiff leather tunics with as many irons strips as could be placed without compromising flexibility. Buckles and straps were secured until all that remained were the helmets that were lined with wool to keep them from slipping. Bridget felt the heaviness of the armor and slumped momentarily and then righted herself.

Walking stiffly now and I can hardly breathe. Still, there is something comforting about the snugness and the sword slapping my thigh. My heart is pounding and yet I feel oddly calm. The men are lined up nicely.

Vortimer felt suddenly odd, as if he was looking at himself from a great distance—the queerest sensation he had ever encountered—much like the time he first touched Varduc.

Oh, no! He cannot feel me or be distracted! I feel anger now, slow and sure. My arms feel light as feathers and as weak. It is much lighter now—soon. The peasants are nervous and I cannot blame them much. "You are here for one thing and one thing only! To kill those who would rob us of our family, our fields. You have not been ordered to die, only to fight! Any man who dies will answer to me!" *That's good! They are laughing, nervous, but laughing. Can't have them too tense. I wish someone would make me laugh. I wish a thousand things!*

It would have been a most beautiful day—it is a beautiful day. Look at them over there, pounding their shields with axes and swords. "They believe that when they die they go to a place where all they do is fight, drink and whore! Let us send them on their way so that we may live! Bone Tear! Bone Tear!"

Yes, they will hear our voices thundering. Now, where are those heads!

Vortimer found the two skulls of the Vikings that had been killed and brought to him the day before. He dropped his shield, lowered his pants and began urinating on them. Bridget's bladder let go. Two horsemen came and each grabbed a head by its wet hair and rode towards the enemy.

That's it! Ride on both flanks and avoid the trench. Now, ride side by side in the center to awaken the wasps...good. That's it, closer, a little closer—now! Strong arms! They almost tossed the heads into their laps! Now, come back slowly and ride towards the perimeter and stir up the hornets on the flanks. I must have their names—a job bravely done. Ah, listen to them bellowing! "Glendon! Is my cohort ready?"

"Yes, lord!"

"That one! I want that one over there!"

Look at him, naked to the waist and with nothing but an axe. There are a few more like him but he is the biggest. Let him think he is a bear! I still hear the men shouting Bone Tear behind me. I pray this never happens again. What does Glamorgan think of all this? Can't worry about him right now—only me, only me.

"Today we will consecrate Bone Tear with blood! Their blood! Their blood!"

No need waiting...best not to let them spend their energy screaming. I am thirsty. I have never been so thirsty! Now! Now!

That's it, let them see the peasants approach first. Glendon has done well to place a few men in the front to keep them steady. They can't go too far or too fast—cool heads and strong arms are what we need—easy—easy. Now the Vikings approach slowly—savages but they hold rank well enough. Which one is their commander? Doesn't matter. Steady—steady—now quicker. Ha, look how they react in kind and now! Yes! Yes! The hornets are having an early breakfast. The big one has barely flinched but his comrades are having a time of it! Listen to the men laugh behind me! Good! Good! Get ready! Be ready! The Vikings are in full charge! That's it, that's it—stop and look confused. Who did Glendon put in command of the rabble? I must reward them personally.

That's it, start to retreat, come back up the hill, back up the hill towards me. Archers steady…archers steady and now! Listen to them sing through the air. They can't raise their shields in time and the wasps are driving them mad! Look at them fall!

Another fusillade of arrows passed overhead as the peasants were now behind Vortimer and sitting on the ground as instructed while his soldiers paired up with them.

Varduc stood next to Alexander, filled with an oppressive melancholy as he witnessed the drama being played out in the field below and as being experienced by Bridget. He gritted his teeth each time she moaned or gave short cries. He smelled the urine she had voided and he wondered how this joining would affect her afterwards. It had nearly driven him mad when he himself did it years ago.

But the young mistress is much stronger than I and is bonded to Vortimer—she will not suffer as I did. His tricks seem to be working. And now the final assault begins! Her body is so rigid!

Vortimer raised his sword and cried out the attack just as the Vikings reached the trench.

The forces slammed into one another with horrific noise as shields, bodies and weapons crashed. The combatants were so close that it was often difficult to raise shield or sword in the crush and that vulnerability could be lethal. Vortimer preferred his shorter sword for that very reason—the longer, heavier weapons had to be raised overhead to deliver a killing blow. In the time it took his opponent to do that, he could get in close and lunge or slash at any unprotected part.

Vortimer's blood was infused with a firey liquor that exploded in offensive and defensive actions with blurring rapidity. He felt himself rocked by the grunting bodies swirling around him. In truth, he was blind to everything that was more than a sword's length away. He would recall little, if anything, and he never remembered any faces—all that mattered was impairing the enemy to the extent that he was no longer a threat. He found legs the most vulnerable target. Twice he severed arteries that sprayed blood and once separated a foot from its leg.

Words were replaced with the howling language of slaughter as gore and blood began to make footing unsure. The carnage continued and twice Vortimer almost stumbled over bodies—friend, foe—it didn't matter; sprawling, even if for a moment, almost assured death. The most difficult thing was being aware of your back as the struggling required frequent pivoting—the weakest and strongest shared this Achilles' heel. It was the duty of Vortimer's cohort to protect their lord's back at all times. Nevertheless, he had trained himself to glance over both shoulders frequently and this had saved his life more than once. It was difficult to remove your eyes from the enemy in front and look for the one in the rear but it was a skill worth learning if you could steel yourself to do it.

The initial crush began to separate and Vortimer saw one of his pikemen rip out the throat of a Viking. Too late, an axe caught the peasant between the shoulder blades. Tall as he was, Vortimer spotted the berserker he was determined to slay. He angled and shoved in the general direction, careful to maintain his footing. He wanted to wipe the slippery blood from the glove of his sword hand but that would mean putting it down and he was loath to do that. He felt a pressure on his left shoulder and a sudden weakness in his left arm caused his shield to droop—but it was nothing.

Glamorgan! Where is he?

The thought flitted through his mind and was crushed like an annoying bug—thinking was dangerous now. The confused melee continued to unfold and as it did, words began to be heard intermingled with the shouts and cries of earlier. It was not possible to tell who had more dead, you fought until you were killed or could kill no more.

He was a giant of a man. Tall and thick, the bare-chested Viking swung his great axe easily, creating a swath around him. Vortimer waited till the axe's momentum carried it full circle before engaging. He thrust his sword but his opponent was as nimble as he was powerful and easily dodged the blade. Vortimer was taken by surprise when the Viking spun around and whipped the axe towards him. Vortimer felt his whole body shudder as it struck his shield. Rather than back off as the Viking expected, Vortimer instead moved in closer and was able to hack his sword against the left ribs. He pressed forward, shoving his shield against the man's bare belly, his sword flailed the air as he was unable to withstand the man's brute strength—he felt his feet begin to slip backward—it was now or never. Vortimer dropped to his right knee, threw his shield to cover his head and swung his blade with all the force he could muster.

The blow from the Viking's axe struck Vortimer's shield with such force that it numbed him from wrist to shoulder—his left arm fell uselessly...but not before he felt his sword crack through flesh and bone of his opponent's left leg. Defenseless and on his knee, Vortimer could only roll blindly, hoping his blow had been disabling and that he did not expose himself to any more danger. His cat-like agility was unusual for a large man but after three rolls he stood up rapidly, no longer able to hold onto his shield. Glancing left and right and discerning no enemy he looked at the fallen warrior.

The blow had severed the lower part of the leg and blood gushed from the stump as he valiantly tried to stand, not yet comprehending the injury. Vortimer took two steps and swung his sword down, splitting the skull. Vortimer was wobbling unsteadily and it took two tugs before he could dislodge it.

I can fight no more. Where is everyone? If I fall I will not have the strength to stand! If I am to die, let it be now.

But no enemy came at him. Vortimer's vision began to return as though a veil had been lifted. Bodies littered the field in unnatural poses but it was the living he looked for. Fighting was now in scattered clusters as two or three men fought one. Dropping his sword, he wiped the sweat from his eyes with his hand that was sticky with blood. Two or three of his men, one Viking.

From his vantage point, Varduc had witnessed the slaughtering and the triumph but could not locate his young master, did not even know if he was still breathing till he heard Bridget croak, "Water."

Vortimer stumbled like a drunken man, refusing help from two men who rushed to his side.

Water! All I want is water, not someone to hold me up!

He tried to swallow but there was no spit. He halted, grasped the shoulder of the man flanking him and with great effort whispered, "Water."

Victory? Triumph? Does it matter? I should be flinging my arms up in the air with joy but that will come later. How come I can't lift my left arm? Who is alive? Glendon, where are you? I can't even speak.

A skin of water appeared as if by magic and Vortimer squeezed the contents into his mouth using his right hand only. He drank in deep long gulps; no amount of water could slake his burning thirst. He stopped only when he doubled over and vomited. Now he drank more cautiously, allowing himself to taste the warm liquid. Clearing his eyes once more and feeling stronger, he walked to the closest cluster of men.

Two peasants, spattered with gore, were jabbing their pikes into a Viking who stood by supporting himself with his sword. He was another big man and blood was seeping from the numerous puncture wounds inflicted by his tormentors who stood in front and behind, enjoying their sport. The man never uttered a word as the humiliating torture continued, each thrust inflicting pain but not bringing him closer to death.

We are animals. Like a cat toying with a mouse. May this never happen to me.

He held out his right hand and called for a sword as he brushed the peasants away. Vortimer stood in front of the man and looked into his eyes. The Viking muttered something unintelligible and Vortimer sensed a great dignity. His eyes betrayed neither fear nor pain but instead a tranquility that Vortimer at once envied. He whispered out the question again and Vortimer nodded at the dying warrior who finally closed his eyes. The Viking gripped his broad sword with two hands and managed to lift it off the ground without toppling; he slowly raised it above his head. Vortimer plunged his own sword through the thick leather and into the great heart—the man dropped. He stood joylessly over the corpse and glared at the two peasants whose sport he had interrupted.

Bridget's sweat saturated her clothes and she began trembling so violently that Varduc barely managed to pull her off Alexander and lay her gently on the ground where she continued to shake. He sat and placed her head in his lap, soothingly saying, "Young mistress…young mistress, are you awake? Are you here with me? How do you feel?"

Bridget opened her eyes slowly and when they focused on Varduc, tried to sit suddenly but fell back as though her muscles had gone flaccid.

Vaarduc chuckled knowingly and stroked her cheek gently as Bridget began an uncontrollable sobbing. "There, there. Everything is well. This is what happens afterwards and nothing I can do will change that. How do you feel?"

In a voice that resembled Vortimer's she said weakly, "Relieved…and my shoulder hurts." She cried till she fell asleep and Varduc wept along with her, careful not to disturb her in any way.

Vortimer saw that vacant stare in his men—eyes that looked beyond and gazed at something far away, just over the horizon. The stench began even before the troops began gravitating towards Vortimer who could not allow himself the luxury of sitting, not yet. Those that walked helped those that could not, the only sounds came from the dying, the living were to exhausted to do anything else. They stood before him, this army of soldiers and peasants and waited to hear from Vortimer himself that they had survived and that victory was indeed theirs. Vortimer needed help stripping off his armor and only then did he truly feel the pain in his left shoulder and upper chest. The collarbone had been broken and a ragged wound snaked down the shoulder. No arteries had been severed, no lungs punctured—he would heal. Someone placed the arm in a sling and that helped dull the pain that increased as the liquor of combat began to evaporate.

Weak beyond words, Vortimer could think of nothing to say, at first. He looked at the rabble in front of him and wanted to cry, but would do that later. He took his time surveying them all and nodded knowingly at Glendon whose head was bandaged.

He raised his right fist and cried out, "Bone Tear!"

The men responded in kind and startled the ravens that had already begun their feast. Men wept and cheered simultaneously. Vortimer waited till the shouting died.

"We shall never forget this day but we are not yet finished. Help the wounded into the carts, dress the wounds as best you can. Who can still ride and fight?"

A scattering of men shouted out.

Not enough to bring me the head of Glamorgan!

"Ride into those woods," he pointed, "and let me know what and whom you find."

The archers who had not taken part in the hand-to-hand fighting drove carts into the field and lifted the severely wounded into them—some dressed wounds and others dispatched the hopeless. The more experienced soldiers produced treasured needles and began suturing their comrades with horsetail. It took some time before Vortimer heard Glendon cursing—all would be well.

"I don't need the ear!" he bellowed. "My hair'll grow over it!"

"You're covered with blood," Vortimer said. "Any of it yours?"

"Some, not much. You have bathed in it as well, I see. Any of it yours?"

"Some, not much. I need to speak with you alone."

Together they walked a short distance from the men who were busy with other things.

"What happened to Glamorgan?" Vortimer hissed. "I want him dead! I want his head! Coward or traitor makes no difference! I want him hunted down like a mad dog and brought to me so I can draw and quarter him! Bring him to me!"

"What's that?" shouted Glendon. "I only have one ear, you know!"

Glendon draped his arms gingerly over Vortimer's shoulders as Vortimer did the same with his right. Their ensuing laughter brought quizzical looks from those who did not know them any better. The two warriors laughed so hard that they were at last forced to sit. They sat silently for a moment as they watched the men.

"Glamorgan is a dead man, lord."

Vortimer grunted. "Do you remember anything?"

"Very little. You?"

"The same. After we have licked our wounds I want to honor a few of the men—get their names if they still live." Vortimer recounted what he could recall as Glendon added his own experiences. Vortimer did not rest till the sun was halfway towards the west. Now he allowed himself the luxury of sitting and drinking water slowly, washing his face.

How appropriate! My right leg and left arm. As helpless as a bug on its back!

Several riders approached.

"My lord! We found these two of Glamorgan's men!"

Vortimer's first impulse was to slay them on the spot but he knew the underlying problem was not with them but with their renegade master. "Your names?"

"Astorious, lord." Said one.

"Maldwyn." Said the other.

"Tell me why you did not fight." Vortimer ordered

The two men blurted out as they had been concealed in the woods, swords drawn, ready to attack, waiting for Glamorgan to give the order that never came.

"What was your lord's state of mind? Fear?"

"No, lord Vortimer, he was angry…has been for some time now." Said the one called Maldwyn. Astorious nodded in agreement.

"Go on."

"When he drinks, my lord talks. He has called you the interloper, sucking pup. Things like that."

"He is your lord yet you remained here, why?"

"My lord, one time we were ordered to escort and protect Princess Bridget, your wife. That order has never been rescinded."

Vortimer mulled these last bits of information deliberately. "Your devotion to my wife is admirable and will be rewarded accordingly. From this day hence, you serve me and me alone! Understood?"

They nodded in unison.

"Go, both of you, to Gwaldner and tell him of our victory. Tell him of Glamorgan's treachery. Further, inform the king that I want all the property and holdings of Glamorgan forfeited to me. Is that understood?"

"Yes, lord."

"Then why are you waiting about?"

The men wheeled their horses about and Vortimer watched as they galloped off into the distance.

The field of strewn bodies was still being culled when Bridget appeared on Alexander with Varduc leading by the reins.

"I do not wish you to see this, Bridget," he said sourly.

Bridget dismounted and gently enfolded her arms around Vortimer "Your shoulder! The sling!"

"It is nothing, nothing. Glendon lost an ear."

Glendon is not my husband, dear man! You cannot even set yourself on Alexander.

"There is nothing more here for you to do," she said bluntly. "We will return to the camp where I can examine that shoulder." Her tone indicated that protest was pointless. Together, Bridget, Vortimer and Varduc climbed towards the crest. Weak, Vortimer had to rest twice.

"Perhaps the finest and most complete victory I have ever witnessed!" cried Varduc. "Poets will write of it and songs of the Iron Dog will spread to the ends of the realm, young master!"

Vortimer smiled wanly and let Varduc carry on while he and Bridget sat upon a thick log and watched as scavengers, human and animal, went through the remains of the Vikings. Savages, but they crafted fine jewelry. Varduc went off to find some herbs for a tea that would dull Vortimer's pain as Bridget silently sliced off his thick, felt jacket. The shoulder began bleeding as Bridget picked out pieces of fabric, dirt and hair—Vortimer remained stoic.

"Is there anything you wish to tell me, Vortimer?"

"No."

"Is there anything on your mind?"

"No."

He is infuriating! There, I think the wound is cleaned out and properly dressed. His breathing is shallow—is it the fracture? What are his needs? I can't read his mind...well, not any more!

Beginning to shiver in the chilled air of evening, Bridget fetched a blanket which she wrapped around the two of them. The men began returning in small groups, most bandaged and limping. A fire was started before them, beer was drunk as goblets were passed, emptied and refilled. They laughed, they sang ribald songs, remembered slain friends. On and on it went, Vortimer even joined in occasionally but for the most part kept to himself.

"My lord! My lord!" A voice cried out beyond the fire's light. "Look what we have found!"

The assemblage parted and two men shoved a youth, a boy actually, in front of Vortimer.

"We were going towards where the bastards landed to check for anything of value left on their ships when we run across this here lad. He's a scrapper, he is! Teeth as sharp as a pup's!"

He was, Vortimer judged, nine or ten, certainly no older. His dress and light features identified him as Viking. He stood erect, fearless, his eyes boring into Vortimer's as the men jeered. Vortimer stood and the insults stopped.

"Who are you, boy?"

He looked at Vortimer but said nothing.

"I said, who are you, boy?" Louder this time.

Nothing.

"Perhaps I may try, young master." Said Varduc who had edged closer.

The stripling looked up in surprise as Varduc spoke to him in a strange language. Taking a deep breath, the boy thudded his fist against his skinny chest and began speaking rapidly. He went on and on in a voice twice his size, punctuating his recital with imagined sword swipes against an invisible enemy. He would have continued had not Vortimer held up his hand. "What is this about, Varduc?"

"You asked who he was and he was telling you, young master. Going back ten generations so far. We are the product of our ancestors, are we not?"

"I only wanted to know his name."

"Ah, then that is an altogether different matter!"

Varduc translated the question to which the boy responded, "Hrolf."

"Take young Hrolf away, then. Feed him, give him something to drink and tie him up while we decide what to do with him."

Hrolf displayed no fear as he was led off, casting one last glance at Varduc and Vortimer.

"How is it that you know their tongue?"

"I would not say I am fully conversant, young master."

"I get more an answer from a young savage than I do from my own counselor."

Varduc remained mute as he bowed slightly and began heading in the same direction as captors and captive.

A cold wind sprung from the north and rapidly grew so that it whipped the fire. Everyone began retreating for the blessed shelter of their flapping tents as the temperature plummeted. Varduc's tonic had helped only a little and Bridget tried mightily to position Vortimer where he was in the least amount of discomfort. Using whatever she could find in the tent, she made him sit semi-reclined.

"So long as I do not move, I am fine," he joked weakly.

"So long as I am here you will be fine!" she retorted.

This sudden, bitter cold was unexpected and Bridget covered themselves with blankets and a skin. Vortimer closed his eyes just once and pain or no, fell immediately asleep. Not even the wind-driven rain that pelted the tent disturbed him. Bridget, just as exhausted as her husband, slept as well.

It rained hard that night—the drops like chips of flint—and the howling wind was mercilessly cold.

CHAPTER TWELVE

The harsh buffeting of the tent walls and the unexpected chill that had crept beneath the heavy blankets during the night awakened Bridget. Momentarily confused, she molded herself against Vortimer, deciding what to do next as she lay in the darkness. Careful not to disturb his uneasy sleep, she draped a blanket over her shoulders and poked her head through the tethered flap.

The gray dawn was thick with rain and heavy snowflakes that were whipped about by the confused wind that screamed through the trees. Bridget squinted and in the dull light watched the tattered tents flay the ground.

What are we to do? What am I supposed to do? Where is Glendon? Varduc? I have never seen such a storm!

Chilled from even this brief exposure, she returned to the relative comfort inside and checked on Vortimer. He was still sleeping and even in the poor light Bridget could see he looked haggard. Bridget tucked the blankets behind his shoulders, mindful of the numbing cold invading her fingers. Vortimer let out a weak cough and grimaced.

"Damn! That hurts!" he said weakly. "Is there anything to drink, Bridget?"

She fumbled about till she located the small cask and poured the water. She tilted the goblet to his lips but Vortimer took it from her. "I am not totally helpless, Bridget. This storm sounds malignant! What is it like out there?"

Bridget described the tempest as he continued to sip his drink.

"I knew you shouldn't have come."

"On the contrary, this proves that I should be here. Now, excuse me while I have to piss." Standing behind and out of Vortimer's view, Bridget urinated gratefully.

I have to go so often now but there is no way I can relieve myself outside!

"What do we do?"

"Not much we can do except wait for Glendon to report. Come beside me and keep warm."

"Can you move your left arm?"

Vortimer tried but the pain was too severe. "Not very much."

"You just stay here and rest, then. I will begin getting our things."

Bridget had not expected it, but Vortimer actually did close his eyes and within a short time had fallen asleep. This, more than anything else, was alarming. It was not like him to fall asleep once awakened. Alone, Bridget began stuffing whatever she could into large sacks, the activity keeping her warm. She looked at the shawl, the one given to her by Vortimer, only that did she fold carefully and wedge in a deep and protected place—no other possession mattered.

Glendon's voice was shouting something unintelligible outside and Bridget went to let him in. He was soaked through, his hair wild from the wind, the dressing where he once had his ear was the color of wine.

"How is my lord?"

"Keep your voice down!" She whispered urgently. "He is sleeping but he does not look good. And he has been coughing. We have to get out of here and back home!"

"Well, we haven't much choice in the matter."

"How so?"

"We never planned to be here long and so we haven't any food. This storm makes it impossible to forage—we can't even light a fire, milady!"

"What does it mean?"

"What it means," said Vortimer who spoke with his eyes shut, "is that we cannot remain. We have to return."

"Why can't we stay?" Asked Bridget.

"The longer we stay, the more we starve. Most of the men are injured in one way or another—the grievous ones left by cart yesterday." Vortimer replied. "No one will get better under these conditions." He coughed. "Only worse."

"No one expected this kind of a storm so early," Glendon muttered. "We've hardly the clothes for it."

Bridget felt a sudden snap of her resolve as their desperate situation struck her full force. "Glendon, get the ruined tents, get all the tents and have them cut up to make wraps for the men! Take our tent and use it to cover one of the carts, we can use it as a litter for those who cannot walk," she turned to Vortimer, "or ride."

"Have them leave everything here. We can make new weapons, shields, and cots. We cannot make new men. Vortimer will ride in the cart and I will lead as you keep them moving."

"But, milady…"

"Mind to have them walk together, hold hands if they must. It bears no further discussion," she added flatly. "No discussion at all. And I want Varduc! I want him here right now! Tell me when you are ready to take my tent so Vortimer can go to the cart. I am going to saddle Alexander."

Glendon glanced at Vortimer and then at Bridget who was positively glaring.

"As you wish, milady." He backed out of the tent.

She returned to Vortimer and kissed his forehead gently. "I have things to do," she said huskily. "Have faith."

"Bone Tear." He replied.

"Bone Tear."

The wind was so violent it almost ripped away the skin Bridget clutched tightly. Leaning forward, she fought to where the horses were tethered. With numbed fingers her practiced hands slapped on the saddle while she stood on the blanket to keep it from being swept away.

This will not do. This will not do at all! I wish I had my gloves or a hat! Anything dry! Anything warm! I have to piss again!

Cold, tired and confused, Bridget had one overriding emotion—anger. Anger at having to fight the Vikings; anger at Vortimer for getting himself injured.

Walking Alexander to the tent, she debated whether or not to go inside.

Vortimer would be with the men. I remember telling him that he had planned for everything, but who could have foreseen this gale! Where is Varduc?

It was all she could do to keep from sliding on the slick grass and twice she had to yank on Alexander's rein to maintain her footing. The wind was pummeling everything that stood in its path and Bridget had to squint to see the forlorn shambles of the camp. The men were colorless shapes in the driving rain and from even a few feet away, impossible to distinguish. She went to as many as she could, patting them on the shoulders and yelling encouragement till she began shivering uncontrollably. When at last the fit had passed, she tried to find her way back to Vortimer as the wind now pushed her.

Somehow Glendon had passed with a cart and she hadn't noticed. In it were several figures wrapped in sodden blankets that even covered their heads.

They look like black cocoons! Vortimer has to lie in there?

"Are you ready, milady?" Glendon shouted. "You walk him in there while we fashion a roof of some sort that won't blow off!"

Bridget nodded before walking into the tent. Vortimer was as he she had left him, sitting quietly.

"How is it out there, Bridget?"

"Truth?"

"Truth is the basis of many things." He laughed weakly and then winced and clutched his left chest.

"It is bad. I can think of no other way to describe it."

"What is your plan?"

"To get us back home as quickly as possible."

"And how will you accomplish this?"

"I am the wife of the Iron Dog! I can do many things," she laughed, "except carry you to the cart. You will have to walk. The most important thing is for you to stay dry as possible. I will help you in there and get you comfortable. We will use this tent to wrap the cart as tightly as possible."

"Bridget," he said solemnly, "keep them moving. Flog them if necessary but keep them moving! Now, let me get up. Hand me that skin."

He wobbled from lightheadedness but then steadied himself as she placed the old goatskin over his shoulders. "I can walk on my own, allow me to do that, at least."

He left the tent and stood upright to the wind, neither bending nor bowing. With his good arm he pulled himself up and found a comfortable place in which to sit. "I have the best of company!" He shouted to Glendon. "At least I won't have to ride that damned horse! And this weather is perfect! It keeps away the miserable flies!"

Glendon was about to begin a conversation but Bridget shoved him away as she secured Vortimer. Their tent was pulled down after its contents had been removed and was hastily affixed to the top and sides of the litter.

Not very pretty but it should shield them from most of the wind and some of the rain. How am I to do this? How can I lead these poor men? I haven't the strength to go with the will! But if we stay here we die! When will this storm pass? What would the Iron Dog do? Where is Varduc?

She watched the wretched column line up behind her as Glendon rode through the ranks. Those with horses carried at least one less fortunate than themselves, even Glendon. It struck her that now she, Bridget of Bone Tear, was to lead. The thought at once dismayed and thrilled.

I can't do this! I can't! But I will! I can do this! I am Bridget of Bone Tear! Wife to the Iron Dog! I will do this! Somehow I will do this!

Clenching her jaw, Bridget nudged Alexander forward into the driving slush.

Horses and men slogged with their heads bent, dumbly following the feet of those in front. Bridget kept Alexander under tight rein, knowing that the sucking mud made each step a strength-sapping effort for both man and horse. She glanced back frequently, making sure she was not going too fast. Small hills tested the band as men pushed and horses pulled to keep the carts from sliding sideways and down to the bottom.

Bridget's body screamed to stop this hopelessly mad journey but her brain told her to go forward, to endure, to lead.

They are my responsibility now. Mine. If Vortimer could win that damned race I can at least do this!

They reached a low lying area with some few trees that stopped the wind somewhat and she took the opportunity to ride down the ranks, encouraging the men forward, always forward. Glendon, she saw, rode at the rear, making sure no one fell behind—she nodded in silence and he replied in kind. Then they started again.

Had there been only the rain or only the icy wind, the trek would be nothing more than uncomfortable—but the combination was deadly. Men, most of whom were in someway disabled by the battle, began falling asleep as they walked—some spoke with phantoms. The wet and bitter cold gave way to an exquisite weariness. If only they could lie down and sleep for a while, they'd be fine, just fine! Glendon was unable to prevent all those who walked to the side to sleep and to die. Those that kept walking were too weak to stop their comrades from that profound slumber. Bridget kept pushing forward.

This is victory? Where is the glory in any of this? Vortimer did not feel triumph! The only elation in his heart was that he was alive! I am so tired, so tired. I have never felt so tired. Maybe if I close my eyes for a bit, just a short time, that's all I need.

Her body was suddenly wracked by such uncontrolled shivering, that it took all her might to remain mounted.

I don't think I can open my hands to release the reins. I didn't see Varduc before. Where is he?

She stopped the column and rode back slowly, peering for the little man on a nag. Spying him at last, she saw that he had Hrolf walking beside him with a rope secured around his neck and tied to the saddle. Varduc looked as forlorn and pitiful as any of the men, maybe more.

"Where is She, Varduc!" Bridget screamed at him! "Where is your Goddess now! Look at us! Look at us! Is this the will of your Goddess? Did we endure the battle only to die by Her hand? Give me that boy! No reason for him to die as well!"

Varduc, for once, said nothing and meekly handed over the rope. Bridget reached down to the boy who reminded her of a wet kitten and scooped him up behind her. He instinctively wrapped his arms around her waist and clung tightly, burying his face into her back.

"If ever you prayed for a miracle, do so now, damn you!"

Bridget returned to the wearying task of leading once more with Hrolf fastened to her like a leech. Perhaps it had been unfair to upbraid Varduc but Bridget was beyond caring about anyone's hurt feelings. She only knew she was doing all she could and he had better be doing the same! The screaming warmed her blood, however, and she felt less tired as they restarted the endless plodding.

How many hours have we been at this? Did I just fall asleep? I only closed my eyes for a moment! How is Vortimer? I'd stop to care for him but I can't! He would not stop for me, much as he might want. We have to get the men back! What happened to Glamorgan at the battle? Why did he not join in the fray? I know there has to be some explanation, there has to be! He loved me! I have to piss again! If I get off Alexander I may not be able to get back on without help and that will not look good, Bridget needing a boost!

She emptied her bladder, not caring whether Hrolf noticed or not—personal niceties no longer mattered to Bridget or to anyone. She fell into an uneasy place that blurred the somewhere between dream and reality, where discomfort and pain were acknowledged but not felt. It was a comforting place where Bridget freed herself from her body and dreamed of a warm bath and a dry bed with Vortimer lying next to her, anxious and prepared to make love. She found it very nice indeed till the apparition shattered her reverie! He was back! The Hooded Man with the bloody hands! Bridget gasped out loud and everything vanished except the residual terror.

Hasn't he left me? It has been so long! And why now? Something is different, what is it?

It took a while for Bridget to realize that the wind and rain had died considerably and that she was now able to see several hundred yards ahead! She looked up and for the first time all day was able to see the sky. She unclenched her hands but it took some time before she was able to flex the fingers. After that she started with her wrists and worked up to her elbows. It was a delight

307

to be alive and enjoy such a simple pleasure as movement and feeling. By the smallest of degrees the weather improved to the point that the sun, though it gave no warmth, was a light gray disc hidden behind sullen clouds. She was even able to look back and see the end of the ragged line that followed.

I have to get off! I have to see Vortimer! I have to! I am his wife!

She clapped Hrolf's thigh to waken him and felt his shivering body give a start. Stopping, she unclenched his hands and lowered him off Alexander where he stood as if awakened from a dream. Bridget's numbed legs had remained in the same position for hours and it took an effort to unstiffen them now. Her body ached with each ungraceful movement and she ended up, not on her feet but on her buttocks.

I don't care! I must see Vortimer!

If anyone noticed the fall, they didn't acknowledge it by assistance or laughter. Only Hrolf, his boyish face grave, helped her up. Bridget started to laugh so hard she almost fell down again. She bent her knees several times, feeling them crack in protest. Confident now, she began walking past the men who appeared startled to see her and the sky—Hrolf followed Bridget closely. Bridget's teeth were chattering but she kept moving on, flexing her arms and neck— encouraging the men to do the same. She came to the cart and began unpeeling the makeshift canopy.

"Hello, Bridget!" Vortimer boomed. "Are we almost there?"

She wanted to scold him for startling her so but his face belied the bravado. There was an unhealthy blush on his cheeks and Bridget knew he had to be feverish.

"Yes. Of course we are almost there. The rain and wind has stopped!"

"Good. Very good. This one next to me died some time back. An interesting man, Patrick. I promised to tell his family he died facing the enemy." He hesitated. "I need some water."

"At once!"

Bridget began walking hurriedly along the men, shaking their shoulders and crying out. Men sluggishly dismounted with much the same results as Bridget She passed Varduc wordlessly till she found Glendon who was doing much the same as she.

"Glendon," she cried. "We need two things and two things only! Fire! We need fires built! Can you do that? Can you find some dry kindling beneath the brush? Second, Vortimer needs water desperately! Can you do these things?"

His dressing was long gone and Bridget saw the stubble that had once been his ear.

"We can do that, I think. Let me get my legs moving again. Are we to camp here, then?"

"I don't know. I only know that we need some warmth!"

"And wine."

Bridget laughed. "Yes! Hurry now!"

"And what of your little kit?" He said looking at Hrolf.

"He is no trouble! Now go!"

Bridget walked more forcefully back to the litter as her legs warmed to the motion.

"Water is coming! Let me remove this man."

"No! Let him be. I will bury him myself by his home."

Bridget was about to protest when a small cask of water was thrust at her. Grasping the side of the cart, she started to lift herself up when Hrolf leapt nimbly inside. Taking the cask, he tilted it against Vortimer's lips and then to those not unconscious.

"I see you have made a friend."

"Forget Hrolf for now. How do you feel?"

"I feel fine, Bridget. Just fine. How are the men?"

"Our line has thinned out some. I don't know how many but there was nothing I could do."

"There was nothing anyone could do, remember that and you will sleep better. Now, what do you propose?"

"That we take advantage of the weather and warm ourselves. Glendon is having fires built as we speak."

"And after that?"

"I don't know," she confessed.

"We should have moonlight and if the sky clears, ride."

"In the dark?"

"Movement is essential! These men are hard as horn! So long as they are moving they will know that there is a destination and that will give them hope. I have to get out of here and move myself!" Refusing Hrolf's hand, Vortimer stood as he shed his trappings and carefully worked his way off the cart. His bad leg was stiffer than ever and his limp was more pronounced than Bridget had ever seen. Still, he walked as nobly as he could with Bridget by his side.

Does anything smell as good as a fire? No, I don't think so.

Dry tinder and wood had been rooted from beneath several seasons of fallen leaves and small fires were crackling happily as the men began warming their hands till they stung. Bridget and Vortimer walked to each group and shared their flames, talking with the men at the same time. Ill as he was, Vortimer put up a noble front as he assured the men that they were capable and strong.

"Know what we decided to call this, my lord? Bridget's Run!"

"I think," said Vortimer, "Bridget's Run will be remembered longer than our baptizing of the ground with Viking blood! She is a hard task master!"

Surprisingly, the men were resilient enough to laugh in agreement; Bridget swelled with pride but remained mute, relieved that all concerned acknowledged the difficulty she was being made to endure. Still, many shivered uncontrollably as they soaked up the fire's heat. Those able to do so scrounged for the least wet firewood and greedily plucked any berries they chanced upon.

Vortimer was immediately aware of the tension between Bridget and Varduc when they came upon his small group and pulled them both aside. "Whatever happened between the two of you must stop immediately! There is no room for disagreement now, understood? We have to do our best to get back to shelter and that will require both your efforts. Varduc, will we have a moon tonight?"

"Yes, young master. She will be waxing tonight."

"Will the sky clear, do you think?"

"I believe that it will, young master."

"Bridget, will you be able to continue at night? It will be colder but at least dryer."

"We will do whatever it takes."

"Good. We will stay here till the men have regained their strength, such as it is. Varduc, I have a slight fever. Warm yourself first and then bring me something."

"Immediately, young master!"

"Will you be all right?"

"Bridget, I did not beat the Vikings only to be laid low by some cough and a sore arm!"

"I was only concerned—you are my husband!"

"I will be fine! Just get us back! I was dreaming of a tub filled with warm water and our bed with dry linens and you lying in it. Make that dream come true!"

No one wants that dream more than I!

Bridget accompanied Vortimer back to the cart where they covered poor Patrick respectfully and made sure the other occupants were as comfortable as possible; they accepted their misery with a stoic nonchalance that Bridget found both remarkable and foolish. Remarkable that they did not complain of their pain and discomfort and foolish in that they truly believed Bridget's Run could get them home before they died.

Except Vortimer—Vortimer will persevere! He must!

Anxious to begin, Bridget fretted as she waited for Varduc to produce Vortimer's tea. That done, the cart was again covered. Hrolf indicated he would stay inside to help the men but Vortimer protested that there was no reason to trust him and so he rode with Bridget again.

The weather had improved considerably—a thin fog whisked over the ground and the sky, though darker, was visible at last. It was still cold and their clothes still sodden but for the first time Bridget felt a spark of optimism where none had been before.

The crescent moon brightened in the clearing sky and cast the faintest of shadows—just enough to prevent walking into trees but not enough to prevent stumbling over their roots. Without hard reference points to judge their progress, Bridget found that time seemed not to exist. Alexander just went on and on and on. The night air was more bitter than before but without the lashing of wind and rain. Bridget felt encouraged when she finally heard some of the men talking amongst themselves.

How is Vortimer feeling? Will he be well? I wanted to hug him so much when he told me of his dream—the same as mine! Yes, he will be safe, I know it. What's that smell?

Bridget picked up her face and inhaled deeply. She did it once more. The night air carried the perfume, however light, of food! Somewhere before them were peasants in their hovel and they were cooking! Bridget's stomach growled loudly and her mouth began watering. She had left all thoughts of eating back when they first broke camp, almost twenty-four hours ago but her body had not forgotten. She peered intensely, trying to spot the fire on which the food (barley soup?) was being prepared...there! A faint orange glow was ahead and to the left. She knew it was foolhardy to risk charging blindly towards the light but it was difficult to restrain that first impulse.

We have come this far—just a bit more patience. There even appears to be a path!

The hut was little more than logs, sod and sticks, and the smell of the chickens and goats that lived inside could not overpower the scent of hot soup. Bridget let Hrolf down gently and she dismounted. She slapped her hand on the crude door and shouted, "We are hungry!"

The man and woman who presented themselves knew that nobles were an odd bunch but that did little to prepare them for what they saw. They knew Bridget, of course, and Vortimer, but did not expect an army to come banging at their door, ever! They bowed, they kissed Bridget's hand and they wailed unceasingly that they should be visited by their lord and lady.

"We are many and hungry. Give us what you can."

They handed Bridget a mug of steaming soup that she carried to the litter as Hrolf undid the ties. Much as she yearned to feel its warmth, Bridget knew Vortimer needed it more.

"I heard the commotion. We must be getting closer. Did you have something?"

"Of course I did! Here, this will make you feel better."

"Varduc's tea helped some. I feel stronger but tired."

Hrolf passed the soup to Vortimer who sipped it slowly. Behind them they heard the rest of the regiment being scolded by Glendon to remain in place or forfeit whatever chance they might have for some of the savory liquid. When he was half done Vortimer passed the mug to Bridget. "Don't lie to me—now, eat."

Bridget downed it in one gulp and said, "It was only a smile lie."

In spite of their cold and hunger, Bridget saw the men maintained their discipline. Some had just a mouthful from a ladle, others a dry crust of bread. The smell of food not only increased their hunger, it also bolstered their belief that they were indeed almost home! Besides, there was not one of them who had not gone hungry before, sometimes days on end! It was not food they craved but the sustenance of hearth and home, no matter how meager.

Glendon reported that there was no food left which caused some half-hearted grumbling from those who hadn't eaten and Bridget felt herself shamed that she had eaten before them—she was stronger than that! She made a silent vow that should this kind of thing ever happen again, she would not eat until her men had been fed. Thanking the peasants and turning, she heard them mutter something about the failed crops but she was already turned and mounting—she never gave it a second thought.

Feeling much better, she lifted Hrolf up onto Alexander and in the silvery night continued Bridget's Run. Even in the depths of the dark and cold, Bridget felt hopeful now that they had met one of their own people.

We must be getting closer. Where will we be when the sun rises? Will we see the fortress? No, I cannot think that far ahead—just keep moving! There will be more peasants as we get closer and that means more food! My hands can still remember the warmth of that mug—so does my belly! I want to get home! I need to be home! Why didn't I ask them how far we were from the fortress? Will Vortimer be well? Of course he will!

And so her thoughts meandered as she led the ragged line into the murky night.

They came upon more hovels and wakened the startled inhabitants with demands for food. Bridget abstained though her stomach grumbled in protest—she and Glendon made sure that those who hadn't eaten, did. Here, too, there were murmurings about the ruined harvest. Only Vortimer was given more and that was by Bridget's hand. Hrolf watched everything keenly, even refusing to eat and instead proffering his portion to Bridget who accepted and at once returned it to the waif.

"I know you would have killed my husband if you had the chance, Hrolf. Still, you are a child and a handsome one, I think, beneath those rags. Drink the broth and warm your little belly."

Hrolf looked quizzically at Bridget as he accepted the mug and then smiled broadly as he drank it. This time, rather than sit behind his benefactor, Hrolf took Alexander's reins and began leading horse and mistress onward. The path was more clearly defined now, even in the scant light and Bridget kept waiting for the dawn that must surely be coming soon. True enough, the false dawn began and Bridget and her followers began recognizing familiar hills and meadows. Some of the peasants began taking their leave and scurried to their homes that were closer than the fortress. There were shouts of encouragement from the men and Bridget knew at last that all would be well.

The pikes! I was supposed to account for the all the pikes! Well, I failed. I don't care! Has any dawn been as remarkable as this?

It was no more a remarkable dawn than the thousands that Bridget had witnessed in the past. The sky only became less black. There were no breathtaking colors and no early promise of a glorious day—all that mattered to her was the light and with that, home. Bridget finally saw the fortress up ahead. People appeared as if from nowhere and now there were shouts of jubilation over their victory but Bridget would have none of it—they fought, they won, some died. The meager happiness she felt was that they had survived the ordeal. There were questions about Hrolf that Bridget ignored and also urgent pleas about missing kinsmen which she also ignored.

They are alive or dead—I don't know everyone here! For your sake I hope they are alive and that you can find them and that you can go to your homes. I want to go to mine! I want to gallop through those gates and carry Vortimer up those steps myself! I want to sleep! I want to be warm! I want to care for my husband!

The last hour had been the most difficult—the anticipation of creature comforts made this last part of the trek unbearable. Her clothes were still sodden, she shivered, her eyes wanted to stay closed—her stomach cried out for food and water—she wanted warmth and sleep. Most of all, paramount, was Vortimer! Bridget needed to nurse him in the most primal way a woman could care for her love. She would endure all the anguish she had experienced during Bridget's Run if only she could care for Vortimer.

I love you, Iron Dog! I love you! In spite of your sullenness and obstinate ways. I know the man that lurks behind those eyes. I know what you have been through, dear man, my husband. My life for yours! No, you cannot die! Not now! I am being foolish, again! I have never lifted a sword in anger nor killed a man—but I now know how you feel. I now know how you have come to be the man you are—so long as I breathe, you will not suffer as now.

The fortress gates opened and Bridget dismounted—the crowd cheering. Glendon rode forward and said he would take care of the men—Bridget could barely whisper her thanks and then asked that Vortimer be led, with her, to the hall. Before dismounting she saw the smith who had made the pikes, he waved. She was too tired to smile.

Vortimer balked at first, wanting to bury his dead companion but Bridget insisted he get out of the litter before he himself would need burying. They were met at the bottom of the steps by the castle staff who were more nuisance than help. Only Gwenthe and Mathilde had the presence of mind to lead the couple up—Vortimer's arm over Bridget's shoulder.

"We can make it from here. Just go and prepare a fire in our room and I want dry clothes and a steaming tub. Don't worry about me, it is your master who needs you now."

It took some time to get to their room as Vortimer walked slowly, coughing wetly. Together, she and Mathilde stripped off his clothes and placed him beneath several covers. The wound on his left shoulder was fiery.

"We need to clean it out, milady."

"With what?"

"Make up some salt water, Bridget, use that and maybe some vinegar. Varduc knows what to use." Vortimer whispered.

"Go find Varduc and bring him here. Will you be all right, Vortimer? I just want to go the bath for a while. I can't feel my fingers or toes!"

"Go and get warm. I will be fine."

Bridget dropped her clothes in a wet heap and stepped gingerly into the warm water that made her toes feel like they were on fire. It took some time but at last she was able to slide up to her shoulders. Her body absorbed the heat greedily. She even put her head beneath the water and later splashed her face as she luxuriated in the warmth. Over in a corner she spied Hrolf who had made himself quiet and small.

He has seen me naked! Who cares? I am certain he has seen naked women before. I just want to stay in here and not move. I did it! I got them all back! We were victorious! So then why don't I feel happy?

She glanced over at Vortimer as he sat in bed with his eyes closed. The blanket had fallen from his chest and she could see the disfigurement of his collarbone near the shoulder.

We must fix that somehow.

Stepping out, Gwenthe asked a thousand questions as she toweled her down vigorously. Bridget stepped into the warmest clothes she could find and then motioned for Hrolf to go into the tub which he did immediately.

"We need some food, Gwenthe. Lots of food and have it brought up here—Vortimer is too ill to walk down to the hall."

"We have plenty of food for now, milady, but don't know about how it's going to last."

"What are you saying?"

"Remember all the grains we had gotten and what we had in the fields? There was nary a place to store any of it when that storm came through and it soaked most of it through. What was in the fields was beat down and is going to rot."

"I'll worry about that later. Right now we need food...and some wine. Where is Mathilde? I need Varduc to attend to Vortimer."

Bridget sat by the fire and breathed in the hot air to warm within as well as without.

I want to sleep so badly but I cannot, there are just too many things yet to be done. Vortimer did what was expected of him—he defeated the Vikings—but he knows precious little about governing. Neither do I, really. If I don't take care of this matter, no one else will. I have to take care of Vortimer, first.

315

It was not too much later when a breathless Mathilde entered with Varduc close at her heels.

"Young mistress," he bowed.

"Sit by me here at the fire, counselor, and share this wine with me. First, I was wrong to speak to you the way I did. I was scared, truthfully. I never did anything so difficult before. I needed help and it seemed as though I was getting none. I apologize." She stared into the fire as she spoke, not wanting to look at Varduc's quizzical face. She asked Mathilde to replenish her goblet.

"Young mistress, I knew you before you knew yourself. There is a mastery and strength that resides in your bones that cannot be denied, not after Bridget's Run!" He looked into the fire and continued speaking quietly. "You and Vortimer have that same spirit, young mistress, and the same failings as well. Do not doubt yourself. Your apology is humbly accepted."

"Vortimer is sick."

"Yes, the Iron Dog is mortal after all. I will do what I can but my wisdom is limited in the healing arts." Together they glanced at Vortimer who was sleeping quietly.

"Can you set that bone?"

"I think so…but it will be painful. I have some rudimentary knowledge after all my years. So many peasants get injured and falling off horses causes the same kind of break. I never had the time to study the herbs and roots of Bone Tear, young mistress. We will get him drunk and set the bone but it is the cough and festering wound that worry me most."

Bridget said nothing, letting Varduc's words seep into her thoughts, waiting in vain for some plan to make itself known. When nothing happened she drained the goblet.

"There is something else." She whispered.

"Yes, young mistress, you are with child."

The confirmation only caused Bridget to look deeper into the flames.

I thought so, but how does Varduc know? It doesn't matter. What to do?

She walked over to Vortimer and gently stroked his face to waken him. She kissed him when he opened his eyes. Taking a goblet, she put it to his lips. "You know what we have to do."

"Yes, I do." He coughed heavily and winced. "Let's be about it."

"First, I want you to drink till you become silly and I can see you smile again, my husband. We haven't laughed together in some time, you and I."

Dare I tell him about the baby? No, better that I wait till he is up on his feet and I can surprise him!

"What are you smiling about?"

"Oh, nothing, just glad to be home and to be warm again. Have some more."

Bridget had two for each of Vortimer's and the two spoke softly, recalling what little Vortimer remembered of the battle; most of all, he spoke of Patrick and Patrick's family. His eyes filled as he recounted their conversations in the dark of the covered wagon.

"We are ready, Varduc," Bridget said.

"I am not as strong as I used to be, young mistress. You and your women will have to help."

Hrolf, who had long ago finished his bath, stood at the foot of the bed and stared mutely.

Varduc positioned Bridget on Vortimer's right and showed her how to place her arms under Vortimer's left armpit and neck. He went over, gently removed the left arm from its sling, lifted it up and had Gwenthe grasp it by the shoulder.

"When I tell you, pull firmly and don't stop till I tell you. The bone has to be pushed down so that the ends can join together. Ready?"

All parties nodded and Varduc gave the order to pull. Vortimer groaned at first, then cried out and cried out again. Everyone broke into a sweat except Varduc whose practiced hands finally pushed the two bones together. Vortimer lay gasping and cursing as the women loosened their grip.

"I thought only the Vikings wanted to kill me."

"Hush, young master. You have seen this done many times before."

"Seeing it and having it are two very different matters."

"True, young master, but now I suggest you keep your arm in the sling and don't move it at all. A splendid job, ladies."

Vortimer's pain diminished rapidly after the bone had been set and the effects of the wine lulled him to sleep.

"What do we do for the shoulder wound and that feverish cough?"

"All I can suggest now, young mistress, is to clean it frequently with vinegar. As for the other matters, I do not know. Have him sit up in his bed and don't let him lie down. I can offer nothing further except some tea which may help."

"Go and prepare some then, I have to think."

Bridget ushered everyone from the room except Hrolf who she allowed to lie on the floor in front of the fire.

I need time to think. When was the last time I slept? Has it been that long? I suppose I did sleep on Alexander. Vortimer is gravely sick; I know that for certain. I also know that there is precious little food for the winter. And I am carrying Vortimer's baby. What else can go wrong?

She sat looking at Vortimer's face in the darkening room, searching it for some clue. At last she stood and went to the nearby table and began writing hurriedly.

Dearest sister, you know by now that we have defeated the Northmen and you also know of Glamorgan's treachery. What you don't know is that Vortimer's wounds are grave and I am afraid for his health. Much of our crops have been destroyed. You have done so much for me already but I need you once more. Come as quickly as you can and bring your woman with you along with all her elixirs. I have need of you. As you love me, fly.

CHAPTER THIRTEEN

Fly to her?

Celestine crumpled up the note and flung it into the fire.

All those months of turning Glamorgan against Bridget and Vortimer, all for nothing! Well, not really—at least Vortimer is wounded. Is he that strong? The Stones promised me opportunities but how to take advantage of this one? They need food and Vortimer needs care. Perhaps Bridget can be separated from Vortimer, but how?

Celestine mulled over possibilities and ramifications; discarding some outright or keeping parts of others, trying to fit them together. She paced the room, talking to herself as she visualized one plot after another. Clearly, she needed to go to Bone Tear. She smiled and began humming.

Fly.

* * *

Everything was in disarray. It was most apparent when Vortimer's fever subsided and he spoke with Glendon and Varduc. The ferocity of the early storm had destroyed what scant crops there were and how to find the means to replace them was paramount on everyone's mind except Vortimer's.

"Glamorgan turned tail and ran, did he?" Vortimer seethed.

"That is the report from his former men, Maldwyn and Astorious. We understand the king has banished him," said Glendon, "but you know how I feel about that, lord."

"Yes, I do. Dead dogs don't bite."

And then the discussion would return to the matters most pressing—food for themselves and grains for the livestock. Vortimer was unconcerned about his own physical condition but Bridget could see how he had deteriorated. The arm wound had neither healed nor worsened, instead it oozed a thin, pinkish fluid that she was careful to clean. He would soak his bedding with sweat each night and it was all Bridget could do to keep it fresh—his robust appetite had disappeared and she found it difficult to get him to eat and drink. His urine had a foul odor

319

and he looked thinner each day, his ribs plainly visible. She herself slept hardly at all, preferring to hover over Vortimer. Bridget vomited almost every morning now but she staunchly refused to tell Vortimer of her pregnancy. They would celebrate the news when he became well.

Where is my sister? I know she will come, she must! How do I tell her that I will be having a baby? She will be furious! Well, I won't be showing for quite some time—she should be long gone by then. What are we going to do? And it is becoming colder each day. Even Gwenthe and Mathilde are cheerless.

Bridget's troubles were suffocating; each waking moment was devoted to any or all of them. Her only solace came when she drank wine (which was rapidly diminishing) or ale each night. Then, all the problems became distant nuisances. Vortimer would heal and they would ride to the sea together, maybe swim. She would find the finest midwife and safely deliver a scrappy boy child. There would be feasts and plenty as envious nobles would come from distant kingdoms to marvel at Bone Tear's prosperity. The early summer would last and last and each day would be more bountiful than the one before. It was a comfortable way to fall asleep—it even dulled the Hooded Man.

It was a cold, gray morning when a messenger arrived to announce that Lady Celestine was but a day's ride away.

Bridget forgot her queasy stomach and pounding headache and directed Gwenthe and Mathilde to light a fire in Celestine's room—it would take a full day to warm it up.

She has to have brought Calgwyn with her, she must! Oh, I can't wait to see her! I mustn't let on about the baby, not at all! Will she be able to help Vortimer? Of course she will. What will she think of Hrolf? I think it best if he sleep in the kitchen. How can I make him understand? At least we have meat. I think I will have cook butcher what she thinks might not survive the winter.

Bridget divided her day between badgering the staff about her sister's arrival and caring for Vortimer.

Are all men as stubborn as my husband? My sister came all this way to help us and all he can say is that he will be fine. He looks terrible and is still weak as a kitten. At least the broken bone doesn't bother him as much. What will she do for him, I wonder? Even with all his wisdom, Varduc is disappointing in the healing arts. There must be someone here who knows about the powers of roots and herbs.

Bridget only drank ale that night; conserving what wine they had for Celestine. Vortimer was sleeping as she sat, feet curled beneath her, before the fire and watched the liquid flames. Everything was going to be fine, she thought. Her sister, as she had done so many times, would take care of everything.

Celestine's arrival was without fanfare and it was all Bridget could do to have her get settled before going to examine Vortimer. Calgwyn was there as well and made many trips, carrying countless jars and vials. Bridget could not recall the last time she had been so overjoyed. It was as if the dazzling presence of her sister melted away the shadows that had been plaguing her. Unable to contain Celestine anymore, she led the two of them into see Vortimer.

"Does he often sleep this late in the day?" Asked Calgwyn.

"He sleeps more than he is awake."

"Does he get up and walk? How frequent are his fevers? Are they worse at night or during the day? What have you been putting on that hideous wound? It is going to scar badly."

Bridget felt greatly inadequate as she answered the pointed questions while she held Celestine's hands in her own.

"Do you think—."

"Of course I can. It will just take time and luck. The only thing that's kept him alive this long is his youth and the strength that goes with it."

"Does he ever get brain fevers?" Celestine wondered aloud.

"Yes, he gets those, too. He doesn't recognize anyone or know where he is. I place wet rags on his forehead to cool his skull when that happens."

Calgwyn left and returned with an armful of jars and small baskets brimming with dried leaves, roots and powders. Not heeding the two ladies, she went about her work on the table.

I'm surprised they didn't try to bleed the poor man! First, that arm. I'll make a salve of Wormwood and Holligold. Probably hasn't eaten a decent meal since all this happened! Well, that will change in a hurry! I don't care who he is!

I know I have Mustard here. A poultice on that chest will loosen the phlegm he's drowning in. Let's see…I'll try the Ash bark with the Willow for that fever and if that don't work, some Eye Bright.

"Your husband is such a handsome man, Bridget. I never truly noticed his features until now." Celestine whispered.

"Thank you, but to me he looks so ill! Can we go to your room to talk? When I whisper like this as he sleeps, I feel as if he really isn't here."

"Of course, poppet. I have to know everything. Everything!"

Celestine's questions were pointed and thorough. First, she made Bridget recount every facet of the battle. Bridget related everything except the spiritual joining she had shared with Vortimer—the trench, the wasp nests, the field strewn with bodies and Glamorgan.

"Ah! Glamorgan has fled, never to be seen or heard from again, dear. It puts father in something of a bind as he depended on him for so much. Who knows or can understand what thoughts lurk in such a person? From devoted vassal to traitor in so short a time!"

"My feelings exactly!" Bridget exclaimed. "I thought he truly cared for me. I even called him 'uncle'. That was how close we were."

Celestine listened in awe as her sister recounted the terrible trek from the battlefield to the castle. "It was terrible! All of it! The wind cried like dying men! I swear, I never want to do anything so horrible again, ever! And now Vortimer is sick and that storm destroyed so much of the crops. I am at my wit's end! We tried so hard and now it appears as if it was all for nothing!"

"Poppet, Have you been using Calgwyn's elixir?"

"Of course." She lied. "Not that I needed that much—preparations were so hectic before the battle and of course he is in no condition now. I am the last thing on his mind."

"He is a man," she chided. "Always remember that. Now regarding those other problems, have a seat."

Celestine produced a carefully folded letter with Therdorous's heavy seal prominent.

"My husband's affairs are far-reaching and he has many friends of considerable wealth and power. That," she pointed, "is a letter of introduction to Lord Justin, himself a powerful and wealthy nobleman. I have had Theodorous notify him to expect your coming and the reasons for it."

"My 'coming'? What do you mean?"

"Bridget, how can I possibly plead your case? You are the lady of Bone Tear, not me! It is your responsibility, yours alone. Besides, you will have to bargain with Justin. He will not yield a bushel of oats unless there is some profit in it."

Bridget sat uncomfortably. Leaving Bone Tear and Vortimer was not something she had foreseen.

"Oh, Bridget! You must really learn how to dissemble if you are to be a lady! Your face mirrors your every thought!" Celestine sounded annoyed. "Yes, you have to go on this mission."

"But what about Vortimer? Who will care for him? Who will watch over Bone Tear?"

"Poppet, I am surprised and hurt by your groundless fears! Haven't I always been here for you? I will care for Vortimer in your absence and quite frankly, there isn't much to administer in Bone Tear. What's his name, that little creature can handle the everyday affairs and Glendon will remain here as well."

In two sentences Celestine had lifted the burden from Bridget's shoulders and placed them on her own. Overwhelmed by Celestine's generosity, Bridget began kissing her cheeks joyously.

"Enough of that now, poppet, enough! You have to prepare."

"I must do this swiftly. Do I need much of an escort? I think not. There are two men of Glamorgan's that are sworn to me and I think I will take young Hrolf, the experience will be good for him."

"Whatever you think best, Bridget. Now, let us go back to your quarters and I will help choose your clothes. Justin's is a fashionable court and it would not do to dress poorly."

Together the two sisters began sorting through Bridget's garments as Calgwyn continued preparing Vortimer's tinctures.

"You must wear only your finest, Bridget. Where do you keep them? I am certain that you have better, no?"

"I have never had much reason to wear finery." Bridget replied. "Besides, why do I need to dress uncomfortably?"

"Have I taught you nothing? Lord Justin is a man—need I say more?"

"But I am married! Vortimer is the only man in my life!"

"Bridget, I know that. We all know that! I also know that provocative attire can obtain more from a man than the most reasoned argument"

Together they continued pulling apart Bridget's meager apparel—finally choosing two. Calgwyn informed them that she had readied Vortimer's drink and that it would be best to wake him. Returning to his room, Bridget sat on the bed as Celestine and Calgwyn looked on. Bridget stroked her hand across his cheek—she could feel the warmth radiating from his forehead. He opened his eyes in that dreamy manner which always made her uneasy. Vortimer, vibrant and strong, was now listless and helpless.

"We have company, Vortimer. My sister is here and she has brought medicines for you."

Celestine took this moment to sit on the opposite side of the bed and held

Vortimer's hand in hers. "We are so very grateful and in your debt, Vortimer! I would have come anyway because I care so much for the both of you. Here, I am going to hold this to your lips and I want you to drink it down quickly." Vortimer did not speak, instead he drank the bitter liquid and grimaced.

"I believe," he said, "that should be used to kill fleas."

The sisters smiled but Calgwyn was not amused.

Let him think what he wants! But right now I am the only person capable of keeping him alive. His eyes are glassy but they must be beautiful. Even my lady seems to notice. Best not to think too much on that—just do my business.

Celestine and Bridget doted on Vortimer as Calgwyn proceeded to apply a poultice to the arm. He winced initially but then found it soothing. The news that Bridget would be leaving was unsettling, however.

"Are you certain you have to leave? I hate not being able to do a damn thing!"

"Ah," said Bridget, "then you are not annoyed with me so much as yourself, Vortimer. I have learned many things from you and from my sister. I know I can do this thing and do it well. It is much like 'Bridget's Run'—I never wanted to do it, thought I could not, but did. Allow me to do this for us; allow me to make you proud."

Vortimer mulled the situation over but the fever was making concepts slippery, much like trying to grasp an eel. Why argue when it was easier to agree and be allowed to sleep? It all made perfect sense. Every thing would fine.

"Have your women pack up your things, Bridget. We can go to the hall and plan your journey. Vortimer is resting and Calgwyn can watch over him for now."

Together they went down and Bridget found it joyless, cold. Where once she and Vortimer had eaten and laughed with their men, now was merely a large room, barren, dead. She tried to shake off this dismal feeling, could not, so ignored it and sat with Celestine. Summoning Glendon and Varduc, they waited for their meal to be served. It was a simple meat soup but hot and hearty and it picked up her spirits. She thought of the man upstairs all the while and twice Celestine had to prod her to pay attention to all she was telling her.

Glendon and Varduc arrived together and were invited to sit and eat as Bridget outlined her intentions. The two men said nothing to contradict her, knowing that Bridget had no other recourse.

"It is a good thing you do, young mistress. I have the fullest confidence in your abilities and know you carry a heavy burden."

Don't you dare hint at my being pregnant, Varduc! Celestine is far too clever and astute to be tricked. Having her wrath now would be a perilous mistake—we need her.

"It is the least I can do and the young master and I have faith in your abilities to make decisions. You love him almost as much as I."

"That we do." Said Glendon. "Now, as to where you are going. It is a hard ride, at first but the further south you are of your father's, the better the roads become. You cannot make the trip in two days of hard riding but there are inns along the way."

"Tell Maldwyn and Astorious that they will be my escort and have them ready. It is necessary I have a packhorse and Hrolf can ride on that. We will be leaving long before sunrise, so mind they are rested and ready."

"And how long does my young mistress think she will be absent?" Varduc asked.

"I will be gone as long as it takes. Promises and good wishes will not fill bellies. I will see that the carts and wagons are loaded and on their way before I return."

"Perhaps," said Glendon not discourteously, "we should call you the Iron Bitch?"

"It is a name I would carry with pride and fitting because that is how I feel. The Iron Dog is ill, let the Bitch take his place."

Her pronouncement was delivered with the same authority as when she prepared to do Bridget's Run, Glendon remembered. He admired it in Vortimer and was struck with Bridget's ability to instill the same unflappable confidence. The gold flecks in her green eyes glowed with determination. "It will be done, milady."

The two men left and Celestine used this time to begin informing her sister all that had been happening. First, her father was overjoyed at the victory. He knew Vortimer was the right man for the task. As far as ceding all of Glamorgan's holdings to Bone Tear, he was less enthusiastic. "You see, poppet, father needs the proceeds to bolster his own forces. He has promised that there will be an accounting after winter and before the next planting."

"The next season is a lifetime away, Celestine. Father sent us here only with the promise of Glamorgan's help, nothing else, and that failed! We deserve more recompense for that bit of treachery! If we had lost then father would have nothing!"

"Again, Bridget, this issue can only by settled by you."

Bridget fumed indignantly that her own father, the man whose fault this all was, could be so ungrateful. "Perhaps a powerful Bone Tear threatens him. As if we would ever consider such a thing."

"You might not but what about Vortimer? Tell me such things have never happened and I would call you a fool!"

"Forget about all these impossibilities for now!" Bridget threw up her hands in disgust. "How is the abbess? How is she treating the wounded we sent her?"

"Bridget, you asked me to get here as quickly as possible, not to be your emissary!"

Bridget accepted the rebuke with a half-hearted apology, knowing that Celestine, as usual, was right. Hadn't she made the arduous journey as swiftly as she could? Bridget knew her sister's dislike for physical discomfort and who knew what she thought of Bone Tear's humble chambers? Bridget was about to apologize for her ingratitude once more but Celestine put her fingers over her mouth. "Not another word, poppet. You have undergone a great deal; I understand that. Now, let me hear no more misgivings and let us plan your trip, instead. You will certainly need to spend at least one night at an inn, maybe two. Whatever you do, make sure you hire someone to announce your arrival the day before you get there. And be sure to wear something dignified when you arrive. It would be unthinkable to arrive dressed in your riding habit."

Bridget nodded appreciatively, recognizing Celestine's greater insight into the ways of courts.

Things used to be so simple. I used to ride and dress the way I wanted, not caring what anyone thought. Was I wrong in this as well? When will Vortimer be better? I cannot do all this on my own. He never cared how I dressed. At least I don't think he did. Would he want me to wear dresses and gowns all the time? Soon I will need larger clothes.

Celestine encouraged Bridget to use this opportunity to meet and become acquainted with as many men and women of high standing as possible. "You will find that in spite of their wealth and power, all they desire is greater wealth and power—it is their singular passion, trust me. Now, as to my responsibilities when you are away—I will first and foremost care for Vortimer, no? I will also manage your household which appears to be in some need of discipline, I think."

"I happen to maintain a very fine household but the preparations for the battle and the subsequent events have been very distracting! I just can't seem to focus on problems any more." Bridget protested.

"All well and good, Bridget. Your triumphant return will be to a much changed Bone Tear."

"Celestine," Bridget grasped her hand, "I trust you in all things but most of all, I trust you with my husband. I hate having to leave when he is this ill, you understand? Were it not for our desperate situation I would never even think of leaving!"

"I know, I know." Celestine commiserated. "However, we do what we are called upon to do. I just want you to know that all will be well here."

The sisters spent the remainder of the day planning Bridget's undertaking as Gwenthe and Mathilde went up and down the stairs with Bridget's things. Glendon appeared once more to announce that all was in readiness for her journey tomorrow. "Those two men will spend the night here and be at the ready, milady. I don't know them well but they seem like a good lot."

Bridget shuddered at the thought of having to leave. Like everything else, it was all happening too quickly. Once again, things were out of control and all she could do was to move forward and not fight the forces propelling her towards yet another unknown. Looking back, recalling the innocence and freedom of her youth, was a comfortable exercise in futility—it did nothing to alleviate the problems nipping at her heels.

In spite of her sister's confidence, Bridget felt herself become blanketed by an overwhelming sadness. Pregnant, confused and doubting her ability to accomplish yet another mission to salvage Bone Tear, she only wanted to be held by Vortimer and hear him tell her that all would be well.

Vortimer, I need you desperately. I want you to hold me and make me laugh. I need your strength to fill me. Remember that day I was so angry when you ran that race? Remember how we made love that night? And the times that followed? I have your child inside me, conceived in our perfect union. I was not meant to be the Iron Bitch, Vortimer. It is not in me. I only do what must be done. I love you.

"Where is your head, poppet?"

"Oh, nothing." Bridget smiled. "Just getting my thoughts together. Tonight will be my last with Vortimer and I wish to go to him now."

"Of course, dear. Calgwyn and I shall retire to our room and she will instruct me in his care. I want you to sleep well, Bridget. You need your strength."

Together they went to Vortimer's room where Bridget herded Calgwyn, Mathilde and Gwenthe out. Her women went downstairs to make sure all her things were in order; Calgwyn and Celestine retired to their room. Alone with Vortimer at last, Bridget again felt the heaviness well up as the daylight evaporated.

The fire no longer gives warmth and its shimmering only makes this desperate situation more unnerving. Dear Vortimer, why did you have to get so hurt? I hate you for putting me in this position!

She sat on his bed and gently kissed his forehead. Calgwyn had cleaned his face and she did not taste the salt of his fever—he smelled clean. Not caring whether it was proper, she insinuated herself beneath the blanket, longing just to feel the touch of his body next to hers.

I love you. I love your baby, our baby! I love Bone Tear. I love your infrequent smile. I love your gray eyes that can become hard as steel or like smoldering ashes. I love when you talk with me.

"I love you."

"And I love you, Bridget." He whispered as he held her left hand with his right. "I remember that first night I met you, vividly! I thought we would never survive!" He chuckled. Bridget laid her head on his shoulder and then kissed it. "You stomped your foot, I believe."

He loves me! I know he is not feverish and this is no game—I can feel it in the way he said it

"You were quite infuriating. You can still be infuriating!"

"You confuse me with Varduc, Bridget. Now he can be maddening!"

They reminisced about their tumultuous beginning and subsequent skirmishes and the longer they spoke, the brighter and warmer the room became to Bridget. Sick as he was, Vortimer's simple words as he held her hand in his, beat back all her misgivings and fears. "I knew from the time you won that horse race, you were special. A person to contend with. Now listen closely, you go as Bone Tear! I have faith in you—it is time you have faith in yourself."

They kissed long and softly, neither wanting the moment to end. If she could, Bridget would have crawled inside Vortimer's body—anything to be closer, a part of him. Still short of breath, that eternal kiss ended with his coughing abruptly.

"Are you all right?"

"I am fine…never better."

"I have to leave very early. Would you be more comfortable if I slept over there?"

"I want you to stay here next to me." He replied.

That was how she remained and that was how they slept.

The next thing Bridget felt was Mathilde gently squeezing her shoulder.

Bridget was awake at once and felt refreshed and flush with optimism; attuned to all that was around her as her nerves crackled with anticipation. She carefully removed herself from the bed, placed two logs on the rosy ashes and waited for them to catch fire before returning to look at her husband's face one last time.

May this simple fire keep you warm till I return. I long to kiss you once more, husband, but the baby in my belly and you must sleep. Remember last night. I can do this.

She turned and went out the door without looking back.

Celestine's heart was tripping as she waited impatiently for her sister to come down the stairs. Sleep had been impossible as Bridget's imminent departure seemed to be taking far too long.

The Stones promised me an opportunity and now it is almost at hand, almost within my grasp! I cannot let my excitement show. Look at her descending those steps! I swear she has gained weight! She does have a determined air about her, I grant her that. All I have to do now is look concerned and compassionate, the perfect sister!

"Celestine! It is black outside! What are you doing up so early?"

"Please, poppet! How could I not see you on your way without one last kiss? You look exhausted. Will you be able to go?"

"Celestine, I brought the men through Bridget's Run so I can certainly do this." She responded firmly, peeved that her sister still thought her frail and weak.

"Of course, dear. Here, have something to eat and I will tell you our plans."

Bridget devoured the poached eggs and bread as Celestine outlined Vortimer's care. Calgwyn, along with Mathilde and Gwenthe, would care for Vortimer during the day: changing his dressings, seeing that he ate and drank and took Calgwyn's elixirs. Too, they would challenge his pride, make him get up and walk.

"And I will care for him as he sleeps, poppet. I lack the skills and to be honest, I do not do well with sick people. However, I can sit quietly by the fire at night and listen if he should need some help—Calgwyn will be right next door."

Overcome, Bridget wiped her mouth with her sleeve before kissing Celestine's hand.

"There, there, Bridget. It is the very least I can do."

It would not be wise to do it tonight. Maybe the next?

Gwenthe took that moment to announce that the horses were ready. Celestine felt her heart trip an extra two beats. Forlorn, she took Bridget's hand and walked her to the door where Maldwyn and Astorious were standing respectfully.

"Wait! Where is Hrolf?"

Astorious chuckled. "He is already horsed and waiting, milady."

Celestine allowed Bridget to hug her close as each protested their love and faith one last time. "All will be well." Said Celestine with a smile. "All will be well."

Bridget allowed Maldwyn to lead the way down the steps as he carried a torch—twisting and fracturing her ankle would be disastrous. Celestine was fairly quivering with anticipation as she headed back towards her room where she awakened Calgwyn who slept on a pallet by the fire. "Bridget has gone and I think it best that you see to Vortimer. I have hardly slept all night and am going to retire for a few hours more."

Calgwyn was up immediately, straightened her clothes and left silently. Alone, Celestine removed her garments and returned beneath the covers.

The Stones promised me a child and opportunities. This is all truly a part of their plan—I can feel it in my bones. Why else would I have Calgwyn and learned much of her skills? I would never get my hands filthy by pulling up roots but at least I know which herb does what. It is simply a matter of choosing the proper amount and when to give it. I would love to get this over with tonight but it would not be wise. Better to be patient and like a cat, have some sport with its prey. It is too easy—best to be vigilant. Would Calgwyn suspect? Perhaps, but what of it? No, I will weep torrents and tear at my hair when he dies! I will neither eat nor sleep and make myself haggard. And what of Bridget? The convent? Theodorous could make some bargain to purchase mercenaries for father in exchange for Bone Tear. That will require some manipulation.

Celestine fell asleep with a smile even before the sickly dawn began.

The breaths of horses and riders were vaporous plumes in the chilled air as the quartet rode steadily onward. The packhorses prevented them from going too rapidly but that was for the best as they had a long journey before them—driving the horses to fatigue would be foolhardy. Bridget rode in the fore as her two escorts followed close behind. Hrolf was managing to stay atop his mount without much difficulty. The ride held no pleasure for Bridget and it reminded her that it seemed like an eternity since she last rode for the simple joy of it. The last good thing she had done was to lie next to Vortimer last night and hear "I love you" from his lips. Other than that, the last few months had been tedious and fatiguing.

But there is the baby! Won't Vortimer be thrilled? He will make a fine father; I know he will! What will we name him? Who will he look like? Oh, I hope he looks like Vortimer! Will my breasts become overly large? Do we get a wet nurse?

Bridget entertained these sweet thoughts of the future, preferring them to the bitter reality of the present. Daylight had finally begun but the dull rays promised no warmth.

* * *

Celestine napped intermittently throughout the day, preparing, she reminded all who listened, for her vigil. She visited Vortimer's room several times and watched as Calgwyn made him eat, drink and walk. He coughed up large amounts of gummy secretions into a rag as the searing pain from the split collarbone brought him to his knees more than once. Celestine was desperate for the sun to set but reminded herself to look patient and sad for poor Vortimer. Calgwyn laid out the various libations she had prepared and showed her mistress which ones were to be given and when. "This one is for sleep?"

"Yes, milady. I have hardly let him rest all day so he should sleep like the dead tonight."

"Really, Calgwyn. That was a very poor choice of words, I think."

"You know what I meant, mistress. He will sleep well and deeply."

"And this one is for his fever, yes?"

Calgwyn nodded.

"See that I have a proper chair by the fire, then. I shall hardly rest at all, I think. Oh, and have some food brought up for me in case I get hungry during the night."

"As you wish, mistress."

Celestine returned to her room and lay down once more, praying for the gloom of night which came at its appointed time. She walked into Vortimer's room just as Calgwyn was giving him something to sleep. He greeted her groggily and she smiled in reply as she went to the chair that faced his bed.

"He needs something for his fever as well, milady."

"I shall give it to him. You may go rest now. I will summon you if the need arises."

Calgwyn bowed out of the room and closed the door quietly behind her.

Everything was quiet in the castle. The cold months froze activity and commerce as much as it did ponds and lakes. Tradesmen left early and it was too uncomfortable for roving vendors to find customers who now stayed inside. No evening birds cried and crickets no longer chirped. The icy grip of winter was closing and whether they survived its throttle was in the hands of Bridget who was miles away on her desperate journey. The only sound was the murmuring fire.

Celestine studied Vortimer as he sat sleeping in bed; the blanket that had been pulled up to cover his torso, now slipped to just above his waist. The wavering flames gave his scarred skin a honey hue that glistened warmly. She watched as the light and shadows played about and defined his muscular arms and shoulders. The hair on his chest was a soft shadow that lightened towards his belly. Though his face was thinner, Celestine could still discern his deep eyes that were hidden in shadow. Even in repose, his well-muscled neck looked strong and sturdy. She quietly placed another log on the fire to see better. She stared hard and long at the figure before her, so different from her husband.

Opportunity.

Celestine giggled at the impossibility of what she was thinking and stopped herself abruptly.

Why not? They promised me a son.

She went to the table where scores of jars sat with their medicines. There was one that Calgwyn had mentioned haphazardly one time, a certain mushroom. Had she brought it?

Here it is!

Her hands were trembling as she unsealed it. Taking a large pinch, she mixed it with the brew for sleep.

Best if he remains feverish.

She brought the bitter liquid to Vortimer and gently pressed it against his lips. "Here," she whispered. "Time to drink this. Time to sleep—time to dream."

Vortimer, his eyes still shut, almost gagged as he drank it but managed to swallow the whole thing. Celestine returned to her chair and began her observation anew as she placed her hand between her legs.

I am such a slut! Wet already. How can I tell when the mushroom has muddled his brain? How long will it last? How ironic that his reality will seem but a dream dreamt by many men.

She continued stroking herself unashamedly before him, unconcerned that Vortimer might awaken or notice. Celestine brought herself to the brink two times...then stopped to regain her composure. Her senses were acutely receptive to everything in the room—the smell of the fire mingled with her own scent, the whispering of the flames, her thudding heart—everything.

She moved from the chair to the bed and sat by Vortimer's good right arm, her pulse racing. She ran her index finger across his forehead, along his eyebrow and down over his jaw and throat. Celestine did this several times, getting to learn the texture of his flesh and to see if he would awaken. She moistened her finger from between her legs and stroked his lips with it so very softly—still he did not waken.

Encouraged by his stupor, she began running her hand over his chest and shoulders—reveling at the strength she felt beneath his smooth skin. Vortimer moaned weakly as she began caressing his nipples, noticing how they stiffened just like hers. She put her lips by his right nipple and gently began licking it as her fingers rolled its brother between them. She heard Vortimer gasp and then mutter something unintelligible.

This is just a dream, Vortimer. A wonderful dream!

She held the nipple with her teeth and gently tugged at it and then released. He tasted like a man should. Celestine did this several times before her mouth began moving across his chest, licking and sucking slowly—fanning her own smoldering desires. Down his belly now, she darted her tongue into his navel and then licked it wetly. From the corner of her eye she saw that the blanket had risen where before it had been flat.

Would that you were mine, Vortimer. Well, tonight you are!

She pulled the blanket down roughly to his thighs, now certain that he would not awake. He was not fully erect but Celestine had no doubt as to her abilities. She cupped his testicles with her hand and gently began squeezing them. Again, Vortimer moaned but not in pain. His pelvis began to rise and then lowered as Celestine put her mouth over his shaft.

She felt it harden in her mouth as she went up and down on it slowly, mimicking the quivering cleft between her legs. That she had this power only increased her appetite and she began sucking him hungrily as his breathing now stopped and hitched.

Mustn't do this too much. Don't want to waste what is so clearly destined to be mine!

Celestine straddled the recumbent Vortimer whose eyes were half-opened and sightless. Pulling up her skirt with one hand, she grasped his throbbing shaft with the other, placed it between her damp lips and sat on it. Her hips convulsed for a few seconds and then stopped as she caught her breath—glorying in the feel of Vortimer deep inside her—she whimpered. Placing her hands on her thighs she began rocking forward and back rhythmically, dancing to the old song of men and women. Celestine did not know how often she crested—it seemed as though it was one continuous orgasm that became stronger and deeper—she knew it would be like this. She wanted to cry out as the jolting ecstasy ran though her. Vortimer now began to stir and she felt him pulsating with each thrust, matching her own. He began to cry out but she covered his mouth with her hand just as he gushed inside her. Man and woman stopped, both gasping weakly.

Every facet of the encounter had excited Celestine to a degree she never dreamed. The impossibility, the reality, the inherent danger and the sinfulness of it all had whetted her lustful craving like nothing before! She willed herself to calm down as she sat there, looking at Vortimer's sightless eyes.

Well done, Vortimer! Bravo! Magnificent! A pity you will never know the pleasure we have given each other, brother-in-law.

Celestine gingerly dismounted and felt his juice begin to run down her thigh as she stood by the bed and looked down at him, noticing the sticky fluid covering his testicles and partially erect member.

Oh, this will not do at all! It is not wise to leave any trace.

Kneeling by the bedside, she began sucking and licking him clean, delighted that it did not taste at all unpleasing—perhaps another time. Satisfied that she had licked him as clean as possible, she covered him and returned to the chair as she tucked her feet beneath her. Celestine closed her eyes and hummed as she fell into a delicious slumber.

* * *

The inn, Bridget thought as she lay in its vermin-filled bed, was the grandest example of filth she had yet to encounter—and one of the noisiest. The din from the drunken patrons below filled her room, unfiltered by the thin and poorly joined floor boards that allowed light and shouting to leak through. She had never been to a place like this before and was greatly disappointed, hoping it would be comfortable.

It was not uncommon for highwaymen and thieves to take advantage of unescorted and foolish travelers and three times Bridget swore she saw dark figures lurking in the shadowed forests that crowded the road. The militant bearing of her escorts, with their dangling swords and no-nonsense expressions, persuaded any scoundrels to wait for easier prey, however. Escorting wealthy merchants and businessmen had become a thriving, though dangerous trade for many young men, as thieves could sniff out their inexperience and unwillingness to protect their rich employer. Robbery was rampant and Bridget thought that most of the highwaymen were now in the room below her, clapping the shoulders of tomorrow's victims.

"I'll take care of the innkeeper, milady." Maldwyn had said when they first bulled their way in.

"You have nothing to fear." Added Astorious.

The reality was that Bridget was stiff with fright. The inn was the first place Bridget had ever seen the commoners mingling shoulder to shoulder with wealthier drunks. Her guards pushed the rabble aside as Bridget followed in their wake.

"My lady needs a room, your best room."

"My rooms are all taken."

"Throw them out or Lord Vortimer will be very displeased when he learns his wife was treated with such inhospitality."

The innkeeper's jaw dropped. "The Iron Dog?"

"The Iron Bitch is here and if we do not get a room immediately we'll have this cesspool razed!" Astorious threatened.

Pulling aside an overly large woman, the flustered man told her to remove the current occupant and ready the room for Bridget. Her countenance and thick forearms left no doubt that this would pose no problem.

"Would milady care for something from our kitchen?"

The squalor of her hosts and the stench wafting from the bodies and walls made Bridget decline, though famished.

"Something to drink, perhaps?"

Well, they can't ruin ale.

It was watered down.

That was more than an hour ago and Bridget, hungry and miserable, tossed fitfully in the bed.

What is Vortimer doing now? I pray he feels better. I know Celestine will take care of him for me. He will be so excited when I tell him about the baby! What will it be like to have a big belly and swollen breasts? Will he still love me? Will I still be able to ride? What I wouldn't give for some warm bread and honey.

Bridget felt the rumbling in her stomach.

Is that you, my child? Or is it just hunger? Oh, I will have so much to tell you about your father and Bone Tear. How our first meeting was so disastrous! Your father is so handsome and strong, he really is. I will teach you how to ride, my love. Maybe they will call you the Iron Pup!

This last thought caused Bridget to giggle uncontrollably and in that moment all became well again. Bridget reflected on the absurdity of her position and began laughing once more. Confident at last, Bridget fell asleep with a smile. Maldwyn, who was sitting guard outside her door, thought he heard snickering from within but decided it had to be his imagination. Better, he mused, to be inside than out in the stable with Astorious and Hrolf who were guarding the horses.

* * *

"I had the strangest dream last night, Varduc."

"And what was that, young master?"

"I can't really recall but it was somehow very pleasant. It was as though I was awake and yet sleeping at the same time. Strange."

"Fevers can do that to a man, young master. You know that well enough."

"But I feel more tired now than ever."

"Young master, perhaps no one has told you, but you are sick! The young are not accustomed to having maladies and it shocks them to the core when they discover just how mortal and frail they really are. Your color appears to be a bit better today; whatever it is these women are doing, is working."

Calgwyn beamed from the table when she heard this and then went back to her preparations. She thought her mistress looked particularly radiant this morning, in spite of having spent the night watching over Vortimer. Whatever the circumstances, Calgwyn returned to her work. Yes, his color had returned somewhat but there was no way he was yet out of death's shadow. She had seen too many men, young and old, snatched while they were on the mend. Her charge was Vortimer and he absolutely had to be saved! Calgwyn considered herself fortunate in that she had the resources of Bridget's women as well as Varduc and her mistress. Still, she knew that his survival was in her hands and knowledge. She would give him his bitter brews to drink and apply his dressings and get him up and about, no matter his protests! Deep down she knew that her job was to keep him alive till the body healed itself—Calgwyn would not allow him the luxury of surrender.

"It is time to walk!" She exclaimed.

"Walk where?" Vortimer protested.

""Around the room three times and then down the hall. Later on we shall try the stairs!"

"Bitch!"

"Iron Pup." She mocked.

* * *

The following day, Bridget arose feeling better than she had in weeks, at least in her mind. Physically, she felt ill and bloated. Hungry as she was, she declined

336

having a morning meal and instead insisted that they all leave before dawn. Hrolf had hardly wiped the sleep from his eyes when he found himself once again upon the back of the packhorse. The day was cold and now gloves had to be dug out; they cracked through the thin skin of ice on the muddy puddles as they rode.

Winter is upon us way too early. How is Vortimr this day? Is he awake and filled with his obstinate ways? That would be a good thing, I think! I hate seeing him so weak and docile. I am famished!

Bridget's earlier misgivings about her ability to accomplish the mission decreased the further south they rode. The threatening gloom of the woods slowly gave way to open fields and pastures. Real villages, not the random collection of shacks and hovels she was accustomed to, were seen more frequently now. Though modest, some structures were two stories, their gleaming whitewashed walls in sharp contrast to the dark, shorn earth.

Someday Bone Tear will look like this, only finer! We still have so much to do! We need only get through this winter. I will do this thing. What is Vortimer doing now? Are they taking good care of him? Of course they are! He will be so proud of me! I hope the next inn will be better than the last. I have to remember to take out better clothes so that I can present myself correctly. What will this lord be like? How great will his castle be? Do I have that letter of introduction? Yes, it is wrapped with my shawl, Vortimer's shawl. I will certainly wear it my entire stay.

I will relate all of this to you, my son and you will see just how silly your mother was for fearing this undertaking. Hrolf will be your older brother!

With that thought still in her mind, Bridget pulled Alexander over and rode next to the lad and began pointing to the trees, clouds and sky as she said their names. Hrolf's face brightened with the attention and imitated Bridget, often stumbling over the pronunciation but repeating it till perfect in his uncannily sonorous voice.

* * *

How ironic that I have given myself to two men, both of whom are lame. Would that my husband had the bad leg and Vortimer the ineffectual cock. My sister does not know how fortunate she is. I have never been so bored and so anxious at the same time! The sun cannot set quickly enough. He gave no indication of what transpired last night, not an inkling. Control is the word. Give the mushroom time to work its magic and hope that his fever remains constant or increases. Is there too much risk in getting him more active? Probably. Certainly. Still, I want him to take me! I want him to crush my lips with his mouth. I want him to hold my breasts and kiss my nipples. Vortimer, I offer myself to you!

Celestine brooded by the window and glowered at the sun.

The Stones never promised anything more than an opportunity. I must content myself with that. I will have a son, Vortimer's son. And to think that I was going to kill him, how foolish and willful of me! I never dreamt it could be that incredible, never! A pity Bridget doesn't have to visit the Pope! I know I could make Vortimer mine in time.

The thought of being a wanton tantalized Celestine and her pink button began throbbing, needing to be caressed once more. She rubbed herself, but it was a poor substitute for what was next door. Celestine dejectedly went back to her bed, perhaps to nap before her night vigil began. She nodded when the insistent, lulling voices told her to be patient.

Calgwyn's hand was barely on Celestine's shoulder when her eyes snapped open in the dimly lit room.

"It is time, milady."

"Yes. Of course it is."

Celestine was ready to bolt out the door but regained her composure and instead yawned. "How was he today?"

"Much the same, milady. The fever comes and goes, he ate a little and walked raggedly. He will sleep well tonight."

"Oh, I am sure of that, Calgwyn. Here, you may sleep in my bed. Tell me, have you heard any whisperings?"

"Whisperings, milady?"

"Nothing. I suppose I was dreaming. Is everyone else in bed?"

"Aye. No one awake but you and me."

"Very well. I will go and pray over my brother-in-law as he sleeps."

Throwing off the covers, Celestine escaped quietly from her room and entered Vortimer's. Taking her place by the fire, she again studied Vortimer's naked torso as his chest rose and fell with each breath.

Damn! I shouldn't have sat so quickly!! Best to give him his teas now and allow them to work.

With sure hands, Celestine made the adjustments to the liquids. This time, just to be safe, she added a pinch more of the mushroom before giving it to Vortimer who drank it groggily.

Making herself comfortable once more, Celestine contented herself with listening to the fire and looking at how Vortimer's strong neck flowed into and across his shoulders.

A long journey for my tongue but worth it! Now, just to be patient. I can feel how wet I am already! A bitch in heat is what I am, nothing more. But I do have a purpose and if the sacrifice be pleasurable, so much the better! I tend to like his short-cropped hair; it exposes more of his face. Not a classically handsome face but easy on the eyes. I remember the night I first saw him, he looked so bewildered in a boyish sort of way but intriguing. What a mating we could have made, Vortimer! Still, you are not wealthy, at least not in gold. I have money and land and the power it bestows. And, unlike my husband, I have the guile and will to use it. Do you have the same backbone, Vortimer? If I were a man I would crush my foes outright but as I am a woman, must resort to stealth and intrigues. Which of us is stronger, then? Could I dispose of Bridget and Theodorous? Perhaps they could acquire the same affliction? Or, better still, one have an unfortunate accident while the other wastes away!

Celestine continued her reverie, twirling her golden hair with her index finger as she waited for the potion to drag Vortimer into oblivion. She wanted desperately to touch herself like the night before but, like a dutiful bride, was saving that exquisite pleasure for her husband. When at last the voices whispered that it was time, she stood and softly stepped out of her clothes.

Naked this time, she walked to the bedside and gently lifted the blanket down, exposing Vortimer to her hungry gaze. Even in repose it was easy for her to appreciate the power that resided just below his white skin. Celestine glanced at his hewn right leg and found it exciting; it made him more vulnerable. She slowly walked around the bed and hummed, looking at the naked Vortimer from every angle, smelling the masculinity that drifted from him till she could taste it. The fine hairs of his chest tapered down his flat belly to just below his navel, like the head of an arrow.

The fire did not give light, instead it radiated wavering shadows that played over and along his body. She sat on his right and gently traced her fingers along his scalp, temple, cheek and neck. Vortimer did not stir as she continued across his shoulder. She did this several times as she hummed delicately and then began with her tongue. Slowly, she ran it over his shoulder and then across the wide expanse to his neck, savoring the salty sweet taste. Her tongue licked along his ear and then explored it slowly. Vortimer moaned, but not in pain.

Delighted, she positioned herself so that her mouth could explore his chest while her hand cupped his testicles and gently squeezed them. She kissed his nipple at first and then began to suck it before holding it between her teeth—all while her hand opened and closed on the fleshy sack she so reverently held. Bolder now, she began running her nipples across his abdomen and flank, making them tauter and more sensitive with each swipe. Groaning, she felt the hunger begin to overwhelm and devour her, still, she was steadfast—her mouth not yet sated.

He was already stiff when her mouth arrived and a heavy breath exploded from Vortimer's mouth. Rolling her tongue along the head, Celestine noticed how it tasted differently than the rest of him—she needed more. She slid her mouth over and down on him, taking it as far in as she could before gagging. Up and down, her eyes opened, she caressed it with her mouth until she felt his hips begin to anticipate each lunge she made.

Celestine was incapable of putting it in slowly when she at last mounted him and instead sat firmly down, grunting as she felt it slide in so easily and deeply.

She sat quietly for a moment and watched as Vortimer's lips moved wordlessly, his eyes open just a slit. Grasping his right hand with hers, she pressed it against her breast while undulating her hips. At times she took it away to lick his palm or suck his fingers, never ceasing her gyrations. Frantic now, her pelvis pushed harder and quicker, clamoring to be filled. Celestine began to whimper till at last her innards seemed to explode in a dazzling wave of ecstasy that left her weak and breathless. She collapsed forward and rested her head on Vortimer's chest while her own sucked in deep breaths. Celestine took time to compose herself and realized that Vortimer was still stiff inside her—she smiled dreamily as she repositioned herself before starting over.

If the sacrifice be pleasurable, so much the better.

* * *

The filth of the first night's inn was in no way repeated with the second. Bridget found the patrons to be better dressed, more civil and no unseemly odors assaulted her. The innkeeper maintained cleanliness and service with his nimble daughters while his two thick-armed sons made sure no one became too boisterous or belligerent. They could become as drunk as they wanted, just so long as they did it quietly.

Famished and cold, Bridget's party was seated at a roughly hewn table close to the cheery fire. In charge, Bridget ordered meat and wine—it didn't matter what kind or meat or wine—just so long as it was plentiful. She watched as her two guards instructed Hrolf in the pronunciation of various objects and food and was gladdened by their acceptance of him. He repeatedly made several errors in pronunciation but was diligent in his exercise. Maldwyn and Astorious were generous with their praise when he said something correctly.

The steaming venison, thick with gravy and a loaf of crusty bread were placed on the table along with two large flagons of wine and four goblets. Hrolf stood and poured out the wine for all. After sitting, he solemnly raised his wine and in the sweetest voice intoned, "My lady, Bridget."

Her two escorts saluted the Iron Bitch in the same fashion and clapped their hands on the table, congratulating the young boy who was smiling so proudly he looked as though his face could split!

How adorable he is! Truly, he was meant to be here! Vortimer was wrong! They are not all savages. How is Vortimer? I sense that he is being well cared for, I know it! Oh, to have this over and done with and to be by his side once more. I cannot believe I am so hungry—it looks like we are racing to see who finishes first, like ravenous dogs! This man sets a good table. I hope my room matches his fare.

"Maldwyn," she asked as she chewed. "Find out how much further to Lord Justin."

"I already have, milady. Naught but two hours from here."

"Then find someone here who can announce our arrival tomorrow. This was suggested by my sister and it makes sense, does it not?"

The large man pushed back his chair and went straight to the innkeeper and whispered urgently in his ear. The man nodded and Maldwyn was about to put two coppers in his hand which he adamantly refused. Huffing, he came to Bridget's table and announced that he was indeed honored to have Bridget, wife of the man who defeated the heathens, at his inn. "My son will ride before the cock crows, milady. Pray, tell Lords Vortimer and Justin that you have found my humble accommodations fitting." Clapping his pudgy hands, he indicated to his daughter that this table required more wine and food. Bridget thought it best not to argue, besides, she was still hungry and his wine was excellent.

Enlivened by their surroundings in a place far from home, the quartet feasted as they soaked in the fire's warmth and wiped their plates with the crusty bread

I wish you were here with me, my husband. You, me and the baby in my belly.

Bridget could eat no more. Holding her goblet, she toasted Vortimer and his health, slightly slurring the words which made her giggle happily.

I will sleep well tonight, my husband. May you do as well.

The innkeeper's wife arrived early next morning, carrying hot bread and butter on a heavy tray which she placed on Bridget's bed before waking her. She allowed Bridget to eat in privacy, promising to return to help her dress. All Bridget could do was to thank her profusely before attacking the food.

I am so hungry? Is it because of the riding, nervousness or the baby? It tastes wonderful! Oh, I feel so good!

Returning with two lit candles and a heartfelt smile, Marta at once began brushing Bridget's thick hair before helping her put on a more presentable wardrobe. Feeling refreshed and confident, Bridget was beaming as she pulled Vortimer's shawl over her shoulders.

I don't care how cold it is! I will arrive as grandly as I can. Besides, the sun will be up and that will help.

Walking to the horses, Bridget felt the eyes of the inn upon her and she stood that much taller. Turning to the innkeeper she said, "Bone Tear appreciates your hospitality, sir. It will not go unrewarded." With that, she mounted the waiting Alexander in one easy movement and led her trio of followers down the road towards her destiny.

It was a much grander castle than she could ever have imagined. Large blocks of granite set the foundations for the walls of hewn stones and timbers. Up and up the massive walls went, thick and impenetrable. Bridget's eyes widened at the largest structure she had ever beheld! It was magnificently foreboding and dwarfed both man and beast. Bridget allowed her escorts to ride in front and announce her arrival to the guards who stood at attention by the massive gates

Vortimer's pyramids could not be larger than this! And they have banners flying by the ramparts! I want this for Bone Tear! Wouldn't Vortimer love this? And so would the baby! I must choose a name and soon. Well, we can choose the name. The guards are all dressed similarly and smartly—perhaps we can do the same? Oh, Celestine, I thought your exaggerations were imaginary—forgive me! I must feign complacency and boredom, how? Best to focus on Alexander's ears. Hrolf's jaw has positively dropped to his knees!

A flurry of servants led by a distinguished looking man upon a strong black horse came up to Bridget. "Lady Bridget, mistress of Bone Tear, wife of Vortimer the Iron Dog, I am Marius, chamberlain of Lord Justin. Permit me to welcome to you and your party." He bowed.

"We are honored, sir."

Pointing and barking orders, he had her escorts led off to their accommodations. "Fear not, milady. They will be by your side shortly. I am charged with making you as comfortable as possible during your stay. Whatever you need or desire, you need only ask."

"Your lord is a gracious host, then?"

"Aye, and his lady as well! She begs to see you as soon as you refresh yourself."

"It would be impolite to do otherwise, no? A guest has certain responsibilities and duties."

"Then, Lady Bridget, permit me to lead you to your quarters."

They threaded their way through the narrow passages as footmen shoved pedestrians rudely out of the way. Bridget so badly wanted to gape at Justin's castle but restrained herself, preferring to focus on Marius's back. They arrived at last to what Bridget decided was the great hall—solid stone with thick doors and ornate hinges. They dismounted and Marius escorted her through the immense portal where they were immediately joined by two young women.

"These two will be your serving women, day and night. It is not proper that I should lead you to your quarters, they will. Your baggage and garments should already be in your room, milady. I have already ordered that a bath be drawn so that you might refresh yourself after your journey. Will that suffice?"

Walking through the largest room she had ever been in, Bridget nodded. In spite of her finest clothes, Bridget felt decidedly shabby.

No earthen floor here! This could hold ten of Bone Tear and still have room for my father's! What will Hrolf think of all this grandeur? Oh, I do like how they have the banners draped from the walls!

The two young girls led her up to her room as Marius bowed graciously. Bridget was once more impressed by the size and furnishings of her chambers.

Someday we will have a castle like this!

The servants helped remove her clothes, all the while remarking on Bridget's beauty that was so enhanced by her shawl. She stepped gingerly into the tub and was at once soothed by the scented and oiled water—an indulgence she had only heard of. She watched as the two girls chattered like jays as they unpacked her belongings. When that task was completed they focused their attention on Bridget—washing her hair and asking questions like excited children. Where was Bone Tear? What was it like? Did the Vikings actually have horns? Who were the handsome men escorting her? And the young boy?

Bridget answered politely, enjoying the company of women once again. She asked questions as well. How old they were, their names. What was Lord Justin like? His lady? Feeling wonderfully refreshed, she stepped from the tub and was vigorously dried before given a thick robe to put on as she sat by the fire. Bridget closed her eyes, letting the girls dry and brush her thick hair.

I cannot recall ever having indulged myself like this! I have to find out what they use to scent the water—rose petals?

"When will I see Lord Justin?"

"That will be tonight, milady." The younger giggled.

"My lord is out with the hounds and his companions, milady. There will be a grand feast tonight. I know, however, that his wife, Lady Athene would like to speak with you at some time."

Athene! Named after a Greek goddess, but goddess of what? Beauty? Wisdom? I can't recall! She is probably so elegant and beautiful and I feel so tawdry—even these poor girls are better dressed than me! Well, I was not sent here to be beautiful, the Iron Bitch is here for more practical reasons! I wonder what she looks like?

Bridget finally tired of being groomed and sent the two girls on their way after telling them that she would be delighted to see Lady Athene at her pleasure.

What is Vortimer doing now? Is he up and eating or sleeping? I would to God that I had some news! I am certain he is well; he has to be getting better! This is such a grand adventure but hollow when not shared. I do miss him so! I need him, I truly do. Not for his thoughts but simply for his touch, his smell.

Two sharp knocks on the door jarred Bridget from her thoughts. "Enter."

A bustling, rotund woman with a round face entered. "Ah, there you are! Lady Bridget, permit me to welcome you to our home! Was everything satisfactory? Your bath hot enough? I trust those two silly girls didn't prattle too much!"

She had a face and manner that were guileless and energetic; a face that exuded warmth and intimacy; a face that made you glad to look upon. She was, Bridget judged, twice her age at least and a good deal shorter than most.

"Forgive my ignorance, lady, but who are you?"

"Forgive you?" She cried out with the greatest mirth. "You should forgive me for not properly introducing myself! I am Lady Athene, mistress of this castle and wife of Lord Justin. That is who I am and what I am about is to finally meet Celestine's sister! Oh, you two don't look hardly alike, praise be! Couldn't bear to have all men staring at you all night, including Justin! Ah, but you do have some wildly wicked eyes—they and your hair are your most outstanding features! Simply lovely! Here, stand and let me have a proper look at you."

"Lady Athene—"

"Tut, girl! I was a woman long before I was a lady! Let me just look at you! Damned if you aren't tall! I am so glad you don't stoop! I have heard a great deal about you and Vortimer and Bone Tear. Tell me, is it all true? But you must be famished; I know I am. Olgren!" She bellowed. "Fetch us up some food and drink!"

Bridget could do nothing but smile as her hostesses' exuberance filled the room and uplifted her spirits. Athene's pudgy fingers quickly ran over Bridget's hair and across her shoulders. "Nope, nothing like Celestine. You do have some muscle, child! Have you any children? Hips like that——."

"Please, Lady Athene! You are making me laugh! No, no children yet."

"Well, in due time. Now, sit and tell me all about this Bone Tear. Odd name for a place—but I like it."

Bridget sat back on the chair as Athene faced her from across the table. Beginning with her first meeting of Vortimer, she related the story to her entranced hostess. Some soft cheese and wine were placed before them and Bridget only stopped talking to eat and drink. For her part, Athene asked pointed questions in between mouthfuls of food—questions about Bone Tear, the battle, Vortimer's wounds.

Bridget sensed a keen shrewdness lurking behind Athene's jocular familiarity, however. Her queries were intelligent and probing.

Celestine did say to learn how to hide my feelings and emotions—perhaps if I smile? What would Vortimer do? Dear Vortimer, no sense of subtlety. I am the Iron Bitch.

"Forgive me Lady Athene, may I make an observation?"

"Athene," she chided.

"Very well, Athene. Are we bargaining, you and I?"

"Dear child, of course we are!" She chortled and drank deeply. "You don't think we own all this," she swept her thick arm around, "because of Justin, do you? You know how men are, involved with seeing who can piss the furthest! Idiots! We'd all be a lot better off if they used their brains instead of their cocks! The key to wealth is taxes and commerce, Bridget. Tax the peasants just enough to let them till the land and then take the proceeds and invest in trading!

"And I?"

"Justin listens to me, dear. Oh, he will draw himself up importantly and ask particulars but I am the one he listens to and I will tell him that an arrangement with Bone Tear would be to our advantage for many reasons—not least of which was keeping the Vikings at bay!"

"We are in your debt."

"Nonsense, child! I am not doing you a favor, I am perfecting an arrangement between our two lands. Grains and feed for what? You do have abundant sheep and large fields, do you know not? We will decide upon the number of bales of wool and casks of honey."

"Business tires me, Bridget, it really does. I will let you rest now so that you can look your best for tonight's feast. We have many guests scattered throughout and you might find them amusing dinner companions. I will send in those two silly girls to help you dress when it is time. Let me see those eyes of yours once more. Ah, there is a liveliness in them that your sister lacks. Rest well, dear!"

Bridget stood to bow but Athene disregarded that as nonsense as she waggled her way out the door.

Well, that was an interesting woman! Have we completed bargaining yet? I suppose not. I only want to get this over with and go home! Still, I told them that I would see the carts loaded and on their way to Bone Tear. Two days? Three? Longer? Commerce? I hardly know what the word entails. Perhaps I should just try to rest and enjoy this respite. Ah, there is still some unfinished wine!

Bridget appreciated such bounty and made sure it did not go to waste or into the bellies of the servants. Contented physically and emotionally, Bridget allowed herself the luxury of a rare midday nap which was ruined by her hooded tormentor.

The blood smells more pungent now than ever! The hands! The damned hands of blood! Whose are they? Where is the Hooded Man? Where is he?

So real was the dream that the blood smell still tickled Bridget's nostrils for several minutes after she had awakened.

* * *

Celestine was in her bed while Calgwyn and the others administered to Vortimer's needs during the day.

His 'needs', how droll! Ah, Vortimer, what about my needs? The needs of your midnight lover! Just the thought of our little sins makes me drip.

How can it be that I once despised the very thought of you? The sound of your name grated upon my ears! Did you know I once thought of poisoning you? What a tragedy that would have been! The Stones promised me a child but never did I suspect that you would be the cause of the worm that is now growing in my belly.

Fate has a way of making things right, doesn't it? I married a man who gave me wealth and power and you married Bridget for Bone Tear! It is almost time for us to take this course that was plotted ages ago. Allow me to navigate, dearest. Theodorous drinks and stumbles all the time so it will come as no surprise when he snaps his neck on our stairs, poor dear.

It would be far too suspicious for Bridget to have an accident and almost impossible for me to plan. Too, she is strong as an ox, so poison might raise suspicions. How do I rid you of her?

Celestine rolled on her other side.

Why is it that the most obvious and easiest ideas are always the hardest to attain? My sister should become pregnant! No one would question her death at childbirth, no one! Yes, it will be easy to convince her. No, that won't do. I will just not replenish her elixirs. You, Vortimer, will take care of planting the seed and I will see to its fruition. So many infants die before they have even sucked—so sad. I will be there to comfort you, just as you will comfort me on the death of my husband. I will spend a week, a fortnight and a lifetime for you Vortimer. We shall marry—it is the only way for our son to be nurtured.

And you will make love to me with your eyes opened, my name and nipples on your lips as we shake the ground with our lust. Bridget will become a sad memory, like one of your scars. Theodorous is already a memory to me, no longer worth remembering.

It is an agony to lie here in bed during the day, knowing that only a wall and the sun separate us. You shall have me tonight and all that follow.

* * *

Try as she might, Bridget found herself having a difficult time getting into the gown, even with the help of her two servants.

Have I gained this much weight already? I feel like a sausage! Vortimer is going to despise me! Well, I won't be here long. I wish I could wear something more comfortable, anything! At least my hair looks presentable. What am I doing? I am the Iron Bitch! I don't care what I look like! Then how come I do care? I am pregnant and not just some old sow! Oh, let this damned night be done and let me return home!

Angry with herself, Bridget stood as erect as she could, if she could not be the most elegant then she would at least be the tallest woman there. She heard the sounds of music coming from Justin's Hall as her two girls led her down. It was the grandest Great Hall she had ever seen! Men, women, servants—there must have been three, perhaps four hundred people milling about. Some danced merrily as others laughed, shouted and sang. The women, Bridget noticed sourly, were indeed very elegant.

The Iron Bitch looks like a bedraggled cur.

"Ah, there you are, Bridget!" Cried Athene who grabbed her hand and began pulling her through the jumble of bodies. "You look radiant! Simply radiant! Is it the air from the north that gives you such marvelous skin? Wherever did you get such an exquisite shawl? Absolutely stunning! I wish I was as tall as you! It'd make it much simpler to get through this damned rabble! Here, come meet my husband."

Bridget had not known what Justin, lord of this castle, looked like. Still, she was surprised to see a rather elderly and portly gentleman with no outstanding characteristics other than his very small eyes. "Ah, Lady Bridget! Mistress of Bone Tear!" He grasped both her hands in his and bowed easily. "Welcome to my castle."

Bridget curtsied. "We are honored to be your guest."

Athene and Justin took Bridget by her arms and escorted her to a quiet corner.

"We know why you come here, Bridget, Mistress of Bone Tear. There is no dishonor in seeking assistance. The only dishonor is in not giving it. Know," said Justin, "that we shall grant your requests. All that is left is to discuss the terms. I have a fondness for your father and Vortimer's reputation is legendary. I have a desire to cultivate some agreement between us. With this in mind, I should ask you to join me in dance! No on will doubt your virtue in dancing with an old man and besides, I want you to enjoy yourself while here! It is my burden as host!"

To not dance with Justin would be an insult, Bridget knew. Besides, she no longer had the worry about her mission! Grabbing a goblet of wine from a passing servant, Bridget downed it in a throaty gulp and allowed the lord to lead her to the floor. It was a merry tune and Bridget at once found herself moving easily to the rhythms and laughing with her partner who was nimble of foot.

Vortimer! I did it! We will be safe and we will survive—nay, we will thrive! How I wish you could dance! Maybe if you took something for pain and drank more wine!

Spinning and twirling, Bridget forgot the tightness of her gown and all the troubles of Bone Tear momentarily—there was nothing but the drums and lutes. She twirled her head and ran her fingers through her thick hair and looked at Justin seductively which brought a round of applause and laughter from the onlookers. Justin thrust his hips in a crude mating motion and the spectators laughed merrily. It was a marvelous dance and Bridget spied Maldwyn, Astorious with Hrolf between them, who were looking on.

I may be the Iron Bitch but I am also Bridget—and Bridget loves to dance!

Justin was breathless as he laughed and spun while others clapped to the rhythm of the music.

"My dear, this old man has had enough! Perhaps you should find another partner?" He said breathlessly.

"With all due respect, I am very much a married woman who is far from home. While the reality of my virtue may never be doubted, appearances can cause tongues to wag."

"Well, right you are, I suppose. Here, have another goblet. The workmanship and detail of your shawl is quite extraordinary! Wouldn't care to sell it, would you? No, I suppose not and can't much blame you.

"Now, here is our table and your place is here." He pulled out a chair. "Sit back and refresh yourself. We will be joined by my wife and other guests of note at which time we shall discuss terms over a superb dinner. Now, however, I must beg your leave and return to the madness of being a host."

In spite of Justin's warm welcome and the milling throng, Bridget felt so terribly alone and vulnerable. It reminded her of the way she felt during Bridget's Run.

I am being so foolish! This is nothing to Bridget's Run! No one is dying and we are so well protected from the elements. Still, I suppose it is because I am a stranger.

Looking about, she waved over her two men and Hrolf.

"Is everything all right, milady?"

"Of course. It is just that I wanted to see how you three were faring."

"We are doing fine, milady, but I think the young one misses you. He's a bright one, he is. Can really hold his drink, too!"

From somewhere they had furnished the young boy with tight trousers and a heavy linen shirt that was secured with a braided leather belt. He even had a fine pair of soft leather boots which he displayed proudly. "Boot!" He cried and lifted his foot so Bridget could examine it closely. Laughing, she hugged Hrolf and kissed his forehead.

You, and the memory of Vortimer are all that I have right now, Hrolf. I can only begin to imagine how you must feel! We are both strangers now. My, but the girls will make quite a fuss over you, I think. You will be a good brother, won't you? Yes, I believe you will be. Vortimer was wrong, there is no savagery in your eyes or heart. You are just a silly boy in spite of those grave eyes. Is that why I am so fond of you? That you are like Vortimer whose serious countenance veils a boy who wants to come out and play?

She dismissed both men and kept Hrolf by her side. Together they watched the laughing dancers, Bridget keeping time with her foot as Hrolf grinned at the spectacle. A young, dark-eyed girl came up to them and in a halting voice asked Hrolf if he wanted to dance. Hrolf looked at Bridget gravely. She laughed warmly and pushed them towards the floor as the girl grasped his hand.

Yes, they will make a fuss over you, I see!

Bridget watched with amusement as the two children danced haltingly but with enthusiasm. A man on the floor caught her eye. Of average height and slender, he was as elegant and graceful a dancer as she had ever beheld. His entire body blended seamlessly with the music—but he was far too handsome.

He almost looks beautiful. He certainly would have made a stunning woman. He does move so well!

She studied him carefully, noticing that the only time he looked at his partner was when he whispered in her ear which made her giggle. Other than that, he glanced this way and that, in a bored fashion. The dance completed, he left her without a word as Bridget watched him swagger through the crowd. Several people, most of them women came up to chat and she watched as he replied with a quick and disarming smile. Still, he was decidedly the handsomest man she had ever seen.

Decidedly arrogant, though. Far different from Vortimer, thank goodness. This man has a studied delivery—each motion or smile is well-practiced, precise. I don't think he and Vortimer could survive in the same room.

She smiled at the memory of the first night she saw Vortimer. Dark and brooding but with an air of confidence, content with who he was, all others be damned. And his smiles and frowns were genuine. Bridget lost sight of the pretentious man as the dancers began anew—instead, she continued drinking the excellent wine as she watched Hrolf and his partner spin and twirl as children do.

Couples began arranging themselves at the table while Athene bubbled and introduced them to Bridget who smiled in return. "My dear, you must try this venison. Our cook performs miracles!" It was the finest meat Bridget had ever tasted, spiced with herbs Bridget had never encountered. "Justin makes sure we get our share of the spice trade, Bridget. Marvelous, isn't it? You look like a woman who enjoys her food, nothing like your sister at all! Here, taste some goose with the gravy."

Bridget was enjoying herself now, glad to be able to converse with others who asked after Bone Tear and Vortimer. Hrolf rejoined Bridget and picked from her plate as he stood mutely behind her chair, wide-eyed.

"Bridget, allow me to seat our young friend next to you. This is Augustus." Said Athene.

It is that arrogant dancer! Augustus? No, it can't be the same person!

"You know, Athene, that Lady Bridget and I might have become much more than just table partners."

"Really?"

"Yes, I saw her watching me as I danced earlier—we might have been dance partners! And you know that dancing is very much like making love."

"Shush, Augustus! You are incorrigible! Now behave yourself and act like a proper gentleman for a change! You are embarrassing my guest."

"A thousand pardons to you and to Bridget, Mistress of Bone Tear. I have never been one to politely hide my feelings behind some veil. Isn't that right, Lady Camilla?"

An attractive woman across the table chided him playfully for his arrogance before returning to the conversation with the man next to her.

He does have elegant hands—not a scar or scratch on them. He is wearing scent!

"Augustus, if you do not behave yourself I will be very displeased." Athene reprimanded.

"Of course, my dearest hostess. I do not want to be sent to my room without dinner…or alone."

Bridget's plump hostess threw her hands up in mock despair before joining her husband. Unsettled by his brash behavior, Bridget looked straight ahead and drank her delicious wine deeply.

"Why so cold, milady? I hope I did not offend. Truth be told, I know a great deal about you! You are aware, of course, that you and I might be sharing the same bed."

"Excuse me?" Bridget choked.

"Of course! Had your father not chosen that cripple, you and I might have been man and wife. Perhaps lovers!" He laughed out loud at his witticism and looked quickly about to see if others had enjoyed it as well. All eyes turned to look at Bridget and she felt every single one of them.

"I have come to know, sir, that things happen for a reason and always for the best. That my father chose Vortimer over you was certainly no mistake and I doubt that we could ever have become lovers. And though Vortimer may be lame, I assure you that all his other parts work quite nicely, indeed!" This rejoinder brought appreciate guffaws from several who shouted, "Well done! Well done, indeed!"

"So you say. A pity you haven't had a complete man to compare him with."

"Not a pity, sir, an honor." Bridget said lightly as her emotions seethed.

Hide your true feelings! That is what Celestine said. Just smile and counter his barbs with equanimity. Vortimer could crush the life out of this fool with one hand.

Large platters of highly seasoned mutton were brought out and distracted the combatants and onlookers momentarily. It was the most delicious food Bridget had ever tasted and she ate mightily.

Have to eat for two, now. Whatever is this spice? I must get some.

"Lord Justin, whatever is this unique flavor?" She asked innocently.

"It is called garlic. I am glad you like it!"

"I have acres of this herb," muttered Augustus. "It is quite a valuable commodity, is it not? And I have so many other profitable ventures."

Bridget ignored him and instead sunk her teeth into the succulent meat whose juice dribbled down her chin—and the wine was still superb. Bridget belched appreciatively as did many others. The rest of the assemblage had also sat down to partake of the great meal and sat on long benches as compared to the chairs at the table of Justin.

Not unlike our own practice. I must get more of this 'garlic'. I wonder if Justin might supply a cask? No, it must be terribly expensive! Perhaps a handful? I just want to get away from this peacock.

Lord Justin chose this moment to begin questioning Bridget about Bone Tear—how many acres were plowed, the number of inhabitants, sheep, hogs and timber. Luckily, Bridget's knowledge paid off handsomely. Too, she could not help but brag about Vortimer's conquering the Vikings and how this action, which benefited all, cost dearly.

Justin nodded appreciatively, his eyes sharp as thorns as numbers swirled through his head. "Very well, you have a strong grasp of Bone Tear and I am pleased at the breath of your knowledge. We shall send you twenty carts of milled grain and fifty barrels of peas and beans for the inhabitants. For the livestock, fifty carts of forage. For you, as you have shielded us from the savages, two casks of garlic and one of pepper. In return, we require one hundred bales of wool and fifty casks of honey. The wool may be paid over two years—wouldn't want you naked."

Bridget thought it over for an instant and nodded in agreement. It was not an unfair bargain.

"That is not the way I hear it, my lord." Said Augustus.

"What do you mean?"

"I happen to know that Lord Glamorgan, banished by his liege, claims that it was he who defeated the Vikings and that Vortimer was given the victory only to keep the kingdom intact."

"That," Bridget jumped to her feet, "is a damned lie! I was there and I saw the whole affair! Would you be calling me a liar?" She shouted.

"My dear lady," August said easily, "I only repeat what I heard with my own ears, nothing more. I have also heard," he turned to Justin, "that Glamorgan is trying to raise an army to take back what is rightfully his. This might put your agreement with Bone Tear in jeopardy."

Bridget felt the heat rush to her face as her hands clenched with anger at the absurd but damaging lies.

Calm! Keep calm! How can I listen to these damned lies while my blood boils? Glamorgan, that traitor! How dare he? It was not enough that he fled but to spread this nonsense!

"My lord," she said as she turned to Justin, "forgive my outburst but it is the only recourse I had after hearing such drivel." Sitting, she continued, "My husband's valor in past battles is beyond reproach, you know that. I also know that you are an honorable man and a bargain has been struck. Bone Tear will keep that bargain in spite of these outrageous lies."

"An agreement has been struck," he replied. "And I will not falter in my end of the agreement."

The awkward silence that had blanketed the table dissipated as the meal continued—Bridget kept the rage under control but it was hard, damned hard.

"Tell me," Augustus asked innocently. "Does Vortimer still tell everyone I injured his leg on purpose? If so, he is a liar as well as awkward. Perhaps he has lied in other matters as well?"

"Really? No, he never mentioned how he injured his leg but it is very slight, I assure you. Odd, I never thought of him as awkward."

Bridget's blood screamed for revenge! The rage that had been seething began to bubble and Bridget's temples pounded—her fists clenched and unclenched as she smiled dumbly. "Tell me, where is Glamorgan now?"

"He stays at an estate of a friend, not an hour's ride from here. Frankly, I am surprised he isn't here this evening." Said Augustus innocently. "Ah, the musicians are returning! Would you care to dance, milady? You may hide your passion well enough from the others but I sense your fiery spirit. We might have made a fine pair, you and I." He whispered.

"I think not," she whispered in return. "And if you do not remove your hand from my leg—."

"What? Will you slap me? In front of all these people? How would Bone Tear look then? Foolish, I would think."

"I am a married woman."

"You are married to a cripple, three day's ride from here! Tonight there is only you and I." Augustus slid his left hand up higher on Bridget's thigh, the table hiding his groping.

I have prayed for this moment.

"Please remove your hand."

Augustus grinned innocently and instead advanced his hand closer to Bridget's crotch. Slipping her right hand beneath the table, Bridget began

353

stroking his fingers as she smiled. "I am Bone tear. I am the Iron Bitch." She whispered lightly as she stroked his middle finger with her hand. "The Iron Bitch is not in heat."

Clamping his finger tightly now, she bent it back with all the force she could muster and Augustus let out a pitiful wail. All her energy, weight and strength was focused on her steady grip as she bent the finger back towards the wrist. Augustus kicked the chair out from beneath him and began crying out as the occupants of the table immediately surmised what had been going on out of their vision—they watched with dark amusement. Augustus' troubles were now apparent to the others in the hall who began laughing rowdily as he begged for her to stop, his assured manner much changed.

Bridget looked darkly into his eyes and in a voice that only Augustus could hear said, "I am Bridget, wife of Vortimer and mistress of Bone Tear. I do not care for you or your manners or your wealth. So long as I am here, I do not wish to see your silly face again. I will not tell Vortimer of this insult or you would be a dead man. Will you leave my sight or must I snap this finger off?"

Augustus merely shook his head, his face red and sweaty. Bridget released the finger and he immediately rose and strode away swiftly, followed by the laughter of the hall as he held his left hand with his right.

"I apologize," said Bridget to Justin, "if I behaved improperly, but we do not dishonor wives in Bone Tear."

"Well put!" Cried Athene who raised her glass in toast to Bridget. "Well put, indeed!"

"Augustus may well put it some place else." Bridget said with a trace of a smile.

The diners roared with laughter at Bridget's quip and slapped the table with their approval—except Lady Camilla.

The feasting continued and Bridget's fury seemed to diminish to her new comrades but inside she remained a cauldron of venom.

That wretch Glamorgan! How dare he insult Vortimer and challenge Bone Tear like this? Something needs to be done and done quickly! What would Vortimer do?

One part of Bridget's brain began formulating a plan, a brazen one, while the other engaged in the social politeness that was required. She was glancing at the whirling dancers and did not see the servant who came to the table with a note for Lady Camilla who read it and left quickly.

Augustus knew that the pain in his finger would be gone in a day, two at the most, but the scourging laughter at his failed seduction would be with him forever. He knew this repulsion, this public failure, would be the topic over many a cup in the years to come. His mild disdain for Vortimer and Bridget swelled into a black loathing as he paced his room, swearing and cursing. If he could not have Bridget, he would at least have revenge. He had not succeeded in bedding every woman, but neither had any humiliated him. She and her hobbling husband would know his wrath. He picked up a scrap of paper and began scribbling painfully.

Bridget remained with her hosts as long as politeness dictated before leaving them, blaming fatigue. Finding a quill, she began writing even before all the details were thought out.

Uncle,

Greetings from my father. I bear you news that cannot be written—know that it is about your restoration. We must meet somewhere in private, some place far from eyes and ears. Draw where we shall meet on the back of this page and return it to the bearer without a word—make haste. Tomorrow would be best—tell no one if you value what I have for you.

Bridget

Bridget's hands were trembling at the enormity of her plan as she sealed it and handed it to Maldwyn who was waiting outside her door.

"This is for Glamorgan, your former liege. He is but an hour from here. Make casual inquiries as to how to find him and go there immediately. This is to be handed only to him—do you understand? Only Glamorgan. Say not a word and wait for his reply and then return to me, no matter the time. Do you understand? Not a word to anyone."

The young soldier had long given up trying to figure out the minds of his betters and though puzzled, took the letter and bowed silently away.

Is this the right thing to do? Is there any other way? I am Bridget, the Iron Bitch, wife of Vortimer, lord of Bone Tear. Soon to be a mother! How dare Glamorgan threaten us! He deserves whatever he gets! Still, this is so dangerous! I have never even thought of anything like this, much less carried it out! Still, I have Bone Tear and Vortimer and my baby to care about now-I mustn't fail—I will not fail.

She paced her room, the conflicting emotions ebbing and flowing. Bridget's sensibilities were being trampled by the audacity of the scheme and with all her might she willed herself to be calm and think, just think.

That is what Vortimer did! I remember how he acted when planning against the Vikings.

He and Glendon thought of things that could go wrong and how to overcome those obstacles. I must do the same.

Glamorgan can accept or not. If he agrees to the meeting, what next? I must go alone but disguised somehow. Maldwyn's cloak has a man's cut to it! And I must not ride Alexander, a white horse is too conspicuous—Maldwyn's horse, then? Do I tell him that Alexander seemed a bit lame?

The longer she thought, the calmer she became as the pieces of her plan slowly came together. That she had the will to complete it she only doubted for a few moments when she suddenly thought of her soul.

There is no sin in killing an enemy. I am grateful he was not here! That would be discourteous to Justin. The success or failure hinges on two things—he accepts to meet and that it be alone. Where is Hrolf, poor dear? I need some wine and badly to steel these nerves. No, I mustn't. I need a cool head. Damn Glamorgan! Vortimer could have gotten killed! How is Vortimer doing? Is he being well taken care of? I am sure that Celestine is taking care of all his needs. Do I tell him? I don't know. First, let's get it done and worry about that later. I hope he is well enough when I get home. I can't wait to tell him about the baby! He will be thrilled! Glamorgan even puts my unborn child at risk! How dare he! I loved him, I truly did! He was my only friend when I was a little girl—but I am a woman now! What was it they once said? 'Dead dogs don't bite'.

Bridget heard a whisper of a sound and a timid knock on the door. Walking over she spied a sheaf of paper had been slipped beneath. It was fine, rare paper and delicate.

Dearest Lady Bridget,

You left far too early and quickly—almost to the point of rudeness, dear girl! True, that scoundrel's outrageous behavior would rattle anyone!

I should like to meet and speak with you privately when you have the opportunity this evening. I am two doors down on the left. I require your company.

Lady Camilla

Bridget struggled to remember the authoress—there had been so many people at the table and the din from the party blurred everyone. That, along with the subsequent events and goblets of wine, made her memory hazy. The note lingered in her hand as she decided what to do.

Cesestine is far better at this than I! How would she handle such a summons? The writer is a lady and wealthy, for sure. This paper must cost a fortune! And she 'requires' my company, which is nothing but a polite command. These people are rich and powerful, possible future allies of Bone Tear and potentially valuable. Yet, I must not rush over like some common maid at her mistress's bidding. I could use some diversion this evening.

She laughed to herself, thinking that she could use many things this evening! She fumbled among her clothes till she found her brush and began pulling it through her hair. The sun was just below the horizon now and her room was darkening as she found a taper and lit two candles. There, in the furthest corner she discovered that Hrolf had curled up on a discarded blanket, sleeping sweetly.

I really must pay more attention to Hrolf! I am not accustomed to being a mother so I suppose I should learn. Do I waken him to tell him I am going or let him sleep? He drank quite a bit for a boy and was dancing wildly, wasn't he? I wonder if that girl taught him anything he doesn't already know? Hard to tell with these Vikings. Best to let him sleep, I think.

Bridget sat patiently on her bed—it would not do to rush breathlessly to Lady Camilla's room. Try as she might, she could not recall the woman at all—still, it was heartening to have an ally in a place of strangers. Deciding that enough time had elapsed, Bridget straightened her hair and dress and quietly opened the door to the dark corridor. She knocked timidly on the heavy oaken door which was at once flung open. "My dearest Bridget, it is so kind of you to come!"

She must have been stunning when she was younger! She is beautiful even now, though. Yes, I remember her from across the table.

Bridget thought her own room was grand but it paled in comparison to that of Camilla's. First, it was far larger and better lit with several thick rugs on the floor. The headboard on the bed was carved with figures depicting a hunt and there was a large table upon which sat a large flagon and two finely wrought goblets.

"I am so glad that you could come here this evening, Lady Bridget, very. I am just brimming over with questions and would so like to get to know about you and Bone Tear more intimately. Pray, be seated and make yourself comfortable."

She was, Bridget guessed, in her forties, maybe more, but unlike any older woman she had ever seen. Immaculately quaffed, the great lady was adorned with gold and jewels of a kind that Bridget had never seen. Unlike Athene, Camilla had a figure that rivaled her sister's. Bridget felt decidedly bovine in comparison, like a shapeless, too tall lump.

"I appreciate your invitation more than you might know, milady."

"Oh, it is nothing child, nothing! You do me the honor, I assure you! I could scarcely hear you all night, you know and the less we say about Augustus, the better! I could not help but notice that you are a woman of strong appetites, vital.

Help yourself to the wine, dear. I do not stand on ceremony in my own apartment, ever. Be so kind as to pour me a glass, also. That's a dear. We hear so little of what happens in the wilds; tell me of you and Vortimer, I must know everything!" She sat across from Bridget and clicked her goblet against Bridget's. "Just between you and I, two women of destiny. And you must tell me about your shawl! It was exquisite! How ever did you come by it! Good thing you didn't wear it here to my room, I might not have let you leave without it!"

Bridget only laughed and began talking about her father, her betrothal and marriage. Lady Camilla had that gift of being able to draw out the details without seeming intrusive. Besides, Bridget felt inclined to talk, her tongue lubricated by the countless goblets of the sweetest wine she had ever drunk. Camilla listened attentively with an encouraging smile. And Bridget spoke truthfully and without adornment, omitting the more personal aspects of her relationship with Vortimer.

"My dear, you have had quite a life for one so young. And as you have told me much, I feel obliged to share my experiences with you, but only if you permit me a small absence for matters of state. Help yourself to the wine, it is my own, you know. Justin has great taste in many things but his appreciation of a superior vintage is lacking. I shall return shortly."

Bridget thought it odd that lady Camilla had to leave so suddenly but dismissed it as something great people must do. Not feeling offended, she escorted Camilla to the door and then returned to her wine.

I never knew such jewels could exist! I know nothing of the world and everyone else does! How can she wear so much heavy gold? It is best that she left for a bit, allows me time to think of tomorrow. Tomorrow, when all my problems will be laid to rest once and for all! I think Vortimer will be pleased with the outcome of my agreement with Justin. He better be! How is he doing? Still with fevers? I hope not. This wine doesn't warm the belly so much as it muddles the head—I must really stop now! My thoughts must be as crystal clear as my purpose. Perhaps if I just close my eyes a bit and rest. I will hear her as soon as she opens the door.

Bridget did not fall asleep, instead she thought of Glamorgan and what the morrow would bring. Would he see her at all? Would she be able to carry out the grisly work? She no longer thought about the rightness or wrongness of the thing because to her mind it was only a matter of survival, plain and simple; survival of Bone Tear, Vortimer, herself and the child in her belly. Did Vortimer give a whit about how many men he had slaughtered? His nightmares were not about the dead but of the battle themselves. Bridget was certain that Glamorgan no longer cared about her but she would have to hide that, distasteful as it was.

She heard a great many muffled voices in the hall with laughter and little cries of surprise—even some clapping as the remnants of Justin's party made their way to bed.

Over and over she played out various scenes in her head until frustration set in. She sat upright and was about to write a small note to Lady Camilla who just then happened in. Her hair was no longer perfect but slightly mussed and her face was flushed as though she had run up the long stairs.

"Ah, there you are, Bridget. Forgive me for not entertaining you as I wanted but things just happen, it seems, and we are powerless. Do be a dear and pour me out some wine."

Bridget desperately wanted to know what her urgent leaving was all about but knew it was impolite. Camilla would tell her if she wanted—it was not her place to question. Sitting down, Camilla regained her composure and began relating some aspects of her life to Bridget. A widow, she was independently wealthy with vast estates to manage which, she said, she did with an iron fist. "Men think of us as soft and that misconception is our strength. A resolute purpose combined with cunning can accomplish much more than some buffoons wielding swords. In Vortimer's case, however, he has never had much of a choice, has he? Kill or be killed, no? Well, now that he has Bone Tear perhaps you may teach him the art of manipulation."

"Manipulation?"

"Bridget, dear, appearances are reality to the unknowing eye."

They spoke for several minutes more, Bridget wanting more than ever to return to her room but Camilla did not appear to want to excuse her just yet. The castle was completely quiet when Camilla poorly stifled a yawn.

"My, it is late, isn't it? You must be tired of listening to this old woman prattle about nonsense, dear. Get the backbone to tell me you wanted to go to bed!"

"Lady Camilla, you are the one speaking nonsense now! I have found you to be stimulating and educational and I know that you would be a most welcome guest to Bone Tear as soon as our dwelling goes from being a fortress to a home."

They stood, kissed and hugged as Camilla led Bridget to the door. She looked up and down the corridor before letting Bridget pass, however.

Odd behavior. Perhaps it is just a quirk.

Bridget flung herself onto the bed gratefully and closed her eyes.

How does Voertimer sleep so easily on the eve of battle and in miserable tents? I hope he is sleeping better than I. How much longer before I know my destiny? What would Vortimer do? He would plan and think of all that could go wrong and make allowances, that is what he would do. I have to get out of these clothes! I feel like I can't breathe.

It took time for Bridget to remove the tight gown and bodice without assistance but worth the effort. Looking into the dark corner, she saw Hrolf's dim outline sleeping soundly. Moving quietly, Bridget found her most comfortable tights, tunic and put them on in the dimness.

I can feel that my ankles and wrists have thickened. When will my belly start?

She went back to her bed and waited, attempting to determine when she should have her answer. It had been just past dusk when Maldwyn departed and he was in unfamiliar territory. It would be black when he returned, so he would have to ride slowly. Waiting was the most difficult part—and Bridget did it, alone in the inkiness until she heard a muffled rapping at her door.

Maldwyn looked frigid and grim in the half-opened doorway.

"I rode as fast as I could, milady, but the roads are not known to me."

"I understand and I am grateful for your efforts this night. Did you have any trouble?"

"None, milady." He whispered. "Though my former lord was mightily surprised to see me."

"Did you do as I asked?"

He reached deep into his cloak and handed over the now crumpled letter.

"Excellent. Now, two more things before you retire. My cloak is too light for the cold and I wish to go riding tomorrow—may I borrow yours?"

He took of the heavy cloak and handed it to her wordlessly.

"The second is this, Alexander was getting a slight limp and I wish to ride tomorrow. Please saddle the horse of Astorious for me now."

"It will be done, milady." He bowed as she shut the door quietly, her heart racing. Going to the closest candle, she unfolded the letter to find a crude map drawn on the back and 'before noon' in thick letters. Bridget stared hard at the map, focusing her attention on memorizing every road, lane and brook. Satisfied, she placed it on the dying fire and watched it flare and then expire into charred flakes.

Resolute, Bridget felt an awkward sort of elation now that she no longer had control over the events she had set in motion. She would either succeed or fail and failure was something the Iron Bitch would never abide. Finding a chair,

Bridget sat in front of the fire and smiled as she pictured Vortimer playing with his son. It was a pleasant interlude and it enabled her to pass the dark hours.

It was before dawn, the darkest time of the night when Bridget stirred. She pulled her hair back and tied it loosely behind. She slid on the thick riding boots and then groped among her things for her knife and dagger. As mistress of Bone Tear, she carried both, never dreaming that she would ever need them. Securing them tightly to her belt, she put on the heavy cloak which fit perfectly and pulled the cowl over her head before leaving.

I should stoop a little bit and hang my head down—drag my feet as if I have just woken.

There was no one in the corridor and only a few sleepy servants in the hall who were still cleaning after the festivities of the night before. If anyone noticed the tall stranger ambling out the door, they paid no heed. Guards were posted outside the door but their concern was with those trying to get in, not out. Bridget grunted deeply as she passed them, her breath billowing in the cold air. Keeping her head down, she was still able to find the stable without a problem and found Astorious's horse tethered and saddled.

I wish you could go with me Alexander but you are far too conspicuous and this work requires I not be noticed.

Mounting in one fluid motion, Bridget wheeled him about and rode slowly towards the gate. A thin snow began to fall but Bridget knew it was the kind that would disappear with the first sun. The eastern sky was just starting to lighten as Bridget left the castle of Justin. She rode methodically and slowly, not wanting to bring undue attention to herself—though she could not be invisible, she could be a faceless, dark rider on a dark horse. As the castle began to disappear, Bridget allowed herself to look up and around at her surroundings.

The snow was leaving a crust on the well-beaten road and the crowing of cocks was the only sound disturbing the silence. She rode calmly but prepared to bolt at a moments notice. Glamorgan had already shown what he was made of; he could do so again. Bridget's remaining concern was that he be alone and that would not be determined till later. Though her mind was at ease, Bridget felt something was not quite right, odd.

Is there some magic going on? I have never been here before and yet I have a sense of the familiar—as if I have smelled this air and rode this way. I think there should be a small bridge around that bend.

There was a bridge. After that there were boulders and creeks that suggested they had been seen before. Bridget ascribed this unsettling feeling to her imagination that was strained taut by lack of sleep, Glamorgan's map and the desperate enormity of her plan.

Maybe it is because I am pregnant? What did Camilla say about women being cunning and resolute? What would she think of me now, I wonder? There comes a time when action, bold and bloody is needed. The map pictured a winding logging trail—.

Bridget had no trouble distinguishing landmarks that had been drawn on the map as the light improved. The dull sun allowed her to see that there were no fresh tracks in the snow that had now stopped. The trail was rough and little more than a wide path with overhanging branches she swept aside. Coming to a bubbling brook, she stopped for a moment to listen. Nothing. Except for the gurgling water there was a heavy stillness. Bridget was again overcome with the sensation that she had been here before.

Nerves, nothing more. I am beginning to feel the way Vortimer felt just before the battle. Purposeful action. Clarity. The air smells so sweet. There is the fork ahead with the birch thicket.

There was something else, a single set of hoof prints leading deeper into the silent trees. Bridget stopped once more to savor the moment—its smell and sounds, its dark silence and menacing beauty. Her heart pounded heavily and all the memories of her life were put away on a small shelf that was in her brain, hopefully to be recollected, if not…

The winding path went on and on and Bridget had to remind herself to breathe as the tension continued to build. She was startled when it finally opened into a large clearing that was surrounded by trees, empty except for a horse standing idly by and Glamorgan who sat on a rotten log.

"Bridget!" His booming voice was smothered by the silent trees, as if they alone were meant to bear witness.

Bridget dismounted warily and stretched by the perimeter of the circle.

"Glamorgan."

"It pains me deeper than you know not to hear 'uncle' from your lips."

"It pains me to be here, as well." She replied and walked closer. "I am no longer a little girl, Glamorgan."

"Aye. We are not the people we once were." He said ruefully.

Bridget saw that the old warrior had aged badly. His eyes, once so proudly defiant were rheumy with the friendship and solace he sought in his cups. Even at this early hour, Bridget could smell the stink on his breath.

They stared at one another, their exhalations bellowing quietly.

"Before I tell you the news from my father, I have to ask this one question: why?"

He waited a moment before speaking and paced back and forth as he spoke, staring at the muddy ground.

"It was your father, Bridget! It was your father's fault all along. Not you, not Vortimer, but your ungrateful father who drove me to what I did. I deserved Bone Tear! Me! Glamorgan, who stood by your father all these years! It was me who picked up the pieces of your father's mistakes! Me! It was me who kept the snapping wolves from his door when I could have turned with the others and destroyed him! I was loyal, Bridget. Loyal to the end. And then he gives Vortimer the land I coveted! I didn't even want the whole damn thing! All I even wanted was your father to do right by me—I wanted him to be loyal to me!"

Bridget allowed Glamorgan's tirade to continue—hearing the words but not comprehending them—only getting a sense of how he felt betrayed. His face was florid with righteous anger and he was breathing heavily as he sat back on the log, his head held up defiantly. She walked up to him, placed her hand on his shoulder and kissed his forehead. Bridget walked behind him and began stroking his grizzled head with her left hand as her right found the knife handle deep within her cloak and tightened on it, her thumb against the hilt.

"I've spoken my piece. Now, what word do you bring?"

In one motion she grabbed a handful of his hair and snapped his head back as her right whipped out the knife and plunged it deep into his neck behind and below the ear. With a grunt she pushed the knife forward and to the left.

Bridget had never seen blood explode as it did from his severed arteries. It spurted against her arm and up over her head. He thrashed his heels on the ground and made thick gurgling sounds as the blood pulsed out in thick, red arcs. She continued to hold his head until his struggles and wet breaths stopped entirely. She held onto the hair that was now slimy with blood and lowered him gently, almost carefully to the ground. Bridget averted her eyes from the gaping wound and instead stared at her boots.

No! No! It cannot be! It must not! The boots in a bloody pool! That coppery smell! My hands! My hands! They are my hands! It was me! I am the Hooded Man! Look at my hands!

Bridget moaned and began crying as she looked with horror and disgust at her hands. She walked around the lifeless corpse as if it were nothing and instead stared at her hands. She began wiping them on the heavy cloak and then stopped.

That will not do, will it? Just stop for a moment and think. I am so thirsty. I will drink from that stream. I can wash there as well. Stop for a moment, collect my wits.

Bridget was going to sit on the log but there was no spot that was free from the rapidly congealing blood. Steam rose from the small pools and rivulets. She walked over to the horse and held on to the reins for support as she trembled and began weeping, no longer holding back the frantic emotions that had plagued her for half a day.

I can't even wipe my face with my hands! It was me all along! No one else! All those fears I had, thinking that I was going to be killed and it was me that did the killing! That was why this place seemed so familiar! Is this magic? Does it matter? The deed is done. The deed is complete. Now, what next?

Bridget's plan had ended with the slaying of Glamorgan and went no farther. Her actions had to be immediate but could not be rushed.

Who killed Glamorgan? Highwaymen! Does he have a purse? I must stay composed.

She walked over to the body and began feeling through his thick clothes for some money, anything. Finding none, she went over to his horse and round a small leather bag tied to the pommel with a few gold coins. She placed it in her cloak.

I can release his horse when I leave. Now for me!

Bridget shrugged off the cape and was dismayed to see heavy splotches of blood that she knew would make stiff crusts when dried. Her boots were also soaked with the stuff. Bridget waited and listened—not a sound. Made confident by purposeful action, she walked back to the small stream and began washing her face and hands in the frigid water, then drank. She vomited once and then drank once more, ridding her mouth and throat of that bilious taste. Next, she threw the cloak in and began walking on it, cleaning both it and the boots at the same time.

If I had really been clever, I would have brought a change of clothes. I did not think there would be that much blood and with such force!

Bridget should have been chilled numb but wasn't. The sodden cloak was so heavy that she had to drag it from the water. Fixing one end to a tree, she began wringing it with all her might. She did this several times, getting out as much water as he could till the great garment was somewhat manageable.

Face. Hands. Arms. Cloak. Gold. Dagger and knive. Boots.

Bridget looked around once more, every nerve now sharpened to an extraordinary degree. Satisfied with her work, she untied Glamorgan's horse and mounted her own. It was hard going with the heavy cape but she managed. It was much quicker leaving than going and the sun was beginning to shine more brightly. Bridget untied her hair and began riding confidently on the main road towards the castle.

I went for a ride in a new place with an unfamiliar horse—how foolish of me! I was lucky not to break my neck when I fell. Look at me, soaked!

CHAPTER FOURTEEN

Vortimer was becoming increasingly edgy and ill tempered as he healed, pacing about his room like a caged animal. In his mind the sickbed had become a bier and he was loathe to lie in it. His restlessness delighted Calgwyn who continued her ministrations, and exasperated everyone else except Celestine who smugly now thought it unwise to continue her nightly vigil.

I am not sick! I told them all I was fine and I am, except for this damn bone! How long will it take to heal fully?

His appetite had returned and the fevers subsided; his gestures and motions were sharp, impatient. Celestine was the only one able to calm him, it seemed. Indeed, it was not surprising to see them engaged in long conversations that were punctuated by easy laughter and bracketed with comfortable looks between them. Vortimer sought her company after his increasingly perturbing meetings with Varduc who spoke of nothing but the diminishing stores and the coming Yule.

Yule, Christmas! Does it make any difference, after all? The longest night of the year and the beginning of the new! Will we be forced to beggar our way back to her father for a few crumbs? What if Celestine is right? That he hoards enough stores for Bone Tear and more? After all that I have done, he denies me! Perhaps Celestine could intercede? No! I will not have a woman do that for me. If the food is there, I will take it as payment for services rendered! Still, he is my lord and I have never betrayed any liege. No, I am no Glamorgan!

The memory of Glamorgan's deceit furrowed his brow and his face became dark and threatening—only Celestine could lighten his spirits when he brooded over the betrayal. Then there were the gnawing memories of the battle itself as bits and pieces of the mayhem surfaced. Vortimer startled easily, at times he wanted to be alone and cry as the memory of the brave Patrick and so many other newly dead appeared unbidden. They had been companions, he knew their names and now they were just shadows, corpses rotting. Coming so close to

Death was unnerving—and this last encounter was the worst of all. The guilt of breathing and walking as his comrades lay in the hard earth was unbearable—again. And then there was Bridget.

At night, alone with only his thoughts, Vortimer attempted to find solutions for his perplexing agitations. When ill, he was helpless and now that he was healthy he remained helpless still—subject to the whims of whatever Fate held in store. He felt more alone now than ever and was weary of it. He wanted to strike out at some adversary—that was how problems were solved—but these foes were not bone and blood. The Iron Dog raged and snapped with impotent frustration and accomplished nothing—and then there was Bridget.

In the quiet moments Vortimer realized he missed Bridget terribly. Unknown to him, he smiled at the thought of her. He yearned to hear her voice and robust laughter and the way she seemed to make things easier; her energy for living and love of motion. There were times he had looked deep into those dark green pools that were her eyes, attempting to fathom the passions that roiled there. He missed the smell of her, the way he would cup her breast after making love. He visualized their lovemaking, each time more wondrous than the ones that preceded. Together they were learning the nuances of each other's body, when to yield and when to demand, the time to surrender and the time to conquer. He recalled the comfort he felt during their last night—the gentle peacefulness of being together, of being in love.

Love. Not something he had given much thought about before Bridget, what would have been the point? Vortimer felt destined for a shallow grave beneath some crusty plain—she changed all that. More than a wife—Bridget was the promise of a future. He more than loved her—he needed her. He needed to be made happy by her and needed to make her happy. It was marvelously, wonderfully confusing.

I have had women before but none could make me laugh or make me so angry. And yet there is contentment when we lie in bed, her head on my shoulder. Varduc was right and I have been so wrong! I would never have thought I could fall in love. I never thought I could do many things.

Bridget must get back home and soon! What better time than Yule to plan our dreams? The start of a new year and the beginning of a new life! We don't need all the nonsense that goes with it, just she and I.

The days of waiting crept by as night grew longer and the temperatures plunged.

Shadowy snows fell frequently and the sunlight no longer had the strength to melt it all. The only cheerful voice in all Bone Tear, it seemed, was Celestine's— even Calgwyn noticed how her mistress's temper and bitter tongue had diminished. Though her headaches came more frequently, Celestine's whinings had ceased and she took it all with a shrug and a bemused smile. For three straight days she did not prepare her hair as had been her custom and she now devoured her food, like Bridget.

Vortimer was in the hall with Celestine and Varduc when it was announced that a messenger with a package had arrived.

Bridget! It must be news from Bridget!

"Send him in! Don't let him stand in the snow!"

Vortimer's face was laughing excitedly as the neatly bound package was handed from the messenger to Varduc to Vortimer.

"Let's see it, man! Give it here! News at last!"

He ripped off the thin cords and unfolded the fine leather. In it was Bridget's jeweled shawl, lightly perfumed, and a note. He read the letter slowly and paled. Across the table, Varduc watched as Vortimer's countenance changed in rapid succession. Disbelief, hurt, sadness, rage, anger.

"No!" He thundered. "No! Never! Impossible!"

"What is it, Vortimer? What is the matter?" Exclaimed Celestine who was startled by the anguished bellowing.

"What is it, young master? Trouble?"

Vortimer gained control after a few moments and whispered dejectedly, "No, no trouble at all. No one is to come to my room unless bidden." Head down, he stormed away from the surprised group. Celestine was the first to retrieve the note he had left behind.

Vortimer—here is Bridget's shawl. I simply had to return it. I trust you will find your wife much more experienced, if not improved, than when she left your bed.

How is your limp?

Augustus

Celestine suppressed a triumphant shout and instead handed the damning letter to Varduc.

Yes! Yes! The scoundrel did it! I have no idea as to how he managed to do Bridget but he succeeded! He will be repaid but not in the coin he desires. Oh, this is simply thrilling! What next? I need Vortimer's ear—he must not be allowed to do something foolish.

"How could my sister do such a monstrous thing, Varduc? How? What will become of Vortimer?"

"This is impossible!" He said unconvincingly. "It is just not in Bridget's nature, particularly now."

"You see the proof before you! Oh, I feel as you do, betrayed."

* * *

Bridget had never been happier. Even the foul weather could not dampen her blossoming optimism. The carts were strung out behind and she was heading home at last, her triumphs paving the way for future bliss. She was giddy with anticipation to be home and to crush Vortimer in her arms. She would humbly accept the congratulations from the others regarding the foodstuffs from Justin but longed to hear Vortimer say, "Well done."

Her joy was boundless, no longer shackled by the fetters of self-doubt that had held her for so long.

Everything! Everything I have done in the past has led up to this very moment! How exciting to be alive! I feel like I could fly! Oh, that I could do that, straight to Vortimer! Will I be able to ride Alexander when I am bigger? I will miss galloping through the meadows but he will understand. Perhaps Alexander could sire our child a fine pony? Well, time enough for that!

I am the most fortunate of women; our baby growing stronger each day! Child, I don't know your name yet but you will be closer to my heart than you are right now. I will hold you in my arms and suckle you as Vortimer enfolds the two of us in his. I will need a midwife, child, to usher you safely. Maybe your Aunt Celestine will give me Calgwyn? I don't even know if she is capable of that.

What would your father want for you? A life better than his, no doubt. I don't want you to become a scarred and broken warrior. I don't even want your father to do it any longer, he must not! He, we, have seen enough blood for a lifetime! Glamorgan's death was a necessity, child. He deserved what he got and I have no guilt about doing what needed to be done to keep my loved ones free from harm. A wild sow would do no less!

Will Vortimer wonder about my weight? Well, it is his fault and I will make him apologize! I think, child, you will be born in early summer, around Beltane, the finest time of the year. You were conceived in love and will be born the same way and I will cherish each breath you take.

Supremely confident, mistress of her destiny, Bridget thought back as to how she had overcome Vortimer's two adversaries, Augustus and Glamorgan. She chuckled when she recalled the whimpering Augustus on his knees. She dwelt on Glamorgan abstractly, glossing over the wetness of his retribution and the part she had played in it.

They were so right, 'dead dogs don't bite.'

And I have even made allies in Justin, Athene and Camilla! Camilla even helped me pack my things—not just an ally, a friend. Perhaps we can visit one another when all this fighting stops. Vortimer was right, all he wanted was peace, perhaps now he will have it.

The cold fog muffled sight and sound so completely that Bridget was startled when a group of twenty or so horsemen appeared suddenly—men of Bone Tear!

An escort! Vortimer sent me an escort!

"Bridget of Bone Tear?" Their leader said sharply.

Bridget was about to respond when she was abruptly cut off.

"You are to leave this party at once and follow me under guard."

Maldwyn and Astorious began drawing their swords.

"Stand fast!" He motioned to the pair. "I am under orders from Lord Vortimer! You were her escorts? Vortimer wishes to question you two directly."

"What is going on? What is this all about?" Bridget cried out.

Two riders flanked Bridget and rudely grabbed the reins from her hands. The leader pointed to three others who joined their comrades.

"Don't let her use the horse, she can ride like the wind! You know where she has to go, so do it."

"What is all this abo—."

Bridget was led into the fog before she could finish. Glancing over her shoulder, the last thing she saw were the carts being led away. Her guards were grave and Bridget knew it would be pointless to protest or ask questions.

What is this all about? He said it was under Vortimer's orders? How can that be? What is happening? Wait, didn't Celestine bring up the idea of Vortimer rebelling against father? No, that is just absurd! Glamorgan? Do they suspect me of the murder? But these are my men!

The befuddled Bridget allowed herself to be led off but sat tall, confident that whatever was amiss would shortly be set right.

* * *

Vortimer had shut himself in his quarters and raged in profound silence. To cuckold him was one thing, but to do so with Augustus was unbearable! He wanted to rip Augustus apart with his bare hands but knew in his soul that the fault lay with Bridget, she alone. He had given up asking why she did it; it didn't matter. He shook his head in hurt and disbelief that she could wound him in this way. Vortimer kicked chairs and generously heaped his wrath on Varduc. It was Varduc who had promised that Bridget would be his greatest ally and look how terribly wrong he was! Vortimer ached with despair, he scarcely ate or drank. Only Celestine was able to melt away his melancholy and it was she who suggested Bridget be sent to the abbey pending the divorce.

Divorce! I loved Bridget! How can all this be happening just when everything seemed to be going so well? Damn her, her father and Augustus! Damn Varduc for misleading me! What will become of Bone Tear? Divorce is easy enough. I don't need anyone!

Though he knew it was unreasonable, Vortimer wanted to throttle Maldwyn and Astorious himself, crushing their necks till the small bones cracked beneath his thumbs. No one, not Glendon nor Varduc, had ever seen Vortimer so dangerous. They were used to the lord who kept his own counsel. They spent the ensuing nights together, each expressing shock and disbelief over Bridget's betrayal—wondering what would happen next; Varduc never mentioning Bridget's pregnancy. This alone, he thought, should have kept her from another's bed. Still, he never ceased to be perplexed by women. Who knew how their minds worked? That they could give birth was mystery enough! Varduc attempted to stretch out for the truth with his spiritual tendrils but it was as though they became hopelessly tangled.

Of one thing was Varduc absolutely certain—that Vortimer's love was so deep that he had forgotten the underlying principle of Life—the mutability and fragility of it. Varduc sighed morosely. Vortimer had become more than a son to him and Bridget a daughter—he hated to see either hurt but accepted it grudgingly. The Goddess would do as She thought best for Her plan, not his. Still, if She could be convinced…

The brimming carts began arriving the following day but there was no joy in Vortimer's heart, just resentment as it reminded him of Bridget. There was just one more perfunctory task to perform before he would begin seeking a divorce. Summoning Celestine, Glendon and Varduc, he waited alone in his quarters, making certain that Gwenthe, Mathilde and Calgwyn remained working far from earshot in the hall. When everyone was convened he sent Glendon to bring in Maldwyn and Astorious. "No one else knows of Bridget's treachery." He muttered. "Let us hear the truth from these two."

The two bewildered men were at last brought in to face Vortimer who was doing his best not to glower. "You were charged with safeguarding my wife, were you not?"

They mumbled in the affirmative.

"Did either of you lose sight of her?"

Both men looked down on the floor until at last Maldwyn mentioned the time Bridget borrowed his cape.

"Borrowed your cape, for what?"

"Milady said she wanted to go riding in the morning and her cape was not warm enough."

"Anything else?"

There was a long pause before Astorious spoke up, telling Vortimer that Bridget had used his horse for the ride.

"So, Bridget leaves wearing your cape and riding his horse, correct?"

They nodded.

"And she was gone for how long?"

"She was back around noon, lord."

"So, she had a full morning to herself. Anything else?"

Maldwyn hesitated before mentioning the condition in which he received his cloak back. "She said she fell from the horse, lord." He said lamely. Seeing Vortimer's mood, he thought it prudent not to mention the letter to Glamorgan.

"Very well, go."

Vortimer sat mutely, visualizing Bridget and Augustus squirming on the cape they had thrown on some forest floor. He looked about the room, defying any of them to dispute Bridget's infidelity now that they had heard the damning truth. "I will divorce Bridget. All her holdings will forfeit to me as lord of Bone Tear. What needs to be done?"

"Shall I tell my sister of your decision, then?" Asked Celestine.

"How can the two of you share the same blood, Celestine? I have judged badly. Yes, tell the bitch she has been granted her wish to serve the Christ—he can have her."

"Glendon, see the stores are fully protected and distributed equally. She kept a list somewhere, locate it and use your best judgment."

"Varduc, I do not want to see you again till I call you. Is that very clear? I wish to be left alone for now. What has happened will soon become common knowledge but I do not want to hear any more of that whore. Now go."

Vortimer, I know your heart is breaking right now and I am so sorry but it will all be for the best, my love! I promise to make you forget everything about my sister in a very short time. Let she and I fall to our knees—she to pray and I to take you. It will be Vortimer and Celestine from now on. I will leave for a few weeks, first to see Bridget and then to care for my husband. Did she actually do it in some woods with Augustus? How I would have liked to have seen that! I didn't think she had it in her. Well, obviously she did!

Celestine laughed silently at her play on words as she and Calgwyn began gathering their belongings for the journey home. "No, leave a few things here, Calgwyn. Who knows but that I may return soon?"

* * *

It was all Bridget could do to maintain some sense of reason at the abbey. Unceremoniously shoved inside, she ran straight to the abbess who greeted her with open arms. "We have not seen you in a long while," she scolded lovingly. "Why the tears, child?"

"Mother, I do not know why I am here! There is no reason for Vortimer to treat me in this way! I have missed you so much but things have been happening so quickly I scarce know where to begin."

"Ah, I see. Well, Jesus loved the prodigal son and I am sure He has room in His heart for the wavering daughter as well. Come, let us go to the chapel."

Together they kneeled—Sister Maria silently bemoaning her inflamed joints and Bridget wondering if this was divine punishment for murdering Glamorgan.

If this was a loving god he would have kept me from all this trouble. No, if he wanted to punish me for killing Glamorgan then he is an unjust and spiteful god! I do not repent, I confess no sin because none are present.

The pair remained on their knees until the aged nun could no longer stand the pain.

This wretched climate does nothing for these old bones except vex them! What am I to do with Bridget? Something is gravely amiss for Vortimer to send her here. I must remain neutral until this plays out. What will become of her fortunes?

The old nun placed her hand on Bridget's shoulder and painfully pulled herself up as Bridget dutifully followed.

"You are most welcome to remain here with us, my child. I have had a cell prepared for your stay. You needn't follow the regimen of the other sisters, my dear, you are not of the order. Just be comfortable and pray."

Bridget was then escorted by one of the novice's to her new quarters. It was stark and windowless with only a crucifix hanging above a hard cot—what light there was came from a sputtering candle, there was no fireplace. Bridget sat in the joyless room and wondered how she could have ever thought about joining. She wanted to pray but stopped short—she would not become a hypocrite. Jesus had never answered one prayer before and she doubted He had an ear for her now.

Besides, I was named after a goddess, not some bloodless saint! The priests may have altered my name but they have not changed me!

For two days Bridget fumed in her cheerless room, leaving only to eat the meager meals, her patience and hope dwindling. Now, she worried that perhaps something had happened to Vortimer and Bone Tear! Why else hadn't she heard something, been given some word?

It was on the third day that a forlorn Bridget nearly jumped out of her skin at a timid knock on her door. A scrawny as a stick novice, silent and sallow beckoned for Bridget to follow. She was led into the chapel, empty except for Celestine who stood in the rear.

"Celestine! Celestine!" Bridget cried excitedly as she rushed into her sister's arms. "What is going on? Why am I here? What is the matter? No one tells me a thing and I am frantic with worry!"

"Bridget, Bridget, I know what it is like to be a woman and to be desired. I never thought that you—"

"Why are you talking in riddles? Tell me what is going on before I burst!"

"Vortimer discovered the truth about your dalliance in the woods."

Then I should be given a hero's welcome and not this imprisonment.

"That does not tell me why I am here! It took all my strength to do what I had to do! It is impossible that he could know! How?"

"It took all your strength to tumble with Augustus? Is he really all that virile? I would have thought Vortimer much more of a man, wounds and all."

"Mate with Augustus? That prissy peacock? Is the world going mad? I thought you spoke of Glamorgan!"

"Glamorgan? Said Celestine. "What does he have to do with any of this? I speak of Augustus who sent your shawl to Vortimer with a note begging it be returned to you and that you would be much improved upon your return?"

"My shawl? I never gave it to him! It was in my room ask Lady Camilla! She helped me pack my things and—"

In one blinding instant Bridget knew why Camilla had befriended her, left mysteriously and returned disheveled. She started to swoon but Celestine lowered her gently on a bench.

"What is it, poppet? What?"

"Betrayed! I have been betrayed by scum and forsaken by my husband who believes them!"

"I have not betrayed nor forsaken you, Bridget. Now, tell me what happened and perhaps I can make this right."

Bridget related how Augustus brazenly attempted to seduce her and how he nearly lost his finger for it. Celestine nodded impassively but imagined how the humiliation must have crumbled Augustus's towering ego. Bridget had forgotten the little comment Augustus had made to Camilla at the table but remembered it now. She went on, explaining how Camilla convinced her to vacate her room so the shawl could be stolen and handed over to Augustus. "They probably had sex and wiped themselves with it afterwards." She said sadly, feeling so utterly foolish for having been tricked so easily.

"Then, when it was time to leave, Camilla made a fuss about helping me pack and made a mess of things so that I would not notice the shawl missing. That is the truth, all of it."

"Vortimer will not believe you, poppet."

"Why not? He has to believe the truth!"

"What about your leaving the castle disguised and returning with the wet and filthy cape? How do you explain that? No one believes that the great Bridget could fall from a horse. What was it you were saying about Glamorgan?"

"Nothing. I am tired and hungry and confused and frightened. I was not thinking."

Would they believe I could slit a man's throat? What if I showed them where the body was? That would make me a murderess. Is that better than an adulterer?

"I swear on my life, Celestine, that what I have told you is the truth! You must believe me and you must get word of my innocence to Vortimer. He has to trust me!"

"You know his raging temper. I have never seen anyone so resolute, Bridget, I am sorry."

"I cannot stay here! My place is by his side!" She wept. "More now than ever."

"What, Bridget, dear?"

"I am having his baby." She sobbed.

"Whose?"

"Vortimer's, of course! Who else?"

It was a mistake to come here. I knew Bridget would be wretched but I never wanted to see her in such a woeful state. A baby? How will this alter things?

"Does Vortimer know?"

"No, but Varduc does! Somehow he knew."

That damned man-thing!

Celestine held the weeping Bridget in her arms as her mind raced with the possibilities that presented themselves. Vortimer would never believe the child was his, not after so much damning evidence. So what if Varduc knew? Could he name the father? Another thought stabbed through her already reeling brain.

Could Varduc possibly know that I am pregnant? He is clever enough to know that only Vortimer could be the sire. Well, he hadn't even hinted that he knew. I will have to act quickly when I return home.

"Bridget," Celestine looked grimly into her eyes, "wipe your face and listen to me. I must return home but I will make sure that Vortimer learns what you have told me. I cannot promise he will be dissuaded from his course of action but if he has one tenth of the love you possess, he will see the truth. When is the child due?"

"Early summer." Bridget sobbed.

Bridget lied to me! She knew she was having this baby for some time! Well, now she'll pay for it!

"Oh, poppet, everything will be well. I promise to do what is best for both you and Vortimer."

"Will you, Celestine? Will you?"

"You may depend upon it, my dear. Now, I want you to return to your quarters and never give up hope. I have been so long from my own home that I must return to see about some matters there. In the meantime, I will send word to Vortimer of what you have related to me."

Bridget stood and clutched her tightly, still sobbing at the hurt and the injustice of it all—and something else—the intolerable pain of being cast off so easily by Vortimer. She allowed herself to be escorted back to the cell and sat in the darkness, now preferring it to the light of day. Sitting on the cot, she hugged her knees to her chest and moaned in the inkiness as the betrayals and abandonment began their crushing.

Poor, Bridget! Well, she lied to me, didn't she? Still, I hate to see her agonize so. I will return home and begin planning what I must next do. Vortimer will divorce Bridget without difficulty, some gold and a few signatures is all it takes. She will remain in the abbey till the day she dies, shamed and penniless. I know father would never take her back, he daren't. As for her baby, well, children die all the time.

* * *

Glendon came sputtering into the hall where he found Vortimer looking sourly over some notes. "I have wonderful news, lord!"

"Good! We could use some. What is it?"

"Just learned that Glamorgan is dead!"

"Well, that is good news, indeed! We must celebrate his untimely demise this evening, the bastard! What happened?"

"That's the odd part, a highwayman."

"That is odd, a single thief?"

"Glamorgan's horse returned to his stable and they sent out a search party. They thought he might have gotten drunk, fell and broke a leg. They found him with his throat cut. Doesn't make much sense, does it? Still, he is dead and that is what matters."

"Yes, that is what is most important—dead is dead. That he suffered makes it even sweeter. Just one thing, how do they know only one man was involved?"

"Only two sets of hoof prints, I gather. Glamorgan and the other scoundrel. I must return to seeing the grains stored properly, lord. I thought this bit of news might interest you."

Vortimer nodded and allowed Glendon to leave as he thought deeply.

A highwayman on a horse? Never! A commoner on horseback would be noticed too easily. Usually they work in thieving bands, grab the horses and topple the riders over and rob them. They might beat them with clubs or even stab them but I never heard of one that cut a throat. Interesting. More interesting was that his horse wasn't stripped and sold. Still, Glamorgan is dead and we shall drink a toast to the man who saved us the trouble. How was it that he let his throat be slit? Didn't the man fight back at all? You don't get your throat cut when defending yourself.

Varduc rushed breathlessly into the hall with Hrolf in tow. "Young master! Young master!" He piped and bobbed excitedly.

"I know, Glendon has already informed me."

"About Hrolf?"

"No, not the brat! About Glamorgan's death!"

"Glamorgan is dead?"

"Slain is the proper word, I think."

"Well, that is good news, young master! Yes, it is! But I have better! Far better!"

"This seems to be my day for good news." Vortimer said dourly. "What is it?"

"The truth! The entire truth about what happened to Bridget, young master!"

"What does this have to do with Bridget's pet?"

Varduc's expression changed from one of poorly contained agitation to one of the deepest gravity. "Heed me well, young master and listen with care. Hrolf was very confused and frightened when Bridget was taken to the abbey. He is still so poor at expressing himself, particularly where you are concerned. You frighten him, young master. When at last he was finally brought to me, we hardly spoke a word till at last he asked about what had happened to Bridget. Hear for yourself!"

Varduc shoved the defiant lad towards Vortimer. He bowed without smiling, as if expecting some great punishment. Varduc began speaking slowly in Hrolf's odd tongue.

"What are you asking and what is he saying?"

"I asked him if he recalled ever seeing a man called Augustus. He said he did. He told of a great feast when this same man sat next to my young mistress—he describes him well."

"Go on."

They conversed a few more times and Hrolf bent his middle finger back and fell to his knees, dramatically crying out in pain and laughter at the same time.

"From his vantage point by the table, he saw Augustus place his hand on Bridget's leg. You saw for yourself what she did."

In spite of himself, Vortimer smiled as he visualized the ire of Bridget and the agony of Augustus.

"What else?"

"Hrolf had drunk a great deal of wine and danced till exhausted and took himself to Bridget's room where he collapsed on some blankets in a dark corner and fell asleep."

"Damnit! Just tell me what happened!"

Hrolf needed no further encouragement from Varduc and began speaking rapidly, with gestures that indicated searching and fornication. He finished with two words, wiped his brow and waited for Varduc to translate.

"He was sleeping in a dark corner when a well-dressed man arrived. The man was carrying a candle and he saw that it was Augustus."

"Where was Bridget?"

"He remembers her leaving somewhat earlier, thought nothing of it and went back to sleep."

"What happened next?"

"A handsome lady arrives in the room and together they begin going through Bridget's clothes."

"Why didn't he do something?"

"That's what I asked him but he said that they were so richly dressed and important looking that they couldn't have been thieves. Besides, they were all present at Justin's table and it would be a discourtesy to accuse a lord or lady."

"Go on."

"They found the shawl, Bridget's shawl, and began laughing excitedly and then they waited till they heard people outside the room and began to have sex…loudly. The man throws the shawl over his shoulder and steps out where he was met by some people who clapped and laughed. The elegant woman adjusted her clothes and waited till there was no longer any noise and left."

"Why didn't he tell this to Bridget?"

"He was scared for one thing. Second, he thought it was a drunken dream, not real."

There was no sound in the hall, no noise at all. Varduc watched his young master as the truth, the real truth made itself known—but Vortimer did not smile. Instead he whispered in a sinister voice, "Who else knows of this?"

"No one, young master. Just us."

"I have to think."

"About what, young master? Bridget is innocent of any wrongdoing! Go get her!"

"I have to think about ridding the world of this leprous maggot." He hissed. "Boy! Come here!"

Young Hrolf walked up to Vortimer, his head barely reaching the hilt of Vortimer's sword. Removing a dagger from his belt, Vortimer dropped to one knee and handed it to him. "This is for you, Hrolf, a small token of gratitude. Bridget was right when she spoke well of you."

Hrolf looked at the keen point and then at Vortimer. "Bridget," he said flawlessly.

Vortimer turned his head and wiped a small tear away. "Varduc, as you love me, stay close, you and the lad."

The hatred Vortimer originally carried for Augustus had dwindled over the years as time cools even the greatest of fires. In one instant, however, Vortimer was a walking inferno of fury, absolute and undiluted. The problem of Augustus would be solved once and for all. Vortimer accepted his own wounds objectively but that Augustus had compromised Bridget in such a way was unspeakably cowardly and so true to his nature! Vortimer trembled with rage as he pictured the conniving bastard boasting about sleeping with his wife!

I have never hated one man as much as he! I haven't even hated my foes on the field of battle! Oh, I will kill him with pleasure, but how? I cannot drag him into a battle. He would be too cowardly to accept a duel. How then?

Vortimer sat and allowed his blistering rage to subside before he began to think clearly. He would do what he had always done before entering a campaign—he would address the weaknesses and strengths.

It was past midnight and for the third time Vortimer was attempting to copy Bridget's fine penmanship with his thick fingers. Each stroke was deliberate, accompanied with sweat and grunting after each word was completed.

Perhaps he has never seen her writing? Still, it is best to do it this way. How does anyone write so clearly? Ah, I am not made for this sort of intrigue!

But he continued writing each painstaking word until his hand cramped. At times he laughed bitterly. He sat still when the note was completed to his satisfaction and shook away the stiffness. Vortimer was surprised to see that daybreak had begun but he was not tired at all. His blood screamed for revenge and would never allow something so petty as fatigue to deter it from being satisfied.

Gwenthe and Mathilde were struck to find Vortimer awake when they brought up his food. They kept quiet when in his presence now, knowing that something unspoken and terrible had happened between their feared lord and loved lady and it would be unwise to invite his anger.

"Varduc and Hrolf are in the hall. Send them up." He said curtly.

Not hungry, he pushed the food towards the two of them when they arrived. Vortimer watched searchingly as Hrolf ate, wanting to discover just what kind of mettle the boy had. When at last they had finished, Vortimer looked at Hrolf but spoke to Varduc.

"We are going to swear a pact of secrecy, you and I."

Varduc translated and the boy nodded. Vortimer held out his hand towards the boy's dagger which Hrolf handed to him, eyes blazing, fearless.

"On the honor of your father and your father's father and all your mighty ancestors…"

Varduc translated somberly.

"By all the gods of the North and the deep sea, you will tell no one what you saw that night or that you told me. Swear."

Vortimer waited for Varduc to finish and waited for the boy's reply. When Varduc confirmed acceptance, Vortimer took the dagger's keen point and drew a crimson line across his palm. He handed the dagger to Hrolf who did the same thing. Neither flinched. They clasped their bloody hands together, letting the blood oath mingle till it coursed through their bodies.

"Varduc, when this work is done I will make him my vassal."

"Yes, young master—and what is this work that has to be done?"

Vortimer was binding Hrolf's hand and indicated that Varduc should read the letter lying on the table. He roughly bandaged his own while Varduc read silently.

"I will need a white horse and for you to furnish a messenger who will swear, even if tortured, that he delivered that letter from Bridget. I am no longer patient. The sooner it is done, the better."

"There is some risk, young master."

"Life is risk. Remember, not a word to anyone. Perhaps you can use your wiles to make the messenger dream it is the truth—do whatever it takes."

Left alone, Vortimer coldly played out the coming confrontation till at last he tired of it and instead thought of Bridget. He was abysmally ashamed of how he had reacted—he should have known better, he realized too late. What had Bridget ever done to deserve his instant condemnation? The answer was always the same: nothing. He wanted desperately to beg her forgiveness, though it went against everything he had learned. Still, once this chancre had been excised, Vortimer swore he would make amends, paltry as they might be. He wallowed in the swamp of his conscience and then finally shunted it aside—first Augustus.

* * *

What few pieces of gold I have are used for this messenger and a half-day of freedom at a deserted shepherd's shack, some distance from the abbey. Take the Great Road north till you come to a burnt oak and then turn right and at each intersection thereafter.

I write this on a Friday with the hope that on the following you will allow me to commit the crime for which I am being punished. Come alone or not at all.

I await you on my knees.

Bridget

Augustus flapped the letter loosely and looked up at its deliverer. "She gave this to you herself?"

"Yes, lord. She was pitiful determined to send it off."

"It took you that long to find me? Today is Monday, idiot!"

The man stood with glazed eyes and because he was not asked a question, did not answer.

"She told me as to how I was to take the letter back with your answer."

"And if I do not give it back?"

"I was told to remind you of your finger, whatever that means, your worship." He scuffled his feet as he searched for something interesting to look at on the ground.

Dear Bridget, how wonderful that you have finally come to your senses! How could I, how could any man, disregard such an entreaty? I recognized the passion flowing in you as soon as I laid eyes upon you, my dear. Still, I will not trust you entirely. I think I should have you strip first and make sure you are planning no injury. Oh, how delightful that will be, to see you disrobe as I watch. Will you blush? The mere thought is making me hard. How delicious it will be in the flesh! I might just make it back in time for the beginning of Yule.

Augustus smiled and handed the letter back. "Yes." Then closed the door.

* * *

Vortimer took the loathsome letter from the dazed messenger and tossed it into the fire, never wanting to be reminded of its contents. He watched as the edges curled into smoky flames. Vortimer sensed the change in himself and did not like the person he had become. It was he who now possessed those demonic eyes that spit with glee before battle. Revenge was intoxicatingly seductive with its righteous finality and Vortimer drank deep from its well, infusing each fiber with a terrible lust for its completion. Not even Glendon knew why his lord wanted to ride a white steed on that Thursday night.

Vortimer rode as if his life depended on it and arrived at the hut shortly after midnight. He lit a candle that sent the vermin scurrying noisily into their burrows. His shallow breaths billowed as he lit a small fire in the center of the floor, its smoke easily escaping through the decrepit roof. Vortimer rushed about, making sure that the windows were sufficiently blocked so no one could easily spy in. He examined the door last and thought which way to best position himself. He laughed evilly when he recalled the 'fair is fair' of the peasants when engaged in single combat.

Life is not fair, dear brothers.

Satisfied with his preparations within, he tethered the white horse conspicuously outside. Returning, he added some new sticks to the fire and covered himself in loose rags as he sat by the entranceway, his hand clenching the heavy club. He slept with raw nerves and waited for a voice, a whisper, the cracking of a twig or the whinny of a horse—Time had been reduced to heartbeats.

It was barely light when he heard the thudding hooves approaching. They stopped momentarily and then began circling the hovel and then stopped once more.

"On your knees, my dear? I have dreamed of this. This is not the time to be shy. Are you on your knees as you promised?"

Vortimer did not expect this. His dry mouth barely had any spittle. He swallowed hard and whispered in as high a voice as he could, "I am waiting."

"Perhaps I should have you come out here first and remove your clothing?"

"Cold. Please?"

He heard Augustus land on the ground and watched the door spring open.

In one powerful arc the club landed squarely against the shins of Augustus who pitched forward, yowling in surprise and pain. In another instant, Vortimer slammed the club against the side of his head, stunning Augustus but not making him lose consciousness. Vortimer stood up, his breathing coming in short spurts as he kicked the ribs and head heavily, over and over. Satisfied that Augustus had no fight left, Vortimer pushed him onto his back with his heavy boot.

"I have been waiting to do this for hours, years!" Pulling down his tights, Vortimer began urinating on the groaning Augustus who was oblivious to all except his difficulty in breathing and the shooting pain of his legs. His bladder relieved, Vortimer took time to look at the writhing, whimpering figure, deciding what to do next. He never much cared for torture but it was suddenly very appealing—Augustus had not suffered enough. He sat down heavily on the heaving stomach and watched as his enemy fought for air.

Why struggle so? You will be dead soon enough.

Pulling out his knife, Vortimer dug it just below the quivering chin. "Look at me, Augustus. Look into the mad eyes of Vortimer the Lame! Look into the eyes of the man who is killing you! I am the last thing you will ever see."

Augustus clamped his eyes shut.

"Open them or I will pluck them out with my thumb. Will you give me that pleasure?"

Vortimer waited several seconds for Augustus to focus his eyes before pushing the blade slowly upward through his neck, mouth, pinning the tongue on the hard palate and up into the brain. He twisted the knife several times as Augustus twitched violently, almost pitching him off.

That took longer than I thought. Good.

Vortimer sat for a moment to compose himself, the fire of his revenge had been doused but still smoldered and his hands trembled. He went out and stripped Augustus's horse of its saddle and tack and tossed them into the hut. With great care, he placed a heavy pile of dry wood over the body before torching it and the shack. There wasn't much blood to wipe off his hand or the knife. He stood back to make certain the fire would burn like the furnace he wanted.

Vortimer mounted his horse and led that of Augustus to a nearby corral he had passed earlier. He grinned as he imagined the surprise of the tenants as such a gift on Yule.

* * *

Bridget was sitting forlornly, inexorably drawing into herself when she heard Vortimer's booming voice resonate through the abbey.

"Where is my wife? Where is Bridget?"

Mindlessly, she dashed out the door to seek him out, tears running down her face. "Vortimer! Vortimer!" She cried.

She found him in the courtyard surrounded by several of the nuns who were failing at keeping him constrained. He stood there, tall, glowering, and absolutely maddening when she threw herself shamelessly into his arms and began kissing his cheeks, his neck—any part her mouth could find. Vortimer did the same, laughing joyously. It was not possible to tell who said "I love you" the most or with the greatest passion but it was Vortimer who began begging forgiveness.

Bridget stopped for a moment, pushed back and slapped him full in the face with her right hand. He did nothing. She did it with her left. Still, Vortimer did not budge. Instead, he dropped to one knee, took her right hand in his, kissed it, looked up into her eyes and said, "I love you, Bridget of Bone Tear. Forgive this fool."

Bridget dropped to her knees, and began squeezing him so tightly with her thick arms that he found it difficult to breathe. Together they laughed, they cried and the nuns along with the abbess, made the sign of the cross repeatedly, just in case the crazed couple were possessed.

* * *

The castle had gone mad with joy upon Bridget's return. Gwenthe and

Mathilde wept shamelessly as they never thought they would see their mistress again. Glendon and Varduc ordered the slaughter of sheep, pigs and geese—this would be a Yule that none would soon forget! Varduc and Hrolf grinned and laughed with the jubilant Bridget and Vortimer. Varduc alone was able to deduce how his young master came by his reddened cheeks. Never, had there been such a spontaneous Yule! Peasants were invited or pulled into the hall and received the blessings of their lord and lady with dazed expressions of gratitude. Makeshift dances began, ended and started afresh as Bridget twirled in merriment and delight throughout the day, night and early morning.

They made love—Vortimer repentant, Bridget forgiving, as the sun began to rise, bright and crisp.

"I have a gift for my lord."

"You have already given me the greatest gift possible. I deserve no more." He said dreamily.

"I can't give it to you until early summer, though."

"And what gift will that be? What can surpass what we already have?"

"A son."

EPILOGUE

She stood by the window, shutters open, unmindful of the cold. The only sound was of the heavy snow falling. Inhaling deeply, she allowed the crystalline air to purify her and the baby growing within; the promised son. She caressed her belly with both hands as she stood naked, cleansing herself with the night.

How ironic that all my beliefs have changed since I first began carrying you!

At times like this she often heard the Voices of the Stones vibrate within, but not tonight. No, the night was all hers and hers alone.

So magical how the dark makes the world clearer, unblemished by sharp edges. I can see the essence of things unsullied by the light. I can see how wrong I was about so many things.

Celestine thought herself a leaf floating delicately on a brook. Twirling madly about as the water became shallow and then gliding peacefully when it was deep. The wind might push and spin it one way or another but it was the dark eddies that carried it relentlessly forward, even if the way was momentarily blocked by some rock or low hanging branch.

Impediments.

She looked over at Theodorous who snored drunkenly and then returned her gaze outside.

He was the means to this end and will not be missed. What widow's clothing do I have?

Celestine was no longer enraged over Bridget's redemption and now meekly submitted to the reality of it and knew that it served some hidden reason. She was overcome with sadness and wept silently, not wanting to hurt her sister but it seemed inevitable now.

True strength lies in doing what we most abhor.

Then there was the one other obstacle, Varduc.

I will let nothing keep us from our destiny, little one. Vortimer is your father, you carry his blood and my will. No one will stop us.

CPSIA information can be obtained at www.ICGtesting.com
Printed in the USA
BVOW08s0729090416

443634BV00001B/121/P